PROMISE OF DARKNESS

BEC MCMASTER

Lochaber
PRESS

To Freyja, the cutest little distraction
an author ever needs

PROMISE OF DARKNESS

Princess. Tribute. Sacrifice. Is she the one prophesied to unite two warring Fae courts? Or the one bound to destroy them?

In a realm ruled by magic, the ruthless Queen of Thorns is determined to destroy her nemesis, the cursed Prince of Evernight.

With war brewing between the bitter enemies, the prince forces Queen Adaia to uphold an ancient treaty: she will send one of her daughters to his court as a political hostage for three months.

The queen insists it's the perfect opportunity for Princess Iskvien to end the war before it begins. But one look into Thiago's smoldering eyes and Vi knows she's no assassin.

The more secrets she uncovers about the prince and his court, the more she begins to question her mother's motives.Who is the true enemy? The dark prince who threatens her heart? Or the ruthless queen who will stop at nothing to destroy him?

PROLOGUE

Eons ago, the invaders came from beyond the stars.

They traveled through portals that tore space and time apart, riding on steeds that trampled all in their wake. They were bright and glittering and malicious, and while their faces could conjure love in a mortal's heart, their smiles held no mercy.

Fae, they were called.

Beautiful and terrible and heartless.

They rode into a world where magic comes from the earth and from the blood, and where the people worshipped their Old Ones. Where ancient forests loomed, they raised their cities and palaces. And they enslaved those they found on this world, calling them monsters for the ugliness of their forms.

With all their power and magic, there was no means to defeat them.

Except one.

Children were born of the couplings of fae and monsters. Dark, vicious, blighted children that bore some sign of the beast upon them. The bright and shining turned them from their homes, disgusted by the misshapenness of their forms. Others were left on stone altars in the woods for the forest to take them.

Unseelie, they named these children. Wretched filth that was no better than the monsters that loomed in the dark night.

But the Unseelie were gifted with both the power of the fae, and the earthbound magics of their monstrous brethren. And where the Seelie bore few children, the Unseelie bred like rabbits.

The Seelie were so focused upon their ugly brethren they forgot the power of those that sired them.

They stopped placing salt on their window sills, and lighting the Samhain bonfires. There was no longer a horse-shoe of iron bolted above the doors of their homes, to ward away the monsters.

The monsters prayed to their Old Ones and brought them sacrifices. In the darkest hollows of the forests, shadows called to shadows, until an ancient malevolence awoke. Whispers came that the Old Ones had begun to walk the mortal realm again and the Unseelie flocked to their banners. Stones were erected around the places of sacrifice, where blood had quenched the soil. Power lingered there, growing steadily in might, as the Old Ones drew upon the magic within the earth.

A new war began. The Wars of Light and Shadow.

The bright ones won. They trapped the Old Ones within those precious Hallows where power lingers, and forced the Unseelie into exile in the wild lands of the north.

But the Old Ones merely wait.

For they are immortal, and their memories long.

And they know.... That the prison walls are weakening.

—Prophecies of Arcaedia

1

Kill the beast.
And don't disappoint me this time....
My mother's words play in my head in time to the drumming hoofbeats of my gelding. It's a song that's been repeating itself for years, though the verses often change depending on her latest critique. Disappointing my mother seems to be my greatest ability these days.

Golden leaves drip from the trees in a steady tumble as autumn starts its slow, seductive slide into winter. I ease Jaeger to a halt, and he snorts, no doubt catching scent of the rank musk I too can smell.

"I know, boy." I pat his neck as I slip from the saddle, landing lightly on the leaf mulch. Smells like a troll's breath the morning after a feast of decayed corpse.

Late afternoon sunlight ripples over the ground, the wind whispering through silent trees. The forest itself seems to be holding its breath.

Watching.

Waiting.

Drawing my sword, I tie Jaeger to a tree and then creep toward the ruins.

There are eyes upon me.

I can feel them.

"That's right, you ugly bastard. I'm here."

The trail of blood leads directly toward the ruins ahead. Where it fell, the leaves have shriveled into brittle shreds, as if the blood itself is tainted.

The news came from the borders three days ago. An empty hamlet discovered on the edges of Vervain Forest, the woodcutters within vanished. Instead, there'd been claw marks in the door and a bloodied fingernail on the floor inside, as if someone had been dragged out by the ankles.

Other empty cabins were slowly discovered. Tales of a beast stalking the edges of Vervain and whispers of hunters not returning from relatively easy hunts began to grow in strength. Chickens slaughtered in their coops over the summer months, though nobody had mentioned it until it was too late.

It always starts with the chickens.

Banes are violent, magic-twisted beasts, cursed to live in a half-animal, half-human shape. It takes a powerful witch or spell to create them; and to break the curse is both dangerous and difficult. True love's kiss. Eating the heart of the witch. Sometimes another spell will gift them with the ability to remain a man during the day and a beast at night, but magic often sloughs off them.

Which leaves me with one option.

The cold kiss of iron, straight through the heart.

It's my first bane hunt.

Preferably not my last.

"Let's make this nice and easy," I mutter as I slip through the forest with murder—or mercy—on my mind.

Thorns encircle the ruins, some of them bearing spikes as long as my forearm. Poison drips from their tips; they call this particular bramble Sorrow's Tears. It sprang from the ground the night the King of the Sorrows was slaughtered by his new Unseelie queen. Where his people wept, the brambles grew. It's deadly to the Unseelie and excruciating to my kind, though it won't kill us.

How, in Maia's name, am I going to get inside the ruins?

The snuffling of the bane echoes in the distance. No doubt it made its lair deep inside where it will be safe from predators.

Skirting the brambles, I hold my sword low. Demi-fey peer at me from the shadows, their golden eyes vicious and unblinking. Sweat drips down my spine. I'm practically jumping at shadows, my skin prickling at the faint whisper of claws on stone.

"You can do this," I tell myself quietly.

I have to do this. I have to slay the beast at my mother's behest or suffer her consequences.

After all, if it tears my head from my shoulders, then at least I won't have to hear about it for the next ten years.

Or worse.

Girding myself, I follow the bane's blood trail to an overgrown arch. Shadows loom beneath it.

This was once the ancient stronghold of my kingdom, many years before my mother took power. The king who ruled wore a gauntlet coated with pure iron. A literal iron fist. Though the main tower's half-shattered, with stones strewn about it like rumpled skirts, it wouldn't surprise me if the tower once bore a certain phallic resemblance.

My mother overthrew him nearly a thousand years ago.

Nobody even remembers his name—she had it wiped from public record, and no one dared speak it upon pain of death. The years passed, and he faded from memory, crushed to dust just like this keep. Now only the forest remembers him, slowly swallowing what remains of his grandeur.

I wonder what he did to her to earn such a fate, such enmity. My mother is petty and vicious, but to ensure even history forgot him speaks of an enemy she saved her most vengeful acts for.

"This way, Princess!" a voice cries through the ruins. "I can see its tracks!"

I freeze.

Hooves echo on half-buried cobblestones, and then a glint of gold shines through the brambles as a young woman canters into view. Her blonde hair knots into tight braids that circle her head like a coronet. A trio of Seelie hunters clad in hard leathers are at her heels.

Curse it.

The Crown Princess Andraste. Strong. Dangerous. Powerful.

She looks like the epitome of a warrior princess, with a battle-hardened leather corset protecting her slim waist and boots that cling to her calves. A lush dark green cloak wraps around her shoulders, but it's the bow at her back and the knives tucked into her boots that make her dangerous.

Andraste doesn't miss. She doesn't fail.

I might have once called her sister, though it's been so long since we've been close enough for such a word. It's not encouraged anymore.

After all, in my mother's kingdom, there is only one ruler, only one heir.

And I'm not the favored child.

I have to kill the bane first.

Darting up the spiral staircase of the tower, I slip my

knife from its sheath so I'm well armed. I can't afford to rush this and make a mistake, but I cannot afford to lose the chance.

Thighs burning, I make it to the highest level, my steps slowing.

Wounded grunts echo from within the chamber at the top. I slip toward the door, pressing my back to the stone wall beside it and softening my breath. A glance shows the turret room inside, dust and dead leaves covering the floor. In the middle of the room is an enormous, twisted mass of fur and sinew.

It looks like a wolf and a lion had a baby.

Or no, not quite.

There are enormous teeth that don't belong to either animal, and claws over two inches long. It moves like a man, though its spine is curved like a cat's, and it loped along on all fours when we were hunting it.

Blood drips from the wound on its flank where my arrow sank between its ribs, and it licks the ravaged wound, wincing a little.

The movement's so familiar my fingers curl around the knife. The sound it made when my arrow sank into soft gray fur lingers in my memory. A cry. It sounded like a man's pained cry.

No mercy for the monsters, sneers my mother's voice.

But is it a monster?

It was fae once, whispers my conscience.

Aye, and now it's terrorizing local villages.

Year by year, it will lose itself to the curse, until all it craves is blood. All it will hunger for is flesh. There's no turning back. If the curse hasn't been broken yet, then I doubt it ever will be.

This is mercy.

Or at least, that's what I tell myself.

My fingers flex around the knife as I creep closer, picking my way between dead leaves.

The creature freezes.

So do I.

"Schmell you," it whispers. "Coming to finish job." The word comes from an inhuman mouth, but it freezes me right to the core.

There's no reasoning with a bane. All you can do is put them out of their misery and stop them before they slaughter entire villages.

But this one is fae enough still to speak.

The slight hesitation almost costs me.

The bane lunges toward me, muscle rippling beneath its fur. I drive to the side, blade swinging up. Its claws lash out, smashing my sword to the side. The weight of it slams into me, and then I'm going down. Only pure luck—or years and years of practice with my mother's swordmaster—mean that my knife drives into its side.

Stupid. So stupid.

As my back slams into the stone floor, I kick my heels up, driving it over the top of me. Lines of heat sear my thigh as its claws glance off me, but if I hadn't reacted so quickly, they'd be buried in my gut.

Rolling ungracefully to my knees, I scramble for my sword. I have no idea where the knife went. Probably still in its flank.

The bane lashes out, claws swiping my boots from under me. I hit the floor, my hand closing over the hilt as I flip over. Like a turtle on its back, I shove the sword between us, scrambling back across the floor until my back hits the wall.

The beast stretches its spine, eyes glowing an amber

gold in the dying afternoon light that pours through the open arch window.

It laughs, a faint, wheezing sound, as it prowls back and forth. "In trouvle now, little fae."

It's between the door and me, and even though it's bleeding heavily, it's still twice my size. And I'm down a weapon.

Curse it.

I clamber to my feet, forcing my voice full of a false bravado I don't feel. If in doubt... bluff. "I don't know. It seems I swapped the knife for a star-forged sword. I'd say I just traded up."

It snarls and swipes the air threateningly in a mine-is-bigger-than-yours kind of way.

Okay, fine. "Yes, I know. My, what big claws you have...."

"Come closer and see dem," it hisses.

I lunge forward, sword whining as it cuts through the air. Right into the sunlight that streams through the arched window, which blinds me for half a second. The bane avoids the blow, but instead of lashing out and taking advantage of my blunder, it hesitates.

"Prinshess...."

What? My sword hovers in the air. "Do you know who I am?"

Its lip curls as it backs away. "Ish-vien."

Close enough. I stare at it in horror. There's only one way it could recognize me by sight. "Who are you?"

"I am loyal, my princess. I am Evernight," it whispers, holding up one paw, claws curled inward. "Pleashe. Pleashe don't hurt me."

Evernight?

The Kingdom of Evernight is the enemy. Evernight and

Asturia have been at war for centuries. How would it know me?

When I was a little girl, I played games of Strategy across from my mother. Each game was a lesson, and if I played well, I would not be punished. It made me wary, thoughtful, hesitant.... And Mother noticed. *Trust your instincts*, Mother would say, eyes alight upon me. *Instinct is the cold kiss of warning that something is wrong, but hesitation is a death knell.*

And right now, mine are blaring.

It knows my face. My name. And I swear I've never come across an envoy from the Kingdom of Evernight. Mother will barely let us speak its name, let alone encourage mingling.

I lower the sword. "How do you know who I am?"

Movement shifts behind it.

"Don't move," says Andraste, stepping inside the room with her bow drawn.

The bane hisses, rising onto two feet, its hackles lifting. Amber fury rolls across its eyes, driving away any last vestiges of its humanity. All that's left is rage.

"Don't kill it!"

"Did you hit your head? That's what we're here to do."

"Something's wrong." I don't take my eyes off the beast. "How does it know who I am?"

Andraste steps to the side, her bow nocked, the string tight with tension. "Step back, Iskvien."

Before I can even move, the bane roars and rams me. My sword lands with a clatter as I slam onto the stone floor, the beast leaping over me.

An arrow flashes, and it screams.

Then it's upon my sister, driving her into the wall. Andraste whirls beneath its lashing claws, swirling her cloak in a flourish that traps them. She ducks free of the fabric, draws the knife from her right boot, and lunges forward.

It should have been an easy kill, but the beast shoves away from the wall and throws her off-balance.

She staggers back, boots clipping against my side and sending her sprawling. We're both down, scrambling to get out of the way as the enraged monster launches itself toward us.

A hand shoves me in the back as I stagger to my feet, knocking me clear. Claws rake down my arm, spilling blood, but it's my sister who grunts as she barely deflects a killing blow. My sister who pushed me aside.

Curse her. She wants to steal the glory of this kill, but I need to know how the beast knows who I am.

If it doesn't kill us first.

There's no hint of those fae eyes in its monstrous face. Not anymore. Only rage and fury and pain.

I grab Andraste's fallen cloak and throw it over the bane's head. Andraste drives her knife between its ribs just as I kick the back of its knee. For one shining, precious moment, we're moving in unison. A deadly, unstoppable force to be reckoned with.

"Don't kill it!"

Andraste's eyes flicker to mine as she slashes through its hamstring. The bane screams. Her knife flashes, catching the last dying rays of sunlight that glint through the arch, and then it's burying itself in the bane's throat.

"No!"

Blood gurgles from the stab wound. The bane's roar chokes off.

She stabs it again, right in the kidneys.

Those amber eyes lock upon me, breath wheezing from its lungs as it slumps forward. "Prinshess...."

And then the light in those eyes fades, and the beast hits the floor.

My sister turns to me, alight with fury as she wipes the blade on her thigh. "What in Maia's name were you thinking? Were you *trying* to get yourself killed?"

"I was *trying* to discover how he knew me."

Light shimmers around the bane, as though the curse isn't quite done with him. Its fur shrinks, claws sinking back into flesh and becoming fingers right before my eyes.

When the light fades, there's a fae male on the floor, naked and bloody. Scratches mar his back and buttocks, and his blond hair is long and ragged. I can't stop myself from squatting beside him, trying to avoid the growing pool of blood.

I don't know his face.

I would swear I've never seen him before.

But he's seen me, which sends a shiver down my spine. Catching the attention of the vicious prince who rules Evernight is never a wise idea.

There's a chain around his throat, and I slide my hand along its length, revealing a golden amulet shaped in a wolf's snarling head.

"Leave it," Andraste says.

"It knew me," I insist, slipping the amulet free. I don't know why, but I feel the urge to keep it.

"It was Evernight."

"Precisely the problem," I snap, fetching my sword and pocketing the amulet. Won't Mother be thrilled with her now. "A pity you're not going to get a nice fur throw for your floor."

"Haven't you learned anything, Iskvien? We do not treat with the enemy. And we show the beasts no mercy. Both are only likely to get you killed."

"And we wouldn't want that." I slide my sword home with a steely rasp. "Or do we?"

Andraste startles. "I don't want you dead."

Only bowing at her feet.

"There can be only one." One queen. One heir. It's how the Kingdom of Asturia operates. "Let's not pretend I wouldn't be a threat to you if you left me alive." Every scheming courtier in the castle would see me as an opportunity to climb the ladder at court. "Let's not pretend I'm stupid enough to think you wouldn't. You should have waited. You should have let the bane have me."

"Vi." She snags my wrist as I turn to go.

I arch a brow, waiting for her to protest that it's not like that at all. That we're sisters, not a threat to each other. But Mother has done her job far too well.

"I am either Mother's heir or I am dead," I say quietly. "I don't even want the throne. I just want to stay alive. And so do you."

"There are other options."

"Oh, really? I would love to hear your proposition."

Her lips press thinly together.

"Marriage into another kingdom? You know we'd both be merely pawns. And Mother's done too good a job in alienating every other royal court. Besides, I'd prefer to choose my own husband rather than become some petty prince's little plaything."

None of the royal options are anything short of skin-crawling. The fae can be merciless and malicious. Royals never sit on an easy throne, and the truth is, no innocent ever holds a position of power in this world.

Not for long anyway.

Those who rule kingdoms are rarely kind.

"Maybe marriage doesn't have to be a death sentence," she says.

"And maybe that bane didn't intend to kill either of us. Maybe it was trying to give me a hug."

Andraste lets me go. "We're not enemies, Vi. I would protect you."

She doesn't understand. She never will. She's always been Mother's favorite. The one who sits in on council meetings. The one who receives gifts from visiting nobles, as if they already consider her to be Mother's heir.

The one who can wield her own magic, when mine dies on my fingertips in a shower of sparks.

"I wish that was the truth." I miss my sister. But neither of us are children anymore, and I can't afford to forget that. "And I'd stay to help you lug your trophy home, but I think I'd best get a head start before night falls. Got to watch my back out there. The forests are dark and full of monsters."

But nowhere near as dangerous as court.

T wo dresses hang in the closet in front of me, both gauzy and overflowing with far too much fabric. Neither are my preferred style, but that's not the point.

Tonight is Lammastide and appearances have to be met.

Tonight I'm not Iskvien, second daughter of a merciless queen. Tonight I'm an Asturian princess, ruthless in her own right, invulnerable to those who might seek to bring down my mother's court. It might only be silk, but it's armor of a kind, though I'd far prefer a chain mail vest.

"Wear the red," says a clipped voice from the doorway. "It will accentuate your dark hair and olive skin."

My fingers still on the fabric. "Mother. What a pleasant surprise."

It is neither.

She wasn't here when we returned from the hunt. It's been three days. And I know Andraste made her report.

I've been waiting for the queen to make an appearance, and point out all the ways in which I fail her. Queen Adaia is not the type to strike immediately. She likes to let her opponents wait. And each day she hesitates is one more hint of her displeasure, one more sign it's going to be fatal.

Three days…. Not quite a storm of rage that could threaten to tear the palace apart, but a quiet, deadly chill, I suspect. Like the breath of winter down your spine.

I turn as the queen sweeps inside the room, her heavy silver gown dragging over the marble tiles with a rasp. We're as different as night and day, and I see Andraste in the queen's features, which is simply another reminder of whom the favorite daughter is. They share the same stubborn chin and full mouth, high-swept cheekbones highlighting the vaguely feline shape of their blue eyes.

But Mother's hair is wheaten gold, drawn up into a coronet of braids upon which rests her sharp-pointed crown. And she's taller, slightly thinner. More dangerous.

Anyone looking at the two of us might wonder if we shared any blood at all.

"To what do I owe this pleasure, Mother?" It's the edge of impertinence, which is all she will allow. "Won't we be late to the Queensmoot?"

"They'll wait."

"You expect an attack?" Lammastide is the one night of the year when all five surviving kingdoms of the Seelie Alliance come together to bring in the new year. Drinking, dancing, bloodshed, and assassinations are all to be expected.

Because allied we may be, but it's only against a common enemy. If my mother could destroy the other rulers of the alliance, she wouldn't hesitate.

In some part of her mind, she sees herself sitting on a throne that rules over the entire southern half of the continent.

"Sit," she says.

The only option is to obey.

"No attack." She slinks behind me as I take a seat at the vanity. "Or nothing beyond the usual. The Prince of Evernight will be there, after all. He craves my downfall."

Someone's projecting.

"I thought the Unseelie delegation would be the greater danger?"

Five hundred years ago we defeated them in the Wars of Light and Shadow, but the peace has always been tenuous. This recent treaty between Seelie and Unseelie courts is a relatively new development, and if I were my mother's daughter, I wouldn't trust it.

The three witch queens of the Unseelie court are blood-thirsty, vicious, and powerful. If my mother has delusions of grandeur, then they're nothing compared to the Unseelie, who want to cast us all into chains.

The queen lifts the heavy strands of my hair from my shoulders and runs her jeweled claws through it. "Queen Angharad is still bleeding from that last skirmish, and some say she doesn't have the full support of her sister queens any more. She's trying to fight a war on two fronts, so she won't have the courage to cause trouble for us. Focus on the real danger, Iskvien. Those at your back. Those with a knife to your throat." Her claws caress my collarbone. "Those who were never meant to rule the earth beneath their feet."

She's speaking of the two Seelie princes who forced their way onto the thrones of their own kingdoms. The Seelie kingdoms have been matrilineal for centuries—queens are tied to the lands, and the earth beneath them flourishes from the bond. Any kings that sought to elevate themselves were slowly and mercilessly destroyed. My mother considers Prince Thiago and Prince Kyrian's claims to be unnatural, and she's been working on ruining them ever since they proclaimed themselves.

Prince Kyrian never attends the Lammastide rites in person. Mother once mocked him for the loss of the woman he loved, and he swore an oath that if he ever set eyes upon her again, he'd have her head. To uphold the peace, he sends an envoy to the rites in his stead.

So she's talking of Evernight.

Always Evernight.

My thoughts stray to the forest and the bane. The creature who knew me.

And the Prince of Evernight, who rules the dark kingdom.

"What should I expect?" I've never met the prince. These are the first Lammastide rites my mother's allowed me to attend. "Will the Prince of Evernight avoid us?"

"Unfortunately, not. He considers me responsible for the loss of his wife, and I daresay he's still determined to have his revenge upon me. In fact, he's the reason I'm here."

Here it is. I still, like prey catching scent of a dangerous predator as she moves to the side, considering the array of scents and powders on my vanity.

"What does he have to do with me?"

"You're not coming home with us tonight, Iskvien," my mother says, lifting the stopper of my perfume vial and sniffing delicately at the scent within. Her nose wrinkles.

I blink.

"*What?*"

"The Prince of Evernight agreed to a truce over the territories of Mistmere after that unfortunate clash near the border, but it has come at a price."

I feel the edges of the world sucking at me. "What price?"

"There are to be hostages, to prove our good faith. His cousin is to be exchanged tonight, for you."

The jaws of the trap spring shut. I shouldn't have trusted her sweet smile, her gentle touch.

"You bartered me away? Like a fucking trinket?"

The queen's eyes narrow. "Watch your tone, daughter."

Rage fills me, but it's tempered with the quicksilver flash of fear. All these years I've been wary of her temper, but this is.... How do I...?

"It's only for three months," she continues, as if I've accepted it.

The prince could do anything to me in the space of three months. If he thinks my mother killed his wife, then I daresay I'm to be a proxy for his vengeance.

"Is this punishment?" The words erupt from my mouth. "For failing to kill that bane? It was just a hesitation, Mother. Andraste stole the kill. It won't happen again."

"*What* hesitation?"

Andraste didn't tell her?

The queen's face tightens imperceptibly, and her hands come to rest upon my shoulders. The tip of each of her fingers is covered in a silver claw, the points pressing into my collarbone. Thin chains connect them to the gauntlets around her wrist. It's nothing more than a focus for her powers—not that many know that—but the effect is also eerily threatening.

She doesn't say a word.

She doesn't have to.

"Andraste was faster than I," I say swiftly, to cover my misstep. "I thought she'd told you."

"The bane is of little consequence."

I square my shoulders. "Why worry about a ferocious beast when you're throwing me to the wolves?"

"You are not to be harmed."

"Of course not. Am I to be his whore instead?"

She arches a brow at my tone. "You are to be his political hostage, Iskvien. Make whatever bargains you need to, to keep yourself safe. But remember..., his cousin will be in my hands."

And any harm that befalls me will be returned in kind.

"Forgive me, Mother, if such a concept brings me little peace. They say the prince betrayed his queen and murdered her sons. I daresay he'll not hesitate to consider his cousin to be an acceptable loss if he can strike a blow upon you."

"You disappoint me, daughter. I offer you an opportunity, and you throw it in my face."

This is another one of her challenges. *Prove yourself*, she's telling me. *Show me you have the strength and wit to survive.*

"What opportunity?"

"There is a way you could serve your queen while you are there." My mother unsheathes the dagger at her belt and places it on the vanity in front of me.

Star-forged steel. No trueborn fae can wield the iron that lies on this world, but this knife was forged from the heart of a fallen comet, and its iron came from beyond the stars.

As long as I don't touch the blade itself, I can use it.

For a second, I see his blood splashed across the marble tiles of his palace, the knife planted between his shoulder blades. An end to the monstrous lord of the Evernight court, and freedom for those Asturians who've been imprisoned in the war camps. No more fighting. No more endless wars. No more scheming and politicking.

But murder, just the same.

"No," I say abruptly. "I'm no assassin."

Adaia leans down, her face resting on my shoulder and her gaze meeting mine in the mirror. "Perhaps not. But he'd never expect it. Not from you, with your soft heart and those pretty eyes. And perhaps you should consider your people. The Kingdom of Asturia has been at war with Evernight for centuries. Whilst this treaty sparks a fragile truce, it doesn't mean anything. We could end this war with a single strike. We would own Mistmere, perhaps more...."

I push away from her, the hem of my silk wrap brushing against my calves. "Murder, Mother. I'm the first person they'll point the finger at. Who do you think they'll blame? If I kill the prince, then his people will execute me immediately, and their armies will rise against you."

"Not if it's self-defense," she points out.

So now I'm to frame an assassination as an assault by the prince.

"Thiago has no heir," she continues. "Without him, his generals will fight for control of his armies. It will be chaos, and I will crush them."

I notice she doesn't address the part where I lose my head.

"Take the dagger."

It's not a suggestion.

I pick it up, feeling the weight of it. Accepting it doesn't mean I have to go through with anything.

"I'll consider it." I catch a glimpse of my mother's dangerous smile in the reflection as the queen backs away. It wouldn't surprise me if she made this bargain with this end in mind.

"You have an hour. Get dressed and meet us in the courtyard. We ride for the Hallow. Wear the red."

Then she's gone.

Leaving me trembling.

I can't believe she gave me no warning. Or maybe that was deliberate: With a hint of what was to come, I might have been able to flee or outmaneuver this treaty. Now, I don't have a choice. The stamp of the guard's feet as they settle outside my door is jarringly loud, and my mother expects me in the courtyard within an hour.

This isn't merely hesitating to strike a killing blow against a monster.

This is politics, and she will brook no refusal.

But who would I rather face? My mother or a volatile, dangerous prince who might think me a plaything?

My resolve firms. If he thinks he's getting a trinket to toy with, then he had best think again.

The prince of the Kingdom of Evernight is Unseelie to his bones, despite the fact he claims to be Seelie. I can't afford to show him even a hint of my weak underbelly.

And curse my mother, but I'll be damned to the Under-world if I'll let her think me her puppet.

I fling the wardrobe open, both the red and the white gowns tumbling in a frothy mess to the floor. Inside the wardrobe, right at the back, is *the* dress.

It's like a piece of pure midnight was carved from the sky, diamond stars glittering down its silken length. I don't know what urged me to have it made. Mother's right: vibrant colors suit me best. And yet, I'd been unable to think of anything else the moment I saw the material.

Red would be a sign of groveling.

The white is probably what she intended me to wear all along.

But this.... Time to show her I refuse to bow to her whims. This princess has claws. And she's not afraid to use them.

3

The guards are on edge as we take the portal from Hawthorne Castle to the Hallow that lies by the grassy plains of the Queensmoot, where the Seelie Alliance will meet for the Lammastide rites.

It's the only Hallow in the area, which means every queen—and prince—will be using it. Despite their vigilance, there's no sign of danger as we step through the circle of standing stones that guards the portal. Power hums through the ley line it's set upon, setting my teeth on edge, but the night is quiet and dark.

And probably full of surprises.

In the distance, enormous bonfires glow like a necklet of starfire gems draped around the throat of the nearby mountains. The moment takes my breath away. I've heard the court bard speak of the unbroken chain of Lammastide fires that ward against the thinning of the Veil. It's said the fires protect the realm from the Others who occasionally slip through the portals from the Underworld on nights like these, when both worlds pass each other so closely they almost touch.

"If I was an assassin, you'd be dead right now." My sister materializes out of the shadows, tearing my gaze from the mountains.

"The only thing you've killed of late, appears to be a flock of ravens," I point out. "Does mother approve? Where's your pretty gown?"

She wears black leather from head to toe, with a ruff of raven's feathers around her throat. That moonlight hair is braided back fiercely, and silver moons drip from her ears. No dress for her. She's a warrior princess, prepared to hold a sword at someone's throat if needed.

"I'm not here to play nice with the other nobles."

No, I'm the one dressed up like a gift, though the black silk cape I wear hides my starlight dress. I'm not quite prepared to reveal it just yet.

Curse it. I feel like a peacock, displayed on a platter on the dining table.

"You didn't tell her about the bane."

My sister doesn't flinch.

And a thought occurs. "You knew."

Andraste didn't need to tell mother about my failure. She's already won. I'm to be sent as tribute to another kingdom, a sacrifice to peace. The path to being named heir is clear for her without so much as a hint of bloodshed.

It's so well done, I'd almost clap, if I wasn't about to be sacrificed.

"It's not like that," she finally says. "I—"

"It sounds exactly like that. You've won. You barely even had to lift a finger. All that talk about finding another court...."

"Vi—"

"Don't." We both know anything that comes from her

mouth next is insincere. She can afford to be gracious. "You're Mother's heir. That's all that matters."

My mouth tastes like ash. What am I going to do? When I return in three months' time—if I return—what am I coming back to?

It's unwise for a princess of the blood to remain in another's court. It creates too many opportunities for politicking nobles. Too many pathways to dissent. I'll always be a knife held to my sister's throat unless....

Unless I disappear.

"Vi, there are things you don't know." She finally looks at me.

More cursed secrets. I'm starting to realize how peripheral I am to Mother's court.

"All these little secrets," I murmur, twitching at my cloak. "It's starting to make the skin between my shoulder blades tickle."

"You'll understand, one day."

"Oh, I think I understand now."

Andraste's gaze drops to the hem of my skirt, and her eyebrows hit her hairline. "You're not wearing the dress Mother had made for you."

My fingers brush against the midnight-dark silk that caresses my legs. Tiny pinprick diamonds are woven throughout the fabric, so it seems as though a cloak of pure night clings to my body. "I thought the white lace seemed a touch too virgin sacrifice. This suits me better."

"Where did you find it?"

"Find it?" Andraste spends most of her time in hunting leathers. I'd have thought fashion would have been the last thing my sister would ever willingly discuss. "I had it made on a whim several weeks ago. It seemed a little more fitting for the night."

The faintest of smiles plays about Andraste's lips. "Has Mother seen it?"

"Not yet."

I can't explain why I withheld the dress. Only a gnawing sense the queen will not approve.

Andraste laughs. "Oh, I can't wait to see her face when she does. Wait until the last moment to reveal it, or she'll strip you to your skin."

The precise thought I'd had. For a second, some of the old camaraderie we'd once shared whispers in the night.

Of course, she's happy. You won't be around to block her path to being named princess-heir.

My smile dies on my lips.

Only three minutes separate the pair of us, and from the moment we were birthed into the world, we were inseparable. I remember rolling in the grass as children, chasing demi-fey through the trees, stealing into Mother's chambers and trying on her jewelry and her crowns....

I don't know where it all went wrong.

I can't remember a single fight or betrayal that tore us apart. It was a slow creep of realization, I suppose. Leaving childhood behind and realizing my sister was now my competitor.

It was one of my tutors who pointed out the future to me. I'd never wanted the crown. Andraste could have it for all I cared, but my hob tutor had slapped his cane on the desk in front of me one day when I wasn't paying attention and snapped that if I didn't focus on my lessons, then my future was bound to be short and inconsequential.

She'd never hurt me, I protested.

But every ball, I'd see the pair of us on display. Nobles would circle around us, and I realized Andraste was making her own little court.

It soon became clear she was the favorite. The one who began to be seated at Mother's right hand on the dais. The one who was asked for advice in Mother's Round Chamber. The doors would close in my face, and I'd see my sister through them, shooting me a sad, apologetic look.

It's been years since I've seen that expression.

The sister I knew is gone, replaced by this hard, implacable woman. Though she wears no crown, the circlet of braids reminds me of a coronet every time I see it.

"You should make the most of it," she finally says.

"My three months in Evernight?"

"Yes."

I give an incredulous laugh. "I think you've been drinking too much elderberry wine, sister."

"Perhaps it won't be so bad."

Won't be so bad? "Which part?" My voice roughens. "The part where I'm handed over to a monster? The part where I have to bargain for my safety?"

For a moment, Andraste looks like she wants to tell me something.

Then the queen stalks toward us, surrounded by her advisors and guard. The moment's lost.

"Are you ready?" she demands of both of us, though I know she's looking at me.

I can't help myself.

Some part of me always has to challenge her.

So I step forward and brush the cloak from my shoulders, where it falls in a spill around my skirts.

The queen's face hardens when she sees the dress. For a second, rage ignites her magic, and glints of pure gold streak through her irises.

Defiance is her least favorite attribute.

But it's too late now.

I arch a brow in her direction. "I don't want him thinking how nice the red dress looks against my skin, and the white gives the impression I'm some pure little dove ripe for the plucking. Considering I don't have any chain mail in my wardrobe, I settled on the least offensive option."

"Oh, Iskvien." Her jeweled claws capture my chin, the heat of her magic banking in her eyes. "Why must you always defy me?"

"Because I want to make my own destiny, Mother."

"You've already made it," she whispers, the claws biting into my skin. "And now, you can lie in your bed and bear the consequences."

"Mother," Andraste murmurs.

They share a look, and I hate the fact they're clearly communicating something I don't understand.

"Let Vi wear what she likes," Andraste says. "There are too many witnesses."

There's no time for the queen to punish me for the transgression. Trumpets blare, and a malicious whispering wind suddenly springs through the trees, announcing the arrival of another court.

The queen lets me go, her spine straightening. It's one thing to punish defiance, quite another to have it witnessed by the enemy.

I breathe a sigh of relief and glance at my sister. It irks to have to say it but... "*Thank you,*" I mouth.

Andraste gives me a sad little smile.

Time to throw the dice and play the game of my life.

I DON'T JOIN the dancing.

There's nothing to celebrate.

And I can't stand to remain with my mother's delegation, watching as she introduces Andraste to envoys and foreign nobles from other courts.

Instead, I grab two glasses of elderberry wine, drain one, and then sip the other as I weave through the gathering.

There has to be some way to escape this trap, though I'm aware that two of my mother's guards stalk me circumspectively. Running is clearly not an option.

Perhaps the Queen of Aska will take mercy on me and welcome me into her court in exchange for every little secret I know about my mother? Unlikely, though, and my mother would make it her life's duty to have me assassinated.

Painfully.

I'm running out of options when a shiver trickles down my spine; a sense of trepidation hovering in the air, like the lingering portent of a lightning strike about to detonate.

I turn.

For a second, there's nothing there but myriad dancing fae.

Then shadows melt together, forming into a tall, masked figure that stalks through the crowd as if it doesn't exist. It's as if Kato, the god of death, walks among us. But this is no god, slumbering now in the memories of the fae. This male is carved out of hard, heated flesh and practically poured into black leather. Despite my anxiety, I can't help noticing the breadth of those shoulders and the powerful flex of his thighs.

The fae of mother's court flee before him like deer scattering before an approaching predator.

Because that's exactly what he is.

Even I feel it.

Piercing eyes meet mine through the eyeholes of the mask he wears; a feathered raven's beak cascading over his brow. Though no crown graces his temples, power drips from him, leaving me with no doubt of whom I face.

Thiago, Prince of Evernight.

Lord of Whispers and Lies. Master of Darkness.

I hadn't expected the sheer boiling power contained within him, or the shock of anticipation—the feeling I'd somehow spent my entire life drifting toward this single moment. The sensation punches the breath out of my lungs and sets my heart racing.

I've never been afraid of man or immortal, but I suffer a moment of trepidation as I realize the black cloak eddying behind him isn't fabric, but a pair of black wings that hint at his impure heritage. He calls himself Seelie, but my mother claims he has impure blood. And the wings betray him, for no Seelie bears the features of a beast.

I blink, and the wings vanish. There's only a man before me, draped in a black cloak.

But I swear I saw them.

"Princess," he says. The way he looks at me makes me feel as though nothing else exists. "I've been waiting for you."

All night, I'm sure.

I force my spine to straighten. To become steel. *You are an Asturian princess, and you will not yield to the Prince of Evernight.* "Prince Thiago, you honor us with your presence."

His gaze drops, the faintest flicker of—is it disappointment?—marring those dangerous eyes. "The pleasure is mine."

Why, then, do I feel as if I've somehow failed some test?

Perhaps he thought I'd be more welcoming.

If so, then he's a fool.

"I don't believe pleasure has anything to do with it."

His eyes sparkle as he lifts my hand to his mouth, his lips ghosting over the back of it. "Yet."

Oh, so that's the way he means to play.

I tear my hand free, though I can't deny a shiver runs down my spine, and the sensation of his caress lingers. "Ever."

"Did your mother not warn you? I've never met a challenge I've failed to surmount."

"But you've never met me before."

"Haven't I?" Another mysterious smile. "We're to spend the next three months together. Be careful with your challenges. I always play to win."

"Ah, but what precisely are we playing for?"

"Hearts, perhaps."

It steals a laugh from me. Oh, he's so polished, he's practically gleaming. "You think to steal my heart?"

"I don't think that at all. I think you'll give it to me."

"Never in a thousand years."

The prince leans closer. "There you go again, Princess. Opposing me. Daring me. I think I'm going to enjoy the next three months. Very much so."

Of course, he will. He's the one with the power. "Perhaps. You might regret them instead."

"Regret meeting *you*? Never. Dance with me," he says.

I press my hand to his chest. "But you didn't say please."

The faintest of smiles graces his hard mouth. "I never say please."

I've heard that about him too—I can see it in the flex of his jaw, as if a part of him yearns to reach out and take my arm. He's not the sort of male you deny. A warlord, a conqueror, a prince who stole his kingdom from its rightful heirs.

Time to prove I'm no mere pushover. "Sorry. You don't own me just yet."

And then I whirl away into the watching crowd, leaving him staring after me.

4

"Acurious choice of words: I don't own you...."

He finds me within minutes.

I close my eyes, blinking away the afterimage of a bonfire. When I open them, the prince fills my vision. Fire backlights him, shadows cutting harshly against those cheekbones and the playful fullness of his mouth.

The worst part of this entire affair may be the fact that even though he's my worst nightmare, he looks like he stepped directly from my dreams.

"Midnight," I tell him. "The exchange happens at midnight. Until then, I'd prefer to be alone."

I push past, but a hand shackles my wrist.

"Stay," he whispers, his thumb stroking the inside of my wrist. He's big enough that I feel a little overwhelmed. Every inch of him dwarfs me, and his dangerous beauty holds a lethal grace that intrigues me, just a little.

He has the face of a sinner.

The body of a god.

And the touch of a seducer.

I tear my hand free. "I have little choice in accepting this sham of an alliance and my role in it, but do not ever mistake me for obedient. I *will* fight you at every turn, and if you dare put your hands on me again, I'll remove them."

I hate that faint quirk of a smile.

Sliding the mask back off his face, he considers me. The shock of those dangerous green eyes is like a punch to the chest. I don't know why, but my heart is suddenly pounding.

"If your mother abides by the treaty, then you have nothing to fear from me."

It's that *if* that concerns me.

"We don't have to be enemies," he adds, gliding toward me. "And the next three months don't have be a war."

"No, they don't."

But they're going to be.

The prince glances around, and I realize we're drawing attention. Hobs whisper behind their hands, and a pair of fae watch us over the slow waft of their feathery fans.

"*My lady love*," sings a nearby minstrel, smiling viciously at the prince as he bows his head and strums his lute. "*My lady fair. She of the moon, and the gilded hair. Come dance, said he, and extended a hand; But the lady divine, slapped him with her fan—*"

"This way," the prince growls, directing me toward a stand of trees.

"I like that song," I protest.

"Of course you do."

Here in the clearing, we have a semblance of privacy. I tug at a golden cord, and a curtain of vines sweep closed behind us, shielding us from prying eyes. It's been created for lovers, a private nest some lord no doubt intends to use later tonight. But for now, it's a haven.

I don't know what he wants to say.

I don't even know why I followed him.

Except for the lingering desire to take a stand and ensure he doesn't think me a prisoner at his mercy.

"What do you want?" I demand.

"I thought we ought to get to know each other. We're about to spend a significant amount of time together."

"Oh?" I tilt my chin a little arrogantly. "In what way?"

If you intend that statement to mean in your bed, then I will promise you an eternity of ruin.

He reads me accurately. "You have nothing to fear from me, Princess. I don't take what isn't freely given."

I turn away, kicking cushions out of the way as I pace the small space. The dagger seems heavy at my side. "Good. For neither my heart nor my body will ever be freely given." Which begs the question.... "And you still haven't told me what you want from me."

"A chance."

"A chance?"

"A chance to win what you deny me."

My heart skips a beat. "You *do* want me in your bed."

"Perhaps I merely want your heart." The prince's lashes half obscure his eyes, as I laugh. "You place poor value on such a thing."

"Or perhaps I doubt you would submit to my mother's treaty, simply for the chance at my heart." I shake my head. "Especially when you know such a prize is impossible to win."

"Nothing is impossible."

"We are enemies—"

"We don't have to be. We—"

He turns, cocking his head.

I pause.

It isn't just the pounding of my heartbeat—drums echo through the forest, slowly growing louder. A shiver of silence sweeps through the trees, revelry dying like someone snuffed a candle flame.

The Unseelie queens have arrived.

Two of the three Unseelie queens stood on the other side of the battlefields during the Wars of Light and Shadow over five hundred years ago. Though the Seelie Alliance overthrew the Old Ones, turning the tide of the battle, the Unseelie queens yielded but never completely bowed their heads.

Every thirteen years, the Unseelie Queens ride south to the Queensmoot to renew the treaty between the north and the south.

And every thirteen years, the fractured Seelie courts meet to pledge themselves to the accords.

If I have to be the price of this peace, then so be it.

"We will finish this discussion later," the prince tells me, one hand resting on his sword as he strides through the curtain of vines.

I follow him, cursing under my breath. There's nothing to discuss, though his words bring me little ease. This is merely a game to him.

The Unseelie queens bring with them the creeping chill of a breathless body. Torches flicker and then gutter out as an unearthly gloom creeps over the gathering. The fae of my mother's court shift uneasily.

And then the Unseelie clear the trees, and the drums cut off so abruptly, a shiver runs over my skin.

Angharad the Black rides at the head of the Unseelie column, astride a lich-horse woven of old bones and moss. Its foul breath steams the night air, and clumps of dull, matted hair cling to its fetlocks. She wears black silk from head to toe and a crown carved of pure obsidian that swallows the light.

At her side ride Blaedwyn the Merciless and the Black Crow, Morwenna of Isenbold.

Blaedwyn's black hair tumbles down her back, with some of it woven into a pair of horns atop her head. She wears hunting leathers, and the enormous Sword of Mourning is strapped to her spine. Her white teeth flash in a smile as she beholds us, and I remember what they say about her. She lives for the rush of battle and the swing of the sword. This treaty will barely hold her in check, and she no doubt sees us as an impediment or a challenge.

Morwenna looks like the ancient Hag she is.

Her white, brittle hair flows over her shoulders, though her spine is straight and she holds the reins with a firm grip. Finger bones hang around her neck in a malevolent necklace woven to counteract curses. Centuries old during the wars, she's rapidly approaching her twilight, though it doesn't make her any less dangerous. She's the ultimate witch queen, her life bound to serve the Horned One, who is locked away in one of the prison worlds. If she saw even the slightest chance to release him, she'd take it, and damn the world thrice over.

"That old bitch is still alive," my mother says in some disgust.

"Seemingly," Andraste counters. "Perhaps she crawled out of the grave for the accords?"

I say nothing.

The Unseelie horde capers along behind them. Unseelie fae with black bat wings and horns that hint at their impure heritage; leering hobgoblins covered in warts; pale-faced Sorrows with black hair and long claws; trolls and redcaps and beastlike, twisted banes. They're all ugly, vicious creatures who live for blood and flesh.

Some say that millennia ago, the Seelie and Unseelie

were one people, but I can't see any resemblance in the capering, howling mob.

The queens finally arrive on the mound. A tall, impossibly gaunt fae male slams his staff against the stone at his feet, and silence echoes as the Unseelie's howls and screams cut off all at once.

"Angharad brought her favorite pet sorcerer," murmurs a masculine voice at my side.

Someone's determined to haunt me tonight.

I glance at the prince. "That's Isem?"

"Fresh out of the grave by the look of him."

"Let us treat," says Angharad, smiling a devil's smile.

"THERE HAVE BEEN incursions into Unseelie lands," Angharad says, wasting no time as she settles onto the thronelike seat that is set out for her. "Fae warbands that ride with goblin warriors in their ranks. Many of our border villages have been burned, their occupants slaughtered."

"The goblins rule their own clans," the Prince of Evernight interrupts smoothly. "We hold no treaties with their people. We do not ride at their side."

"Do you call me a liar, Prince?" the Unseelie Queen snarls.

He spreads his hands. "I only claim the Seelie Alliance holds no bargains with the goblins. Whoever is raiding your villages does not belong to us."

"*Truth*," rasps Isem, his milky white eyes staring at nothing. "Or the truth as the prince believes it."

Isem is a truth-seeker and was born with the gift.

It's still creepy.

And a reminder that lying in this moment might be a precursor to war.

"The goblin clans wouldn't dare strike us of their own accord," Angharad bites out, her clawed hands curving over the arms of her throne.

My stepbrother, Edain, lounges by Mother's feet, rolling grapes between his beringed fingers. Ever since his father died in a hunting accident, he's been serving Mother in bed, though some say the timelines overlap. "The goblin clans remain leaderless with the loss of their king. Without him holding their reins, who is to say some clan does not ride at its own whim? They're violent, greedy creatures, after all."

Angharad cuts him a furious glance.

"The boy speaks truth," says Lucidia, the Queen of Ravenal. She's ancient and has proven counterfoil to my mother many times over the years. "King Rangmar held his goblins together. None dared step outside his edicts, but he is gone, and the Unbroken Crown is without a head to sit upon as the goblins squabble. Perhaps some clan decided to seek its own fate outside the mountains."

The other Seelie queen, Queen Maren, lifts a goblet to her lips. "Perhaps you should strengthen your borders, Angharad. If the goblins are riding, then I intend to."

Angharad seethes, but she has no option to explore. The Seelie Alliance has swiftly shut her down.

They move on to other topics.

Edain settles in beside me, brushing my hair off my shoulder. We aren't friends, and in other circumstances, I'd punch him in the balls, but he's also aware of that. Pasting a smile on my lips, I lean in to him.

"Interesting," he murmurs, his lips brushing my ear. "Angharad's grasping for reasons to fight. It wouldn't surprise me if these 'goblin incursions' ride at her directive."

The goblin clans are more likely to ally themselves with the Unseelie, after all, and I cannot say I blame them.

"You think she intends upon a war."

"She's been hungering for one for centuries."

I glance down at my hands. The Seelie Alliance is ill-equipped for war at this moment. Though they present themselves as a united front, they're anything but.

Queen Maren and my mother plot together, but Lucidia is a prickle in their socks, and the two princes would rather slit their own throats than stand beside my mother as allies.

The more I discover, the more I realize I need to uphold my mother's treaty with the Prince of Evernight. The entirety of Seelie might depend upon it.

The night wends on, the bonfires dying down as the Unseelie and Seelie courts treat. Promises are made. Whether they'll be kept is another matter.

And there is one last business to attend to.

"Your Highness," the Prince of Evernight says, standing and offering me a hand. "It is after midnight."

The entire gathering falls silent.

I cannot help feeling Angharad's eyes upon me, and a shiver runs down my spine.

This is it. This is the moment.

I push myself to my feet, ignoring his hand. I will walk on my own two feet, an Asturian princess to the last inch.

"This is Thalia," he says, gesturing to the tall brunette at his side. "My cousin. She will tend to you on the journey back to Evernight."

The woman smiles at me, but I have no interest in making friends.

I slice the blade across my palm, staring him directly in the eyes. "Blood to blood, I bind my promise to you. Three months, I will serve as hostage in your court."

The prince slices his own palm. He clasps hands with me, our blood mingling. A shock jolts through me as the power in his blood mingles with something in mine.

"Three months you will be mine." His gaze drifts over my shoulder. "And then I shall return you to your mother's court."

Adaia smirks. "So be it."

I can't help feeling as though something else has been promised between the two of them, for neither of them lowers their gaze until Thalia takes me by the hand and leads me into the mass of the Prince of Evernight's people.

I don't look back.

There's nothing there for me.

All I can do is look ahead.

Three months.

I just have to survive the next three months.

5

"He won't bite, you know?" Thalia says cheerfully.

I glance at the prince's back as we ride toward the Hallow. I've been given a horse, and though the prince offered to help me mount, I took the reins myself and refused his courtesy.

It earned me a faint smile, as if he knows we're playing a game.

"Unless she asks for it," says the other woman at my side.

Her smile's not kind. There are too many teeth in it, and the innuendo raises my hackles. Tall and muscular, she wears her hair tugged back in harsh black braids, and her attire could be a mirror of my sister, Andraste's.

Somewhere out there, a tanner is missing half of his finest leather.

"*Eris,*" Thalia chides, giving the taller woman a pointed look.

Eris. Sweet Maia. My eyes widen. This is one of the prince's generals and his most dangerous weapon.

Surprisingly, she shuts her mouth when the prince's

cousin speaks, even though she could crush Thalia like a glowwyrm.

"Back on your leash," I say through a smile.

The prince lets his horse drop back to my side, and both Thalia and Eris fall back in some unspoken agreement.

Subtlety at its finest.

"Save your breath," I cut in. "You're charming, but it doesn't make me trust you an inch. Quite the opposite, in fact."

He glances at me. "What would make you trust me?"

"Set me free. Return me to my mother's court unharmed. Release me from this mockery of a treaty."

"I will." When my gaze jerks to his, he smiles a little. "In three months' time."

"I hate you."

"You don't know me." There's something sharp in his voice.

"I don't intend to know you. Why are you doing this?" The question has been irritating me all day. "You said I have nothing to fear from you. That you wouldn't touch me unless I willed it. Then what do you get out of this entire arrangement?"

"Besides picturing the look on your mother's face every time she thinks of me?"

"As much as I think you'd enjoy that, I highly doubt you'd have put your kingdom on the line just to spite her."

"Perhaps you should look beyond the surface, Princess. You might see more than what your court whispers about me."

It's true. What I've heard has been less than flattering, which is typical, considering it came from my mother's court. The Prince of Evernight is both demon and night-mare, his name spoken in hushed whispers, just in case their words traveled to him on the wind. They called him the Usurper or the Prince of Darkness.

There have always been seven Seelie kingdoms ruled by queens. When Maia breathed life into the world, she left her seven daughters behind to rule each territory. Each successive queen went through the blood rites that tied her to her kingdom and gave her access to the powerful magic of the land.

The war changed everything.

Two of the kingdoms fell: Mistmere and Taranis. Of the five remaining kingdoms, two were left without their queens —or any of the matrilineal lines.

And so the prince rose. A man who appeared seemingly out of nowhere, serving the previous Queen of Evernight as her warlord before she'd died. He'd won his kingdom through blood and ruin, striking down the queen's sons and claiming her throne for himself.

And he'd destroyed any who sought to rise against him.

But that story was told to me by my mother.

And she has cause enough to believe it.

"No," I say softly. "You're right. I don't truly know what type of man you are."

"Do you want to?"

Know your enemy, my mother's memory whispers in my ear. "Why not? You can start with what you intend to do with me."

"You're right. There's more to this arrangement than I've admitted, but the truth shall remain between your mother and me for the moment. The treaty does have the side advantage of keeping a knife at your mother's throat for three months. She won't start a war when I have you at my side."

You might be overestimating her fondness for me. "So, I'm to reside in your lands for the duration of the time? Rotting in a prison cell? Or free to roam?"

"Are you sure that's what you're really asking?"

"It had better be."

"You will be given your own chambers, and you'll be free to roam the castle at will," he replied. "I don't intend you any harm. I wish you would believe that."

In my mother's kingdom, wishes are worth nothing more than the breath they're exhaled upon.

"Perhaps I find it difficult to believe, considering what happened to your wife."

He hesitates as he moves to dismount. Just a moment of wariness dashing across his expression before he collects himself. "My wife?" The words are cold and hard. "What have you heard of my wife?"

"Only that you lost her," I tell him, "many years ago, and you swore bloody vengeance upon my people for her loss. You blame my mother, so you can understand my reticence."

He reaches up to help me dismount, hard eyes locking on me. "You have nothing to fear from me, Your Highness. I would never repay her loss upon an innocent."

"And my mother? What of her?"

"Adaia's no innocent." His smile turns dangerous as he sets me on both feet before the Hallow. "One day, I will make your mother rue the moment she ever heard of my marriage."

"Even if it destroys her people?" I snort, brushing his hands from my hips. "You speak of not striking the innocent, but you'll have to plow through them on your way to strike down the queen."

The answer is in his eyes. "Only those who rise against me will be considered my enemies. And trust me, Your

Highness. The people of Asturia would not stand a chance were I to truly go to war. You would be wise to warn them against such a move."

"If you were as merciful as you claim, you'd not make such a move in the first place."

The prince leans closer, the chill early morning wind cutting around the imposing length of his body. "Don't mistake me, Princess. I'm not merciful. I'm not kind. And I don't intend to let your mother win this bloody war." He presses his fingertips to my startled lips. "But you and I have no grievance. Now follow me. Anyone would think you were stalling."

I glance at the looming stones.

The second I pass through them, this becomes shockingly real. But I can't afford for him to know I'm nervous.

"Lead on, my prince. I'm not afraid of the next three months. Indeed, quite the opposite. I'm going to make you regret every single second of them."

His smile is swift and makes my heart pound just a little. "You couldn't make me regret your company in a thousand years."

"Challenge. Accepted."

THE HALLOW LOOMS AHEAD of us.

Thirteen ancient standing stones stood on the moor, carved with bronze glyphs in the old language. Each stone is perfectly smooth and polished, gleaming pale in the moonlight. There are twenty-three Hallows in the Seelie lands, used for centuries as portals. They stand where ley lines intersect, a nexus point for the power that bands the earth. Only sixteen of them remain in use. The others were destroyed or altered during the wars, and while the stones still stand in those ruined Hallows, the fae who used them vanished forever.

Now nobody dares.

Each step brings the Hallow closer. I can feel the power within the circle vibrating over my skin. They'll use that power to open a portal and travel to the prince's lands.

But where?

The city of Ceres, on the bay? Or Valerian, the ancient City of the Dead that was half destroyed during the Unseelie Wars all those years ago?

"Gather in close!" Eris bellows, gesturing the rest of the prince's retinue through the lintel stones.

Twenty-four guards and retainers—which was the strict number allowed to attend from each court—make for close quarters. Thankfully, I'm somewhere near the edge, though Eris grabbed a handful of my horse's bridle as if she feared I'd bolt at the last second.

"Tempting," I mutter for her ears only.

"Time it incorrectly and the Hallow will slice you in two. It would be a shame to get blood all over my boots."

Thiago cuts his finger and paints blood across one of the granite faces.

Power throbs through the stones, lighting up all the glyphs. They're written in the Old Tongue that came from the origin world. His voice lifts as he slowly intones the words that will channel that power directly through the Hallow.

Each stone lights up.

"Ready?" Thiago asks.

A flash of silver glints in the night to my right. A movement, a blur, a threat—

I react purely on instinct, shoving the prince aside as the

knife bound for his back drives directly toward me. I snap my palm into the chin of the assailant, feeling something bump my arm. A face glares at me from inside the cowl of its hood, and I grab the assassin's hand, twisting it to try and force him to drop the knife—

And then my blood turns to acid.

A scream tears loose.

The assassin punches me in the cheek, then vanishes in a whirl of smoke, but I'm barely aware of it.

I stagger back, slapping a hand to my arm. Blood wells between my fingers, a slash I barely felt until it was too late. My vision blanches as the pain nearly drives me to the ground.

"After him!" Thiago bellows, catching me as my knees give out.

The prince's retinue fan out, hunting the assailant, but he's gone, vanishing into the trees that surround the Hallow.

I can barely breathe. Barely see.

The whole world is spinning, and it isn't because of the portal. The magic within it is powering down, losing focus as the prince's half-formed spell begins to dissolve.

Thiago picks up the knife, his face savage. "Do you trust me?"

Somehow, I laugh through chattering teeth. "Not even an inch."

"Then trust this: if anything happens to you while you belong to me, your mother has cause to demand my head. Hold out your arm."

I have no choice.

He takes my wrist, and I nearly scream again as the simple touch ignites new agony. Black veins crawl up the skin of my forearm, twisting like poisonous brambles hunting for my heart.

Every fae alive knows what that means.

A Deathbound Blade.

"Unfortunately... for you," I pant, "I think you're... going to lose your... head after all."

All these years, scrambling to stay alive in my mother's court, and it comes to this. A tiny little scratch. An act of mercy, my instincts urging me to react before I'd even had a chance to realize what was happening to me.

My old swordmaster would be impressed with my reaction time.

Unluckily for me, I'm going to end up just as dead as if I hadn't seen the knife coming. There's no means to cure the curse attached to a Deathbound Blade. More dangerous than any poison, the curse will eat my heart alive from the inside out.

And I'll feel every excruciating moment of it.

Someone wanted the prince to suffer.

"How little faith you have in me," the prince murmurs. "Hold still, Princess. This will hurt."

Heat flares from his palm.

The pain wells. I scream again, throwing back my head. It incinerates me from within, my blood boiling as if it's pure acid. Some fae know how to heal, but this isn't healing. He's using his magic to destroy the curse that creeps through my body.

Then it's over.

I come to in the prince's arms, my head slumped against his chest. A warm palm splays across my back, rubbing soothing circles.

"You're safe," he promises.

I hold out my trembling hands. The black veins are vanishing before my eyes. The pain subsides to a dull roar.

I'm going to be sick. "All over your boots," I think I say. I'm not sure. The world is spinning again.

"Get that portal activated!" the prince bellows. His voice lowers, just for me. "I'll forgive you my boots. Just this once."

I blink blearily against his chest. Everything hurts. My brain throbs, and my eyes ache as if I haven't slept in two weeks.

Several fae start chanting, and the stones light up again.

The magic rushes through me like a million ants skittering over my skin. Then the prince is staggering forward through the gush of light and power, his boots finding solid ground on the other side.

When the light finally dies, I manage to lift my head from his shoulder. We stand in a second Hallow, the stones cold and gray and lifeless again, as if the magic has been sucked from them. They'll need at least an hour to recharge, but for now, nobody will be able to follow us.

"It's clear," a hard voice says, and apparently, we're still in my nightmares, for it's Eris. She keeps a hand on her sword as she sweeps the circle of stones until she's satisfied. The others must have stayed behind to find the assassin.

Beyond the stones stretches a labyrinthine city—or the ruins of one. We're on a hill in the direct center, where an ancient palace still stands, draped in snowy skirts.

City of the Dead, it is.

They say Valerian was the jewel of the north once, and as I stare upwards, I see it. The palace takes my breath away. It's carved completely of white marble that gleams beneath the soft wash of moonlight like alabaster—or bone. Graceful arches beckon and lithe bridges arch into nowhere, their ends sheared off.

It would have been beautiful when it was whole. A

palace built to grace the near-constant night that exists so far north.

But the war with the Unseelie ravaged its soul and stole a piece of its heart. As my eyes see past its immediate beauty, I notice the blank holes where windows once stood. They look like soulless pits watching the night. Thorns of the night-blooming Sorrow plant grow up its towers, but no blooms open to the moon, and wraiths flicker in and out of existence on the battlements.

"There's no one here except my servants," the prince murmurs. "We'll be alone. It's safe."

Alone.

With the enemy.

"I can stand," I tell him, pushing at his restraining arm.

His arms tighten around me. "You can also fall flat on your face, but let's not take the chance. Eris, make sure our way is clear."

She shoots me an expressionless glance, then strides down the hill, her hips swinging and her hand never leaving the hilt of her sword. "As you wish, my prince."

And then the bastard carries me all the way to the ruins of the palace.

6

The prince eases both doors to his bedchamber shut and leans against them with a sleepy look in his eyes. "How are you feeling?"

"Like I just took a knife for you," I point out, wobbling a little, though I'll be damned if I show it. Surviving my mother's court gives me a good grounding to face him like this. It doesn't matter how much blood you've lost, you don't dare faint in front of my mother or her people.

Especially not when I'm standing in front of the monstrous bed he just set me down in front of.

"And I'm grateful, but shouting a warning would have been just as effective."

"I'll consider that next time." Along with simply standing aside and letting the assassin complete their task.

An enormous thronelike chair reclines by the fireplace, and thick, woven rugs are scattered across the stone floors. Everything's been made on a scale to both impress and threaten, though there's a sense of luxuriousness I hadn't expected. Silk sheets on the bed. Luscious velvet throws in a dark mulberry color. The silvery ruff of fur just begging me to lie upon it.

A pair of sconces linger by the bed, and a sheer curtain is tied to the wall. Thiago moves to light the candles in the sconces, becoming little more than a shadow behind the gauze, his cloak flaring behind him like a pair of wings. I shiver, wrapping my arms around myself as I examine every inch of the room.

That bed is big enough for ten.

Unfortunately, there's no sign of another.

"Not what you expected?" The prince blows out the taper he used to light the candles, and a ring of smoke curls toward the ceiling. He watches me through it.

It's exactly what I expected.

One bed.

The two of us.

"Where are all the skulls?" I joke, instead. "The bodies of your vanquished enemies?"

"Under the bed," he purrs. "Care to take a closer look?"

There it is. The suggestion we've both been dancing around. "And if I don't care to?" I turn around, steeling my spine. The treaty only requires that I spend the three months in his court. Not that I serve as concubine.

The prince shrugs, slipping the cloak free of his shoulders. It pools around his ankles like a swathe of pure night, then he crosses to the decanter to pour two goblets of wine. "Your loss, Your Highness."

My loss?

I stare into the wine he gives me. "Let us establish some rules."

The prince sinks into his thronelike chair, rubbing forefinger and thumb thoughtfully over the base of his goblet.

"Rules, Princess?" A wicked smile crosses his mouth. "I don't play by the rules."

I ignore him. "What do you want of me?"

It catches him by surprise. "What do you mean?"

I've spent years playing word games in my mother's court. "Come now. Let's not pretend you made this request because you're interested in the pleasure of my company—"

"You might be surprised."

"You want something from me. What?"

"What would you give?"

Nothing. But without anything to offer, I have little to bargain with. "A kiss."

His eyes darken as he considers his wine. "A high price to pay." Draining the goblet, he leans forward. "Once a day."

Once a week would be preferable—or never—but I nod slowly. "Once a day."

"And given freely."

"If you keep your hands off me."

"A kiss once a day, for the next three months. No more, no less, unless you initiate it." He repeats it twice more. "Spoken thrice, my oath upon it."

"My oath upon it," I agree, and feel the magic bind us together. The oath tingles along my skin before slowly evaporating. "And if thus broken, let the bearer's ass erupt in boils. Painful boils."

That steals a startled smile from him. He has no need to agree to my additional terms—the oath is spoken. But he does. "So shall it be." Then he laughs. "Hoping I'll break it?"

"That wouldn't be very kind of me, would it?"

"I do like a challenge. Getting you into bed will be deliciously satisfying, all the more so, when you come willingly."

He's got to be joking. "You think I would *invite* you into my bed?"

Another dangerous smile. "Stranger things have happened."

"You'd have better luck with my mother."

His smile dies. "That's disgusting."

"My mother is beautiful," I point out, relishing the look on his face. Oh, he doesn't like this thought at all. "They say she's insatiable too. And adventurous."

"Please, Princess," he mocks. "Have mercy. No more talk of your mother and her bed. Leaving me for the assassin would have been kinder."

On that we agree.

I cross the bedchamber, avoiding the bed. "So... if you're not intending to take what isn't offered... where shall I sleep?"

He gestures toward the bed. "Right there."

The bed looms, the demi-fey carved into its massive headboard practically leering at me. "But you promised. You swore an oath."

"Did you think these chambers were mine?"

There's a distinct masculine aura to the room. And I assumed they belonged to him.

He watches me with amused eyes. "My chambers are down the hall. Unless you want to share the bed? Platonically, of course."

"I snore like a drunk troll. You wouldn't want to risk your hearing."

The prince smiles again, reaching inside his shirt pocket for something. "You don't snore."

"Oh? How would you know?"

He leans back in his chair. "Because I can read you like a book, Princess. You're a little nervous right now, which makes you bluster and speak a little faster than usual. It's endearing."

Endearing.

I want to murder him for the thought, but my hands wouldn't fit around that thick, muscular throat.

"I'm an Asturian princess," I say in a frosty voice. "You can pretend to flirt, but I'm not falling for it, Your Highness. We are enemies—"

"We don't have to be," he says, in a smoky, sultry voice that could tempt a priestess of Maia.

"Unfortunately, that was written in the stars."

"A prince makes his own destiny. And this war is between your mother and me. Not us."

"I am my mother's daughter."

"I'll try to forgive you for that, if you can forget the fact I'm despicably handsome."

I growl under my breath. He's next to impossible. "I'm tired and I want to go to bed. Alone."

"Come here."

"It's been a long day," I protest.

"Ah, an Asturian queen to her fingertips. You think to renege on your deal so swiftly. Should I be surprised?"

"That you demand so much, so soon, doesn't surprise *me* at all." My eyes narrow. "One kiss."

He hasn't specified where, or how passionate it has to be. I can get through this and keep my dignity, and he'll be forced by his own words to honor the pact and keep his hands off me.

"One kiss," he repeats.

Fine. If he wants his kiss, then I'll give it, but I'll make him regret it.

Letting the borrowed cloak fall from my shoulders, I saunter toward him.

The prince reclines in his chair, watching me with those darkly amused eyes. His shirt's unbuttoned halfway down his chest, and the only sign he feels anything is the way he swallows before his gaze dips down the length of my body.

I suffer a moment's hesitation.

This is the enemy.

But this is also the price I'll pay to keep myself safe.

I rest a hand against his chest, leaning down to brush my lips perfunctorily against his.

Soft lips brush against mine, but he doesn't lean into the touch. I can feel the tension in him, his hands curling around the arms of his chair as if he's fighting to restrain them. It's a heady feeling, knowing that in this moment, I hold all the power. He cannot reach for me. He cannot touch me. Not without permission.

I own him in this moment, and the thrill is a dangerously beckoning lure.

He tilts his face to mine, breath whispering over my lips. I can taste the wine, the heat of him, the barely caged desire....

It's the faintest of caresses, barely a kiss, and we both know it. And yet it holds a taste of the forbidden, a reckless, pinwheeling sensation that feels like I'm skating on ice without knowing how thin it is....

He captures my wrist, and our eyes meet, breaths mixing as I'm forced to hover over him. It gives me the ability to start thinking again.

"If you don't want to sit for a week, then please, continue. I won't mind at all." I can feel his touch like a manacle.

His thumb brushes against the inside of my wrist, and I swallow.

Hard.

"Unless you initiate it," he points out, and that's when I realize my own hand is curled in his shirt, thumb brushing small circles over his chest.

All it would take would be for him to pull me down into his lap, and then I'd be at his mercy. It's a heady feeling, knowing how much power I could wield with a simple "yes" or "no."

And it *is* a no.

It has to be.

"You have your kiss."

Thiago releases me, smiling slightly. "Is that what you call it in your mother's court? Oh, Princess.... What I could teach you about kissing...."

Heart racing, I immediately set a few feet of distance between us. I have little doubt he could. Say what they like about his kingdom and people, they didn't call him the Master of Dreams for no reason.

"I'm afraid I'll have to decline."

"Curious choice of words."

Afraid....

"But there will be other kisses, Princess. Goodnight." He crosses to the double doors, bowing before stepping back through them. The faintest of smiles touches his lips. "Sweet dreams."

And then he shuts the doors, leaving only a single key on my side, which I swiftly use to lock them.

I'm alone with the bed of sinful thoughts.

I don't know why, but I'm suddenly certain these chambers *were* his. It wouldn't surprise me to find it amuses him to have me sleep in his bed. I grab one of the pillows and sniff it, and *ugh*, it smells of him.

Sweet dreams, my ass.

The only way I'm going to get any sleep at all is if I keep my knife beneath my pillow.

Three months. All I have to do is survive for the next three months, and then I'm free. Of my mother's machinations, my sister's scheming, and whatever the Prince of Evernight intends to do to me.

7

I wake to eternal evening.

There's a moment of disorientation as I stare at the canopy of the strange bed I'm lying in, and then it all comes rushing back. The Lammastide Rites. The Prince of Evernight. The deal my mother struck with him.

No sound comes from outside the room, though the clock on the mantle reveals I've slept late. The fey lanterns in the room are slowly warming, as if to provide some sense of normality in this twilight landscape.

Slipping from the bed, I find my trunk of clothes and swiftly dress in my hunting leathers. The knife Mother gave me is wrapped in my shirt, and my hand hesitates beneath its weight. The thought of serving as her assassin makes me feel sick to the stomach, but better to be armed than to be helpless, and I wasn't allowed a sword.

I distinctly recall hearing the prince say I was free to roam as I willed, which means I'm up and out the door before anyone has a chance to stop me.

The palace is empty, though it feels as though something watches me from every shadow. I catch a rush of movement out of the corner of my eyes, which means there are demi-fey there, though whether they serve the prince is unknown. They're wilder fae, nature spirits and ethereal sprites that dance to their own whims. Sometimes vicious, sometimes capricious, entirely unpredictable.

Valerian may be called the City of the Dead now, but it was once known as the City of Dreams, thanks to its cocooning blanket of almost ever-present twilight. Magic kept the ice and cold out, and as I slip through the palace ruins, I realize the spell that shields the city from the worst of the weather must still be in place.

Silence echoes through the hallways.

Snow lingers in drifts on the carpets, as if it crept in through crevices unknown.

There's no sign of the servants the prince promised were here, but there's also no sign of him, which can only be a boon.

It's in the heart of the palace, where snow drifts lightly against the walls, that I realize the true beauty of the place. The enormous inner courtyard is no courtyard at all, but the remnants of a ballroom. Glass shards crunch beneath my boots, and as I look up, I see the broken spans of stone that hint at the remains of a roof.

The moon shines directly overhead. It must have been a glassed roof once upon a time, built to take advantage of the ever-present night skies. A silvery blue light cascades over everything, and what is left of the ballroom mirrors refracts it back until the entire snowy room seems to glow.

A single pair of wraiths waltz slowly around the ball-room, caught by the ravages of time in a never-ending loop. They litter the streets of Valerian, an ethereal reminder of the war.

Its only as they sweep past one of the stone columns that

supported the roof that a small piece of paper catches my eye.

It's tucked inside a crevice in the column, and from this angle the moonlight falls directly upon it. Something about its placement seems furtive.

I pluck it from the stone, unfurling the small scroll.

IF YOU'RE READING THIS, then you're being held by the Prince of Evernight. To escape this tangled web, you must discover what happened to his wife. Trust your instincts.

I FREEZE.

It's written in a style similar to my own hand. Sloped Asturian letters. Someone else from my mother's court, perhaps? Definitely feminine, judging by the looping scroll of the letters.

But who?

Another captive?

Blessed Maia, what if this isn't the first time the prince has arranged for a 'political hostage'? He swore not to touch me without my consent, but who knows what he has in mind? There's a reason he's isolated me from the rest of his people.

One question, however, haunts me. What happened to the woman who wrote this message?

And what does she mean, by finding out what happened to his wife?

It's the sort of thing one doesn't mention to one's captor, especially when I know my mother played a role in her loss.

I'm so engrossed in the message that I don't hear the soft pad of footsteps until it's too late.

"You're up early."

My hand clenches shut around the paper, and I spin to find the prince sauntering down the snowy stairs.

He looks even more dangerous this... morning? The fur hem of his black cloak drags across the snowy steps, and a silver and black tunic glints in the moonlight. There's no hint of softness in that face. Only sharp edges, and the feral glint of hunger in his eyes as he surveys me.

"Was I not meant to explore?" I reply, hiding my fist behind me like I've been caught with my hand in the safe.

"You may do as you like—"

"Except leave."

"You can try to leave," he points out, "which means Asturia breaks the treaty. But I won't stop you."

It's not freedom, though he makes me feel as though I have the run of the castle.

"Here," he says, sweeping aside his cloak and revealing the sword at his hip. He tugs it free of its scabbard and hands it to me, hilt first. "I thought you might enjoy sparring with me."

"You're handing me something sharp?"

"It's less dangerous than your tongue."

I take the sword, examining its edges. It's beautiful and perfectly weighted, with a star engraved on its crossguard. It fits my hand as if made for it. A part of me longs for action. Another part rouses competitively at the thought of fighting him. I want to beat him, even as I consider the breadth of his shoulders and the strength in those arms. He's enormous, but every inch of him is gilded with muscle, and I've seen how lightly he can move. "Thank you. But I think I shall have to decline."

I hand the sword back.

There's no expression on his face, but I feel his frustration. "I promise I'll go easy on you."

"Maybe I don't want easy?" I stride past, boots crunching on the shards of glass until I reach the center of the ballroom.

Thiago takes two steps after me, then stills. "No. You wouldn't. You'd never choose the easy path."

My eyes narrow. It feels like there's something unspoken in that statement. "I want to be alone."

"Dismissed, just like that?" His amusement holds an edge of bitterness. "As you wish, Your Highness. You may consider yourself lucky. Business calls me away for several days. Eris will remain here to protect you."

He turns, sweeping up the stairs.

"Where are you going?" I call after him.

I don't want to be left behind here in these lonely ruins. Even by him.

His head turns to the side, offering me his profile but no insight. "Ceres."

"May I come?"

"No."

My shoulders stiffen. I don't know why he's chosen to bring me here when the seat of his power is the golden city of Ceres. It feels as though he's hiding me away from the world.

"Your loss," I reply, kicking glass out of the way casually.

"My loss?"

"How may I repay my debt when you're not here?"

This time he turns, those enigmatic eyes sweeping over me. "I'll hold your kisses in lieu."

"I consider them forfeited."

"I don't."

We stare at each other, but he breaks first, a smile

dawning on his lips. "Until I return, Princess. Enjoy your stay, but don't leave the city."

The second he's gone, I open the small scroll of paper again.

You must discover what happened to his wife....

The less I see of the prince, the better.

Though I can't help wondering who left this here.

And whether it was meant for me or whether I'm only the last in a long line of 'political' captives.

8

Avoiding the prince is easier said than done.

After all, by my own hand, I owe him a kiss once a day, and while he grants me the grace of his absence for three days, he claims his prize when he returns, leaving me in no doubt as to his intentions.

After the first night of his return, I try to gift my tithe to him in the dining room so he has no reason to enter my bedchamber. A faint brush of my lips to his and then a hasty retreat as I try to avoid the mocking glint in his eyes.

The prince knows exactly what I'm doing, but he allows it.

Which only makes me feel even more like I'm being slowly driven into a trap by the hunter.

Days turn into weeks. Then the weeks glide by. Each day feels like a storm is brewing, though he's often absent. I know the prince wants something from me, but what?

Beyond the obvious.

I'm growing heartily sick of the ever-present twilight. The sun bares its shy face for an hour or two each day, and I spend every moment of its presence basking in its glow atop the tallest tower.

Indeed, I'm dueling with my own shadow one morning when the storm finally breaks.

There's a clatter in the courtyard below, and the enormous iron gates lift by means of a complicated pulley system. Lowering my sword and wiping sweaty hair out of my eyes, I kneel against the stone wall of the turret and watch as the prince rides out.

He's invited me to ride with him each morning, but so far, I've declined. He's also invited me to spar every day, and though a part of me wants to test my skills against his, I dare not.

Restlessness itches along my arms. Maybe this is his plan. Drive me crazy by means of self-imposed exile and boredom. The wind calls my name, and my fingers yearn for a bow. I know he comes and goes—most likely seeing to the business of his kingdom via the Hallow—but apart from the demi-fey, I'm alone. Eris certainly avoids me, and I'm not *that* desperate for company, though the endless silence in these halls is making me question just how far I'll go.

A single hunt by his side.

One ride.

What would be the harm?

The prince's knowing smile comes to mind. *That*. That's exactly the danger. Because he's just intriguing enough to make me want to know more.

He cuts a lonely figure as he canters across the drawbridge. Every morning I've watched him head south into the forests there, where he returns with game. But this time he doesn't turn south. This time he heads north, and he's moving fast.

Odd.

The sun is inching back toward the horizon. It's the worst time of day to be riding so fast, but there's a sense of urgency about him this morning.

And he's heading north. North toward the wyldwoods. North toward the crumbling wall that once guarded the realms of Seelie from the Unseelie. North toward the border.

Something is afoot.

Maybe it's boredom. Maybe it's too many days spent cooped up in this icy, echoing palace, where even the servants seem invisible, but it takes me precisely three seconds before I'm moving toward the stairs.

It's not as though I'm stealing a horse from his stables. He *did* invite me to ride with him, after all.

There are only four horses available, and while three of them are big, rangy brutes that look like they could run all day and not flag, it's the smaller, daintier mare at the end that catches my eye.

"Here, girl," I whisper, holding out my hand for her to sniff my fingers.

She whickers approvingly and butts her head into my shoulder, almost knocking me over. I guess we're friends now.

"Good girl," I say, returning with her saddle. "Want to feel the wind in your face?"

She's surprisingly easy to bridle, and while I'd prefer to get to know her a little better before I mount, I'm aware that every ticking second leads me closer to discovery. Swinging into the saddle, I urge her into the main courtyard.

"What are you doing?" someone calls behind me.

Caught.

I wheel the mare, glancing up. Eris pauses at the top of

the palace wall, a hand on her sword. She arches a brow, as if to say *get your ass back here.*

Too bad I'm a rebellious princess who's spent too long in her icy cage. I shrug, a smile warming me all the way through, and then I wheel the mare and give her her head. The swift clatter of her hooves over the drawbridge is echoed by Eris's startled, "Hey!"

The wind whips past me, and snow flies beneath the mare's heels. It feels as though she shares my eagerness. She's utterly glorious, and for a second I forget the mission in the face of this glimpse of freedom.

Then the sight of hoofprints catch my eye. With the freshly laid snow, it's ridiculously easy to follow the prince.

And he's up to something, I know it in my bones.

Easing the white mare back into a canter, I swiftly follow the trail painted across the snow.

Eris is going to kill me if she catches me.

The thought is somewhat a cheerful one.

An ancient road heads directly into the craggy old forest ahead of me. It's not like the forests of my mother's lands. This one is old, and as I follow Thiago into the trees, I can feel the heavy, watchful sensation of it all around me. Old forests always seem somewhat alive, but this one has *weight* to it. Every so often I catch a glimpse of runes carved into the mossy flank of a tree, and piles of ancient stones mark the path.

The Old Ones walked this forest.

I can sense their power lingering in the earth, and the hum of a ley line vibrates through the air. I've always been able to sense the ley lines, but this one almost seems to whisper directly to me, as seductive as the prince himself.

The mare eases into a walk, her ears flickering nervously, as if she senses my sudden wariness.

Maybe this wasn't a good idea?

My sword's at my side, and my mother's iron dagger is sheathed at my hip, but there could be anything lurking beneath these trees.

I'm almost ready to turn back when I come across the prince's stallion, tied to a tree.

He's here.

I leave the mare in a clearing a hundred yards away and slip along on foot. Whatever he's up to bodes no good for my people. My mother's always suspected he has ties to the Unseelie and that he's working to thwart the alliance. If I can deliver proof to her, then...

...then maybe she'll forgive me for not using the dagger in my boot.

Maybe she won't demand murder from me.

Ahead of me, Prince Thiago paces a snowy knoll, rubbing his leather-clad knuckles. If the sun was acting normally, I swear he'd be looking up, trying to gauge the time.

Someone's late.

But who?

I slip through the trees, inching over the snow as I try to find a closer vantage point. I'm almost to a thicket when a tingle runs down my spine. Freezing, I crouch behind a tree just as the bushes ahead of me part and a rider appears.

The horse is enormous, with a coat the color of midnight and an evil look in its eyes. Steam fogs the air as it snorts, and its hooves barely make a sound.

"You're late," Thiago growls, loud enough for the wind to carry it to my ears.

"Blame your own guards. They're particularly thick along the border at the moment," the stranger replies, swinging down from his mount.

His dark hair falls to his shoulders, and from behind, they're the same size, the same height. That's where the similarities end, though. The stranger wears beads and feathers plaited into his hair, and his long silvery cloak is made from what looks like wolf-kin.

Unseelie. He has to be Unseelie if he speaks of passing the borders.

A chill runs through me. Mother was right. The Prince of Evernight is meeting with the enemy.

"You look frustrated, old friend," the stranger says. "How goes your endeavor with the princess?"

"Slowly," Thiago mutters. "She's being particularly stubborn."

"I thought that was how you liked them?"

Thiago scrubs at his mouth. "I can't help feeling that time's running out. I only have two more months with her."

"You've never failed before," the stranger says.

"There's always a first time."

"And then what?"

Prince Thiago's eyes narrow. "If I cannot woo the princess, then I'll deal with her mother once and for all. I won't let Adaia win."

Woo? Win?

What in the Underworld is he speaking about?

"The game of love is more vicious than any battlefield I've ever been on," the stranger muses. "I don't envy you your masquerade. Though it amuses me to watch it, time and time again. Is it truly worth it?"

Game of love? If the prince thinks he's going to win my heart, then he's been drinking too much elderberry wine. I hold my breath as I wait for the prince to answer.

"Worth every moment of sacrifice," he replies softly. "Worth every night I wake in my bed alone, dreaming of holding my wife in my arms again. I will have her back one day, no matter what I must do. No matter how long I must wait."

"No matter how many times you must woo a haughty, arrogant princess who doesn't care for you?" the stranger drawls.

"Careful."

The stranger mutters something in return, and Thiago laughs.

It's starting to sound like some sort of dream, vivid with all sorts of weirdness. What does it all mean? Wooing arrogant princesses.... How is that meant to bring his wife back to him?

He's not... sacrificing them to one of the Old Ones, is he? Or a god?

And how many times has he done this?

I can't help thinking of the old tale of the prince with nine wives. *Don't go down into the cellar*, he warns his final wife, but of course, she does.

"So tell me," Thiago says, "what is that bitch up to now? My scouts report there's movement across the borders."

"There's always movement."

"Not to this extent. There are banes in the wyrdwoods, hunting for fae flesh. Some of them wear Angharad's sigil. There are goblins in the mountains, and they wear no clan marks. And something is leaving nothing but scorch marks where villages once stood."

The stranger looks away. "There are rumors the Heartless are walking."

My breath catches. Fetches hunt the nights and can twist along shadows themselves. They were never fae, but Angharad cut their hearts from their chests and with it, what remains of their souls. Bound to her will, they're her hunting parties, and nothing escapes their grip. "What are they looking for?" Thiago asks.

"Nobody seems to know. The only whisper I've heard refers to *leanabh an dàn*, but that's a myth, a legend."

It's also the old tongue, brought from the Other world we were exiled from all those years ago. I would love to be able to speak it right now.

Thiago paces, shooting the stranger a sharp look. "Are you sure they said *leanabh an dàn*?"

"As sure as—"

Snow drops from the tree above me, right down the back of my neck. A hiss of shock escapes me before I can smother it.

Both men freeze and turn toward me.

I duck back behind the tree, heart pounding. Just one glimpse, but it's enough to assure me the stranger's eyes are pure black, and small horns curl out of his hair.

"What was that?" the stranger whispers.

Thiago's definitely meeting with one of the Unseelie.

Why? Is the stranger a traitor to his queen?

Or is he planting suggestions in Thiago's head at his queen's behest? It wouldn't surprise me to see Angharad pulling Thiago's strings, though that presumes he's a puppet, and so far, he's given me no reason to think him a fool.

Thiago's answer is a low rumble I can't make out, and worse, it sounds as though it's coming closer. Steel hisses in a sheath as someone draws a sword.

I need to get out of here.

But the snow's going to lead him directly toward me. There's no hiding my tracks, painted across the powder white snow like a beacon.

Looking up, I grab hold of the branch above my head

and haul myself into the fir above me. I chose it because of how dense it was, and now it seems I made a smart decision. Sliding along the branches, I slip into the next tree, and then the next, using them to hide.

I can just make out Thiago as he darts around the first tree, pausing when he finds my tracks.

"Hmm," he murmurs.

"Someone's been listening," the stranger hisses.

"I'll deal with it."

They share a look, and then the stranger draws his cloak tighter. "Make sure you do. I'd rather not have to explain to my queen just why I've been whispering her secrets in the Prince of Evernight's ear."

"It won't reach your queen," Thiago assures him.

It's all I hear, because I'm easing down the tree and using a thicket of thorny brambles as cover as I slip away. The second I put some distance between us, I run for my mare.

Asturia's to the south, where it rarely snows, so I'm not used to such a quiet forest, but I've spent years hunting in the mountains. Learning to move quietly can be the only thing that saves your life when your prey is a vicious predator.

Relief floods through me the second I find the mare where I left her. I'm about to put my foot in the stirrup when a voice calls out behind me.

"Did you enjoy your little excursion, Princess?"

My heart leaps. The mare snorts in alarm and nearly dumps me on my ass. But it's the prince behind me who causes the most alarm.

Thiago leans against a tree, one hand resting lightly against the hilt of his sword. There's no hint of emotion in his dark green eyes. I can't read him at all. But then a faint, mocking smile flickers over his hard mouth, as if he enjoys the sight of my sudden dilemma.

Caught. I have no excuses, and he knows it.

"Actually, yes," I reply, reaching for the mare again. "Nothing like a brisk ride to shake off the monotony of imprisonment."

Thiago moves like lightning, his gloved fist curling around my reins. I can't escape, for he's blocking me in against the horse.

"You should have told me you wanted to go for a ride," he murmurs, right behind me.

I glance over my shoulder. "Perhaps I wanted to go alone."

"These woods are wild and dangerous. You don't know the area, and any stray predator could find you out here."

"*Any* stray predator? Or any stray Unseelie?"

"Ah. So you did see that."

He looms closer, and I press my back into the mare, my hand finding my knife. Before I can draw it, his hand slams over mine, trapping us there. "Don't be stupid, Princess. If you draw that blade, I'll have to take it off you. And while I might enjoy it, you won't."

"Maybe you're underestimating me." I'm smaller than he is, but all my life I've trained against larger warriors precisely for this reason.

Hone your weaknesses, Mother always told me. *And use them to your advantage.*

Right now, I have the element of surprise—judging by his smirk—speed, and the fact that if he hurts me, he'll have to explain himself to the alliance.

In return, he has weight, size, unknown skills, and power beyond imagining. The only way to beat him is to play dirty, and Mother's court has been an excellent training ground.

I let my dagger go, and Thiago's shoulders soften.

"Good choice," he says.

In return, I kick his feet out from under him. I've got one foot in the stirrup when he calls out, "Eliara, fly!"

And the mare takes off as if she's been stung by a whip.

With one foot off the ground, I don't stand a chance. I land on my backside in the snow as the mare kicks up her heels and vanishes. *Mother of Night.* Rolling to my hands and knees, I stare after her in disgust. Treacherous beast.

The prince stands, dusting off his hands and flashing a smile at me. "What is it your mother always says? Revenge is the sweetest spice to any dish?"

He's not angry, but that doesn't make me any less wary. I clamber upright, sinking in the soft snow. "She also says never trust an Evernight."

The prince laughs.

"And never make alliances with the Unseelie."

His laughter dies. "How much did you hear?"

"Enough to know you're up to no good."

"Oh, Princess. I'm always up to no good."

"Enough to know you see me as some sort of means to get your wife back," I shoot at him.

It's like an arrow, straight to the heart. "Hmm." He's clearly trying to remember precisely what he said.

"I'll save you the trouble. You need to woo a haughty, arrogant princess, which I presume is me, in order to somehow see your wife again." Once more, my hand drops to the dagger. "And I promise you now, you're the last male in the entire alliance that I'd ever allow to put his hands upon me."

"But that's a lie, Princess."

Oh, how I hate that smug purr.

"Or have you forgotten our agreement?" He takes a step

closer. "Though technically, I suppose we can say it shall be your lips upon mine."

"Not if you're dead."

"Cold iron, I presume? Straight through the heart." Opening his arms wide, he entices me. "Have at."

There's no point drawing the dagger. I'm not going to kill him, nor am I going to fight him. I have no horse, I'm in the middle of an unknown landscape, and I cannot bear to deal with his smirk if he takes the blade away from me.

Which he will. I know it.

So, I do the sensible thing and bolt for his horse.

"Vi!" he yells, and then he's cursing under his breath as I sprint through the snowy forest. "I swear to the Old Ones, I'm going to thrash you!"

He'd have to catch me first, and if there's one thing I am, it's fast.

And inspired.

Gnarled old trees whip past me. I'm making headway when I swear one of them reaches out with a branch and trips me. Staggering forward, I gain my feet just in time to hear his harsh panting behind me.

A blur comes toward me out of the corner of my eye, and then his heavy weight slams into me.

We hit the ground, snow flying up around us as I kick and scramble. Gods, he's strong. It's like wrestling a bear. I may have overestimated my ability to defeat him.

"Hold still!"

I spin, wrapping my thighs around his hips and sending us rolling. A stick jabs my shoulder, but it's the heavy weight of his body as he flips us that drives the breath from my lungs. I land flat on my back, and there's no escaping him. Curse it. Every furious wriggle only succeeds in ensconcing him even more firmly between my legs.

The Prince of Evernight is between my thighs, and this is not how I planned this at all. I go still, giving in to the inevitable. For now.

Thiago breathes hard, pinning my wrists to the ground. "Well, that was fun—if predictable. Now what?"

Balls, or throat?

He sees my eyes narrow, correctly guesses which one I'll choose, and takes my knee to his thigh, instead.

A grinning leer paints his face and he leans closer until our noses almost touch. "*Pre-dic-table.*"

I want to kill him.

Slowly.

"Enjoy the moment, Your Highness. Because this is as close as you're ever going to get to winning me into your bed."

"Would you care to make a wager on that?" He gathers both my wrists in one hand and then rests his weight on his other elbow.

I squirm. Nothing. "What do you have in mind?"

"Within the three months, I'll have you in my bed, Princess." He brushes his thumb over my bottom lip, his voice lowering to a husky whisper. "*And* you'll enjoy it."

A furious quiver runs through me. Mostly at myself and how much a part of me enjoys that simple touch. I bite his thumb, and he laughs.

"I'll take you up on that bet." It's a terrible idea, but I simply can't help myself. Me? In the prince's bed? No surer bet has ever been won, even if I'm subjecting myself to his relentless chase. "Because my mother will bow at your feet before I'll ever end up beneath your sheets."

"Tell her to practice her curtsy. I want to see her grovel."

Oh, you arrogant ass. "And if *I* win, then you will relinquish the disputed territories between our lands to my mother."

The prince stiffens.

It's the perfect opportunity to show my mother I can be valuable. *Make whatever deals you have to*, she'd said. Imagine the look on her face if I return with the deeds to the borderlands.

An unreadable expression crosses his face. "It's a deal."

He's that confident? I gape.

"Now what?" he asks.

I swear, that smile is going to be the end of me. "What do you mean?"

"How do you escape your thrashing now?"

He'd best be joking. "If you even think about it, I'll kill you in your sleep."

"I quiver with terror." He leans his entire weight upon me, as if to prove there's no means of escaping him. Every rock-hard inch of him presses me deep into the snow.

I barely feel the chill. Perhaps he's got good reason to be confident, because there's a battering ram of indefinite proportion pressed firmly against my thigh. It stops just short of where I want it, and I can't help freezing beneath him. One inch. Just one little twist of my hips, and this would be an entirely indecent embrace.

The son of a bitch is enjoying this.

Worse. There's a small part of me that wants him to make that move.

"Get off me!"

"Ask me nicely, and I might just let you go," he teases, his breath caressing my jaw.

I can see he's not going to let me go. Not without making me beg.

And pride is my weakness. It always has been.

But what is *his* weakness?

The second I think it, I know exactly how I'm going to escape.

The kiss takes him by surprise.

But not for long.

I shove a handful of snow down the back of his shirt, and he yelps, giving me just enough space to kick him off. Then I'm out from under him, whipping his cloak over his head and planting a boot in the middle of his chest.

By the time he fights his way free of the cloak, I'm in the saddle of his mount—an enormous black stallion, how typical—and doffing an imaginary hat to him. "A pity you sent my mare fleeing. It's going to be a long, cold walk back to Valerian, Your Highness."

"Get your ass back here!" Thiago yells.

It's so incredibly childish that I can't help myself. I kick his horse into a trot and yell back, "Make me!"

A snowball hits me between my shoulder blades, but all I can do is laugh as his horse canters away from the clearing.

I do believe I finally won a round.

And look at that. Nobody even drew blood.

It takes the prince four hours to return.

Even after enduring a blistering lecture from Eris, nothing can shake my good mood as the prince limps in under the portcullis.

"I've had the servants draw you a bath, Your Highness," I call down from the guard tower above in the sweetest voice I can possibly muster. "Since I daresay you're chilled to the bone. Of course, they're demi-fey, so whether the water is warm is entirely up to their whims."

He merely smiles.

That's not the expression I was hoping to see.

"You look considerably happier than I expected. What are you planning?"

"You're so suspicious," he murmurs, taking the stairs two at a time. "I was rather displeased at first, but I've had time to think. And I consider today a win."

"How in Maia's name do you imagine *yourself* the victor?"

He pauses before me, all heat and muscle and dangerous eyes. "Because you're no longer afraid of me. *And* you wonder what I'm like in bed."

"I do *not*."

He rests both hands on the railing beside my hips, trapping me there. "No? I'm very, very good, by the way."

There's nowhere to go, no means to avoid him.

"Of course you'd say that." It comes out a little breathlessly. "But I'm sorry to disappoint you. I'm not remotely interested in you or the state of your bed. You're losing, Your Highness. You haven't gained a single inch of ground, so perhaps you'd best forfeit."

"Losing?" He leans toward me. "If you think I'm not making progress, then you haven't been paying attention, Princess."

I press a hand to his chest.

His heart kicks swiftly, making my fingers curl in his shirt. It's too intimate, but I dare not let him come closer.

"You owe me a kiss," he whispers.

"I granted you one in the forest. It's not my fault it was swift and followed by a fistful of snow."

"Hmmm." His heated gaze slides over my mouth.

I go still.

There's something intimate about that look, and every

inch of me warms as if his gaze is a caress. I can't help wondering what it would feel like to let him claim the kiss he clearly desires instead of the perfunctory one I grace him with each and every night.

He smiles. "Lie to me again, Princess. Tell me you're not thinking about it."

I shove at his chest, and though he takes a step back, I fear it's more his doing than mine.

"I would kiss every inch of you, if you'd let me. And I would use my tongue, Princess, until you were begging me for mercy."

Sweet Maia.

I swallow. "If you dared, then I would cut it off for trespassing where it wasn't wanted."

"I love the way you lie to me." Lifting my hand to his lips, he brushes a gentle caress there. "Until tomorrow. Sweet dreams, Your Highness."

The breath leaves me explosively as he strides away. My will may be strong, but my body has begun to weaken. Even now, blood rushes through my veins and my nipples tingle as if they felt his touch.

Curse him.

Because he's right.

I can't help wondering what that mouth would feel like on my body.

My GOOD MOOD evaporates the moment I enter my bedchambers. There's a message resting on my pillow, and it looks exactly like the tiny scroll I discovered in the icy remnants of the ballroom.

I snatch it up, glancing around.

There's no sign of anyone, but I've been gone for hours. Anyone could have left it. Except, Eris is the only other soul in the ruined palace, and I'm fairly certain if she were leaving me messages, they'd be painted in blood upon the walls.

Besides, Thiago gave me the only key. He couldn't have lied about that. Not if he promised thrice.

EVERYTHING IS NOT as it seems, Princess. The only way to discover the truth is to remain close to the prince. Push him. He won't be able to maintain the charade for long, as he's desperate to reunite with his wife. Trust your instincts.

THE NOTE CHILLS me to the bone. The one in the ballroom might have been left by chance, to be discovered by whoever came after, but this was deliberately placed here.

This was deliberately written for *me*.

"Hello?" I call, running my hands along the walls and coming up short. There's no hollow echoing revealed by a rap of my knuckles. No hint of any gaps. It's as though the note appeared via thin air.

I cock my head slowly, feeling something watching me.

The demi-fey are notorious tricksters. Rarely seen, never to be entirely trusted with anything important, but never malicious if you leave them a saucer of milk.

Which I've been doing ever since I arrived, since it never hurts to have the local sprites as allies.

"Did you leave this message for me?" I whisper, sensing one moving behind me.

It's in the room. I know it is.

But there's no answer, and suddenly, I feel a swift breeze course by me, the curtains fluttering.

Alone. Again.

But, as I hold up the paper, I realize I can't be entirely alone.

Because the demi-fey can't put pen to paper.

Someone here in Valerian is trying to send me a message.

9

Discovering what happened to the prince's wife is imperative, now I know he thinks to somehow use me to get her back.

Unfortunately, I don't know where to start. The demi-fey are impossible to capture, even if they'd give me a straight answer, and whoever is sending me the messages is either invisible or a figment of my imagination. Servants, he'd said, but I've not seen even a hint of anything living. There's no one in the castle besides Eris and the prince, and I don't want to draw his attention to the fact I'm looking for someone.

Which means the prince may be my only means of discovering the truth.

Push him, the note said.

After a week of avoiding him, I find him in the stables, muttering under his breath as he slips a sugar cube, of all things, to his horse. He's wearing a heavy fur cloak and stiff-ened riding leathers that hint at armor. Not his usual attire. Hmm. There's a bow at his side, an enormous goblin-forged sword at his hip, and enough arrows to down an entire hunting party of Unseelie.

The prince isn't taking his usual route through the forest, which is perfect. I'd rather play a spy than an assassin.

The second he senses me, he straightens incredulously.

"Good morning," I call, slinging a saddle over the edge of the mare's stall.

"What do you think you're doing?" he demands.

I lead the white mare out of her stall and tie her up. "I'm coming with you. You're the one who insisted that if I wanted to ride, then it had to be with you."

"You're the one who refused," he comments coolly, his eyelids half-shuttered as he takes me in. "You're up to something."

"What could I possibly stand to gain?" I roll my eyes as I swiftly saddle the mare. "I'm bored. Your company is better than none. And I want to feel the bitter wind on my face and see something other than the inside of this cursed palace."

He crosses his arms over his chest. "I would rather you didn't."

"I would rather I did."

"And if I refuse?"

"Why would you refuse? I thought you wanted me to come with you." I pretend to notice his sword. "*You're* up to something."

He stares at me for such a long time, I swear he's going to deny me. "Fetch a cloak, a bow, and some warmer clothes. I'll make a bedroll for you."

"A bedroll?"

"Unless you want to share mine?"

When the Horned One walks the mortal realm again....

"I thought so," he replies smoothly, as if my expression

isn't a complete insult right now. "You have twenty minutes before I leave without you. And pack for a couple of days."

Freedom.

I don't waste any time.

Sprinting back to my rooms, I swiftly lace myself into warmer clothes, and then pause with my velvet-lined cloak in my hands. I don't have anything warmer. I was expecting to be locked away in a palace when I packed, not invited to ride into the snowy wilderness.

And I was so furious at my mother that I hadn't thought ahead.

By the time I return to the stables, I'm dressed, but not as I'd like to be.

The prince tosses a bedroll toward me, then arches a brow. "You'll freeze."

"Some of us weren't prepared for sub-arctic temperatures."

"Then use your magic to ward yourself," he says, leading his enormous stallion out of the stables.

My cheeks heat as I hurry after him. "I'll be fine. Where are we going?"

"Beyond the range of Valerian's warding spells," he points out. "You may be warm now, Princess, but you won't be warm where we're going."

Plenty of opportunity for him to suggest I curl up nice and close. I thought he'd like that. "Asturians have fire in their blood. We run hotter than most fae."

"I know."

It's such a suggestive comment, I can't help but arch my brows at him.

"Ward yourself," he says, "or you're not coming."

The mare tugs at her reins as I stare at him.

Magic and I have never been close allies. I spent years

trying to master the basics, only to have it slip through my fingers at the most inopportune times. It's there, within me. I know, because I can feel it. But accessing it is like trying to capture pure moonlight in my hands. The only thing I have any success with is creating fire.

Sometimes.

"I can't."

"Yes, you can."

"I *can't,* curse you."

The prince turns to stare at me. "What do you mean, you can't?"

I hate having to divulge my worst weaknesses. In Asturia, I shouldn't even have them, let alone admit to them. Never show your underbelly. Never reveal your throat. And never, ever grant your trust to someone who hasn't earned it.

"I can't... ward." I shrug. "It's not one of my abilities."

"Warding is one of the earliest magics we learn," he says.

"Well, I can't."

And if he wants to cursed well push me for more information, then I'll stay here.

Thiago gives me a sleepy-eyed look. I hate the fact I can't read it. "Fine." He steps closer, bringing both hands up to touch my face.

I bat them away, instantly on guard, and he holds them up in surrender.

"I was going to ward you myself."

My hands hover in the air. I need to know what he's up to. Does this have anything to do with that Unseelie spy he met in the woods the other day? Where is he going that will take him away for a night or two?

But I also know that letting him touch me like this is a mistake.

Because his touch is another weakness I don't like admitting to.

Every night I grant him the kiss I bartered, and every night I have to fight the instinctive response that begs me to lean into his touch.

"Warn me next time."

It's consent enough. The second his thumbs brush my cheeks, I feel a warm caress glide over every inch of my skin. It's intimate and sensual and makes me shiver. His magic feels like silken sheets whispering against my skin, and the cool embrace of moonlight. Mine is a gush of hot, electric summer storms, but Thiago's magic is a dangerous, smoky lure.

"Done," he whispers.

I shake his hands off me, trying not to shiver again. "You just wanted to touch me."

"Perhaps." With the faintest of smiles, he grabs his horse's reins again. "But consider, if you will, the fact I wasn't the one who refused to try."

"You think I wanted that?"

Incredible. His arrogance knows no bounds.

"I think you like dancing around the truth. You're awfully defensive for someone who merely doesn't know how to ward."

"Maybe I just don't trust you with the truth."

For a second, his eyes darken, and he turns to me. "Are we going to spend the next three days stabbing at each other with words? Because I need to keep my wits about me and not focused on you. So here are the rules: If you intend to come, then you'll need to keep your mouth shut at all times. And if I tell you to do something, then you don't argue. You do it. Agreed?"

Three days?

"Where in the Underworld are we going?"

"Iskvien," he growls.

"Agreed."

He mounts up. "You're the one who was listening to my private conversation the other day. You tell me where we're going."

I think about everything the Unseelie said, and the breath rushes out of me. "You're going to *Mistmere*?"

The ruined keep was once the capital city of Mistmere Kingdom, which borders Thiago's territories. During the wars, the castle was ruined and the lands blighted by the backlash of magic. Most of the territories were divided by the Seelie Alliance—including the disputed borders between my mother's kingdom and the prince's—but the north was never claimed. It holds direct passage to the north-western half of the continent where the Unseelie kingdoms reside, and anyone who claimed it would need to be able to protect it.

"I need to know what Angharad is up to. Cian claims she's poking about the ruins. I want to know why."

I glance behind him. "I'm fairly certain you intended to go alone. It's almost as though you want the witch queen to capture you."

He snorts. "Get your ass on your horse if you're going to come."

"This is foolish. You need an army to confront her." I'm rethinking my decision to join him.

"I *am* an army," he replies softly, "Anyone else is only a weak flank I would need to protect. And I don't intend to confront her. If she sees me, then I deserve to lose my crown. Perhaps you can learn to be a little quieter this time, Princess? You blunder through the woods like a troll."

A little quieter? "You had no idea I was in the trees above you."

"I didn't need to know. The only road through those trees was the one I'd followed, so I knew where you'd return to. Strategy, Princess. By the time I found your horse, I could hear you floundering through the snow like a crippled bane."

I swear to the Old Ones, I ought to kick him off a cliff.

"Fine." I swing into the saddle. "Let's see what Angharad is doing at Mistmere. Lead the way, oh, dangerous one. I promise I'll shed a tear if a troll eats you."

"If a troll eats anyone, it's going to be you," he says as I ride out of the stables ahead of him. "All those soft delicious curves and tender flesh. Why would he want to pick over my rangy bones and sinew when he has you to salivate over?"

I shoot him a baleful glare. "You'd best be talking about the troll."

There's a smile on the prince's face. "Of course I am, Princess. Because if I were to get my hands on you, it wouldn't be your flesh I'd devour. Nor would I use my teeth. Unless you wanted me to."

Heat blooms in my cheeks. "Then it's a good thing you're never going to get your hands on me."

"We'll see. After all, it's going to be cold out there, Princess. Anytime you want to warm yourself, you let me know."

10

"Why Mistmere? I thought there was nothing here but ruins after the Great Wars," I say as we use the Valerian Hallow to transport ourselves to the Hallow in the mountains above Mistmere.

We had to leave the horses—they don't like portals very much—which means we're on foot. In snow up to my knees. I'm trying very hard to remind myself why I volunteered for this mission.

The prince's dark eyes hood as he glances my way, and I know instinctively he's fighting to form the right words—to tell me just enough truth without giving away his secrets.

"Don't bother finding a means to skirt a lie. It's not as though I can report directly to my mother. Not until spring breaks, anyway."

I stalk past him, but I've only taken two steps when he catches my arm. I look down at the firm fingers locked around my wrist, and then up into those mercurial eyes. Sometimes I forget how tall he is, how powerful. And its not until he touches me that I feel the skim of tension light over my arms.

"It's not that I don't trust you," he says.

"And yet you refuse to tell me a wretched thing. I've seen you and Eris watching me, whispering behind my back. I know you're keeping secrets. Well, I don't care. I have nearly six weeks remaining of this sentence, and then I'm free of your company and you of mine."

His thumb strokes over the inside of my wrist, over my pulse. "Are you certain you'll be free of me?"

I tear my arm free. "Quite."

The faintest of smiles touches his mouth. Thiago leans closer. "And yet, you kissed me last night."

"I seem to recall it being the other way around."

"Let me rephrase: You kissed me. Back."

Heat fills my cheeks, because there's no way I can deny it and not call myself a liar. I'd definitely lingered. "That's beside the point. You don't—"

"What's wrong? It was a good kiss. You've naught to be ashamed about."

"I thought we weren't going to mention it again."

"I don't believe I agreed with that statement." He's definitely smiling to himself. "And you don't give the orders here, in my kingdom."

"We're not in your kingdom," I point out sweetly.

Thiago growls under his breath. "Stubborn."

"Always."

"As to your earlier question—before I had a chance to reply—you were right. There isn't anything in Mistmere," Thiago says, slipping through the forest with the grace of a ghost. "Only the ruins of a powerful kingdom."

"Then why…?"

"Because maybe they're trying to resurrect something within those ruins," he shoots over his shoulder.

"What does that mean?"

"You'll see. It's why I brought you, anyway."

"I didn't think you had much of a choice."

"Oh, I had a choice. I could have chained you in the dungeon."

"You have a dungeon?" I haven't seen one anywhere in the ruins.

"I would have one made if you annoy me enough. Trust me, I'm starting to consider it."

"If you lock me in a dungeon, you will regret it."

"How? You can't even ward. And come to think of it, I've never even seen you use your magic. What are you going to do? Whine at me for the rest of my life? Call me bad names? Or stab me with a spoon?"

"Not a spoon, no."

I reach down and scoop up a fistful of snow.

"I'm starting to like this idea." He's striding along in front of me as if he owns the forest. A smug, insufferable asshole who thinks everyone he meets should kiss the ground he walks upon. "I might even make the chains gold. I think gold would suit your skin. You'd be my very pretty prisoner. If you're nice to me, I might even bring you a book to read."

The snowball shatters on the back of his head.

Thiago stiffens. Then turns. Slowly.

The second I see the look in his eyes, I bolt.

Back the way we came, floundering in the tracks we made. Too late. Something hooks my foot, and I slam face-first into the snow.

Slow footsteps stalk me. "Look at that. I didn't even have to run."

The fucker used his magic.

"If you could ward, then you'd have been able to escape your punishment." The grin on his face is pure evil as he glides toward me.

"You son of a phooka," I spit, wiping snow off my face.

The prince rests his hands on his thighs, a merry smile practically begging for my fist. "I could bury you in snow if I choose, and there's nothing you could do about it."

"I'm patient, Your Highness. I'd sleep very lightly if I were you."

"I always sleep lightly," he replies. "Though you're quite welcome to join me in bed. I'll consider any trespass into my bedchamber to be consent. Your plotting may not work out the way you'd like."

"Fine."Clambering to my feet, I settle into a defensive stance. "No magic."

The prince dusts imaginary snowflakes off his black cloak. "No rules. We can use magic if we like."

"Are you afraid I'm going to wipe that pretty smirk off your face?"

Thiago snorts. "Terrified."

The fight's been brewing for days.

I don't know why, but I feel stretched thin. Dancing around him hasn't solved this.

I toss my cloak aside, then draw the knife. The prince's gaze drops to the iron blade, but his eyebrow merely quirks.

I hate that eyebrow. I hate its arrogance. Its mockery.

"If I draw blood, then I win."

Not even fae magic can conquer iron.

I lash out, the knife cutting toward his arm, but the prince merely sidesteps and blocks the blow.

It's like trying to fight a will-o'-the-wisp.

One second he's there, and the next he simply isn't. I don't know what sort of magic this is, but he moves like no one I've ever fought.

"Curse you."

A thumb digs into the pressure point in my hand, and I drop the knife.

That doesn't mean I give up. I simply spin beneath his hand, slamming the flat of my palm against his side. It's like hitting a stone wall.

Thiago grins at me, as if he's enjoying this. Perhaps he is.

He trips me with his magic, time and time again, even as I try to break through his guard.

"Give up, Princess," he mocks. "You won't defeat me."

I push harder. I can see the knife in the churned-up snow near his feet. I just need to get it. Driving forward, I feint to the side, then dart in to drive my knee into his thigh.

It's the perfect move, flawlessly executed.

Or at least, it should be.

Two seconds later, I hit the snow, the breath slamming out of me. The prince pins me, his shoulders blotting out the weak sunlight.

"Surrender," he says, pressing his weight over the top of me.

"Never."

I expect him to be furious at my defiance, but he's still grinning at me, as if this is the most amusing thing he's seen all day.

"You will never back down, will you?" He shakes his head. "Fine. This is your own fault."

Grabbing hold of me, he throws me over his shoulder as though I weigh nothing at all. I catch a glimpse of a slick of ice to our left, right where he's headed, and suddenly understand his intentions.

"Don't you dare!" I kick him in the midriff, but he merely curls an arm around my legs and traps them. "Thiago!"

"Thiago. I like the sound of my name on your lips." His arm softens, becoming a hand that slides up my thigh. "Perhaps if I heard it again, with a few additions like 'please' or 'I'm sorry I threw a snowball at you,' then I might reconsider my current intentions."

"You pig-fucking merciless prick! I swear—"

A sharp slap on my ass makes my eyes pop wide. *Did he just...?*

"Manners, Your Highness," he says smugly. "Now apologize."

We're getting closer to the ice. *He wouldn't.* We're in the middle of a snowy wasteland, and this will set us back hours.

But his steps aren't slowing, and I'm starting to recognize the set of his shoulders at times.

"If you dump me in this pond," I snarl, "then you're going to have to wait until I dry.""I have a hunting cabin nearby. I could just chain you to the fireplace and return when I've done what I need to."

A hunting cabin? It momentarily sidetracks me. "Why do you have a cabin here, in disputed territories?"

"Because I sometimes like to hunt." He hauls me down into his arms, where I make one last effort to escape as he threatens to heave me onto the ice.

"Fine!" I yelp, clinging to him like a barnacle. "I apologize!"

Thiago stills. "You apologize for...."

Gritting my teeth, I look him in the eye. "I apologize for throwing that snowball at you."

Even if *you deserved it.*

"Good." He sets me on my feet. "Next time, use your magic. It's far more effective than any punch. You'll never beat me without it."

I'm left staring at his back, quivering with fury and shock as he strides away.

The ground shakes, snow shivering off trees and a squirrel fleeing with a sudden squeak. It startles me enough that I let go of the anger I've been building.

Instantly, everything falls quiet again.

Thiago looks back at me.

What was that?

It wasn't the same frenetic energy I've felt inside me but couldn't touch. No, this came from far underground, as if my anger somehow roused a sleeping giant. I can still feel it, stirring beneath the frozen earth like a sluggish river of power.

"Princess?" Thiago calls softly. "Are you coming?"

I bolt after him, suddenly feeling the trees press in all around us.

I can't sense that power anymore, but perhaps that's a good thing.

Whatever it is, it's not coming from inside me, even if I suspect it responded to me.

And it's not fae magic.

MISTMERE LOOMS out of the frozen wasteland of the lake, the ancient keep's spires soaring toward the skies. It was built on a rocky island, a single bridge connecting it to the land. Dawn silvers the skies in the east, but shadows cling to the city, making it look like some sort of eerie graveyard of rubble.

"It's said there was only one way onto the island," Thiago murmurs, crouching behind a rocky outlook to peer down at the ruins. "What do you see?"

I squat beside him, surprised to realize he's actually curious about my opinion. I'm an accessory in my mother's court, hungry for more responsibility, chafing at my reins, and yet denied attending the most basic of councils.

It's strange to realize that it's only here with the Prince of Evernight, that I'm being treated as an equal.

Movement shifts near the other side of the bridge; merely the faintest ripple of a guard prowling the shadows there. If I wasn't looking for it, I don't think I'd have even noticed. "A guard," I murmur. "There's someone guarding the other side of the bridge."

Which is highly unusual, considering the entire place is supposed to be abandoned.

"Some*thing*," he corrects, slipping between rocks and ghosting along the ridge. "Angharad's brought her pets."

Banes.

She's the only queen in the territories with the ability to curse-twist a fae into one of the monstrous creatures and then bind it to her will. Most of them can cast the curse, but reining in such brutal beasts is near impossible.

I trail behind Thiago with my hand on the hilt of my knife. The enormous brindle-backed banes that Angharad wields have been bred to tear fae apart, their teeth capped with iron tips. One bite would burn like poison.

It's a breathless feeling to know Thiago's Unseelie spy is correct: Angharad is up to something.

Which means the prince wasn't lying.

I don't know how to twist that into my mother's narrative that he's working with the Unseelie, when he's clearly trying to stop their queen.

"What now?" I murmur, trailing him through the rocky crags overlooking the ruins and the lake.

"I need to get closer to the city."

Excellent. "How do we do that if she's got the bridge watched?"

Thiago leads me into a narrow ravine choked with brambles. He pauses at the end of it, which leads right into a thicket of thorns. "The truth is, there was always more than one way into the city. When the witch king led his war host south, the Queen of Mistmere evacuated the city of its women and children through this tunnel."

"I thought nobody survived the witch king's attack. And what tunnel?"

"They didn't." Thiago sweeps a curtain of thorns aside, revealing the gaping mouth of a cave. "The witch king's scouts were roaming the hills. The evacuated only made it thirteen miles before they were all slaughtered by a roaming host of banes."

"Then how did you know there's a tunnel?" I stare into the darkness.

"Because I was here to lead them out." His voice turns hard. "Nobody from *Mistmere* survived."

I look at him sharply.

The Wars of Light and Shadow were over five hundred years ago. I knew he was older than that, but it couldn't have been by much.

"My queen sent me to Mistmere to serve Queen Abalonia as a warrior. I was there when the city was attacked, though Queen Abalonia sent me with the evacuees, to try and bring help. Unfortunately, by the time I reached my queen, it was too late."

This would be Queen Araya, whom he later overthrew.

"Come on." He pushes me in the back. "We need to start moving quickly, and we need to be quiet."

"I'm not the one speaking loudly enough to be overheard in Valerian."

His eyes narrow. "Lead on, Princess. Unless you're scared of the dark."

"I have nerves of iron," I shoot back, stalking into the tunnel. "I just thought you'd prefer to lead, considering you're the big, bad Prince of Darkness, with balls of pure steel."

"It's got little to do with my balls. I just prefer the view from back here."

I try to shoot a withering glare over my shoulder, but Thiago lets the drape of thorns go, plunging us into darkness. My heart rabbits in my chest. Fear is a weakness and thus something to be overcome, but I can't help wondering if there's anything else in here, watching me.

"No comment, Princess?"

Be brave. At least you're not alone in here.

I release a steady breath. "Considering I can't see a cursed thing, and therefore neither can you, I don't think I have to bother."

Thiago snaps his fingers, and just like that, a faelight appears in the air over my shoulder, glowing a faint silvery blue.

"Watch out for the nixies," he whispers.

COBWEBS AND SPIDERS.

My least favorite combination in the world. I exit the tunnel right on the prince's heels, trying not to scrape the dusty cobwebs from my face until I know the way is clear. Light spills ahead of us, highlighting the enormous cavern we're in.

I stagger over a cracked tile and a leering face jumps out at me. The sword clears my scabbard, hissing loudly in the stillness of the night, and I'm two seconds away from skewering the beast before I realize it's a troll carved from stone.

Soft laughter echoes behind me.

Heart pounding like I've just run a race, I turn to find the prince bent over as he tries to choke down his amusement.

"Thanks for warning me," I whisper, since he's clearly unconcerned with being found.

I could have had a heart seizure—or worse, screamed—and he thinks this is funny?

"Nerves of iron," he mocks.

I punch him in the abdomen. Hard.

Or at least, it's meant to be a punch, but the bastard barely flinches, capturing my wrist. There's got to be a solid ripple of pure muscle behind his leather body armor, because I think I broke my knuckles.

"Next time, hit something a little softer," he mutters, pushing past me.

"Next time, I'm going to aim for your balls."

He doesn't quite wince.

Instead, he turns around, pressing a finger to his lips in warning as he steps into the light.

Understood. No speaking from here.

I follow him past more stone statues. More leering trolls. Guards, I realize, for the enormous stone sarcophagi between them. We're in the catacombs of Mistmere, though after venturing into the City of the Dead, with all its wraiths and shades, I barely flinch. The roof is caved in, and as I step through the moonlight, I feel a creep of dread down my spine.

Because I swear something just howled in the distance.

We move like wraiths in the night, and Thiago merely assumes I'll follow his lead, gesturing sharply every time he thinks he hears something.

Fog lingers like a soft blanket in the streets, stirring

around our boots. I feel something pulse against my skin, like a far distant drumbeat.

"Do you hear that?" I breathe into the prince's ear as we hover in the shadows under an arch.

He looks at me sharply.

"Drums."

Thiago cocks his head for a long moment, and then slowly shakes his head. "Nothing," he mouths.

I hold my arm out. All the hairs have lifted, and I can feel the pulse of that beat in the night. Strange.

He's watching me as if to ask what I can hear, but I merely shrug. Maybe I'm imagining it. Or maybe it's the beat of my heart drumming in my ears.

Soon we're in what remains of the city. Moonlight gilds the stone, highlighting silver glyphs in the Old Tongue, which must have been painstakingly carved into the stone many years ago. Mistmere worshipped the Mother of Night, if I remember correctly, and there are half moons carved into every available surface.

Queen Abalonia alone refused to condemn the Old Ones to their prison worlds when the alliance banded together to trap them.

She was the only Seelie queen to make an alliance with them.

A snuffling sound echoes through the ruins ahead, and my hand leaps to the hilt of my sword. It's not the first time, but this time, I'm fairly certain the threat is real.

Thiago pushes me into a rubble-strewn alleyway, where I barely dare breathe. Every little noise—even the barest crunch of my boots on gravel—seems to echo hollowly in the fog. He's pressed against me, a solid wall of muscle between me and the threat. If his head wasn't cocked to the side, listening intently, I'd almost suspect this was deliberate.

To take my mind off the danger, I follow the cords of muscle in his throat with my eyes. Every day I brush a kiss against those chiseled lips, and every day he sits there and waits for it, hunger barely restrained by the clench of his knuckles around the arms of his chair.

It's the restraint that affects me the most, I think.

He never says a word, though his eyes hold the heat of a thousand unspoken promises. All the things he'd like to do to me, if I let him.

The snuffling sounds drift away slowly, and I can finally breathe again. Shoulders slumping in relief, I realize my hand is pressed to the prince's chest, and he's no longer focused on the creature. Instead, his gaze drifts to my lips.

We're standing too close together, and with the chill of Mistmere pressing against my skin, I can feel the heat of his body radiating like a furnace. Evening is falling, and I still owe him a kiss.

And for the first time, I almost want to give it.

"Later," he whispers, his breath ghosting over the soft hairs that curl at my temples.

A shiver runs through me. He's very, very good at what he does. And he knows exactly how easily he's getting to me. I can see it in the faint creases that line his eyes when he's amused.

"Never," I whisper back.

Thiago leans closer, his lips tracing the curve of my ear. "Then stop looking at me as though you want to eat me alive."

I jerk back from him. "I do not—"

A hollow throb pulses through me, breaking my gaze from

that dangerous mouth. It echoes through the earth beneath my feet like the first vague trembling of an earthquake. Stronger this time, leaving ghostly shivers over my skin.

"Iskvien?" Thiago asks sharply.

I rub my arms. All is forgotten. "What *is* that?"

"What is what?"

It comes again. Stronger this time. Not an earthquake's tremor, no, but something akin to sonar. It ripples over me and locks hold for a second, as if sensing me amidst the carnage of the city. Then the sensation sluices down my skin like warm water, leaving me trembling.

I stare at my fingertips. There'd been a hint of golden light rippling beneath my skin that time, as if my veins absorbed the... sensation.

Thiago grabs my forearm, staring intently at my expression. "Tell me what you feel."

So I do.

His frown only notches deeper between his eyebrows. "You're sensing the Hallow. It's stronger than it should be. You should only be able to feel a faint quiver by now. The circle focusing its power inward was warded by stones, which lock the power of the ley line within it. The stones fell during the wars."

"That's the Hallow? Wait. Why can I feel it?"

And you can't?

"Some fae are sensitive. Come on," he mutters. "We need to see the Hallow. It shouldn't be active."

The Mistmere Hallow lies in the heart of the city, and all the main boulevards lead toward it. Carved owls stare down from each avenue, their endless eyes staring right through us. The owl is the symbol of the Mother of Night, the Old One that Mistmere and its queen once revered. I can't escape the sensation she's somehow watching us, even though she's trapped in the Underworld.

More banes hunt the rubble-strewn streets. I dart down an alley on Thiago's heels, and he bends to cup his hands, gesturing his chin toward the roof. The second I step into his cupped hands, he tosses me high, and I drag myself on top of the roof. He follows, hauling himself up a stone balustrade with the lithe grace of an acrobat and enough arm strength to make me jealous.

Just in time.

Another bane stalks around the corner of the alley, snuffling the cobbles. It's larger than the one Andraste killed, and moonlight shines off the enormous spiked collar around its throat. This one seems more lion than wolf, a snarling, monstrous creature that looks like a nightmare called directly to life.

Head down, it follows our trail toward the wall. I freeze, pressed flat to the roof.

Thiago stares intently into the alley, weaving his fingers in an intricate fashion. The bane's head jerks up, and it stares into the distance, where shadows flicker over the walls like a pair of people running. In the heavy fog, it's a deft enough illusion to seem lifelike.

Baying loudly, the bane sprints after them.

A dozen voices rise to join it, all of them heading in the same direction. They stream from everywhere, galloping along on all fours, some of them mere stirrings of fog and others flashes of fur and claws.

"Erlking's hairy cock," Thiago swears under his breath. "Whatever she's doing here, she's got the entire city locked down."

"We're not going to get near the Hallow." That we've

made it this far is a miracle. And now— "We're not going to escape. Not now they've got our scent."

"One problem at a time, Princess." Thiago scrambles over the rooftop. "Keep moving."

We circle closer to the Hallow, leaping across alleys and rolling along rooftops. If I couldn't hear the ever-present howling of the banes as they come across various scent trails, I'd almost enjoy the exhilaration of the moment.

It's not until we get close to the center of the city though, that I realize what Thiago's been doing all along.

"You've been leading us in circles," I mutter.

Ever since we exited the catacombs.

He flashes a smile at me. "Scent trails overlap. My shadows have been hauling a shirt of mine all over the city too. Let them track us. There's too many trails for them to follow."

"Your shadows can do that?" Despite myself, I'm impressed.

He arches a brow in a *Princess-I-can-do-anything* look.

Ignoring the howls, we inch closer until we're finally crawling on our bellies across a roof. And what I see takes my breath away.

Mother of Cursed Night.

It's not just a dozen banes. There are nearly fifty of them prowling the ruins. Teams of Unseelie yell and curse at each other, and a pair of huge, lumbering beasts strain against a harness. Canvas tents flap in the night, and a banner flies from the top of the biggest.

A soaring white wyvern, its teeth bared, against a black background.

Angharad.

I catch sight of a shock of white, and realize Isem, her pet sorcerer, is also there. Things just became dire.

"What are they looking for?" I breathe the words into the night.

Thiago's face hardens, his eyes searching the ruins. "They're not looking for anything. They've already found it. *Look*."

Ahead of us, several workmen direct a taskforce. One of them cracks a whip, and the team of creatures harnessed to the crane strain forward. Enormous muscles flex in their backs, and I catch a glimpse of the elegant gold tattoos concealed beneath scabbed-over cuts and whip marks. Goblins, by the look of them.

The pulley systems jerk, and one of the enormous lintel stones around the Hallow slowly jacks upright. It joins three others, though the rest of them lie fallen around the top of the hill.

"They're trying to recreate the Hallow," I say breathlessly. "But... why?"

The circles were created to trap the Old Ones and cast them into a prison realm outside of time.

It was only by pure chance that the Seelie realized such portals could also be used to seek passage between kingdoms, Hallow to Hallow.

When Mistmere fell, its Hallow died. Why would Angharad be going to so much effort to create a portal here?

"She can't bring an army through. Unless she has a few weeks." The portal needs to repower after every transfer, and the more people it transports, the longer it needs to revive. "And this is the worst place to stage an invasion."

She'd be crushed between the Prince of Evernight and the Queen of Aska.

"She's not planning on bringing an army through," he replies grimly.

"Then what—?"

"The only reason she might be resurrecting the Hallow is to bring one of the Old Ones back from the Underworld. This is the gateway to the Mother of Night's prison." Thiago scowls, setting a hand to the small of my back. "Let's move. I've seen enough, and neither of us can afford to be caught here. We need to alert the alliance."

11

I flee the tunnel into the cool night air on the other side of the lake, but I can't escape the dirty sensation of something crawling over my skin. Whatever I felt at the circle lingers like little spiders crawling over me.

Thiago follows, cursing under his breath. "I didn't think Angharad was this stupid."

"They wouldn't let one of the Old Ones out, would they? They couldn't. They've been trapped since the wars."

The Unseelie allied themselves with the Old Ones, and rode at their side, but surely they remember how dangerous they were?

"They would, and they could, if given the right spells." He scrubs a hand over his mouth. "The right sacrifice."

"What do you mean 'right sacrifice'?"

"What do you know of the wars and the Hallows?"

"We were losing," I reply. "Badly. And then King Raen came up with a plan to trap the Old Ones and remove their power from the battlefield. Each King and Queen sent their most powerful warriors to lure each of the Old Ones into a Hallow. Once there, the trap was sprung, and the

Old Ones were flung into a prison world they cannot escape."

"They used an ancient spell and blood magic," Thiago says. "The power required to access the Underworld is immense. A circle of stones to control the power of the ley line; thirteen fae sorcerers standing at each stone chanting; and a sacrifice within the Hallow. A kingly sacrifice, in most cases. They cut the heart right out of Raen's chest in the middle of Mistmere. It was the only way to defeat the Mother of Night, and he knew it."

My mouth slowly drops open. "He offered himself up as sacrifice?"

My mother would never do such a thing.

"The sacrifice is the key," Thiago replies. "If the sacrifice can't withstand the power of the ley line and the Hallow, then the spell is ruined."

"So... how is Angharad going to reverse the spell?" She has the power, but I can't see her sacrificing herself in order to bring back the Mother of Night.

"They need a queen. Or a prince," he replies. "Someone who has a trickle of the old blood in their veins. The power required to break the prison open is immense, but they need someone who was tied to those who created the circle. A direct descendant, preferably."

Like my mother.

Or me.

"But why would she...?"

"Power. Angharad signed the treaty, but let's not pretend she would have any intentions of holding her people to it if she has a choice. It's been a good five hundred years since the war. She's bowed her head all that time, but she must have found the right spell to unleash an Old One." He paces the hill, frustration edging through him. "The Seelie

Alliance is not as strong as it once was. If she brings the Mother of Night back, she'll have direct access to all that power. And we're a fraction of what we once were, even if your mother could be trusted to guard our flanks during a war."

"My mother's many things, but she's not a fool," I bite. "If she doesn't stand beside you in the war, then she'll be wading through Unseelie the second you fall."

"If you think, for one second, that she wouldn't be tempted," he shoots back, "then you're the fool. Adaia thinks herself invulnerable. She *might* just think herself powerful enough to confront the three Unseelie queens by herself. Asturia is far enough south that she might think herself safe."

There's no point arguing. "So, what do we do?"

"We need to alert the other kingdoms."

A howl goes up in the forest.

It sounds close. Far too close. And it sounds almost... gleeful.

My head snaps toward the sound. "Was that—"

"Yes," he hisses, stepping between me and the sound, his hand going to the hilt on his sword.

We both freeze, heads cocked to listen. Hearts pounding and blood rushing through our veins. Every inch of me is on edge.

Another howl echoes.

And this time it's to the left.

They've found our trail.

"Run!" Thiago gives me a shove in the back.

The pair of us scramble up the slope, sprinting through the ankle-deep snow. I sink into a deep hollow beneath the snow, cursing under my breath.

The prince returns, yanking me forward and nearly wrenching my arm from its socket. "Move!"

"I'm trying!"

He merely hauls me out of the deep snow and drags me forward.

"The second we get clear of these trees, we're going to have to move fast," he yells.

As if in answer, an arrow hisses past.

"Curse it." Thiago draws his sword, glancing behind us. "Can you hit that archer?"

I slip the bow from my back and swiftly string it. "If I can see where he is. I don't suppose you'd like to play bait?"

"Funny. Trying to get rid of me already?"

I shrug. "Worth a try."

Thiago gives me a long steady look. "Don't miss."

Then he turns and walks out into the snowy clearing, an enormous target painted against the freshly laid snow.

Erlking's hairy cock. My mouth drops open, then I wrench an arrow from my quiver and nock it.

An arrow arcs into the sky, and I turn and sight into the thicket it came from. Steel flashes at the corner of my eye; Thiago gracefully deflecting the arrow with the stroke of his sword.

I can't see a cursed thing. Nothing moves in the thicket. There might be a shadow to the right, but it might also be a tree root.

"Vi," Thiago mutters, under his breath.

"Hold still," I hiss. "I'm trying to find him."

Movement glides through the bushes near the thicket. There. The bastard's on the move. My arrow tracks the target.

Another arrow flies directly toward the prince, a second hot on its heels.

I ignore Thiago and focus along the shaft. I'm not the archer Andraste is, but I've spent too many hours on a range to embarrass myself now. Blocking out everything but the archer, I release a slow breath and then let my arrow fly.

It hits the archer right in the center of his chest, and he cries out, then slams to the ground. Thiago smashes the second arrow to the ground, breathing hard.

"Nice shot."

"Thanks." I share an exhilarated smile with him, before a baying sound makes my blood run cold.

The archer isn't the only problem we have to contend with.

"How many arrows do you have?" Thiago yells.

"Not enough!" And banes are far more difficult to kill than the fae.

Bolting down the hill, I follow a narrow animal track that winds through the trees. Branches flash past me, tearing at my cloak, and I nearly lose the bow. I'm almost to a clearing when Thiago yells, "Vi!"

A heavy weight hits me in the back.

"What are you *doing*?"

Steel flashes.

An enormous iron maw snaps out of the snow—some sort of bane trap, I realize, as we roll into it—and my eyes widen as the metallic reflection flashes in Thiago's dark pupils.

He flings me to the side.

I slam onto my back as the trap snaps shut. Hot blood splashes across my face as spikes of iron slam through Thiago's chest and pin him there. A low scream thunders from his throat.

Mother of Night....

"Thiago!" I scramble across the snow and grab his hand

just as his knees give out, leaving him pinned in the iron maw.

My hands flutter over the bloody ruin of his chest as he gasps.

"Get... out of here."

I try to tear at the iron trap, but it burns my hands.

A long, mournful howl echoes through the mountains.

My gaze locks on Thiago's, and I see the same knowing slide over his expression, his nostrils flaring.

"They're too... close," he gasps.

As if to mock me, another howl goes up, this time to the north. I spin in that direction, an icy chill running down my spine.

"Vi!" Thiago barks. "R-run!"

Leaving him here.... He'll never survive. Not trapped by iron that will blunt his magic. And he's too badly injured to fight his way free. They'll eat him alive.

It would be the perfect end to the Prince of Evernight, my mother whispers in my mind.

But he shoved *me* out of the way of the bloody trap.

And as much as I hate to admit it, he's never given me a single cursed reason to hate him.

"No."

A fist catches in my cloak. "You need to... get out of here. Find my cabin." He manages to point to the west. "Two miles. Warded. Take some of... my blood for wards."

"Stay still," I growl, setting hands on the rusted metal. My mind's made up. I'm not thinking like an Asturian princess, and I know my mother will never forgive this if she hears of it.

But who's going to tell her?

The burn of the iron sears my clammy skin. I can't help

wrenching them away, seeing the pale white burn marks on my skin. How in Maia's name can he bear it?

"I'm not locking myself away in a warded cabin while they tear you to pieces."

"Then return to Valerian." Thiago tries to move, and red blood gushes from the wounds in his chest as he reaches for me. He cries out, his teeth clenching to trap the sound. "Get Eris. You can't... get me out of this." Dark shadows filled his eyes. "I can hold them off until you get back."

It's a lie. I can see it in his eyes. But why would he lie to me? Why risk *his life* to protect mine? We're enemies. None of this makes any sense.

The banes sound like they're barely a hundred yards away.

"Curse you." I can no more leave him here than cut my own hand off. "Don't move."

"Go," he snarls. "Leave me here."

"No."

"That's an order."

"You may as well save your breath, Your Highness. I'm not your subject, and I'm not going to pay any attention to what you say."

"You stubborn...." I ignore the curses streaming from his mouth as he strains to escape the trap.

No magic can manipulate iron, and I'm not strong enough to touch it or wrench it open.

I swing around, searching for something, anything....

There's a fallen log, with pieces already split up to be hauled away. I return with a thick piece the length of my forearm, then jam the end of the log between the teeth, using my weight to work it between them.

Another howl chills my blood. This time much closer.

"For the love of Maia, run, you fool!"

"I will." I lean all my weight on one end of the log in order to ratchet up the other end. Iron teeth bite into it, shredding the bark, but I'm gaining an inch. Maybe two. "The second you tell me why you'd risk your life for mine."

"Mother. Night." White grooves track his tanned face, an anguished cry tearing loose.

"Nearly there."

It takes all my strength, and I give up on the log, my fingers burning as I yank on the trap's bitter edges. Pain blisters my skin, my stomach threatening to disgorge itself. *I can't do this. I can't. I can't—*

Hold on.

Tears wet my eyes even as my skin feels like it's going to peel off the bone. Iron sickness sweeps through me, sweat dripping down my brow.

The banes' cries grow closer, and I can sense the excitement in their howls as they realize their prey is already down. The last of the sharp iron clears Thiago's flesh, and our eyes meet.

"Move!" I cry, arms shaking as I try to kick the log between the trap's jaw. I don't think I can hold it much longer—

Thiago rolls free, sprawling on the snow at my feet just as my strength finally gives out. The iron jaws spring shut, crunching through the log and shattering it.

There's blood on my fingers. Blood on the snow. Thiago curls over himself, and despite everything, I want to see him sweep to his feet.

Instead, he collapses.

"Get up!" I drag him upright.

"You stubborn, reckless bitch." It sounds like a curse, and yet there's something... affectionate about the words as I sling his arm over my shoulder. Something almost familiar.

"I did *not* just rescue you from a bane trap only to have you fall now. Run."

He staggers forward, his legs threatening to go out from beneath him. "We're not going... to be able... to outrun them."

I know. "We just have to make it to the Hallow."

He collapses in a snowdrift, and I go to my knees beside him. The first flash of a shadow winds through the trees beside me. My head swivels but it's gone again. A scout. And I have no fucking idea where my bow and arrows went.

"Get up."

"Can't," he gasps, one hand clasped to his bloodied ribs.

"Yes, you can." I haul him upright through sheer willpower, but he's listing so badly I know I'm not going to be able to carry him. Why does the bastard have to be so big and heavy? "Are you trying to tell me the Prince of Evernight is going to meet his end here? In the belly of a bane? You'd prefer to be shit out all through these forests?"

His lip curls in a snarl, and he takes a limping step forward. The weight nearly drives me to my knees.

"Why couldn't you be a scrawny half-formed bastard?"

"Because... you like... to stare at my muscles."

There's another flash to the right of me. *Keep going.* We just have to keep going. "In your dreams, Prince."

"Think it's mostly... your dreams, isn't it?"

If he's flirting with me, then he isn't halfway dead. We have a chance.

And then that chance evaporates like the dreams he speaks of. The first bane slinks through the trees in front of us, cutting off our escape route. Another flickers through the trees to flank us, and a low chorus of howls seems to echo from every point around us. We stagger to a halt.

Thiago tries to straighten. "Stay behind me."

"What are you going to do? Bleed on them?"

There's a startled glimpse of green eyes. A low growl echoes behind us. Shadows weave through the trees, barely visible through the softly falling snow. All I can see is the sheer size of the creatures, the slavering menace in their faces....

A high-pitched howl rises. Another lifts its shaggy head, a chilling sound reverberating through its throat.

So, this is it....

This is where it all ends.

I have no more illusions. I can count. Six banes, when two would be a handful even if the pair of us were in any condition to fight.

"Do you trust me, Vi?" Thiago whispers, collapsing to his knees in the snow.

This time I let him fall, trying to draw my sword with blistered, half-frozen fingers.

What sort of question is that?

An ancient hardness cuts over his face as he sees my expression, his eyes turning pure black. "Don't answer that," he says with a soft, bitter laugh before turning to the banes.

Tendrils of shadow sweep around us, as insubstantial as mist. I freeze. The Darkness. I've heard of him using it. With his power, he can cut fae down from miles away, but the price is tremendous, for it's rumored the prince cannot always control it.

And sometimes the Darkness takes a piece of his soul with it.

"Whatever you do," he whispers, "don't run. Don't move from my side. And don't scream."

The banes dissolve from the tree line, stalking us in a low crouch. My breath catches, and I unconsciously step closer to Thiago.

"Come to me," he whispers, droplets of blood marking the pristine snow by his knees. "That's it."

His shadows fan across the snow, snaking around the banes.

"Look at thissh," hisses one of the banes with a coughing laugh. "A wicked prinsh, on hish kneesh before ush."

"Delicioush," growls another.

"Itsh the traitor," rasps another. "The Bashtard."

Another merely snaps, lunging forward with yellowed teeth clashing.

I swing the sword, more of a threat than anything else, trying to stop them from rushing us. They're everywhere. Circling us. Growling under their breath as they watch the sword with yellow eyes.

"Vi," Thiago rasps. "I told you not to move."

"Then do what you need to do."

Tearing open his shirt, he falls forward onto his knuckles. Shadows move beneath his skin. No, not shadows. Tattoos. They writhe with malevolent grace, thick and violent. And then suddenly, they're no longer content to remain in his skin.

"Thiago," I whisper as tentacles of pure shadow lift out of his skin.

"Don't move," he rasps.

The banes slink closer.

I don't know where to look. Every hair down my spine lifts as I face the banes, because I can hear little whispers behind me, as though something lurks within those shadows.

"Rip hish throat out," hisses one of the banes.

"Take him for queen," growls another.

"Why don't you come closer and try it," Thiago replies coldly.

As one, they lift their heads and howl.

And then they do exactly as he suggests, launching forward.

I swing my sword, iron whining in the chill night air. It meets resistance, and then hot blood splashes across my face. I'm about to follow up but Thiago grabs my ankle.

Shadows erupt, plunging us into a cloud of darkness and swallowing the banes whole. Yelps and snarls echo through the clearing, along with the crunch of bones. It's bloody and brutal, and I don't know what's worse, the sound of the banes screaming in pain and rage, or the hissing little whispers that fill the shadows.

"Eat them all up...."

"So sweet the screams.... Tasty, tasty bones.... Crunch them and chew them and swallow them down."

Thiago's arms came around me, pinning me to his hard body as his power tears through the banes. I bury my face against his chest, trying not to listen to the Darkness's devastating whispers.

It's as if the malevolence is alive and comprised of several entities.

"More. Want more."

Something touches my hair, and I scream as I feel its chill whisper down my spine.

"Don't worry," the Prince of Evernight tells me. "You're safe in my arms. You'll always be safe."

The wind whips around us, something hissing in furious demand.

"Not her. Never her," Thiago snaps.

"Prince is weak," whispers something behind me. *"Prince is bleeding. Who is Prince to make demands?"*

"Begone!" he bellows, flinging up his arms.

"Tasty, tasty blood—" Right behind him. *"Wants it."*

His weight leans on me, as if they're sapping him of strength. I catch a glimpse of the strain on his face. The sound of slobbering echoes, and then he screams and hot blood splashes against my cheek.

"Keep me safe," I tell him, wrapping my arms around his neck and pressing my face to his throat. Greedy hands tear at my velvet cloak, and something slices my thigh. "You can do this. You can control them. I know you can. You promised you'd keep me safe."

I don't know what sort of magic this is, but I know now why the queens fear him.

Blood splashes as the creatures take their thwarted rage out upon what remains of the banes. Strain tightens Thiago's jaw, and I press my hand to it, stroking his cheek with my thumb.

"Control them, curse you." I don't know if being torn

apart by... whatever this is... would be better or worse than being eaten alive. "Control them!"

"I'm... trying."

Out of pure desperation, I press my lips to his.

It's as if the sun suddenly rises.

The gloom seems to lessen, and suddenly I can't hear those malevolent whispers anymore.

Thiago stills, his hands clinging to my shirt. And then his mouth is moving hungrily over mine, meeting me with an urgency he's never displayed until now. "Vi," he whispers, shaking in my arms. "Vi." And then a trembling hand is sliding through my hair, curling into a fist, as if he's trying to anchor himself.

The Darkness vanishes abruptly. The shadows dissipate.

I come back to myself, my forehead resting against his as we both pant for breath. He's getting heavier, and I realize he must be almost listing toward me for our heads to touching.

"What *was* that?"

No Seelie fae could have wielded such power. That was pure Unseelie magic, malicious and dangerous. The clearing is splashed with blood and bone and other pieces of flesh I don't want to identify. There's nothing left of our attackers.

There's barely anything left of us.

Thiago's weight nearly drives me to my knees. Before he can answer, he collapses with a groan at my feet.

I kneel at his side, checking his pulse. "Your Highness?"

His skin's clammy to the touch. Dangerously so.

"Thiago?" I whisper.

But there's no answer.

A chill settles on my shoulders. It's so fucking quiet now, without the banes or Thiago's Darkness. I blow into my

cupped hands, then realize the snow settling on my shoulders is starting to penetrate my clothes.

I'm feeling the cold.

Which means Thiago's wards are failing. I need to get us
to shelter. Fast. And then I don't know what I'm going to do.

Wind whips my fur vest and shirt around me as I drag Thiago through the snow.

I made a makeshift sled with his own cloak, and then packed mine around him to keep him warm. My own blood runs hot, but by the time we've gone half a mile, even I'm starting to feel the bitter chill creep into my toes and fingers.

He said the hunting cabin wasn't far, and I found a narrow track through the trees that clearly leads somewhere.

Please, please let it be the cabin....

Behind us, I can make out the distant howl of banes discovering what's left of their fallen comrades. If I don't find shelter shortly, I'll be dealing with more of the creatures, and this time I'm on my own.

The blizzard sweeps cold curtains of snow across the world until I can barely see the path anymore. Every step I take grows harder, my boots sinking into the snow and the weight of the prince growing heavier.

"Curse you, Your Royal Arrogance," I breathe, pricks of

cold slashing my cheeks. "You trapped me with this treaty, dragged me out here, *kissed me*, and then bled all over me. Don't you dare die on me. Don't you *dare*."

Only silence answers me.

"My mother will dance on your grave," I tell him, turning and gripping the cloak with both hands as I haul him. "And I will dance with her. I swear I will. I'll tell the whole world you were eaten by a bane. The almighty Prince of Darkness felled by a mutt." I squat at his side, feeling for his weak pulse. It's still there, but the flicker of it worries me. "I'll make up poems, have them sing ballads about your inglorious end.... What rhymes with Thiago?"

Curse him. Blood wells through the makeshift bandages I applied, melting the snowy slush that settles on his chest. He's definitely getting heavier.

I blink, and don't recognize where I am.

Each step seems slower, heavier. Shaking my head, I find the trail and push on. This has to lead to the cabin. I won't consider any other possibility.

"Don't you dare stop breathing, you stubborn, infuriating bastard."

Or else I'll never know why he saved me.

"You owe me an answer. You owe me..."

Another kiss.

I'm almost about to sink to my knees and rest, my entire body aching with both desperation and exhaustion, when something catches my eye.

A darkened blur looms out of the forest in front of me. The forest clears suddenly, and ahead of me I can just make out the sharp ridgeline of a roof. Taking a small faelight out of my pack, I lift it up and shake it to stir the magic. Pale silvery blue light washes over the gables of an old, weather-hardened cabin. Carved wyverns and leering goblins hiss down at me from the gables. My knees almost give out.

Thank the Darkness.

A sob catches in my throat. Against all odds, I've managed to lead us directly to the cabin.

My fingers are so stiff I can barely open the latch. The dark, musty scent of an unopened room meets me, but I don't care. It's warmer in here. Dry. And I can bar the door against the monsters tracking us, though hopefully they'll lose our scent in the storm.

Thiago stirs as I haul him over the threshold. I slump to the floor with him half-nestled in my lap, desperately trying to see if he's awake.

"Your Highness?"

I shake him.

Nothing.

"Thiago?"

The faintest flutter of his lashes makes me release a pent-up breath I didn't realize I was holding. The prince stirs again, a faint groan coming from his throat.

"Vi?" he whispers.

I'm so relieved I could kiss him. "We're safe. I found your hunting lodge. Are you in pain? Are you cold? Can you feel your fingers? Your toes?"

His head lolls to the side, his eyes rolling up in his head, but somehow, he catches hold of my fingers. The faintest smile graces his hard mouth as he rouses again. Then he winces. "Told you... that you couldn't keep your hands off me."

Of all the things....

I rest my forehead on his. "I swear to Maia that I will drop you in the nearest snowdrift—"

"No, you won't."

I half-laugh, half-sob. *No, I won't.*

"Why? Why did you come after me? You knew the trap was there, didn't you! Why sacrifice yourself for me?"

"I made a promise," he whispers, smiling through bloodied teeth. "To always protect you."

Always? A chill runs through me, one that has nothing to do with fear. "What does that mean?"

More cursed unanswered questions.

But his eyes roll back in his head, and there is no answer.

And if I don't move swiftly, there never will be.

The hunting cabin is freezing.

There are wards carved into the doorframe, ancient fae glyphs I barely recognize, but I wet them with his blood. Instantly, I feel them awaken, protecting the cabin from intruders until the magic in his blood dwindles or the glyphs weaken.

I can't feel my toes in my boots, and for a hot-blooded Asturian with summer in her veins, that's a troubling sign. Shivering, I cross to the hearth, finding a fire already laid. The current simmers in my blood, a mere spark. I grit my teeth and call fire to life, setting the tinder blazing.

Light flares, revealing a rough-hewn log cabin decorated with heavy furniture that is draped with decadent furs. Four chairs. A table. Two chests of drawers. A bed.

It will do.

Blood stains the hard slabs of muscle in the prince's chest, and his shoulder is ravaged. He desperately needs healing. I cut his clothes from him to examine the wounds. The edges are gray and ashen with iron poisoning. Some of the smaller gashes are working to heal themselves, but slug-gish blood pools around the larger, deeper wounds.

But it's the black bruises that decorate his arms and back that worries me. They look like teeth marks, if something with a million razor-sharp teeth that size existed.

I find a clean shirt in one of the chests and bandage his wounds as best I can. The chill of his skin bothers me the most.

There's no possible way I can lever his enormous body up onto the bed, so I drag the quilts and blankets down onto the fur in front of the fire, creating a warm cocoon.

If I can get him dry and warm, hopefully he'll last long enough for his people to find us.

Of all the ways I expected this day to end....

"Just so you know, I'm not trying to get you naked for my sake." A part of me is certain his eyes will blink open again the second I have him bare to his skin. He'll smile at me mock-ingly, as if to say he knew I wouldn't be able to resist him.

Except, there is no smile.

No hint he's even breathing beyond the faint flicker in his throat, let alone aware.

"Thiago?"

His head lolls bonelessly to the side as I release his chin.

I curse under my breath as I strip his leather breeches down his long legs. Every inch of him is bloodied and bruised with those horrible mottled suction marks, and I still can't look at the gaping holes in his chest. It hurts too much to think of him never mocking me again.

And it shouldn't hurt.

He's the enemy of my people.

The prince who holds a blade to the throat of everyone I love.

A monster.

Except, he hasn't hurt me. Not once. He's not taken advantage of the treaty beyond a single stolen kiss each day —and if I'm being honest, I don't hate it that much.

Iron poisoning often ends in a fever, but... had he drained himself too much in trying to defend us? *Me?*

I touch his skin, but every inch of him feels frozen.

And I'm dangerously warm.

Don't you dare even think it. "You are not getting naked with the Prince of Evernight."

The silence echoes accusingly.

If he dies, then I'll bear this burden on my conscience.

He *did* save my life, after all.

Slipping out of my shirt and breeches, I pause with my fingers on the hem of my short chemise. It's not as though he can take advantage of this moment of weakness, but still....

I slide under the fur cloaks with him. My chemise shields me from the press of his naked skin against mine, but I'm desperately aware of how close I came to dying today.

I can't help a shiver as I wrap my arms and body around him. Every inch of him is like ice. I'm practically glued to him, rubbing my palms against his arms to try and force his circulation to warm him.

"If you die," I whisper, "then you'll never realize you finally got me in your bed."

There's no answer.

∽

HE's no better by morning.

Black shadows darken the veins near his deepest wounds, rousing my worst fears.

I rest my head on his chest, listening to the racing beat of his heart. *Iron poisoning.* The fever will be coming. And with his wounds barely knitting together, I'm not certain he'll be able to survive it.

This calls for drastic measures.

I remove his bloodied bandages, washing the wounds clean. Still raw and bloody, which bodes ill. Fae heal from practically anything. This should have been smooth, unblemished skin by now.

The fire of my magic would burn the iron poisoning from his blood. If I could summon it....

"I really hope you're not relying on this," I whisper. My magic is erratic at the best of times. Healing is a gift through my mother's bloodlines, which makes it easier for me than most, though at best, I can heal minor scrapes and bruises.

There's no answer.

The tattoos on his chest swirl over his pectorals like shadows, dark and inky. They look like they're about to separate from his skin and envelop him, the way his magic did earlier. I reach out tentatively, placing my palm over the worst of those puncture wounds. I've seen that symbol before. Seen those tattoos? An aching pain lances behind my eye, and I gasp, pushing away from the thought. The ache subsides with a weary grumble, but the threat of it remains.

Setting my palm over his bandages, I risk letting a little of my power stir through the wound. A gasp parts his lips, and those sultry black lashes flicker against his tanned cheeks. Dangerously green eyes blink open.

"Vi?"

Thank Maia. "You son of a bitch. I thought you were dying."

"Sorry to... disappoint," he rasps, and I grab the cup I filled with water and tip it to his lips, cupping the back of his neck to help him drink.

Thiago collapses back on the furs, the muscles in his throat straining as his chest heaves. "What happened?" He blinks, turning his head. "Where...?"

"I found your hunting cabin. And I saved your life."

"So, you did." He laughs, but it dies suddenly, and he repeats, a little more softly, "So you did."

"Don't think I'm not going to hold it over your head. You owe me."

"A life for a life." His eyelashes flutter against his cheeks. "You didn't leave me."

It has to be the fever dreams. "Of course I didn't leave you. I— I can hardly uphold my side of the treaty if I left you to die in the snow."

"Don't leave me." His fingers twine with mine. "Not this time. Don't ever go."

I stare down at our linked fingers.

He doesn't know what he's saying.

"I can't promise that." There's just enough of Maia's blood in my veins to make oath giving dangerous. "You know I can't promise that. But I'm not going to leave you here to rot. It's not as though I know where we are, or how to return to Valerian."

Thiago turns his head restlessly. "Don't leave me."

"Here, you're burning up." I reach for the cup of water and a damp cloth.

He thrashes, seeking my hand.

"Curse you, stop!"

There's no calming him. Sweat dampens his brow as he

flings his arm out. I have to practically throw myself atop
him to calm him.

"I'm here! I'm here!" I capture his hand, press it to my
cheek. "See? You're not alone."

Thiago relaxes back into sleep, but I can sense the restlessness within him. Whatever ghosts haunt him, they wield
sharp whips.

I can't help thinking of his wife and the hatred he bears
my mother. He's never told me how the queen took his wife
from him, but it's clear it affects him still.

I lie down beside him, hesitantly resting my head on his
shoulder. "I won't leave you. Not until we find help. I
promise."

This is one promise I can keep.

AFTER ANOTHER FITFUL NIGHT, the second morning brings
change.

I'm pacing outside the cabin, wondering what I'm going
to do with the prince, when a voice calls hesitantly from the
other room, "Vi?"

Mother of Night.

Rushing back inside, I find the prince struggling up onto
his elbows. I managed to get him onto the bed yesterday,
and he looks like he can barely escape the nest of blankets I
created. "You're alive."

"Of course, I'm alive." He looks irritable.

Rust-colored blood mars his bandages, and those
wicked-looking tattoos seem to leer at me. I offer him fresh
water, which he gulps thirstily.

"Don't tell me you thought I was dying." His voice might
sound like it's coming from a raw throat, but there's a

twinkle in his eyes.

"I was hoping." I say with false bravado. "I nearly left you behind twice."

"No, you didn't." He looks around, hazy recognition dawning in his eyes. "My hunting cabin."

A disbelieving laugh escapes me. "Of all the paths I picked to follow, I somehow led myself straight to it."

"Mmm," he murmurs. "Fate works in mysterious ways."

There's something about the way he says it that makes me look at him sharply. "Surely, you don't believe the old tales—that I was meant to find this place."

"What do you believe then? We're in the middle of a fucking forest, Vi. Do you think you just happened to stagger upon the right trail, when I'd given you no more than a general direction?"

The thought *has* plagued me.

"Maybe the demi-fey led me here," I reply with a shrug. "I was half-comatose myself."

And they've been known to lead strangers to safety in trying circumstances.

Of course, they've also been known to lead them to their doom.

There's no other answer I *can* believe.

"Maybe." He rubs at his temples. "How did you get me here?"

I proceed to tell him about the past two days.

And, of course, he lifts the furs and glances down, then arches an eyebrow. "Did my Shadows destroy my clothes, or did you finally succumb to my charms?"

"What charms?" I growl under my breath as I push to my feet. "That's exactly what happened. When you were unconscious, I could no longer contain myself and tore your

shirt to shreds. Don't worry. You're definitely more irresistible when your mouth is shut."

His eyes narrow.

"And it wasn't as though the cold made you any less a
man."

That shuts him up.

He pushes upright, the heavy muscles in his shoulders
flexing as the furs fall into his lap. "I guess you won't mind if
I do this then." Throwing aside the furs, he slings his legs
over the edge of the bed.

Crossing my arms, I arch a brow as he pushes to his feet.
If the bastard thinks me a very maid, here to blush and
stammer just because he has his cock out, then he's sorely
mistaken. "If you're trying to impress me, I'd suggest you
wait until you're not covered in blood."

He suddenly sways and nearly goes to one knee. Only a
last-minute grab at the bedframe saves him.

"No, please," I say. "Don't kiss my boots in gratitude. I'm
not one for genuflection, though I must admit, there's something about the thought of having you on your knees in
front of me that gets me quite hot under the collar."

Thiago pushes away from the bed. "Is that what it takes?
Because there's a lot of things I can do on my knees that'll
put a smile on your face. And it doesn't involve kissing your
boots."

Heat sears my cheeks. Someone's recovering well
enough. If anything was going to convince me he's not going
to die on my watch, it's this.

"Where do you think you're going?"

"I need to... clean up."

He manages to make his way inside the wash chambers
without a single comment about me washing his back.

"You're welcome," I mutter under my breath.

When he returns, he's draped in a blanket he's managed to wrap around his lean hips. It does nothing to disguise the chiseled vee of his hips and the tented suggestion behind the fabric.

He has, however, peeled most of my bandages off.

Every inch of him is smooth, flawless skin once again.

"You healed yourself." It's the sort of thing one isn't encouraged to do, as healing draws upon the power within a body and he's barely recovered. "You shouldn't have."

"Someone had to." Thiago sinks onto the bed. Despite his lack of cuts and bruises, he's doing his best to resemble an animated corpse.

"I did my best."

"And I'm grateful for it. You saved my life."

"Don't tell my mother." I flash him a weak smile.

"I promise."

And I realize that in the last few days he's gone from enemy to... wary ally in my mind. He was right. I'm no longer afraid of him, despite the threat of the Darkness that lurks inside him.

He saved my life. I saved his.

There's an uncertain feeling inside me.

I may be a princess in my mother's court, but I've always been expected to hold my own. The guards are there for our protection, but if someone attacked me and I failed to defeat them, then my mother would have shed few tears for my loss. Weakness, she would have called it. I'd have been better off dead.

But the prince didn't hesitate to push me out of the way of that trap, though he had to know he'd not make it himself.

Nobody has ever risked anything for me.

"Now," I say, clearing my throat and trying to shrug away

the gratitude, before it overwhelms me. "How are we going to get out of here?"

"We're not," he says, slumping back onto the bed. "We're going to wait. I'm in no condition to walk, let alone fight. Eris will find us."

"I can hardly wait."

The faintest of smiles touches his lips, but then it's gone as he surrenders to sleep.

15

"Tell me about your wife," I whisper as Thiago sits on the edge of the bed the next day, dark shadows beneath his eyes.

Instantly, he tenses. "Why?"

"You started a war for her. She had to mean a great deal to you."

And yet he kisses *me*. Every time he looks at me, I can see the heat in his eyes. The want.

It's confusing.

"I loved her. I still do. And I always will." He captures my hand. "I would burn the world to ashes to have another moment with her. To see her look at me one more time with eyes full of love. But that doesn't mean I will have that moment."

I tug my hand away. It's a little too disconcerting to see the pain in his eyes. This is love, something I've only seen from afar. I don't want to picture the Prince of Evernight softening for a woman. I don't want to imagine my enemy suffering, but I can't help asking, "How did you lose her?"

There's the coldness again. The mask. "Your mother took her from me."

Suddenly, the enmity between the pair of them is starting to make more sense. This bitter war is a tangled affair, covered in thorns vicious enough to draw blood. It's been building for decades, and at this stage I doubt there's anything that can stop either of them from striking again.

I'd hoped there could be a solution to the war, perhaps a means to make amends, but it's quite clear there's only one way to end it.

One of them has to die.

Silence lingers, broken only by the sound of my fingers on the linen bandage I was unwinding.

"What's wrong, Princess?"

"I don't think your wife would have approved of me. Of this."

"This?" His eyes are suddenly as piercing as a hawk.

"You know what I'm talking about." My fingers fumble the bandage as I weave it around his waist, trying to ignore the hard slabs of muscle that brush against my fingers. Heat lingers beneath his skin like a banked furnace. A part of me wants to drown myself in that heat. See if it will ignite just as I think it will. "Trading kisses for a day's peace."

"You do realize, you were the one who offered a kiss. I never intended to push my advances if they were unwelcome. You would have been safe without your oath. I told you several times that you were safe."

My chin jerks up in surprise.

For the first time since I've met him, his smile is suddenly radiant, lighting his entire face. And then he throws his head back and laughs, as if it's the merriest jest.

The Prince of Evernight tricked me.

"Are you saying I bound myself to kiss you once a day for no reason?"

"You seemed so determined to get your hands on me. I could hardly demur."

"You son of a bitch!" I punch him in pure indignation.

"Ouch." He claps a hand to his shoulder as if the blow made an impact. But he doesn't stop laughing.

And it's ruining me.

His sinfully dark looks I can handle. The smoldering smiles and wicked glint in his eyes are deliciously tempting, but ultimately a hurdle I can resist.

But that hint of vulnerability, the small glimpses of a completely different man beneath the dangerous exterior are virtually irresistible.

His laughter slowly dies as he sees the look in my eyes. "My wife would never have wanted me to be alone forever. She would not deny me a kiss, a moment of happiness."

I think about that.

There's no jealousy in this kind of love. I can't help thinking that if I had ever found it—and if I were lost to my lover—then I would never want to see them spend an eternity in loneliness.

No, there's no jealousy in his wife's terms, and yet I feel the smolder of it deep in my own chest.

Because I've never felt that kind of love and I yearn for it.

Thiago captures my chin with one hand, holding me there just long enough for there to be no mistake about his intentions. "And speaking of kisses, you owe me. Two, if I'm counting correctly."

The thought is gone, my moment of jealousy shattered. "It's not my fault you were unconscious. And how do you know I didn't claim a kiss while you were?"

"I'd know." His voice roughens as he leans closer, the heat of his breath stirring over my lips. "I'd *know*, Princess."

A mere second exists in which I could turn my face away, deny him the taste of my lips. Until now, he's been content to let me set the pace. I owe him a kiss, but I know what he intends is no mere brush of the lips. He has that look in his eyes—a conquering warlord, set upon claiming as much as he can take.

And yet...

I don't turn away.

Maybe it's that earlier thought still lingering like a ghost. I can't have what he speaks of, and yet I can taste this mockery of it. Just for a few seconds I can pretend.

A dangerous smile softens his mouth, and then he swoops down and captures a soft gasp on my lips. Steel fingers brand my chin, locking me in place, and his other hand slides through my hair, cupping the base of my skull in a proprietary claim. But it's the hot lash of his tongue that melts me inside.

Dangerous.

This is far too dangerous.

And yet, I could no more resist him, than I could pluck the moon from the sky with my fingers.

This time there's no denying there's more to this moment than an oath I made. I want him to kiss me, purely for myself and no other reason.

And as my fingers curl through his hair, I stop resisting. There is no Asturian princess in this moment. There is no Prince of Evernight. We're just two desperate bodies, yearning for each other.

I break away with a gasp, my heart hammering in my chest. "That was worth at least two kisses."

The prince's fingers stroke lightly over my wet lips. "As you wish, Your Highness."

But his smile is sleek and knowing.

He doesn't need to demand another one, for he knows I finally gave in.

There's no coming back from this.

And I need to.

LOUD BOOTHEELS ECHO on the veranda to the hunting lodge.

My heart kicks right up into my ribs, and I lunge for my knife as the door slams open, a pair of broad shoulders filling it. The man who enters wears battle-scarred hunting leathers, a ruff of heavy fur guarding his throat.

My knife doesn't waver. He looks far too pretty to be Unseelie, but that doesn't mean he's an ally. I certainly don't recognize him.

"Who are you?" I demand.

The stranger's eyes slide over me curiously, and then his lips quirk and he glances over my shoulder at Thiago. "I expected to find you in dire straits, judging by the amount of blood you'd lost between here and Mistmere, but here you are, lolling about in bed with a handsome wench."

"*Wench?*"

They both ignore me.

"Took you long enough to find us," Thiago says, swinging his legs over the edge of the bed. "Did you take the scenic route?"

"Oh, you know me." The stranger's grin widens. "Ran across a few remaining banes and took care of them. Had a slight sweat up, so had to cool off." He shakes his tousled hair. "Looking this good doesn't just happen, my prince."

"Alas," Thiago replies dryly.

"I take it you two know each other." Some warning would have been nice before I made a fool of myself.

Thiago pushes to his feet, clad in only his leather breeches. Those swirling black tattoos across his chest can't hide the creep of iron poisoning that lingers like darkened bruises. "I have that misfortune, yes."

"Misfortune," the stranger snorts. He winks at me and bows. "Finn Archellion, Your Most Beautiful Highness. Slayer of giants. Rescuer of damsels—or in this case, princes —in distress. And hunter unparalleled—"

"Master of Arrogance," Thiago drawls.

"Perhaps he's been spending too much time with you?" I point out sweetly.

"Careful, love. Or I might just tell him how naked I was when I woke up."

Finn's eyebrows shoot up. "Don't stop. I'd love to hear the story."

I smile at the prince through my teeth. *Breathe one word of it, and I'll punch you in the balls.*

He winks. "I'm afraid that's between the princess and myself."

Finn sighs. Thick dark hair brushes against his shoulders, and his eyes are as blue as an alpine lake. I don't know which god blessed this kingdom, but if there's one thing Evernight has, it's an abundance of beautiful men.

"What happened?" Finn asks. "Apart from waking up naked? Eris told me you were heading for Mistmere and that was half a week ago. She's been... upset."

"How upset?" Thiago demands.

Finn coughs into his hand. "Drastic measures were required. Hence why I'm here and there's not a slaughtered trail of Unseelie leading to your door."

There's something they're not saying about Eris.

She's no friend of mine, but I'm not quite certain what her relationship with the prince is, precisely.

While I'm fairly sure she'd drop me off the nearest cliff if she got the chance, I don't think it's entirely jealousy. She doesn't look at Thiago as if she wants to eat him all up.

And unless you're blind, it's the only way to look at him.

The two men clasp hands as Thiago swiftly explains, and Finn's smile fades abruptly. The pair of them share a look that clearly says they'll discuss it later before Thiago turns back to me with a faint smile. "Luckily for me, the princess decided to have mercy on me and dragged me here."

"You can't have annoyed her too much then."

"I didn't like my chances trying to explain to Eris what had happened if I returned without him," I reply dryly, testing the waters.

Finn throws his head back and laughs. "A good argument. Eris would have been frothing at the mouth."

"So, what now?"

The prince shrugs into his shirt, wincing a little. "Now, I need to speak to the council. Whatever Angharad is up to, she needs to be stopped. And I doubt I can do it alone."

16

The flames flicker to life in my fireplace the second I walk through the door of my bedchambers at Valerian.

I freeze. There's no point denying I'd seen it; my mother can always sense the truth.

Squatting by the hearth, I glance over my shoulder, then wave my hand through the flames, muttering the appropriate linking spell.

My mother's face ripples into view. "The prince appears to still be alive."

Ah, good morning, Mother. "Keep your voice down," I whisper. "One of the prince's warriors doesn't trust me. She watches every move I make."

"She?"

"Eris."

My mother smirks. "That filthy half-bred mutt. How can the bastard prince even claim to rule a Seelie court when he takes in such scraps?"

Perhaps that's why his people are so loyal to him. Because he fights for their right to exist and cares little for their breeding or species. But there's no point giving voice to my thoughts. Because Adaia's definition of loyalty only seems to extend to that which is offered to *her*.

"I see your knife hasn't left its sheath."

"I... can't get near him," I lie. "Not with her watching me."

Adaia's eyes narrow. "You could stop a war, my daughter. None of our subjects need die—"

"I don't think he's interested in a war—"

Adaia's sneer cuts me off. "Your weakness is showing. Does he woo you with his charm? Whisper his hopes for peace in your ear, even as he amasses his troops?"

"I've seen no sign of any army—"

"And where is he keeping you? Golden Ceres? The City by the Bay? Or has he got you locked away in Valerian?"

There's no need to answer.

Adaia's smile widens viciously. "What is he trying to shield you from? What is he hiding? This is why you must think with your head, Iskvien, and not your heart. He will try and turn you against me. He will use you in this petty war between us. Don't doubt that for a moment. He's not interested in you. You're just a pawn he can play with."

"Careful, Mother. He's beginning to sound interchangeable with you."

It aches, deep in the cavity where my heart should lie.

A little bit for the prince who charms and flirts with me, but mostly for the mother I've long since lost favor with. And I try to tell myself I don't care, but a part of me *does* want my mother's approval back.

"We're all pawns to our kingdom's whims." Adaia's lips thin in displeasure. "Prove to me you can be trusted with your heart, and perhaps I'll allow you to be the one pulling your own strings. Do your people a favor. Kill him. Before he twists your heart against your own kingdom. Your own family."

"This isn't the right time, Mother. Angharad's been seen in Mistmere. She has her Unseelie army trying to right the stones of the Mistmere Hallow. We think she's trying to access some of the Mother of Night's power—or perhaps to free her."

Silence.

"Angharad sealed the accords with her blood. She cannot go against them."

"I saw her with my own eyes, Mother!" I can see it doesn't matter. "If there is any war beckoning on the horizon, then it is with the Unseelie hordes. We will need our allies, if we are not to be overrun by Unseelie. We will... need the prince."

The queen shakes her head in disgust. "I had hoped you could retain your senses. I'd hoped he hadn't gotten to you yet. But I see my trust was misplaced. He's already twisted you to his whims."

"It's not—"

The queen waves a hand, her image flickering. "Kill him. Or do not bother answering my summons again, for I will be done with you."

And then she vanishes.

I HEAD DOWNSTAIRS FOR DINNER, still aching in every muscle in my body.

Voices drift from the dining room.

"This wasn't just an attack," a strident female voice points out. Eris. "Angharad was prepared to counter any scouts. With that many banes in place, she's being even more careful than usual."

"What I want to know is how she got past the fucking borders without being seen," Thiago snaps. "Queen Maren and I have enough patrols on Mistmere's northern flank to spot a grouse trying to sneak through."

"I haven't been able to ride the borders while Her Highness is here," Eris replies, "and Angharad probably knows it. If you give me a few days, I can ride north and see what's going on. I left Hainard in charge, and he's a solid captain. He should be doing his job."

"No. No," Thiago says with a sigh. "I need you here. Especially if Angharad is plotting an invasion."

"Your powers keep them in check," Finn says. "She's testing you. She won't consider a full-blown thrust unless she's certain she can defeat you on the battlefield. If they know you were weakened—"

"I'm not weakened," Thiago counters with a snarl.

I press my fingers to the crack in the door. There's a chamber beyond, and I can see the prince pacing, dressed in strict black as always.

"Those wounds should have healed by now," Eris says. "The iron is still in your blood—"

"I. Am. Not. Weakened."

"Do *they* know that?" It's Finn, resting his knuckles on some sort of round table as he glares at his prince. "The Unseelie aren't our only cause for concern. If word of this gets back to Adaia...."

"She'll attack," Thiago says, in a weary voice. "But it won't get back, because only the three of us know about it."

The door is wide enough to see Eris and Finn share a look.

"And the princess?" Eris suggests.

"She wouldn't do that," Thiago replies.

"Are you sure?" Clearly Eris isn't as certain. "She's still her mother's creature."

"She's never been her mother's creature. No matter what Adaia's tried to mold her into, Vi's always rebelled. She doesn't have her mother's ruthless heart, nor Adaia's ambitions. She won't tell her mother, because then she'll feel guilty. She doesn't lie very well."

His certainty is a shock.

I didn't realize he'd been studying me as thoroughly as I've been studying him.

"I just need time for the iron to drain from my blood," Thiago tells them. "Until then, I'll keep my magic to a minimum. Nobody in Ceres will know."

I clear my throat loudly enough to announce my presence and step through the door. Instantly, Eris scowls, but Finn's smile widens.

"Princess," he says. "You look much recovered after your bath. I barely recognize you. A bedraggled warrior went into the steam rooms, and a radiant woman emerged in her place." He pats his cheeks. "Perhaps I should try it."

Thiago gives his friend a quelling look.

"There's not enough water in the world," Eris mutters, "to transform *you*."

"We're just about to eat," Thiago says, coming forward to draw out a chair for me. "We were discussing tomorrow. We're going to Ceres. I need to contact the Alliance and set a few things into place to counter Angharad."

"Am I included in that 'we'?"

"Yes." Thiago eases my chair back in as I sit. His knuckles graze my bare shoulders, and I think he's almost about to rest his hand there before he thinks better of it. "I need Eris, and I can't afford to leave her behind to guard you."

My heart skips a beat. I can't avoid hearing my mother's words in my ears. There's something he's not telling me, and somehow, I know I'll find the answers in Ceres.

"I'll be ready at dawn."

THE PRINCE INSISTS upon blindfolding me for the journey to Ceres, which only engages my curiosity.

I barely have time to think about it though, as the second he engages the Hallow, my stomach decides to reverse itself. This doesn't feel like the trip to Mistmere. It feels like the Hallow itself is sucking at me, trying to drain me of my magic. I try to shield, but I'm on my knees before I know it, and my head aches.

"Here," Thiago says, resting a hand on my forehead.

Instantly, the power drain is gone.

I come to on my knees, breathing hard. "What *was* that?"

He swings me up into his arms, which I really should protest, but don't have the strength to. "You've been travelling through portals regularly. It affects some fae more than others, particularly if they're not warded against the power of the ley line."

I know he thinks he's telling the truth, but I can't help thinking he's wrong.

Something about the Hallow didn't feel right.

WE SEEMINGLY CLIMB A THOUSAND STAIRS, and I catch the

sound of servants bustling through the castle, before the prince sets me on my feet and whips my blindfold away.

Light stabs at my eyes. I wince, but I can also make out a woman sitting in what appears to be a circular tower room.

The last time I saw Thalia, she was wearing red, but now she's in a green gown that's more daring than anything I've ever worn. Gold lace epaulets rest on her shoulders, with a heavy golden cloak made of thin metallic scales that drapes to the floor. Dozens of golden chains loop around her throat and cross her bodice. It's the most elegant gown I've ever seen.

The tall, exotic beauty shares some of the same features as the prince, such as his thick dark hair and almond-shaped green eyes. But it's the way she claps her hands together and smiles at me that takes me aback. "Your Highness," Thalia says, sweeping toward me and taking my hands. "I'm so glad to meet you again. I thought Thiago was going to keep you locked away in that gloomy old city forever."

"So did I." For some reason, I'd thought her the cousin that was supposed to be traded to my mother in exchange for me.

There must be another one.

I don't know why, but I want to smile back at her. Her welcome feels genuine, and her smile is infectious.

"E," she says, turning and giving Eris an enthusiastic hug. "I missed your glowering face."

"Ugh," Eris says, pushing her away and brushing herself off, as if to rid herself of Thalia's enthusiasm. "What part of 'I don't hug' did I not make clear?"

"Sorry." Thalia winks at her. "I forgot you don't like being touched... unless it's by a fae lord with an enormous cock."

"Erlking's hairy balls," Finn mutters under his breath. "*Thalia.*"

"What?" she asks innocently. "You should have seen it. I burst into Eris's rooms, thinking—as usual—she'd be alone, and there's this enormous—"

"No, no, no." He claps his hands over his eyes. "I am *not* going to even picture it. I refuse."

"Speaking of hairy balls—"

Finn throws a cushion at her, and Thalia bursts into laughter even as Eris winces.

"Beware the Prince of Evernight's most dangerous allies," Thiago says dryly.

I don't quite know what to make of it.

My mother's advisors and generals are all stiff, malicious bastards who wouldn't dare break into a smile.

"Where's Baylor?" Thiago asks.

"Frightening small children?" Finn replies.

"Dangling miscreants off the tower?" Thalia suggests.

The doors slam open, and a rugged warrior wearing battle-scarred leathers and an enormous helmet stalks inside. "Drilling in the yard with the rest of the guards," he says, "because someone around here has to actually do his job." Then he notices Eris and tips his head to her. "Excluding my favorite little menace."

"Little?" she scoffs.

Eris appears to have a sense of humor. Who knew?

"Vi, this is Baylor, the last of my generals."

"Or first," the enormous warrior says, dragging his helmet off his head so that a tumble of golden hair brushes against his shoulders.

It's like looking into the eyes of a dead man.

A shocked gasp escapes me as I stare at a mirror image of the bane Andraste killed.

"Vi?" Thiago frowns as he notices my reaction.

Indeed, everyone in the room is staring at me.

"I...." I need space to breathe and a moment to think. "Sorry." I press my hands to my temples, flinging a weak smile at the prince. "I think I haven't entirely recovered from the trip through the portal. My head's aching."

Thiago pushes to his feet. "Do you need—"

"No." I wave him off. "I'm fine. I just need to rest."

In the privacy of my rooms, where I'm not staring my guilty conscience in the face.

I don't look back.

But I can almost feel them exchanging glances.

17

The amulet is exactly where I left it, buried among the mess of silver and gold in my jewelry chest.

I don't know why I kept it.

I never expected to see the dead bane's family—which is what this Baylor must be. No, I threw it in my jewelry chest and then forgot about it.

Until now.

The gold feels warm beneath my touch as I turn the amulet over. I know who they are now. Baylor and Lysander, the shapeshifting twins who are two of Thiago's generals. They were legends during the wars and served the Grimm himself before turning their loyalty over to the Prince of Evernight when the Grimm was locked away in a prison world.

It's strange how Thiago seemingly collects such misfits.

Baylor and Lysander served an Old One, Cian's Unseelie, and Eris is....

I don't know what Eris is.

Not fae. Or not wholly fae.

Then there's the prince himself.

The right thing to do would be to return the amulet to Baylor and tell him what happened to his brother.

But how do I tell him my sister killed Lysander? How do I admit I shot him too?

There are legends that speak of him. Eris, Baylor, and Lysander have always been considered Evernight's most vicious generals. Baylor the Blackheart, they call him, though he's as golden of hair as Andraste is.

If he discovers his brother is dead by my sister's hand, then there's no guessing how he'll react.

The walls of my tower room seem to close in upon me. One of the servants escorted me here so I couldn't take any detours, and I know there's a guard standing at the door. Clearly the prince doesn't want me wandering through this castle, which makes me wonder what he's hiding.

I haven't felt this alone since I arrived here.

It doesn't help that every time I unearth a clue, another question forms.

Why is the prince treating me like a dangerous enemy that needs to be locked away in my rooms while we're here? Why did he blindfold me through the portal? It's clear he doesn't want me here in Ceres, and only the threat of Angharad made him bring me. But what doesn't he want me to see?

And how did Lysander recognize me that day in the forest?

A soft rap comes at the door, making me jump.

"Come in," I call, snapping the lid of my jewelry case shut.

Thalia enters, carrying a tray covered with a purple cloth. "I thought you might be hungry after your journey."

The thoughtfulness surprises me. "Thank you."

"You're welcome." She lays the tray on the bed between us and sits down.

A swift glimpse reveals an Asturian beef stew with hot bread rolls that still steam from the oven, slabs of butter, a pair of honey cakes, and a handful of grapes. All my favorites on one tray.

It's either impressive or unnerving.

"The prince has clearly been paying attention," I murmur, plucking a grape free and popping it in my mouth.

"He notices everything," Thalia says, rolling her eyes. "Especially when you don't want him to notice."

"Either that or he has an agenda."

She smiles. "That too. Don't ever think he's not up to something."

"I don't."

I tear into the bread, slathering butter over it and then dunking it in the stew. "Sweet Maia." It's so good, though I haven't eaten in hours so anything would taste amazing right now.

"Baylor's not that scary," she murmurs after an appropriate pause.

Aha.

Clearly, Thalia takes after her cousin, for he's not the only one with an agenda, it seems.

"He didn't scare me," I tell her. "I wasn't feeling well."

"You went white as a wraith," she replies, "the second you saw him."

"He *is* the Blackheart, is he not? My mother's generals piss their pants when they hear they'll be facing him."

"I didn't think you'd be the sort to be afraid of him. And he may be this big, gruff bear, but he's perfectly housebroken." She flashes a smile at me. "If you think him scary, you should see the orphaned kittens he thinks nobody knows he's got stashed in his rooms. He takes them saucers of milk every night, but the demi-fey think it's for them, so they've been stealing it. Now he's set traps for the demi-fey."

She bursts into a peal of laughter, as if she's picturing it.

I can't help myself. A reluctant smile tugs at my lips. I don't know why, but I feel as though I've known her forever.

Thalia reminds me of Andraste, and how things used to be.

The second I think it, my smile dies.

Thalia rests a hand over mine. "I understand. It must be overwhelming to think yourself the pawn between two courts."

"No, it's just.... I miss my sister. I miss my home. And even then...." It was never truly a home. It hasn't been for a long time. "Have you ever felt as though you don't belong anywhere?"

"Yes," she whispers, and her fingers curl through mine. "When I was a child, I was... unwanted. The fae are rarely fertile, and my mother had a brief fling with a mysterious man on a beach one night. His seed took, and here I am." She shrugs, but I can see she hasn't escaped the weight of her past. "I'm the bastard offspring of one of the saltkissed. My grandmother tried to drown me at birth. As you can imagine, I never had a home until I arrived here."

"Your grandmother?" Thiago's grandmother?

Thalia shudders. "An evil bitch if ever I've met one. She's dead now. Sometimes I spit on her grave."

Tugging another piece of bread from the roll, I pop it in my mouth. "When I was a little girl, I spat in my mother's teapot once. She would have killed me if she ever realized."

"Your mother does make my grandmother seem a benevolent soul," Thalia admits.

I offer her a grape. There's not much to say to that.

At least she didn't try to drown me at birth.

That I know of.

"So you're half saltkissed?" Does that mean Thiago has the sea in his veins too? Or is it through her maternal bloodline that they share blood? "You were alive during the wars?"

The Father of Storms created the saltkissed many an eon ago, gifting his worshippers with the ability to breathe underwater and to have voices that could sing a sailor to his grave. Most of them were female worshippers, which is typical—I'm sure they "worshipped" him in a particular way—but a very prized few were males.

Most of them were trapped in the prison world with him when they bound him to the Hallow that resides on the rocky Isle of Stormhaven in the middle of the Innesmuch Sea.

The ones who remained in this world lost their powers.

I'm told that sometimes you can still hear them, pouring their rage through a conch shell late at night.

"Yes, I was alive during the wars," Thalia mutters. "I was living in Unseelie territories then, trying to eke out a living. It wasn't a pleasant time. I'd been exiled by my grandmother and found myself hunted by every type of creature who can be found in those forests. Thiago found me after the wars, locked in a cage in the goblin caves. They liked my voice and used to make me sing for them by stabbing me through the cage with their spears until I relented. My powers were starting to mature, and Thiago could sense me out there in the world somewhere. He didn't know who or what he was feeling, but he came for me. He rescued me. And I've been by his side ever since."

I feel a little embarrassed. "I think your grandmother might be worse than my mother."

Thalia picks at my bread roll. "If you knew the things I know about your mother, you might not say that."

I daresay I wouldn't.

It's surprising how easily I believe her. Mother's always claimed Evernight is ruled by a circle of vicious, power-hungry bottom crawlers who dabble in the dark magics of the Unseelie kingdom, but I've seen little in the way of evil brewing, and after being raised in her court, I think I'd recognize it.

The moment's a breathless one.

What if we Asturians aren't the ones on the right side of this entire war?

Did my mother push us into a war against a kingdom that'd done nothing wrong?

It's been brewing for so long, a series of brief skirmishes that the Alliance holds in check from full-blown war, that I can barely remember what started it. She hated him for taking power, and she sent her armies into the field against him when he made a claim for Mistmere, but it wasn't until recently that their enmity spilled over into a blood feud.

His wife.

The thought stabs at me. My mother took his wife from him, and he's never forgiven her.

"I didn't scare you off, did I?" Thalia jests. "You look like you're going to throw up on the grapes."

"I'm fine. Just dwelling on... unpleasant thoughts."

"Well, I suppose we were talking about your mother. That's as unpleasant as topics of conversation come."

I pick at a grape, rolling it between my fingers. I've tried to discover the truth, but to no avail. When Thiago locked me away in Valerian, he severed my connection to the world. But now.... "Tell me something.... How did the prince meet his wife?"

Thalia rears back. "I think you'd best ask Thiago that."

"I'm asking you."

She hesitates. "Princess—"

"Vi," I insist.

"Vi," she says, meeting my eyes. "It was thirteen years ago—"

No wonder I can't remember. I would have been barely seven or eight. Eight, I think. My birthday's near the autumn equinox, though I haven't celebrated it in years.

"They met at the Lammastide rites," Thalia continues, her voice growing wistful. "He loved her the moment he saw her, and she must have owned the same feelings, for they married three days later. Why are you asking?"

"No reason." I see her eyes narrow. "Beyond the fact we were speaking of my mother, and I was thinking of the war between our kingdoms."

"Adaia resented the marriage. She wanted to see him suffer, but here he was, happy for the first time in centuries," Thalia mutters. "They'd clashed over the Mistmere territories several times, but war only erupted when she stole the poor girl away. She wanted to hurt him, and she succeeded."

"What happened to her?"

"I... I don't know. The queen only ever sent... pieces of her back."

It makes me swallow. "Fine. My mother's the evilest bitch in the entire Alliance. I win."

I can't help thinking of the prince.

He loved his wife.

And my mother destroyed her. Imagine opening a box and finding the finger of your loved one? Or worse....

My mother's been known to send hearts instead.

"Seeing me must cause him no small amount of pain," I whisper. Imagine looking into the eyes of your enemy's daughter every day? "I can't believe he doesn't hate me for it."

"He's treated you well?" Thalia asks carefully.

"I nearly expired of boredom, but that was the only danger." Indeed, he's been kinder than I probably deserve. And all I've offered him are sharp words.

"There's time to make amends," Thalia says, pushing to her feet. "Perhaps if you gave him a chance, you might find those amends aren't really so bad, after all."

I throw my last grape at her. "You're as bad as he is."

And while the attraction between us threatens to overwhelm me, I don't want to be some pathetic substitute for his poor dead wife.

"Of course I am," she says with a smile. "We *are* related. And I think it's time for him to pursue happiness again."

"You overrate my charms."

"You underestimate them," she points out. "Sleep well, Princess. And call me if you ever want to speak. I think we're going to be great friends."

"I'd say you have impeccable taste, but then you seem to like Eris too."

There's something about Thalia that wins a smile from me, regardless of how hard I'm trying not to.

She grins. "Eris is my dearest friend. But she's emphatically loyal to Thiago. She thinks you're going to break his heart and get him killed."

"How can I break his heart when he's already given it away?"

Thalia pauses. "Love is a renewable resource. You can destroy the source of it. You can twist it, and curse it, and deny it all you like. But you can never completely obliterate the possibility of it. All you have to do is be open to it. He gave his heart once, Vi. It doesn't mean he can't give it again.

It will always beat for her, but perhaps it can beat for you too?"

"I was under the impression he was trying to use me to get her back."

Thalia blinks in utter surprise. "How in Maia's name did you ever dream up such an idea?"

It's on the tip of my tongue to tell her about the letters.

But I still don't know who penned them or what the author means by any of it.

"It doesn't matter. It's probably… something I heard in my mother's court."

"Don't believe anything you hear in your mother's court," Thalia says in a droll voice. "It's either poison or lies. What did you think he was planning? Did you think he intended to sacrifice you to Kato in order to fetch her from the Underworld?"

The thought did cross my mind.

"No," I scoff. "I don't know. I hadn't… thought much of it."

Only every night since I overheard the prince talking to Cian.

"The prince means you no harm," she says. "I wish you'd believe me."

I wish I could too.

But, as kind and charming as he's been, I can't help feeling as though he's watching me too.

He *is* the Prince of Evernight, after all, renowned for his ruthlessness. And he's hiding something from me. They all are. Even Thalia, with her friendly smiles and her tray of food, is clearly seeking to placate me.

I don't know who to trust.

Eris, perhaps.

She's the only one not hiding her feelings toward me.

"Thiago's going to contact the alliance tonight," Thalia tells me, pausing by the door. "You may as well get some sleep, he said. He'll see you in the morning." She rolls her eyes. "Hopefully your dreams tonight are a little nicer than they clearly have been."

No kiss.

I don't know why that bothers me.

Every night, I've brushed the most perfunctory of kisses against his lips, and every night he's merely watched me with those knowing, knowing eyes.

But she's left me with much to think about.

"Hopefully," I say.

"Until tomorrow then," she calls, closing the door behind her and leaving me with the pressing silence of my suspicions.

And my lonely, lonely bed.

I DREAM of being hunted through a vast, shadowy forest by enormous black hounds. Howls echo to my right, but when I bolt down a narrow trail, there's a shadow snapping at my heels.

There's no escape.

The Grimm and his hounds are on my trail, and I know I can't outrun them. Breath panting, lungs heaving, I shove at the thorns that slash at my arms and clothes.

"*Rest, Vi*," comes a whisper, and I swear I feel a hand brush against my cheek.

Another howl cuts in from the right.

They're everywhere. The entire pack must be following me.

"*No. You're safe here. The hounds won't dare follow you.*"

There's a kiss to my forehead, and then the world starts to dissolve around me.

The forest starts to open up, and I can hear the hounds baying in the distance. They seem to be falling behind, and as I stumble into a sunny clearing, I fall to my knees and pant.

The Grimm only rides at night.

And he's locked away in his prison world, trapped for all eternity. It's just a dream. It has to be a dream. Except that one of the hounds looked like Baylor, and I don't know how to tell him the truth.

"*The truth?*" This time the whisper sounds startled.

I sit bolt upright in bed, covered in a cold sweat. My heart is racing, and judging from the tangle of my sheets, I've been thrashing.

I could also swear I wasn't alone.

There's an indentation on the sheets beside me, and when I reach out to touch it, it's still warm.

"Thiago?" I whisper.

Nothing moves. The breeze blows through the gauzy curtains by the window, but I'd be able to see something in the hazy moonlight, wouldn't I?

Tossing aside the sheets, I search the room. It's empty, but when I return to the bed, I can still feel the ghostly press of lips to my forehead.

He was in here, I'll swear it.

And worse, he was in my dreams.

And now he knows.

18

The Alliance is planning to meet via astral projection.

It's rare they meet in person—the rites only—and with tension lingering between several of the kingdoms, it's probably a wise decision.

I hurry inside the enormous tower chamber Thalia leads me to, steps slowing when I see the six enormous throne-like chairs set in a circle around the room. Five I can understand, but six?

The polished marble floor is inlaid with thousands of bronze glyphs. Light streams down through a hollow circle in the middle of the ceiling, landing directly in the center of the circle.

The prince stalks out of the columns, and I catch my breath, slamming to a halt. I've been dreading this confrontation all morning.

"Your Highness."

Nothing. No sign he knows about Lysander's death. Instead, he wears a faint frown. "Such formality this morning. I thought I was only 'Thiago' now?"

I take a slow step forward. Was it all just a dream? Or does he truly not know? "You are always Thiago. *Prince* Thiago."

The faintest of smiles flickers over his mouth. "Rebuild your walls, Vi. It only makes me more certain I breached them."

Relief fills me. I still don't know how to tell Baylor the truth, but I'd prefer not to have the decision forced upon me. "Now I know where you get your arrogance from. You tell yourself lies, each and every day."

Thiago gestures to the chair by his side. "As much as I'd like to play this game, we're about to have company. Sit."

"You want me to sit with the Alliance?"

"Yes." A faint smile curls over his mouth. "Don't you want to watch your mother turn an interesting shade of red?"

"Tempting as that may be... I would prefer not to draw her ire."

"You don't think you've already drawn it?" He gestures for wine, and Thalia begins pouring two cups. "Besides, you're my witness. You're the only other person who's seen what is happening at Mistmere. They won't believe *me*, but they can't dispute you're not my ally."

Oh, I see. "Now you're throwing me to the wolves. I thought we'd sued for peace following the hunting cabin, but you were merely biding your time."

"Sit, Vi. It's just a chair."

"You are merciless, and I shan't forget this," I tell him, sinking reluctantly onto the chair. "Check your bed tonight. You might find a nasty surprise in it."

"If you're anywhere near my bed, then it can only be considered pleasant," he murmurs as the bell hanging in the tower above us begins to ring.

It's a sign of an incoming guest.

The Queen of Aska forms right in the stream of light, her long dark hair looking ethereal in the silvery light of her astral form. She tilts her head to us, eyes locking on me and narrowing slightly, before she moves toward the chair to my left. "I assume you have due cause for calling a meeting, Evernight."

Queen Maren is the reason we ward ourselves at night with woven dreamcatchers over the bed. If the bells in the catcher tinkle, it's said she's tampering with your dreams. Sometimes, she'll send her winged dream-spawn to seduce a sleeping soul, and steal their lifeforce, night by night.

When I was sixteen, I served a year in her court as her lady-in-waiting.

I don't trust her, at all.

"Cause enough," Thiago replies coldly, slipping into the mantle of prince.

It's interesting to note that he sheds that mantle with me. I hadn't even realized I was given insight into the inner workings of his mind, rather than dealing with this imperious bastard.

The bells ring again and the stream of silvery light misting in the center of the room turns into Lucidia, the Queen of Ravenal.

Her white hair is a shock of startling light in this ethereal form, and for a second I see a smooth oval face overlaid over her wrinkled features. A queen in her prime, as she must have been many, many years ago. Then she flickers and becomes the old crone I know.

Sinking into her chair, she curls her gnarled hands over the arms. "You had best not be wasting my time, princeling."

"I don't intend to."

The bells ring again, and tension fills the room.

It's either the prince's ally, or an enemy.

My mother appears, and apart from my fireplace, it's the first time I've been face-to-face with her, as it were, since she sent me here.

Enemy, then.

Adaia looks every inch a queen girding herself for war, clad in a long metallic dress created from scales of silver. Rings glitter on her fingers, and she's wearing the Crown of Thorns as well as what looks like half a stick of kohl.

She glances at me, then stiffens.

One of the most enjoyable aspects of the prince's court is the fact there's no need to stand on formalities. I'm tired of being her little peacock. Though I'm not Andraste, partial as she is to polished leather and practical braids. I do like pretty things.

The berry-colored tunic I borrowed from Thalia is my compromise. Beneath it, I wear tight black leggings and leather boots that are laced to my thighs. Adaia's dagger resides in the sheath at my hip—her eyes light up when she sees it—and several heavy gold cuffs rest on my wrist. Thalia even gave me a circlet of golden thorns I can wear as an armband.

"Please," says the prince smoothly, gesturing to the remaining thrones. "Take a seat."

My mother seats herself directly opposite him.

"This is Alliance business," she says, ignoring me. "What is she doing here?"

"She's my witness," Thiago replies.

"Witness?" My mother smirks. "Do we dare trust her account, after she's been with you for over a month? We all know how seductive you can be, how... convincing."

I sense him stiffening at my side.

"It's not as though I'm the one who likes to toy with people's minds," he says, "and use them as pawns."

"You should speak carefully of pawns," she replies. "You were the one who bargained with her life. You were the one who began this."

"And I will end it."

My mother's eyes blaze. "You little upstart. I look forward to finishing this. When my daughter stands by my side and watches you squirm on my hook, I will know absolute satisfaction."

"I'm right here," I say through clenched teeth. "If the pair of you would like to talk about me as if I'm not, then perhaps save it for later. We wouldn't want to waste the alliance's time."

Queen Maren watches me with a considering look. "The girl hardly looks beguiled, Adaia. How frustrating for you, Prince. You've barely managed to gain a foothold."

"Patience holds its own rewards," he says.

I can't help feeling as though I'm the bone thrown between a pair of snarling dogs. "Stop it. All of you. I am nobody's pawn. And I will not be used to amuse you all."

Silence falls.

Every single one of them stares at me as if I'm an amusing dog who's performed a trick.

"The die was cast. The game begun," Queen Lucidia murmurs, "but now the players intend to make their own rules. It shall be interesting to see how this will end. I think... I will back the girl."

"It's all very amusing, but this is a waste of my time," Queen Maren says. "Where is Kyrian? He should be here by now."

We wait.

The bells remain silent, motes of dust shivering through the air.

"Perhaps he's avoiding *me*," says my mother, with mock sincerity.

"I cannot understand why," Queen Maren murmurs.

The two share a smile.

"The request said midday," Queen Lucidia growls. "You have ten more minutes. I have important matters of business to attend to."

And so, Prince Kyrian's chair remains empty.

Thiago's frustration spills out of him. No doubt he hoped his one ally would be here to stand at his side. In a realm filled with queens, the pair of them are considered brutal upstarts, and the three queens will be disinclined to believe him.

"The request was sent," Queen Maren says. "His absence speaks to his lack of care. Begin, Prince. We're all dying to know what this mysterious summons is about."

Thiago wastes no time. He cannot afford to. "Angharad is trying to resurrect the Hallow in Mistmere."

Queen Lucidia sucks in a sharp breath. "She wouldn't dare."

But it's Queen Maren that leans forward with glittering eyes. "Have you any proof?"

"None beyond what I've seen with my own eyes."

"So we're to take your word for this?" My mother sneers. "The word of a prince who murdered his queen's rightful heirs?"

"The word of a prince who dueled those heirs for his throne," he corrects. "My word has been good in the past. Or are you calling me a liar?"

The pair of them stare at each other like cats contesting their turf.

Instantly, I can see this meeting deteriorating until it's nothing more than accusations and insults.

"I saw it," I call.

The room stills.

Four pairs of eyes turn to me, and my mother's hold murder.

"I saw it too," I repeat. "The Hallow stones are nearly all standing. Angharad had tribes of captured goblins working pulleys, and a couple of enormous trolls. The entire city was guarded by banes wearing her sigil, and her banner flew over her tent."

"Did you see Angharad herself?" Queen Maren asks.

My mother's fingers drum, one by one, on the arm of her throne.

"No. But Isem was there."

"How close did you manage to get?" Lucidia demands, her blind eyes staring straight through me.

Not close enough. I know what she's asking. "We were half a span away. On a rooftop. But it was there. The Hallow was risen."

"When you say you saw the Unseelie queen's tent there," Queen Lucidia murmurs, "was the banner over the tent waving in the wind?"

What?

"Why does that matter?"

"Illusions are the prince's gift," Queen Maren murmurs. "How are we to know if what you're saying is the truth? If you were closer, then you may have been able to see if the scene was real."

"Illusions are difficult to control on such a large scale,"

Queen Lucidia adds. "It's the small things that slip. A banner standing still in the breeze. The lack of scent of rank, unwashed troll. The echo of a bane's howl."

A muscle in Thiago's jaw pulses. "First, I'm toying with her mind, and now I'm conjuring illusions to fool her. What an elaborate scheme I have planned."

"What you're suggesting speaks of war," Queen Maren replies coldly. "We merely wish to ascertain the truth before we commit to an action that will drag the entire alliance into a bloody battle none of us wish to fight."

"You also speak of Mistmere, and those territories have long been disputed," Queen Lucidia adds. "The game is already afoot between you and Adaia. It ends in a few brief months, which makes this the perfect time for a distraction."

"Angharad has signed the treaty," my mother adds, "with her own blood. To break it means instant death. So why would she encroach in lands not her own?"

"As I recall, she turned away to slice her wrist," Thiago snaps. "I certainly didn't see if it was her blood that dripped into the cauldron, or her servant's. I'm not the only one with the gift of illusions."

"But you have an interest in Mistmere," Lucidia says.

"What possible cause does Angharad have to raise the Hallow?" My mother arches a mocking brow. "The Old Ones are trapped. And she has her own Hallows in Unseelie lands if she wishes to travel."

"Nor did she serve the Mother of Night," Maren adds. "She was bound to the Horned One."

It seems as if they're working in tandem against him.

Realization dawns: they are.

I told my mother about Mistmere, and she came

prepared. But why would she do this? Does she not care
about the Unseelie threat? Or does she think it may rid her
of her most dangerous enemy?

"I don't know what her interest in Mistmere is formed
of," Thiago says very quietly. "Perhaps you can ask her."

We're getting nowhere.

He warned me this meeting would be frustrating, but
I've never truly witnessed the pettiness of the alliance.

How in Maia's name did they ever drive the Unseelie
back?

"If it was an illusion, then it was a grand one," I tell
them. "I felt the power of the ley line igniting. The heat of a
bane's blood splashed across my cheek, and the sensation of
their teeth drove into my flesh. I could feel the warmth of
their breath on my skin, and the shiver down my spine at
the sound of their howls. I know you struggle to believe
him, but what if he's speaking the truth?"

I turn to Maren. "You share a border with the Unseelie
kingdoms. Both you and Evernight will be the hardest hit if
Angharad is truly plotting something."

She and Lucidia share a look.

"And the alliance still hasn't recovered from the last
war," I continue. "Mistmere is an empty land frayed at the
edges by the claims of several others kingdoms. The Mountain Kingdom of Taranis lies fallow, its scorched plains
peopled by monsters and howling winds. All that's left are
the four kingdoms represented here and the Isles of
Stormhaven, where Prince Kyrian resides. Unless Angharad
builds a fleet, he's the only one of us who can consider
himself safe."

"Do you think we're unaware of our geography?" my
mother sneers.

"No. But I'd prefer not to kneel before Angharad," I say,

deliberately painting a picture my mother will despise, "and if we continue with this bickering, I will be. I may not agree with Prince Thiago on all matters, but I know what I saw with my own eyes. And if you don't trust me, then send an envoy to see for yourself. Send Andraste."

My mother's eyes glitter with unspoken reprimand.

She's too full of spite and enmity to care whether the alliance falls.

But my words do damage where I didn't expect them to.

"Your daughter provides wise council," Queen Lucidia murmurs.

"We shall each send an envoy so we may each make a decision we trust," Queen Maren agrees, and I can tell that she, at least, is picturing her northern borders.

"So we shall," my mother pronounces, sweeping to her feet. "And now, if this mockery of a meeting is done, I have things to do."

With that she sweeps into the circle of light spilling through the roof and vanishes.

I WAIT until we're alone in Thiago's inner chambers before I turn on him.

"Is there something I should know about this treaty?" I demand. "The queens seem to think this is some sort of game being played between you and my mother."

"It was a game, and I bested her," he replies. "That's all you need to know."

I'm tired of hearing those words.

Tired of knowing *nothing*. Locked away in a city of wraiths where there's no one to even speak to beyond the prince. Blindfolded and led here, where I'm effectively locked away again, a princess in her tower.

"How kind of you to tell me what I do and don't need to know." The words sound like they came from my mother's lips.

Thiago shoots me a hard look. "I would tell you more if I thought I could trust you."

"Who am I going to tell?"

"Oh, I don't know." He tugs at his collar, loosening the top two buttons of his black velvet doublet. "Your mother, perhaps."

"She's at Hawthorne Castle by now."

"Perhaps you can whisper the words to your grate then," he says, his voice as smooth and rich as midnight.

He knows.

It stills my tongue. Forces me to straighten. "Listening in, were we?"

"The demi-fey told me. You're not the only one who feeds them milk and honey. Besides, I did warn you that you were predictable. It's a trait you've inherited from your mother."

I want to ball my fist and drive it into his abdomen, though his half-vicious smile warns me against such a thought.

Instead, I pace, ignoring the rustle behind me as he drapes his cloak over one of the chairs.

"If you want to continue to take your frustration out on me," he growls, "then I should warn you. I'm not feeling entirely playful today."

"Neither am I," I snap. "They don't believe us."

"They are warned." Thiago merely pours me a goblet of wine, his face expressionless. "That is all that matters."

"Doesn't it bother you?" They practically called him a

liar to his face and accused him of manipulating me. And I'm the gullible fool dancing to his tune, according to them.

"I expected it," he replies, handing me the wine. "The Alliance couldn't find its own ass with both hands and a faelight as bright as the sun. If one queen says something, then the others will immediately find her words suspect. Kyrian and myself, more than the rest."

"Because you're male."

"Because we both claimed our thrones by rule of might," he replies, tipping the goblet to his lips. "Not by bloodline."

His throat muscles work as he swallows.

I understand what my mother sees when she looks at him now. All the old tales say only a queen may rule, but Kyrian and Thiago took those lands through sheer might. Fae queens are always born, their talents and powers nurtured, their magic linked to the lands they will one day rule. And when an heir is chosen, the lines of power are locked.

But the two princes broke the rules.

They have no ties to their lands, and yet their kingdoms are flourishing.

I think of my stepbrother, Edain, and the way mother quashed his powers by binding him to her and sweeping him into her bed the second her consort was dead. I used to hate it, but I think I understand now.

The Lords of the Marsh are bound to serve her will, their powers muted by the blood contracts they signed.

And of the other nobles, she accepted their sons and daughters into her court to serve as pages and ladies-in-waiting. Some might say hostages would be a better term.

She culled every female in the land who might prove a threat.

And she's hobbled every male who might have ambitions.

But, thanks to Kyrian and Thiago, she must now wonder, every time she looks around her court, whether others watch her and whisper. She must always be on her guard now, both within and without. She is a queen who rules through fear and threats, because they're all she knows.

And it won't matter what Angharad does, she'll never see beyond the threat of the two princes.

I want to throw the fucking wine in the fireplace. "The alliance are fools."

A wry smile touches his mouth. "Careful. I'm one of them."

"Not you. You're...." I wave a hand at him.

"I'm...?"

"A little less foolish," I amend.

"Come now," he teases. "Don't hold back."

I stare at him. *You're dangerous and powerful and ruthless, and yet you're also the man who saved me from a bane trap. You're the man who always has a piece of apple for his horse. The one who rides out singlehandedly to see the truth for his own eyes.*

"You're a prince," I tell him. "And you rule with a firm and steady hand."

"How... generic."

"It's not." I can't believe I'm about to say this. "My mother rules with spite and ambition. Queen Maren rules with secrecy and lies. And Lucidia's people only know hunger and harsh taxes, for she is frugal and bitter." And, if the rumors are to be believed, she is weakening. "You rule with acceptance. I've seen the court that flocks to your banners. No other ruler in the alliance would have allowed Eris to grace their halls. Or Baylor. You think of the future.

You fear the past. And today, you tried to reach three power-hungry queens to convince them to work together to face a dangerous threat, even when they sneered at you and insulted you." I hesitate. "You're a better ruler than every queen in that chamber, and that's what they fear."

There's a stillness to his frame, as if he's absorbing those words.

I think, for the first time since I've met him, that I've rendered him speechless.

"And now, if you're done with me, I think I should seek my bed." The weight of the day's frustrations itch along my skin. And there's a certain sense of closeness in this moment, as if we've both got our shields down.

I'm not sure it's wise to stay.

"I'm not done with you."

He moves suddenly, every inch of him rich with motion, with intent.

"What now?" I demand, realizing he's closer to me than I expected.

"Now?" he murmurs, taking the goblet from my hand and setting it aside on a table. "What do you think?"

The afternoon light is fading. And with the onset of night comes the payment of certain promises....

"You spoke like a queen today," he murmurs, tilting his head down to look at me. "Don't think the others didn't notice."

"My mother didn't like it."

"Your mother doesn't like any of us. Trust me, you're in elite company."

That old, familiar tension pools in my stomach as he steps closer.

Every night it's been like this.

A promise owed, and a debt claimed.

Thiago presses one hand to the table behind me, his hard body caging me in. Leaning forward, his breath whispering over my lips, he pauses.

I can't look away.

One move and he'll claim my mouth. I know he will. He wants to. I see it in his eyes, those ever-present fires stoked with every nightly encounter between us. There is all manner of sin in those eyes. They promise me exquisite pleasure, and they demand complete surrender.

It's that last one I have a problem with.

But he never takes that step.

He always waits for me to make it, as if this is a game, and every time I push my piece into play, he's the one who secretly wins.

I owe him a simple kiss. Just one. And every night they've been the briefest of brushes, my lips to his.

"What are you waiting for?" he whispers, his other hand reaching up to hover an inch from my breast.

I can almost feel that touch on my skin.

You.

I close my eyes against temptation and give into the inevitable, lifting on my toes and brushing my mouth against his.

Thiago leans closer, the heat of his body hovering between us. His wrist brushes against my hip, his hand flexing with the desire to touch. But it's forbidden. Without my word, he cannot.

I feel his frustration in the tension of his body, the trembling of those hands. It's taking everything within him to restrain himself.

And I don't want him to hold back.

When my lips meet his, I can tell instantly that this is different. He feels it too. The moment stretches out too long, and it's as if he senses my hesitation. His tongue brushes against my mouth, begging for more, and I can't help myself.

I give it.

Inch by inch, he steals away my willpower. *Open*, his mouth urges, and then his tongue is slick against mine and there's a gasp trapped in my throat. I melt into that hard body, trembling hands coming to rest against the hard slab of his chest.

More, his lips demand. Desperation and hunger ignite within me, and it's like my body has a will of its own. My fingers curl in his shirt, and Thiago captures my mouth, eating at me as if wants to devour me.

Yield, his body insists, and he pushes back, hard, until my ass hits the table, and one hand clenches in my hair. I'm drowning in the taste of him. It feels as though a dam has burst, and it's both too much and not enough.

I break my mouth from his, breathing hard.

Slowly, the world comes back into focus. It's still not enough. I want more. It's been a long time since I've had another's hands on my skin, and never like this. Never burning through me like wildfire, threatening to destroy every last hint of control I own.

Gentle hands stroke down my sides, and every inch of my being wants to grab a fistful of his hair and tug his face back down to mine. He can see it too, heat darkening those green eyes until they're practically smoldering.

"Vi," he says, reaching for me.

I shove away from him, my hands going to my branded lips. This was a terrible idea.

Because I want more.

Because I don't think one taste will ever be enough.

"Goodnight," I call, forcing myself to haul out the

daughter of Queen Adaia and cloak myself in my role as an Asturian princess.

She's cold and regal and invulnerable to kisses.

Her heart doesn't race.

"Until tomorrow," Thiago says softly, and as I close the door behind me, I know those words will haunt every hour of the night ahead.

19

I t's after midnight when I realize I'm not going to be getting any sleep tonight.

With a sigh, I toss my blankets back, grab a silk robe, and escape into the tower. A cup of warm milk might do the trick, though I have no idea where the kitchens are, or even if I'll be allowed to visit them.

After all, I'm the enemy, aren't I?

It's one thing to be dismissed by my mother, quite another to realize Thiago's keeping secrets from me too. I don't know when I started to trust him, but to realize he doesn't return the sentiment feels like a knife wound to the chest.

The hallways are empty, though I feel the stir of one of the demi-fey shooting past, and golden eyes blink at me from the ceiling before vanishing in the sprawl of carved leaves that embellish the cornice.

"Do you know where the kitchens are?" I whisper.

Movement shifts out of the corner of my eye. One of the demi-fey weaves around a marble column like a cat wending its way through a pair of legs.

I haven't been here long enough to cultivate them, but they're curious little beasties.

"I want some warmed milk. And if someone were to assist me, I might be able to leave some milk out for them too."

Three shadows bob closer. The little sprites are creatures born of the elements; they have the curiosity and intelligence of a cat, though they don't seem to understand concepts like honor, or truth, or treachery.

"Maybe even some honey...."

One of the sylphs' forms grows more solid, until she's blinking those amber eyes at me. Tugging at my robe, she leads me to the left before vanishing in a swirl of wind.

I feel them herding me, scampering through the fretwork as if it's a forest. Others join them, curious now. All I need is a pipe, and I might as well be the famed Piper of Haggelund, luring the sprites from a town they've infested.

My smile fades when I realize I'm no longer alone.

Voices echo down the hallway, and light glimmers like a beacon.

This way, says the push of those invisible hands.

I forgot to request a secret way to the kitchen, where I wouldn't be seen.

It's too late now.

I can hear someone arguing, and the silence of the night is empty enough for those voices to carry.

"—and when do you plan on telling her?" a female voice asks.

"When it's safe to do so." The frost in that voice belongs to Thiago. "She's barely begun to trust me. I can't risk it. Not yet. We're barely through the first ring of curse work."

"You have five weeks." Definitely Eris. She wastes no

time with words. "Five weeks to finish this, or the game ends forever."

"Thank you, E," he growls. "I wasn't aware of the looming deadline."

"The princess is stubborn." The first voice sounds like Thalia's. "She knows you intend to use her to get your wife back."

"And what did you say to that?"

"I told her it must have been a lie formed in her mother's court. I'm not a fool, Thiago. She believed me."

Breath going shallow, I can't stop my feet from creeping closer to the door ahead and that faint crack of light.

I trusted Thalia.

She won me over with a handful of smiles and a platter of bread and grapes. I should have known better. I've never let anyone get so close to me so quickly, but there was something about her that seemed instantly trustworthy.

Erlking's balls, I'm an idiot.

It's her voice. She told me the blasted tale herself. The saltkissed have the ability to lure anyone into a trap with their voices, even when you can see it coming. Perhaps there's some magic left in her, something that makes her believable.

"Today was dangerous," Thiago continues, sounding closer than I expected.

I freeze. He must be on the other side of the door.

"The Alliance queens couldn't stop themselves from gloating about it. I know she's starting to suspect something." He sighs. "If I could just get her to trust me...."

"It will come," Thalia tells him. "It always does. You'll win her heart."

"But will I do it in time?" he murmurs. "Today was a misstep. I can't allow her near anyone else just yet. I could almost see her starting to put together the pieces, and the meeting cost me what little trust I'd managed to gain."

"You can't keep her locked away forever."

"Not forever, no. Just until it's... safe."

"And yet, you can't ignore Angharad," Eris points out.

"This is the worst fucking time for that bitch to be making her move," he snarls.

"I'm sure she consulted her oracle," Finn says dryly. "Perhaps you should send her a letter requesting an extension of time. Five weeks please, Angharad, before you make your move. I just need to seduce a certain princess."

"Perhaps we should send Angharad a knife and someone to plant it in her throat." Eris's voice suggests she's thinking of doing the task herself.

"Tempting," Thiago mutters, "but her sister queens might take exception to that and decide to focus their full attentions on us. We're prepared for war, but not against the entire Unseelie horde."

Invisible hands brush against my shins, an impatient little face forming near my feet. I almost forgot the demi-fey.

This way, it seems to tell me. *The milk is this way.*

I shake my head.

Thiago's too close to the door. Any movement might alert him that I'm here.

"Fuck the princess," Eris says. "It might solve all your problems."

"Woo her," Finn adds. "Fucking's all well and good, but in my experience, the way to a woman's heart is through soft kisses and gentle words."

"Considering how empty your bed is," Eris replies, "I'd hardly consider you the expert."

"Ah, my dear," he practically purrs, "you're one to talk."

"That's why I have these," she replies sweetly. I don't

need to see her to know she's waggling her fingers. "I don't need a man."

"And I would love to prove you wrong," Finn replies, "but I fear it might grow awkward if you were to fall in love with me."

Eris snorts. "You overestimate your abilities."

"Is it possible for you to focus?" someone else growls, and I suspect it's Baylor. "Or are we going to have to separate the pair of you again?"

The demi-fey returns, pulling impatiently on my robe.

"Not now," I breathe, pressing a finger to my lips.

Eyes narrowing, it bites me.

I hiss out a breath, lunging backward. The demi-fey vanishes, but the damage is done.

"What was that?" Thalia demands.

Footsteps whisper over marble. I see a shadow pass over the floor, and take one step back just as Thiago jerks the door open.

Our eyes lock.

His flare wide in surprise before he freezes. "Your Highness."

It's clear I've interrupted a war council of sorts, and my first instinct is to back away. But that's the princess who's spent too many years watching doors shut in her face at her mother's court.

And I'm so fucking tired of being kept in the dark.

"What's going on?" I demand.

"I thought you were in bed," he replies.

"Clearly."

"You should return."

"There's a lot of things I should be doing," I retort, "but I have this terrible habit of not listening when I'm told to run along."

"How much did you hear?"

I'm tempted to say everything, but if my mother taught me anything, it's to never give the game away. "Something about empty beds. The words were a little muffled though, so you may have to repeat them."

He glances over his shoulder, eyelashes brushing against his cheeks. The light behind him does marvelous things to his features, but I harden my heart.

The bastard's been lying to me from the start.

He needs to seduce me, and I, fool that I am, fell for his sad story about his wife. I fell for his kiss. For his smile. For the way he allowed me to join his meeting today. It's all been one big ruse.

Never again.

"What are you all doing up so late?"

"Plotting," Thalia calls.

"We were discussing the meeting today and the result of it," Baylor adds, and I catch a glimpse of him, one foot kicked up on the chair in front of him.

Instantly, my eyes dart away. I'm not yet ready to face those particular demons. "I shall leave you to it then."

Thiago stares at me for a long moment, then slowly pushes the door open wider and steps back, gesturing me into the room. "Join us. If you dare."

I don't belong here.

This is Evernight. Not my own people. We have to be enemies, no matter how many silky smiles Thiago gives me.

I think that's what bothers me the most. I'd started to like these people. I'd started to drop my guard, only to hear them plotting behind my back as though I am just a pawn in this war.

Well, it's time to create my own destiny.

My mother was right.

The prince can't be trusted, but if he *thinks* I trust him....

"It's none of her concern," Eris bites out, and the words are enough to make me step inside the room like nothing else might have.

"E," Thalia snaps, pushing out of the fur-lined chair she was reclining in. The smile she gives me is far more welcoming, but I can't help remembering her words. "Iskvien's more than welcome here."

Some sort of tension drifts between the two women. That same old silent argument I always feel I've just walked into.

Eris's lips purse, and she looks down at the map-table in the center of the room.

"If you're speaking of war, then yes, it's my concern," I tell them. "I have my people to think of too. And I may be able to convince my mother the threat is real if I know more of what's going on."

I can't allow my people to suffer if my mother decides to abstain from this coming war with the Unseelie from pure spite.

I circle the map-table. It's extraordinary. All blues and greens and browns. Valleys carved into the timber, and rivers snaking their way through the grassy plains of the Horde to the North-west, with snow-capped mountains rising out of the map, tipped with white. Little gold castles stand up from the map where the main cities lie. I see Hawthorne Castle ringed with thorns, and Ceres gleams by the sea. To the north, Valerian stands like a bastion of strength, a far cry from its current state. I've never seen a map like it.

Little red flags mark the wilderness in the north, beyond the mountains. The Unseelie kingdoms. A chill runs through me. There are considerably more flags than I'd expected. "There's so many of them."

"The Unseelie have always bred like rabbits," Eris says.

"Some say they're not as pure blooded as we are," Finn adds, "and their mixed blood makes them more fertile."

"These are Blaedwyn's lands," Thiago says, gesturing to the eastern side of the map, where the flags have a ravaging white wolf printed on them. "And these are Angharad's." He points to the larger swathe of flags in the center, with their hissing white wyvern. "And far to the west lies Morwenna's kingdom."

Those flags are black.

"What are the silver circles?" I ask. They look a little like coins.

"The Hallows."

You can almost see the path of the ley lines. A Hallow can only be built along one of them, though the nexus point where they meet provides the most magical energy. The origin Hallows—the ones that trapped the Old Ones— stand at each nexus point. It's where the Veil thins between worlds at each equinox and solstice, where creatures from other realms can step through into ours, even if it's only for one night.

There are significantly more of them in the Unseelie kingdoms.

"The Unseelie allied themselves with the Old Ones, where we sought to crush their worship when we found it," Thiago says. "Most of the Unseelie Hallows have been used as places of worship for centuries. They brought tributes there, and gave sacrifices, and over the years the power in the Hallows began to grow in response." He points to one of the silver coins in Blaedwyn's territories. A golden pair of antlers is stamped onto the face of it. "This is where the

Erlking stepped from his realm into ours, leading the Wild Hunt with him. This is where he's trapped." His finger moves to the far north, where a horned skull replaces the antlers. "This represents the Horned One and his prison." On toward a hound. "The Grimm." To an icy crown. "The Frost Giant." South toward a ghostly, howling face. "The Wraithenwold." Toward Morwenna's lands. "Red Mag. The Raven King. Bloody Mara." He's turning south now, toward our own lands. Toward Mistmere. "The Mother of Night." Into the forests that adorn my mother's kingdom. "The Green Man." South to the Isle of Stormhaven. "The Father of Storms."

There are only two origin Hallows left.

One in Queen Maren's kingdom, and one in Queen Lucidia's.

I finish for him, "The Dreamthief. And Mrog the Warmonger."

"Do we know whether they'll sustain the powers they had if they reenter this world?" Thalia muses. "They were once worshipped as gods, and belief in a god is a power of its own. After all these years, surely their powers are dying with so few left who make sacrifices to them?"

"It's not just the sacrifices," Baylor says, scratching at his stubble. "What do we leave on our window sills on Samhain?"

"Salt," Thalia replies.

Eris shrugs. "Iron shavings."

"Why?" Baylor asks.

I've never truly thought of it. It's simply tradition. "To stop the Wild Hunt from entering your home."

"We hang mistletoe in the entrance of our doors," he says, "because mistletoe is fatal to the Erlking. Some peasants in the western marshes prefer to hang horseshoes there for good luck, and they forget that once upon a time, it was to repel the Hunt."

"What do you hang above your bed to prevent the Dreamthief from stealing your soul away to the realm of dreams?" Thiago asks.

"Webs woven with iron beads to trap him," I whisper, starting to realize what they're both suggesting. "It's not worship, but it is belief. We believe in the Old Ones' powers every time we take steps to counter them. We're granting them strength as we do it."

Eris snorts. "And if they find themselves weak, then they'll simply tap into the ley lines' powers and drink up all that delicious magic until they look like Finn at a banquet."

Finn lobs a blueberry at her head. "Elegant and exceptionally handsome?"

"Bloated with enough mead to drown a ship."

"So they'll retain all their old powers." Thalia circles the map, sliding a silver Hallow from its nexus point. It's stamped with the trident that the Father of Storms wields. Flipping it in the air, she stares at the picture grimly. "I do not want to meet the Father of Storms. They say he shackles his saltkissed and sends them to hunt at his edict. They were his hounds of the sea, and while my bloodlines are diluted, I would very much not care to test the theory that anyone with salt in their blood must answer his call."

"We all have certain ghosts of the past we don't want to see again." Thiago stares through the map, and I wonder which Old One he's picturing. "The Alliance will take its time ascertaining the truth of what Angharad's doing at Mistmere, but I don't intend to sit here, twiddling my thumbs." He rubs a silver Hallow coin between his thumb and forefinger. "Baylor and Eris, I want two companies of warriors standing at the ready. The second I give the command, they need to be prepared to take Mistmere."

"Of course," Baylor rumbles, and Eris simply nods.

"Thalia, my sweet, sweet Thalia," Thiago says, capturing her hand and lifting it to his lips. "Evernight must be prepared to face a war. I want more grain shipments coming in, and instruct the armory to increase production—"

"I do know what I'm doing, Thi," she drawls. "Any spies in the city will know what we're preparing for, but at least we'll be ready."

"Finn." Thiago turns to the affable rogue.

"I know," Finn sighs. "I lost the trail near Vervain Forest, but he has to be out there somewhere. I'll find him. I promise."

Every inch of me stills.

"This isn't like him," Baylor says gruffly. "If it was Finn, I'd say he was led astray by a particularly handsome widow or a grape festival. But Lysander knew the risks. He knew the importance of his mission. He wouldn't just vanish without due cause. And it's been a year now."

"His mission?" I dare to ask, surprised the rest of the room can't hear the thud of my heart.

Baylor glances at me. "Forgive me, Princess. But my brother's task is for the prince's ears only."

"A year." Eris looks uncomfortable. "Do you think—?"

"No," Baylor snaps. "I don't. I would know, somehow. And you're suggesting someone out there has the capacity to kill my brother. Lysander is the best of us all."

He was.

I want to be sick.

I don't know why Lysander was sent to Vervain Forest, but he somehow ran afoul of a witch powerful enough to curse-twist him into a bane's form.

And then he died.

Words bandy around me, plans for war and provenance. I can barely keep the horror off my face.

"This is the last communication I had from Lysander." Baylor slides a folder of papers across the table toward Finn. They spill from the folder, and I capture them with a swift hand.

Thiago reaches past me and slams his hand on the papers before I can see more than a glimpse of them. "These are not for you, Princess. I'm sorry."

I lift my hand and let him take the papers. "Don't be."

There's a coat of arms in the top corner, though I only catch a glimpse of it. A basilisk or a wyvern rears its serpentine head, which makes my thoughts race. Several of the nobles near the borders of Asturia use a similar creature as their emblem, and three of them are within a stone's throw of Vervain. I'd have to get a better look to see what else was on that shield to know precisely which of my mother's vassals is writing to the prince.

I can't stay here any longer, listening to Baylor argue about his brother's lack of recent communication.

"I think I'm of little value here," I murmur, pushing to my feet.

Instantly, Thiago rises and draws my chair back. "You might be surprised."

I grace him with a wan smile. "I'm tired. It's been a long day, Your Highness."

His eyes narrow. "You called me Thiago when we were at the hunting cabin."

"I called you a lot of things." And I lowered my guard for one dangerous second, only to find he'd driven a fatal blade into my heart. Despite the words I overheard earlier, I'm still recovering from those days together.

Because I... liked him.

I trusted him.

And I hate the fact my mother was right. I hate the fact the prince is only using me as some sort of weapon against my mother. I hate the way they all jest about seduction as if I'm some fool to be lured into his bed.

Never again.

"I'll walk you back to your—"

"That won't be necessary," I say abruptly, cutting him off. There will be no more late-night conversations. No more kisses that extend beyond what is owed.

No more teasing smiles.

No. If the prince is up to something, then he leaves me with no choice. I need to know what he's up to before I can decide what to do about it.

And to do that, I need him to think nothing is wrong.

I force a smile and brush my fingers against the back of his hand, because two can play at this game. "Sweet dreams, Your Highness."

It's become a private little jest between us, but now it's a weapon.

Thiago lifts my hand to his lips and purrs, "Trust me. They will be. Goodnight."

20

I hurry along the hallway hours after I heard the prince seek his own bed, glancing over my shoulder. There are no guards in sight, but that doesn't mean there aren't eyes upon me.

And the last thing I need is to be caught right now.

I pause in front of the prince's audience chambers, then slip a makeshift lockpick into the lock and flip the tumblers. It's a skill I acquired when I was a youth with an insatiable appetite for reading. Sadly, I used it mostly to break into the locked section of the library.

I'm inside before anyone has a chance to investigate.

I need information to send back to my mother's court to prove I'm right—that Angharad is the true threat.

And I need to know whether I can truly trust the prince.

What is he hiding?

I circle the map table where his people sat. There's nothing there. I rifle through the shelves. Books. Treatises. Scrolls I don't have time to investigate. I need to find that letter and work out what Lysander was doing near Vervain. I shake a locked box. Something rattles. Not the letter, but it wouldn't be locked away if it wasn't important. I slip the pick inside the lock.

From princess to thief.

Perfect.

It pops open with a click, and then a necklace spills into my hands. My breath catches. Thick, gorgeous diamonds circled by golden thorns. It looks like half the stars in the sky are woven into the gold mesh.

The necklace is mine.

"Where did you get this?" I whisper, barely daring to touch it. My grandmother gave it to me for my thirteenth birthday, and I wore it every day until—

When did I lose it?

I can't remember.

And that ache in my temples starts to pulse.

I lift the necklace with shaking hands, draping it around my throat. It fits perfectly, the weight of it so familiar my heart aches. Turning toward the window, I catch a glimpse of my reflection and swallow hard.

Why in the name of the Old Ones does the Prince of Evernight have my necklace?

Is my mother right?

Is this all just some elaborate ruse to make me dance to his tune? When did he take it? Or did someone else close to me steal it?

Rage bursts through me, and I clench the necklace in my fist. I need answers. And I need them now.

I SLAM both hands against the doors leading to the prince's chambers.

They hit the walls with a bang, and the prince startles

upright from the chair where he'd been examining the bandage wrapped around his chest. There's a bowl full of bloody water on the table beside him, and it looks like he's been cutting open his wounds to drain the iron poison from them.

I don't care.

I saved the bastard's life once.

Now he owes me some answers.

The prince straightens to his full height, arching a mocking brow as he reaches past me for his shirt. "I thought you were asleep."

"Clearly."

"Come to beard the wolf in his den, my love? You ought to tread carefully, you know. I might think you're just trying to catch me naked. Again." Thiago reaches up, brushing his knuckles against my lip, his gaze dropping to my mouth as if he's dying to replace one touch with another. "You've already paid your part of the bargain today. Don't tell me you'd forgotten."

"Kiss this," I snap, thrusting my clenched fist toward him.

It makes him snap his head back, which gives me enough opportunity to escape the jail of his body. I reel into the center of his chambers and then stop, realizing I've trapped myself.

I've never been in his rooms before, and if I thought my bed looked sinful, then it has nothing on his. For one thing, it's *his* bed, and I know those sheets have seen all his sins.

Looking at the bed is no safer than looking at him.

And it only makes me angrier.

"Enough with the games." My fist curls around the necklace, and I shove it in front of him. "Why do you have my necklace? My grandmother's necklace? Why were you keeping it in your audience chamber?"

He pauses, then slowly resumes slipping his arms into the sleeves of his shirt. "I see. You've been digging around in places you shouldn't have been."

"Oh, don't make this about me. You stole my necklace."

"I didn't steal it." His lip curls in a half-snarl.

"No?" I pace around him in a half-circle. "Then who did? One of your lackeys?"

His mouth thins. Clear evidence he doesn't intend to answer me.

That does it. I cast about me and see his dagger, resting in its sheath. Lunging toward it, I unsheathe the steel with a rasp and turn to press it to his throat as he moves to grab me.

Thiago freezes, his rugged chin tilting sharply as the vicious tip of the blade digs into his tanned skin.

"You tell me what is going on. Right now."

He visibly swallows, a stubborn glint lighting those wicked green eyes. "Or. There's usually an 'or' in this case."

"Or," I say, in an icy voice, "I'll bury this blade up to the hilt."

He pushes closer, the blade drawing blood. It trickles down the smooth column of his throat, drawing my attention to the hard planes of his chest and those rippling tattoos that constantly shift. "You won't do it."

"Don't be so sure."

"If there's anything I know, it's this: You don't have the spirit for murder. You're not your mother. Despite everything she's done to you, she's never been able to tarnish your spirit."

"Stop speaking as if you know me!"

"Stop acting as if I don't."

I swallow. My back meets the edge of the windowsill, and the prince rests his knuckles on either side of my hips, trapping me there.

"What are you going to do now?" he taunts. "Kill me? I'm sure your mother would relish the thought of my blood splashed all over the carpets."

It's too close to the truth.

"Considering your warlords would have my head, I think it unwise to pursue such a plan."

"They would never hurt you." His voice turns rough. "They would never dare."

"It's not as though you'd be there to stop them."

We stare at each other for long moments. And then I curse and drive the dagger into the wall.

"That's better," he whispers.

He's between me and the exit, so I bolt for the doors leading to the chamber next to his.

"Vi!" he yells, snatching at my wrist.

It's too late. I'm through the doors, staggering into a world of muted blues clearly lit by the moonlight streaming through the windows. There's a bed, a massive chest, and a daybed by the windows with a scattering of books upon it.

A female room, judging by the glimpse.

It's just a glance that undoes me, a swift flash of white catching the corner of my eye as I look for an escape.

But I skid to a halt as if punched directly in the chest, my jaw dropping open as I stare up at the painting that resides over the bed.

The woman in the painting is gowned in pure starlight as she breezes through a forest lit by night-blooming flowers, throwing a flirtatious glance over her shoulder at the man following her. Thick, dark hair ripples down her back, a circlet of golden thorns adorning her throat, and diamonds dripping into her cleavage.

Me.

It's a painting of *me*.

Wearing my starlit gown, my hair bedecked with flowers, and my grandmother's necklace around my throat.

"What mockery is this?" I can't catch my breath. It can't be real. It's only been weeks since the night of Lammastide. Not even a master could finish such a massive, lifelike portrait in such a short amount of time.

I spin toward the doors, wishing I'd kept the dagger. "What does this mean?"

Limping forward, Thiago presses his good shoulder against the pair of wooden doors. He looks somewhat wary, but hints of frustration and resignation darken his brow. "I didn't mean for you to find out so soon."

"Find out what?" The room is starting to spin, my breath coming swiftly. The ache in my temples increases as I glance at the painting again. "What is going on?"

The bedchambers are directly beside his. It's the position his wife—or mistress—should hold.

He holds up his hands in a placating manner. "Vi, calm down."

Pain lances through my temples, and I gasp, clutching at my head. It hurts. It hurts so much. The room is spinning now, threatening to bring me to my knees.

"Just breathe," the prince whispers, sounding dangerously close. His shadow sweeps over me. "It will ease in a moment, Vi."

"What's going on?" I dart around the bed, desperate to escape now. "Don't you dare lie to me. Tell me what you mean. Why is there a portrait of me in your *wife's* bedchamber?"

The muscle in his cheek jumps, and for a moment I see a hint of pure fury light through his eyes. Then it flickers and dies as he leans closer, his cruel face showing hints of frustration. "Because, my dearest, you *are* my wife."

21

I can't have heard that correctly.

I spin with a gasp, retreating against the door. "What did you say?"

"You heard me."

Instantly, it feels like a crown of thorns suddenly tightens around my temples, driving those wicked spikes deep into my skull. A scream escapes me.

I go to my knees, pressing my palm against my eye socket to try and still the pain. *Mother of Night*. Whiteness obliterates my vision, and I swear someone is driving a blade right through my skull. The world vanishes, leaving nothing but pain.

Nothing but the throbbing drumbeat of "*You are my wife*," echoing in my ears.

It lasts an age.

And just when I think it might very well kill me, I feel the thorns start to dissipate, the pressure finally easing.

Gradually I become aware of a warm body pressing against my side, and the flat of a palm skimming my back.

"Breathe," whispers the Prince of Evernight. "Just breathe, Vi. You're through the worst of it."

I turn my face against his thigh, sucking in a shuddering breath. Every inch of me remains knotted tightly, but the pain is easing. The world around me begins to seep back into my vision, apart from the very centers, which remain white. Blood drips on the floor, and I feel it running hotly down my lip. My nose. My nose is bleeding.

"What happened?"

"The spell that binds your memory has a rather unpleasant sting when it's shattered." He tips my chin up with firm hands, examining my face. "It's nearly killed you before."

It feels like it came close to killing me now.

I can't hold my head up. Everything hurts. *Everything.*

My wife....

I can't even dwell on what that means, for the mere thought brings pain back upon me with a vengeance.

"I've got you," he says, sweeping me into his arms.

I can't fight it.

Instead, I turn my face into his shoulder and suck in a lungful of that familiar scent as he strides toward the door.

It seems like eons before my head stops splitting.

The prince offered water, but all I want to do is vomit it back up. Finally, once my stomach stops threatening to rebel, I manage to push myself onto my elbows.

I'm on the bed in his—*my*—bedchamber. Dried blood crusts on my lip. My nose stopped bleeding ten minutes ago, and the bloodied remnants of his shirt on the bedside table show how much I've lost.

Thiago leans on the fireplace, staring into the flames. There's no sign of the charismatic prince who greeted me at the Lammastide bonfires. Shadows carve harsh lines into his face, and his eyes are dark and brooding. It should scare me, but I can't fight the dull ache of familiarity every time I look at him, and now I know why.

Husband.

He's my husband.

I press my hands to my temples, but the answering ache feels like the dull aftermath of a migraine, and not the excruciating torment of a knife to the brain anymore.

It's unthinkable. How can I even reconcile his words with the truth? I have no recollection of our marriage. No hint I've ever known him, beyond certain scents and words tugging at my mind like elusive will-o'-the-wisps.

And the vague familiarity of his kiss.

I must have made a sound, for Thiago looks around sharply.

"You're awake."

"And alive." Somehow, I manage a hint of a smile. "Barely."

His face darkens. "Don't joke about that, please. The first time the spell shattered, you nearly died in my arms."

"Spell." Of course, it's a spell. I've had a taste of the remnants of a shattered spell turning back on me before, and it felt like it had burned my bones from the inside. This was worse. A thousand times worse. I was certain my brain was dribbling out my ears at one stage. No wonder my nose is still sluggishly bleeding. "I don't understand. Who cast the spell? What does it do? How…. You and I…?" I draw my knees up to my chest. "Why didn't you tell me?"

I steal another glance at the painting. At the way that possessive hand curls toward me in the painting. A ghostly echo of that touch whispers over the same skin, and a sudden flash of Thiago's firm lips darting down to press against mine steals through my mind.

I gasp, and the memory shatters, chased away by a surge of pain.

"Because somehow, she makes you forget, and to remind you only causes you pain. Physical pain." His face twists with anger. "I didn't want to hurt you. To scare you."

"Scare me?"

"You've run from me before."

And it hurt him. I can see it all over his face.

"How did we even meet? *When* did we meet? I don't remember any of it."

"You never do."

My heart starts to kick harder, and I can feel panic blurring the edges of the room.

"I'll start at the beginning." He pushes away from the fireplace. "My people have a custom. When we are twenty-five, we go through a rite of passage into adulthood, where, if Maia favors you, she will give you a glimpse of your future mate. The first time I saw your face was in the waters of Maia's temple, and I vowed then and there that I would find you. One day. Though it was another six hundred years before I first caught a glimpse of you in the flesh.

"I've spent centuries fighting your mother over Mistmere, and the night the Seelie and Unseelie kingdoms drew together to forge a pact was the first time I laid eyes upon you. You were dancing by the fires, radiant in midnight silk with your hair flowing down your back. I couldn't breathe. I'd spent hundreds of years searching for you, and there you were. Right in front of me." He takes a step toward me, pausing when I inch back. "I had to have you. I had to know you. And the world was overflowing with celebration. We were both half-drunk on elderberry wine and victory. And we danced, and we kissed, and when the moon hovered on the edge of the horizon, I laid you down in the heather and made love to you.

"It wasn't until the sun rose that I caught a glimpse of what I'd missed all along. I was tracing my fingers down your back, and there, right along the curve of your spine was a tattoo. All those roses and thorns, interwoven with the Asturian crest. You weren't just from Adaia's court. You were from her loins." His head lowers. "The woman I'd spent an eternity searching for was my enemy's daughter."

It sounds like a lovely fairy tale.

And I have absolutely no recollection of any of it.

"I couldn't just let you go. You were my gift from the goddess, and one doesn't simply walk away from that, no matter how difficult the path ahead might be. I tried to make peace with your mother, but she would have none of it. And you were... determined to defy her. We were married on the third and final night of the rites," he tells me. "We both thought Adaia would have to accept the marriage once it was done, and the alliance witnessed it."

I know my mother too well.

"She would never accept such a betrayal." Not from one of her daughters. She'd have done everything she could to tear us apart.

"She didn't. But she couldn't defy a marriage that was witnessed by the gods themselves. She offered me a choice. I could have you for three months before I must return you to her, or there would be war. The Seelie accords would be broken, and I would be forced to take you by force. And worse, the Queen of Nightmares sided with her. The alliance was threatening to fracture down the center. Kyrian stood by my side, and Lucidia refused to take part. It would have thrown the entire alliance into chaos.

"So, I accepted her deal. Three months with you every time we finalize the accords. And then I must return you to your mother."

The treaty she'd spoken of all along had not been made to prevent war. It had been made to prevent him from having me.

"I thought she accepted the deal with too much grace," he says. "I should have known she would find a way to revenge herself upon both of us. When you were finally returned to me, you looked at me as though I was a stranger. You had no memory of us. I tried to tell you the truth, and the spell she'd cast nearly broke your mind. You came close to dying, and when you woke, you ran from me. I had to lock you away. It took me months to earn your trust. You kissed me only once before I was forced to return you, and the next time you came, I did not dare tell you the truth. Not at the risk of losing you to the backlash of the spell. I had to wait until I could see you again. And I had to be patient with you when I did. I had to earn your trust before I could tell you the truth. Given time, memories start to leak through. The spell weakens with each memory gained. Eventually, it's safe to tell you."

"How many times?" I feel sick. "How many times, curse you!"

Expression slides from his face as though a shroud has obscured it. "Twelve. This is the thirteenth time you've come to me with no memories of us."

The room is spinning again.

"*Thirteen.*" It comes out on my breath. I push to the edge of the bed, suddenly unwilling to lie there any longer. I need to move. Pace. It sounds like the most outlandish story. And yet, knowing my mother as I do, I can see how it *might* happen.

It sounds exactly like something she would do.

"I'm only twenty," I breathe. "I only returned from Queen Maren's court a couple of summers ago, after serving her as a lady-in-waiting."

"You're thirty-three." Thiago's expression softens. "I'm sorry, Vi. Your sister was named princess-heir thirteen summers ago, and you've been locked away in your mother's court ever since. It's all just an elaborate ruse to... keep your memories locked away."

I can't breathe. My lungs simply won't open.

It's not just him my mother stole.

Thirteen summers.

Gone.

All those doors slamming in my face.... My mother turning to Andraste at every opportunity, flaunting it. It wasn't just a ruse. It was all a game, and I'll bet my soul she enjoyed every moment of it.

I want to scream.

The constant fear I've felt, knowing my future depended on who was named heir. Trying so desperately to earn my mother's approval, when it was an impossible task. Andraste knew. And what was it she'd said? Perhaps I should enjoy my time with the prince.

Oh, Maia. My knees buckle beneath me.

The prince is there in a second, catching me before I hit the floor, but I can't stand to have his hands on me. Not in this moment.

I push him away, fighting free.

"No! Don't. Don't touch me."

I'm not ready for his compassion.

It will break me.

He stiffens, and I realize I've escaped to the other side of the bed, my arms wrapped around my chest as if to hold myself together.

We stare at each other like two nobles facing a duel neither of us wants.

"There were letters," I whisper, trying to sort through everything. "Someone was leaving me letters in Valerian, urging me to trust you. Who writes them?"

I'm desperately afraid I already know.

A feminine hand in sloping Asturian cursive.

"You write them, Vi. To remind yourself of the truth. And the demi-fey leave them for you to find."

Imagine writing those letters, knowing I'm going to lose all recollection of him.

"So when you spoke of seducing me, in order to get your wife back...." They were speaking of me.

"Every year she grants me three months with you. And every year I must... must win your heart." He looks down then, at his curled fist. "And every year you promise me you will not forget me."

And then I do.

I'm not the only one who's faced years of this. I'm not the only one who's lost more than mere memories.

I remember the way he looked at me that night by the bonfires, as if waiting for me to recognize him. I'd thought him disappointed in me at the time, but now I know the truth.

That look was the loss of hope.

"I'm sorry."

"It's not your fault," he says. "It's never your fault."

None of this makes sense.

But I know this prince.

He's stolen dozens of kisses from me in the past weeks.

He's never taken more than he was owed, merely waiting patiently for me to come to him.

"Will you let me hold you?" Thiago whispers, stepping closer.

This man feels like a stranger to me. But I can't deny the heat that exists in the inch between our bodies draws me. I can't deny that fluttery feeling deep within my abdomen.

Without thinking, I reach out, hesitating once before pressing my hand against his chest. The fabric of his shirt melts against his skin, and suddenly his heart is beating hard beneath my hand. It calls to me, teasing at the little magic I own. I might not know him, but I know *this*.

I jerk my hand away, but he catches it, that piercing gaze searching mine as if he can see my very soul.

"Don't be scared."

"I'm not." *I'm confused.* How did Adaia steal those memories? Is this real, or is it a terrible nightmare?

But it feels real as he leans down, his face looming into view. I've kissed him so many times, but I can't stop myself from freezing, not this time.

Because this time, there's so much more to it than a simple bargain.

"Sweet Goddess," he whispers hoarsely. "Just this once. Please, Vi. Please let me kiss you. It's been so long."

And I surrender, closing my eyes and curling my fists protectively in front of me as I tilt my face to his.

His mouth crashes down over mine.

A gasp escapes me, and I soften into his embrace as his tongue slicks against me. It's a kiss meant to consume me. A kiss that speaks of loss and yearning, as if he's spent every day of the past nine months counting down the moments until he could hold me in his arms again.

Each time I've pressed my lips to his, gracing him with

the mockery of a kiss, he's been patiently restraining himself.

I've seen his fingers curled around the arms of his chair and felt the stiffness within him. Every inch of him was always rock-hard and aching to prolong our embrace, though I'd always thought it the threat of breaking our bargain that held him at bay.

This is the prince set loose of his ties.

This is the stranger who feels so familiar.

He's a storm of passion and fury finally unleashed, and I can't think. I can't breathe. I can't resist.

"Oh, gods." I come up for air, and his mouth is on my throat, teeth grazing the delicate skin there.

Firm hands grab my ass, and then he's grinding me against him. Want and need conspire to undo me.

Thiago picks me up by the back of the thighs, wrapping my legs around his hips. Two steps and then he's slamming me back on the bed. My fingers curl in his shirt, and I can't breathe, but it's for an entirely different reason than before.

He claims my mouth again, and it feels as though my skin's too small to contain me. I'm burning up, my body igniting. Sweet merciless Maia, but I don't know if I can handle any more of this.

It's only then that I smell the smoke.

"Wait!" I gasp, pushing against his chest.

It's too much.

And that burning sensation.... I think I'm actually setting the bed on fire.

Pain lashes through my chest, my magic gushing up within me. It's always been a trickle, but this feels like the floodgates have finally opened.

"Vi?" He lifts his head.

The smoke dampens down, and when I press a hand to the bedspread, I feel heat lingering in the quilt.

What was that?

My hands tremble. And the press of his body is overwhelming, lighting my veins on fire again. Or perhaps that's my magic. I don't understand any of this.

"I just need... room to breathe. A chance to think."

The prince pushes to his feet, his face forcibly expressionless. "As you wish, Your Highness."

And then he vanishes through the doors of the bedchamber as if an entire pack of banes were on his heels.

And I don't have the breath to call him back.

22

"So how do we break the curse?"

I spent all last night tossing and turning in my bed, thinking about everything the day revealed.

And now I'm angry.

I know exactly where to find the prince, too. Every morning, he trains with his sword. At Valerian, he dueled with Eris in the shattered ballroom. But here.... It takes me only a few minutes to track him down in the solar at the top of the tallest tower. Swords ring and curses grunt, but with my words, the entire room goes still.

Thiago pauses in his attack, breathing hard as he steps away from Baylor. Sweat mars his shirt, and I can see those writhing black tattoos painted across his skin beneath it. "Wife."

It's such a jarring word, but this time, I'm prepared to face it. "Your Highness."

I'm not yet ready to call him husband.

I don't know if I ever will be.

"How do we break the curse?" I repeat softly.

Eris watches from one of the window arches, wearing a

brown leather corset, knee high boots, and a golden armband that highlights her dark skin. Her black hair is bound back this morning, and the second she saw me, her eyebrows rose and haven't resettled. There's a cat nestled on her knee, and she slowly resumes stroking it.

"We don't," Thiago tells me, his words clipped as he lowers the sword. "We've had you examined by every sorcerer and witch this side of Unseelie. The curse is knotted so tightly around you that any attempt to undo it will only destroy your mind. You felt what it was like to merely learn the truth. This will kill you."

"So, we just let my mother win?"

We just let her steal away my life, year by year?

"You will remember me. One day," he says sharply. "You will break the spell, I have no doubt of that."

"And in the meantime?" Another truth assaulted me during the night. It was so easy to call fire last night. I barely even thought it, and my magic was sweeping through me. And Thiago had been so certain I could learn to ward. That I could wield my magic. "I forget everything, don't I? This curse steals all my memories. It steals my hold on my magic. Doesn't it?"

His gaze lowers as he wipes an oiled rag along the length of his sword. "Yes. It steals everything."

I knew it, and yet, the blow still staggers me.

I want to set the fucking world on fire.

"Vi," Thiago warns, stepping closer.

Smoke curls through the air. My clenched palms feel hot.

"Control it," he warns.

I can't. I'm burning up again, and this time there is no way to tamp it down. It flares through me, like a phoenix bursting to life in my chest. Hot and violent and screaming with rage.

Flames burst into being around me. I am pure, molten fire.

They rage in a circular inferno, and too late, I realize he's warded me so none of my magic can escape.

"Control it," he barks.

I can't.

My hair whips around me, my skin cracking apart as the fire consumes me. All my life, all I've ever wanted is my magic, but this is terrifying. It's so much. Too much. A dam that's burst its banks, and nothing I can do will force it back inside me.

"Breathe, Vi. Think of kittens. Soft, fluffy kittens.'

Kittens?

What in the Underworld is he talking about?

But in the next second, I realize the flames are dying down.

With a desperate wrench of willpower, I swallow it all back down, letting it consume me instead. All the hatred and the anger, and the... grief.

I end up on my knees, panting, holding my hands in front of me. They're whole, the skin unblistered, but I swear they were on fire bare seconds ago.

"Kittens?" I manage to rasp.

Thiago kneels, capturing my hands. "I needed to distract you. You lost control of your emotions and hence your magic. Anger and hate will only exacerbate the lack of control, and you'll end up burning the city down if you don't yield to it."

My entire being is shaking. I can smell the smoke again. Feel the heat drying my throat. "I don't know how. She took *everything.*"

"And we will take it back," he says grimly. "Trust me, Vi. Trust me. You're not alone. I won't let you deal with this alone."

He presses his lips to my forehead, and a wave of coolness slides over my skin. It's his magic, dark and foreign, but it feels like drenching myself in water.

The heat and rage abate, and finally I can breathe again.

"I offered to teach you how to ward once," he tells me, hauling me to my feet. "The offer still stands, though I will extend it to teaching you how to control your magic. If you want?"

It's not so much a matter of want as a matter of need. The entire room stinks of smoke. "Do I have a choice?"

"You always have a choice."

"Did I have a choice when you and my mother made this foolish bargain? Did I have a choice when she told me I was going to be your hostage for three months?"

"Eris. Baylor. May we have some privacy."

It's not a question.

Baylor glances at me, glances at him, then stalks past, hurrying down the stairs as if he doesn't want to be privy to any part of this conversation. Eris moves a little slower, sauntering across the floor.

"Good luck," she drawls. "I hope you both manage to keep your eyebrows this time."

Then their footsteps are echoing down the stairs.

"You're angry," Thiago says.

"Would you not be?"

He shrugs. "Yes. But I don't have the luxury of allowing myself to lose control. That's the first lesson, Vi. Power such as ours is not merely a gift, but a responsibility."

It's all I've ever craved, but I can't help looking at the charred marble that surrounds me.

"Let me help you," he says.

"You want to help me?" I turn toward the sword rack and take one of them from its sheath with a steely rasp. I need to do something physical, to rid myself of this rush of blood roaring in my ears. "Then fight me."

"I don't think that's a good idea."

"I don't care if it's a good idea or not. She took my magic from me. She took my memories. Everything. *You*." Meeting his eyes, I tip my chin up. "I don't remember you. You say I loved you. You say I was your wife, but it feels like you're talking about someone else."

"Do you think I don't see that in your eyes every time you look at me?"

It wasn't just me who'd lost something.

"How can I trust anyone when everything that's ever been said to me is a lie?"

"I wasn't the one lying to you," he says.

I cross to the center of the tower, the sword weaving figure-of-eights in the air. "Really? Because it feels like a lie of omission. All these days, you've been flirting with me, smirking at me, driving me crazy.... Knowing what I've lost —what I had *taken* from me—for thirteen *years*—"

"Do you think I enjoy it?" The muscle in his jaw ticks. "Having you look at me like I'm a stranger? Every year you tell me you won't forget me, and every year when you return, you don't even know me."

"That's *not* my fault."

"I know." A frustrated sigh escapes him as he draws his sword again. "I know. But it doesn't matter. It doesn't change."

"You said you have no doubt I'll break the spell. It doesn't sound like it."

A growl curls through his throat. "I have faith in you. I have to, Vi. There is no other option."

"There has to be something we can do. I won't accept this. I won't just hold my breath and hope for the best." I can't live like that. I need to do something, and if we fail, then at least we tried.

"Considering the alternative is watching your brains trickle out your ears, I don't want to take that risk."

"It's not your choice," I remind him.

And then I attack.

The swords meet in a clash of steel that vibrates up my arm. Maia help me, but he's ridiculously strong. I'll never beat him in a full-frontal attack.

I turn into a series of sharp ripostes and disengages, trying to lure him into a trap. But he's prepared, and merely arches a brow when I suddenly lunge forward.

The truth burns: he's toying with me. Not fighting me with all his skill.

Rage ignites within me.

A kick takes out the side of his knee, and I throw myself into a flurry of strokes. It feels good to let the anger wash through me. I don't have to worry about pulling my strokes —it's somewhat gratifying to realize he's forced to use all his skill now to keep me at bay.

"Getting tired?"

A fierce smile flashes white teeth at me. "I could do this all day, my love."

He lunges forward, forcing me back with a flurry of fancy footwork.

I don't know where it comes from, but as I parry his blade, driving it toward the ground, I step into him, hooking my foot behind his calf. His body slams into mine, but he's off-balance enough that I manage to kick his feet out from under him.

We both go down, the swords flying free. I hit with an *oof* and then I'm rolling. Twisting my hips to lock my legs around his and reaching for the dagger at my belt.

I put the knife to his throat with a snarl as I straddle him

For several seconds there's only silence.

The urge to strike dies down, leaving me breathless. Leaving us both breathless.

"There she is," he whispers, lying flat on his back in surrender.

There's a moment where something inside me urges me to slash my blade across his skin, to see if he'll still smile then, but somehow, I rein it in. I don't know where this anger has come from.

Thiago stills, his green eyes hooding with heat as he clasps my thigh. He tilts his head arrogantly, revealing the vulnerable skin of his throat. "Go ahead. You have me at your mercy, my love."

"Stop calling me that."

"My life is yours, my heart, my soul. It always has been, from the second I saw you, curse you. If you want it, all you have to do is take it."

My heart skips a beat.

"And if I don't want it?" I whisper, glaring down at him.

A thumb brushes against my inner thigh, and I suck in a sharp breath. Thiago's dark eyes hood as if he knows exactly what's going through my mind. "I thought we weren't going to lie to each other anymore? Or to ourselves?"

I throw the blade away with a clatter, then try to push to my feet, but he's not done.

One hand locks around my knee, pinning me atop him.

The other snatches at my wrist. I sprawl forward, slamming both palms against his chest and breathing hard.

Two hundred pounds of healthy, solid male lies beneath me. My nails curl into his chest, ruching the fabric of his shirt and drawing a hiss from him.

It had been instinct to touch him like that.

Perhaps something rising from the depths of my subconscious. My body recognizing what my mind doesn't remember.

Want. Need. Furious desire.

But with it comes a flood of uncertainty.

I tear at his grip on her wrists. "Let go of me."

"Aren't you tired of running?"

"Aren't you tired of chasing me?" I snap, and see the words strike him like a whip lash across the face.

Thiago finally lets me go, rolling out from under me and finding his feet with fluid grace. The muscles in his jaw are locked, his expression turning hard. "Perhaps you're right. Perhaps I *should* let you go."

I clamber to my feet, wanting to take the words back somehow.

But it's too late.

They're out in the open, flaying the protective armor from around his heart. I can see it in his eyes as he turns for the door.

Words can be sharper than steel, and this time I've drawn blood. The worst thing is, the wound sharp words leave can often be far more lethal than any blade. They linger, fester. They're never forgotten, even long after a flesh wound has healed.

"Wait," I whisper as the doors slam shut behind him.

It's not in me to be unkind, but I have been.

This has to be hard on him too.

What would it feel like to see your wife look at you as if you were a stranger, year after year?

"Fuck." I kick the dagger into the wall, and it hits the floor with a clatter.

I want to lick my wounds in the privacy of my rooms, but that's cowardice speaking.

And an Asturian princess doesn't back down from a fight.

Nor does she leave others to repay her debts.

23

If I think too long about it, I'll falter.

So, I don't. I stride inside the prince's bedchambers, letting the door slam behind me, an apology on my lips.

And then I stop in my tracks.

He's in the middle of washing himself. Stripped to the waist, all that glorious skin bare for my hungry gaze as he drags a washcloth across his chest to remove the sweat our fight evoked. Golden candlelight caresses his skin, painting it with ripples of gold.

The second I walk in, his gaze jerks to mine, and he freezes.

Mother of Night. I curl my fingers into a fist. *Resistance, thy name is futile.*

I can still feel his fingers brushing against my thighs and the shackle of his hands on my wrists. But seeing him like this, suggestions of shadows behind him flaring like dark wings, makes every ghostly sensation dancing over my skin more intense.

Thiago slowly resumes washing himself, heat smoldering beneath those thick lashes. The shadows behind him vanish as if they were never there. "I thought you made your feelings clear."

"I'm sorry," I say.

Because my brain's not working very well right now and words fail me.

He slowly lets the washcloth drop into the basin, his face giving nothing away. "For what?"

I can't meet his gaze, so I turn and pour us both a goblet of rich Mercian wine.

"For not remembering you. For not being what you want me to be. For... what I said before." I set the wine to my lips and swallow hastily. "I've spent all night wondering if I can trust your claims. I keep thinking, what if you're merely trying to trick me? To use me against my own people? Against my own mother?"

"Did she ask you to kill me?"

I nearly knock the goblet over. "What?"

He casts the washcloth aside and prowls toward me, dark eyes gleaming a cold, merciless green. "She often does, you know. I'm never quite sure if it's a test for you to earn her trust again or a way to twist the knife she buries in my heart every time you look at me as if you don't know me. Probably both. Adaia never likes to waste an opportunity."

"N-no, I— I...." My hands shake, but I don't dare look at them.

It's true.

It's all true.

My mother put that knife into my hand and whispered murder in my ear. She knew what she was sending me to do. She knew if I succeeded, then I would be standing over the body of my husband.

Helplessly, I look to the prince. I want to make sense of

this new world I've found myself in, but he's a whirlpool, spinning me further into confusion.

"I don't know you," I whisper.

"Yes, you do."

Thiago stops just shy of reaching for me. Water beads on his skin. I lick my lips, half tempted to touch him. *This* is the only thing I can make sense of.

"No. I'm done playing this game. I'm done *chasing* you, as you say." He captures my chin and tilts my face to his. "So stop looking at me with those eyes, Vi, unless you mean to cursed well do something about it."

I press a hesitant hand flat against his chest. His heart kicks right beneath my palm, causing my breath to hitch.

But he makes no move to touch me.

To reach for me.

And I understand then. If I want him to kiss me, then I have to make the first move. If I want his hands on my skin, then I have to put them there.

"I *hate* this." I brush my palm down his chest, confused by the heat of his skin and the urge to wrap myself in his arms, when he feels like a stranger to me.

"My chest?" he teases, but there's a hint of roughness in his voice, as if he can sense my hurt.

The humor startles me. "You know I don't hate your body."

"Don't you?" This time, his voice is a purr. His knuckles brush against my hips. "I do know you look at me quite often. Even when you profess to hate me."

"You're the one parading yourself in front of me at every opportunity."

He's getting closer, leaning into me. We stand before each other, his breath stirring over my skin and tension igniting the air between us.

"If it's any consolation," he whispers, "it gets better."

"Do they ever return?"

He pauses.

"My memories. Do they ever return? Do I ever remember the past?"

Dark silky lashes obliterate his eyes. "Only snatches of it."

Thirteen years' worth of memories. Gone.

It's not their loss that hurts so much—you can't miss what you can't remember—but the fact she stole them aches.

And maybe that's the reason I stroke my hands down his chest. I need something to anchor me, and right now, that's him.

"Help me remember, then," I whisper before pressing my lips to his.

He brushes his lips across mine—a feather stroke of a touch that leaves me hungry for more. I turn my face to chase his touch, but he draws back. Taunting me. Teasing me. The message is clear.

I bite his lower lip, nibbling on the soft flesh in a clear response. *Just try and resist me.*

Our mouths meet again, and this time he captures my wrists as he bites me back.

Dark eyes burn as they lock on me. "Oh, Vi." He slides a possessive hand behind the base of my skull and then hauls me toward him.

Our lips meet. Fuse.

It's the kiss that's been promised from the moment I met him. The one I saw in his eyes every cursed time he looked at me. Both sweet and achingly hot. Demanding. Wanting more than I thought I could give.

I stretch up on my toes, my palms sliding over the ripple

of his abdomen as his fingers curl in my hair. Then there's no more time for thought. No chance for regret. He hauls me against him as if the dams have finally broken, unleashing the fury and passion within him.

Then I'm in his arms, my thighs straddling his waist as he lurches to the right.

I gasp as my back meets the bed.

This is more than I'd intended, but as he kneels between my thighs, I can't find the breath to protest. For all that my mind holds no memories of him, my body seems to have no such qualms.

"Does this help you remember?" he breathes in my ear, his tongue lashing against my lobe as his entire weight settles upon me. "Or this?" He rocks against me, the hard grind of his erection lined up right where I want it.

Oh, sweet gods.

I arch my head back, the lash of sensation obliterating all rational thoughts. "Maybe.... Or maybe you should continue."

The rasp of his stubble brushes my throat as he kisses his way south. "How am I going?"

"Definitely... coming back to me," I gasp as that hard, callused hand finds the curve of my breast, palming it with rough urgency.

Then his hot mouth is trailing across my breast, his thumb finding my nipple through my shirt. I gasp as pure sensation arcs through me like a lightning bolt. His mouth follows his thumb, and I catch a fistful of his hair as he suckles on my nipple through the linen. *Sweet Maia.* Whatever history we might have shared, he clearly knows my body as intimately as he knows his own.

"How's this?" he breathes, looking up the length of my body with a devilish smile on his lips.

"Sweet goddess." I drag his face to mine, capturing that wicked mouth before it can do any more damage.

Our lips fuse, and I can feel the passion igniting between us. Thiago ravages my mouth like a drowning man seeking water. My nails rake down his bare shoulders, digging into pure muscle, and a groan tears from my lips as he sinks between the cradle of my thighs, rocking against me.

It's too much.

Hard fingers stroke their way up my thigh, and his gaze locks upon mine as if in challenge. Back and forth. Back and forth. Knuckles questing their way higher until I'm holding my breath, trying not to squirm. Trying not to rock my hips against him.

"The first time I fucked you, we took no time for such niceties," he tells me. "But the second time, you stole away from your mother's court and met me in the ruins of Hammerdale. You told me you couldn't betray your mother unless I promised you my heart. So I gave it to you then and there. Forever, Vi. Forever mine. And I won you over with soft kisses"—like the one he presses against my jaw—"and gentle touches"—those knuckles brush against the leather covering my thigh—"and the hot lash of my tongue, right... here."

I nearly die as his touch finds me.

He rubs those fingers between my thighs, and I've never hated my leather breeches more.

"Your mother proclaimed me a thief, Vi. But I never stole a thing that wasn't freely given. And I never will."

The touch vanishes.

"Don't you dare stop." I grab his wrist.

"No?" He bites at my lower lip, his thumb brushing back and forth over that seam, igniting a million nerves. "Then beg me, Vi. Beg me to shatter you. Beg me to break you. Beg me to make you scream."

Yes. I throw my head back, arching my spine. "Please, oh, *please.*"

He tugs at the leather of my breeches, jerking them apart roughly, and then his fingers slide beneath my waistband, slipping between the wet crevice until they find me. "Beg harder. Tell me how much you want my touch. Tell me how you can't live another moment without it."

Fuck. "Harder. More. Please. Please, Thiago."

He has his fingers inside me, and he fucks them there mercilessly, one hand pinning my wrists to the bed, and the other wreaking sweet torture.

I thrash and buck, my breath coming in sharp, harsh pants.

I see a thousand stars, biting my lip so hard I want to scream. And then he's doing exactly as he promised. His thumb presses down ruthlessly, and I don't even have the breath to beg for more. I shoot over the edge, shattering into a million tiny pieces.

He holds me through the aftermath, his face burrowed against my throat and his own harsh pants landing wetly on my skin.

Slowly, he lifts his head, capturing my gaze, and then he brings his glistening fingers to his mouth and sucks my moisture from them. "I hate every fucking moment of this curse, except for this one. The moment of surrender."

My head falls back on the bed. I don't know how I've managed to retain any of my wits at all. "How many times have we done that?"

His eyes darken, and I can sense his pain in the roughness of his voice. "Far too many times to count."

"If it's any consolation"—I let a trembling hand skate up

the plane of his chest, brushing my thumbs against the roughened stubble of his jaw—"practice makes perfect."

He nips at my fingers, then lowers himself onto all fours over me, his massive arms caging me in. "Are you asking me to continue?"

I think about it.

In my mother's court, sex is often used as a weapon or a political maneuver. I learned that lesson when I was eighteen and Etan of the Goldenhills taught me I couldn't trust a honeyed tongue or a passionate kiss. While the other women of the court enjoyed such pursuits, or laid their own, I was somewhat choosier.

Sex isn't just a means to an end for me. Nor is it a means to answer the questions that brew inside me. I need those questions answered first, before I allow him to take further intimacies.

"I—"

He presses a finger to my mouth. "You don't need to say it. I can see it in your eyes."

Thiago leans down, replacing his finger with his lips as he presses the softest of kisses to my mouth. My resolve is just beginning to weaken when he finally breaks the kiss.

A dark smile curls over his mouth as he pushes away from the bed. "Let me know if you want to test your memory again. Until then…. You'd best get dressed, Vi. Before I forget my promise to give you time to remember me."

A pent-up breath explodes from me as he strides toward the chair where his shirt lies. But it can't slake the furious burn of unfulfilled desire.

"You bastard."

Thiago laughs as he snatches up his shirt. "Your move, Vi. It's always been your move."

24

I t takes me several days to recover from the onslaught of the curse breaking. I spend those days either sleeping or roaming the battlements of Ceres, looking down at the town.

I know now why Thiago kept me locked away up here.

There are too many people in the town who know who I am. All it would take would be one slip, and then the curse's steely trap might have snapped shut and driven me mad.

It reminds me of my mother's court. Doors slamming in my face. All those nobles and emissaries glancing at me from a distance before they were whisked away. It was never obvious how closely guarded I was, but my mother ascertained I was kept away from anyone who might reveal the truth.

All those lonely hours in the stables or in the library were merely another sort of prison.

"Vi," Thiago calls, breaking me out of my reverie. He's striding along the battlements toward me. "The others are in my war chamber. Do you think you're ready to join us?"

After days of mindless recovery, I'm ready to rejoin even my mother's court.

Or not quite.

Surely, I'm not that desperate for company.

"I would love to."

He escorts me inside, and I can feel the tension in his silence. We haven't touched since that day. Nor have we kissed. Sometimes he looks at me as if he's still silently counting how many kisses I owe him, but I haven't dared broach the subject.

I needed time, and he gave it to me.

The others are gathered in the audience chamber.

"Welcome, my princess," Finn says, bowing again as if we're meeting for the first time. I don't know where he's been, but it wasn't in the city.

"Is he always like this?" I ask Thalia.

"Always," she admits, rolling her eyes. "Finn would flirt with your dead grandmother."

Eris mutters into her wine, "Though his favorite flirtation is with the mirror."

Finn shakes his head.

"I can't quite remember why I missed you, Princess," he says. "Or these moments where the three of you decide to cast such vile lies upon my innocent ears."

"Someone has to contain your enormous sense of arrogance," Eris tells him.

"And that someone is you?" he asks coolly, stealing her wineglass and draining it before she even has a chance to snatch for it. "If you were any other woman, I'd be questioning just what your fascination with challenging my pride is."

"It's a good thing I'm not any other woman," she points out, just as coolly. "And it amuses me, nothing more."

"Nothing less," Finn murmurs.

Eris looks like she wants to stab him.

Thalia gives me a quelling look that clearly says we'll speak about it later and tucks my arm through hers. "We've all missed you, Vi. Thiago said you needed time to recover, but I was starting to suspect he'd locked you away so he could have you all to himself."

I can't deny her words.

They must assume we.... That everything is back to the way it was.

"I have news," Thiago announces, as if he's eager to divert their attention too. "Finn managed to rendezvous with Cian along the borders."

So that's where he was.

"And?" Baylor asks.

He doesn't join the teasing, and I can't help noticing he sits a little way away from the others.

"Cian claims Angharad is sending her Heartless south to search for something called *leanabh an dàn*," Finn says. "She's satisfied with her progress with Mistmere, but apparently this *leanabh an dàn* is a crucial step in her plans. She needs to get her hands on it."

Baylor's tapping fingers still. "Are you sure that's what she called it?"

"He's sure," Thiago replies.

I wrap my arms around my middle, uncomfortable at the thought of listening to one of the Unseelie. "Can we trust him? What if it's a trap?"

"We can trust him," Thiago replies. "His loyalty is to me." He turns back to Baylor. "My knowledge of the Old Tongue is rusty with disuse. I'm translating it as *child of destiny*, but I'm not sure what that means."

Baylor scrubs at his mouth.

I've been trying to avoid him since he arrived, but his eyes shift to me as if he's aware of it.

"There's an old myth that there were children born from the seed of the Old Ones," he says. "The children of destiny. Of fate. Of power. But.... They were hunted to death once the wars were over."

"But aren't the Old Ones locked away?"

"Why do we light the bonfires on Lammastide?" Baylor asks. "Why do we sing the old songs on Samhain? Why do the stones guard the Hallows?"

My mouth tastes dry. "Because the Veils thin on those nights, and their prison worlds align with ours."

"It's rumored the Old Ones can walk this world twice a year," he continues. "Beltane and Samhain. Their powers are muted, and they're forced to return by morning or risk seeing their soul cleaved from their bodies, but it's possible."

"We bound their souls to the prison world," Finn explains. "It's how they were trapped. Their souls cannot pass the Veil."

"Am I the only one in this room who wasn't born when they walked the world?" I ask.

Everyone exchanges a look.

Baylor, Finn, and Thiago have clearly known each other for years. There's a hint of brotherhood between them, though Thiago is clearly the leader.

"I wasn't," Eris says gruffly. "But I've seen the ruins and heard the stories. It's enough to know they shouldn't return."

Thalia shrugs. "I was very young."

"So somewhere out there, a child was born from one of the Old Ones," Thiago murmurs, a strange intensity lighting his eyes. "Perhaps even several children. And Angharad wants to get her hands on one of them."

"What would that mean?" Eris demands. "What sort of threat are we looking at?"

"The Old Ones were immensely powerful, their magic drawing upon the ley lines," he replies. "Any child could potentially do the same."

"We'd be facing them again," Finn says, looking horrified.

I hold my hands up. "We don't know that any child would be a threat."

"How could they not be?" Baylor demands.

"I'm not as concerned with any child," Thiago says. "If they're out there, then they haven't yet reached their full potential or we'd know of it. No, I'm more interested in what Angharad wants with them."

"Their power," Eris snorts.

"Their ability to control the ley lines," adds Finn.

"Their link to the Old Ones," Baylor says quietly.

It's this last statement that causes the room to fall quiet.

"Could they do that?" I ask.

"The Old Ones had worshippers who could act as a conduit of their powers," Thiago replies. "I don't see why any child of theirs wouldn't be able to serve the same purpose." He frowns. "Angharad worshipped the Horned One. If she wants this child—these children—then it's for a purpose that bodes ill."

I know enough to know the Horned One is the last Old One the world wants to see again. The Unseelie King, Hyperion, served as his conduit and sought to rule the world, driving his followers south to conquer the continent. Angharad was once his lover, and she'd do anything to see him resurrected.

Though Hyperion fell in battle, Angharad stole his body away, and there are rumors she keeps him entombed on a mythical island in the north, which was warded away from the ravages of time. There he slumbers in the Gray between life and death, with his crown still resting upon his brow and his hands clasped around his sword.

Waiting for her to restore him.

If she somehow accesses the Horned One's power, then she could bring Hyperion back. I never lived through the wars, but I can see them painted in a swift blur of prediction. Blood. Death. Catastrophic blasts of magic. More cities would fall. Thousands would die. The Horned One would walk again.

And this time, he'd be prepared for any trap.

"What do we do?"

"Find the child," Baylor says, "and kill them."

"No." There has to be some other way. "How could we blame a child? It's not its fault it was born to such vile creatures." I turn to Thiago helplessly.

He meets my gaze, but there's no help there. Only cold, implacable resolve. "It's entirely possibly any child would be an adult by now. They could even be centuries old, though I suspect we would have felt the stirrings of their magic by now if they were."

Is it any better to kill an adult than a child?

Especially when they've done nothing wrong except for having the misfortune to be born to a cursed bloodline?

"Ah, I see. We only protect the innocent when it suits us."

His lips thin. "If the loss of one innocent can prevent an entire fucking war and stop our worst nightmare from walking this world again, then yes. We could end it, Vi, before it's already begun. All we have to do is find the child…. I see it as a necessary loss."

I press my hands on the table and lean toward him.

"Well, I don't. There's nothing to say this offspring will help Angharad or free the Horned One. What if it uses its powers for our side?"

"Where's my Asturian princess now?" he demands. "Think with your head, not your heart, Vi. Angharad's a vicious bloodsucking vulture. She doesn't need this child's consent. All she needs is to be able to get her hands on something that has the power and the blood link that can bring the Horned One back and resurrect Hyperion. Innocent or not, I don't want to take that chance."

"You know," I say hotly, "that's the first time you've ever sounded like my mother."

He draws back as if slapped.

Silence falls across the room.

Even Eris studiously avoids my gaze.

"I may disagree with your mother on most things," Thiago says in a quiet, deadly voice as he pushes to his feet, "but when it comes to the Old Ones, she and I have very similar feelings. You weren't born when they walked the earth. You don't know war. You've never lost your entire family to their cults of sacrifice. All you see is a child, a single child, that might stand between an entire world and its fate. Perhaps you should consider that future? Because if we don't make a small sacrifice now, then what sort of world will that child grow into? What sort of torture and punishment will it know if she captures it?"

"There has to be another way."

"If you think I wouldn't take it if there was, then you don't know me at all." He turns away from the table, cloak flaring around his ankles as he strides toward the doors.

They slam behind him, leaving me alone with a roomful of his allies.

And a hard lump in my throat.

I'm not wrong.

I'm not.

But neither is he.

To rule is not a gift, one of my tutors once said, *but a burden.*

"Well," Finn says, all four feet of his chair hitting the floor as he leans forward, "that was fun."

"You have a warped idea of fun," Eris mutters. "It's not enough to face the Queen of Thorns on one flank, now we have to worry about that pasty bitch in the north and some sort of spawn with the power of the Old Ones?"

"Eris, my love," he says, lifting her hand to his lips. "While I adore your smile, I've not seen it in an age. We're alive. We know what Angharad is planning in a general sense. And we can stop it. And of course, let us not forget the sheer entertainment gained from watching our mighty prince tremble in the wake of his princess's wrath."

I share a look with Eris. "So glad I could amuse you."

"Oh, it's not you that amuses me." He winks. "I've watched this play out a dozen times now, and every time, it plays a different tune."

"Sometimes you shouldn't open your mouth," Eris says and rolls her eyes.

"I think, for once, I'm in agreement with Eris."

Then I turn and escape the room before my suspiciously hot eyes embarrass me.

It's Thalia who comes after me.

I sit on the edge of the parapets, staring out over the golden city of Ceres. Fae bustle through the city, going about their lives completely unaware of the argument we had today.

These fae will die if Angharad and her forces attack the city. Or perhaps they'll march to their deaths in the north.

We could end it, Vi, before it's already begun. All we have to do is find the child....

One death balanced against many. Can I even blame him for suggesting it?

"He's on edge," Thalia points out, seating herself beside me. "It's bound to make him short tempered."

"He's been like this for days," I mutter.

She peers at me. "He's worried about the deadline. It always wears on him."

There are only four weeks left until I'm to be returned to my mother. Three months sounded like such a long time when she announced this treaty, but now each day seems like the tick of a clock heralding our doom.

Four weeks to fall in love with him.

Four weeks in which to hope I'll remember him when she takes me back.

Four weeks to break this fucking curse.

"I don't want to hurt him," I whisper. "But how can I let him do this to a child?"

"It might not be a child."

"Does it matter?" I meet her eyes. "Whatever age it is, it's not its fault."

"Why does it bother you so much?" she asks. "Your mother's court is ruthless. She's known for making decisions like these for the good of her people."

I don't know the answer to that.

Or maybe I do.

"My mother's used me as a puppet for years," I tell her bitterly. "I know Thiago thinks this is the best course of

action, but... he didn't even think there might be another
option. Nor did he ask for my opinion. He just made the
decision. Judge. Jury. Executioner. I know what it's like to be
pushed and pulled on the whims of another, my life not my
own." I bow my head, resting my chin on my knees. "There's
a little piece of me that feels as though he's talking of me
when he speaks of this *leanabh an dàn*. Some poor bastard
out there is blithely unaware his life is about to end, and for
what? The pure, unfortunate luck of his birth? It's not fair."

"Thiago's never cruel." She rests a hand on mine. "And
he's used to making these decisions by himself. I don't think
it's deliberate. He's never ruled with you by his side. He's
never had the chance. It's not that he's not listening to you."

"So I should just accept his judgement on this matter?"

Of course she's on his side. She's his cousin.

"Pffawh. No!" Thalia waves a hand in horror. "Let him
grovel. He'll come around once he's had time to release
some of his stress." A grin lights her face when she sees my
dubious look. Before I can move, she leans forward and
hugs me. "I know you don't remember me, but we were
friends. And I love watching you twist him in knots each
and every time. The pair of you were made for each other."

For the first time in months, I feel as though I've finally
found an ally. Maybe some of my memories are creeping
back, for I'm not normally so swift to relax around strangers,
but I can't help leaning into her hug.

"He still seems a stranger," I confess.

Thalia draws back, waggling her eyebrows. "You can fix
that."

Heat crawls up my cheeks. "Are you sure you're not
working on his side?"

"If it's any consolation, you seem to enjoy being in his
bed as much as he does."

I can't help thinking of all that naked skin on display while we were stuck in that hunting cabin.

"Maybe I *should* make him grovel."

"On his knees," Thalia suggests, with a wicked grin that reminds me of the prince so badly, I feel a little twinge somewhere in the vicinity of my chest.

"Now I know the pair of you are related."

She laughs, then pushes to her feet and stretches. "Come on! Let's go raid the kitchen. The head spriggan is an old friend, and I smelled the delicious waft of some of her pastries as I was heading up here."

THAT NIGHT, there's a knock on my bedroom door.

"Come in," I call.

I was expecting Thalia, come to bring me a cup of warmed milk and honey, but the prince strides in as if he's master of my bedchamber.

He pauses by the window, hands clasped behind his back.

"What did you want?" I can't forget our earlier argument, or the way he stormed out. Nor can I forget the aftermath of what happened in the tower.

And neither does he, judging by the heated look in his eyes.

"I won't apologize," he says. "I have my people to think of. Every fae in this world will suffer if this *leanabh an dàn* isn't found before Angharad can get her hands on him or her."

I close the book with a sharp little snap. "And I won't apologize for what I said either. I do think the life of one child, one soul, is worth more than a sacrifice. Surely there has to be some other way to prevent this."

"Which is why I'm here," he tells me. "I will give you two weeks to help me find this *leanabh an dàn* before I decide its fate—"

"Before *you* decide?" Incredible.

His eyes light with wicked fire. "Before *we* decide its fate. To do that, we need to know more about Angharad's plans."

"Your friend Cian can't tell you?"

"He's currently busy," Thiago replies, "and I don't want to risk his deception within the Unseelie court."

Interesting. Cian must be highly placed in the Unseelie world if he's close to Angharad.

Slinging my legs over the edge of the bed, I sit up. "Then how are we to discover her plans?"

"We're going to Stormhaven," he says.

Another slap in the face.

Prince Kyrian rules the Isle of Stormhaven. "Do you... think that's wise?"

"Kyrian's met you in the past. You were never friends, but he won't harm you. Not unless he wants to face me."

"But why Stormhaven?"

"Can I trust you not to share this information with your mother?"

"Right now," I reply coldly, "the only things I want to share with my mother are my thoughts on this entire arrangement. Loudly. I'm not her little puppet anymore. I'm no one's puppet"—this with a warning glare in his direction —"and she hasn't bothered to contact me again."

He leans back against the doors. "Kyrian is the Master of Storms. He has a device that can see and listen through any droplet of water in the realms. He can spy on Angharad for me."

That's a powerful weapon in the wrong hands, because, while I've heard of sorcerers being able to use mirrors for such a purpose, you can always ward them.

Water is everywhere.

"When do we leave?"

"At first light. I'll wake you at dawn," he promises, turning toward the door. "Be ready."

He's halfway through when I can't bear it anymore. This odd sense of tension looms between us, and I don't know how to break it.

"Wait."

He pauses there, glancing back. "Yes?"

My heart starts racing. "I owe you a kiss."

"I thought you needed time."

I don't think time's going to make any difference to the mess of confusion in my head, but maybe this will.

I close the distance between us and, pressing a hand to his chest, stretch up on my toes. "Are you declining my offer?"

Thiago's eyelids hood his eyes, his breath whispering over my mouth. "Never."

"Thank you." I whisper the words against his lips. "For listening to me about this *leanabh an dàn*."

And then I lean into the kiss.

His mouth softens beneath mine, dangerously carnal in its allure.

It's a different kiss than the one we shared when I nearly set the bed on fire. This one is soft with longing, and I can feel the anger in him softening, all his harsh edges easing as he leans into me.

The heat of his mouth is becoming familiar. More so when his hand slides down my spine and cups my ass aggressively. The action grinds me against him, and I break the kiss with a gasp.

It's more than I expected.

And the look in his eyes says he'd like to throw me over his shoulder and slam me down on the bed if he could.

Or against a wall, where I could wrap my legs around his hips.

Or maybe those are just my thoughts, tempted by the solid heat of this male and the promise in his eyes. *Dangerous, dangerous, dangerous.*

This time, there's a smile on his lips when he sees the effect he has on me.

"Sweet dreams, Princess," he says, lifting my hand to his mouth and brushing a kiss there, his eyes shining with feral intensity.

He's picturing it too.

I know it.

I curl my hand into a fist. Thalia suggested I simply enjoy what he's offering, but some part of me can't help feeling as though, if I make that decision, I'll send the pair of us hurtling to a final, desperate conclusion.

25

The next day, Thiago leads me to the chambers that house the Hallow. It's in the second-tallest tower of the palace, overlooking the sprawl of city below.

I peer through the arched windows, hungry for the sight of his city. Golden Ceres is known as the City of the Dawn, and with its rough-hewn sandstone, golden banners, and gleaming blue rooves, it looks it. The sea glistens in the distance, and gulls wheel through the air. It teems with life, a stark contrast to Valerian.

"This is the political center of Evernight," the prince muses, resting a hand on the arch at my side, his body caging me in the open window. "Though I often feel more at home in Valerian despite the snows and the wraiths."

"You feel like you belong in your City of the Dead?" It's a strange confession to make.

He glances toward me, the sharp lines of his cheekbones giving him a feral sort of beauty. There's an untamed wildness to his features that's both alluring and unnerving. I can't help feeling as though he'd shed this skin if he could, with all its courtly trappings, and reveal the real man beneath.

"Ceres was built by my queen," Thiago says softly, turning his gaze back to the city. "Those golden banners aren't mine. If you look closely, you'll see the rising dawn emblem upon them."

My gaze returns to them, understanding exactly what he's not saying.

This city may belong to him, but some of the fae here will never accept him.

"Some of the city folk call me 'abomination' when they think I can't hear them." His voice drops to a soft croon. "Sometimes I walk the city in a cloak of illusions, and I hear them talk of the old days when the queen ruled. Of her legitimate sons. Prince Emyr was a monster, and Prince Arawn no warrior, but to hear the fae speak of it, both were heroes. They forget the day Emyr had forty craftsmen strung up for protesting the new taxes. They ignore the little girl he rode over when she didn't move out of his way fast enough. Everywhere he went, he filled the ground with coffins and the streets with blood. His mother despaired of ever breaking him of his arrogance and cruelty, but she merely sent him to different posts in the hopes he'd stop. That's the monster they call the True Heir."

"History often softens the stark reality of the truth."

"And I'm an impure bastard who murdered the rightful heirs and stole their mother's throne." This time, his smile holds edges. "When Emyr was a golden-haired warrior with a smile that could light up a room."

"I think your Emyr would have made a wonderful consort for my mother." I wrinkle my nose. "It's always the blonds."

"You bear a grudge? It wouldn't have anything to do with your very blond mother and sister, would it?"

He's caught me out.

"All my life I hated my hair," I admit. While Andraste looked like a perfect little replica of Mother, I was the ugly, dark cuckoo in the nest. "I paid a travelling peddler forty gold pieces when I was twelve to chant a spell that would strip the color from it."

"What happened?"

"The color faded and the peddler moved on. I was delighted. Until I woke the next morning to find my hair had fallen out. It was all over my pillow, and my mother was furious at my stupidity." She'd ordered me shaved bald, and I was locked in my rooms, with only a nurse for company, until it grew back. "If it's any consolation, I find *myself* partial to green eyes and dark hair."

Thiago's gaze darts to mine. "Do you?"

The tension in his shoulders softens as I press my back into the stone of the arch, turning my entire body toward him. "Do you think I'd stand in an open arch with my enemy behind me if I wasn't bedazzled by his pretty eyes?"

"I thought we were past the 'enemies' part of this?"

"I'm still considering the notion. I don't know what comes after 'enemies.'"

"That's easy." His voice grows rough. "We kiss. We argue. We fall into bed. We fuck."

My cheeks heat. I'd wondered if he'd mention that.

Thiago brings his hand to my cheek, brushing his knuckles against the smooth skin there. "But you're the one who makes that decision. I won't steal into your bed, Vi. You're the one who's going to have to do that."

"I'm sorry."

"Don't be. You only just woke to the truth; you're entitled

to feel confused about it all." He gives a sly smile. "And for every day you make me wait, I'll repay you with an hour of sensual torture."

Help.

I stare at him breathlessly. "Doesn't that behoove me to make you wait longer?"

Thiago leans closer, stealing a soft kiss from my lips. "That depends." He takes a step back, finally giving me some space to breathe. "On whether your willpower is stronger than temptation."

It's not.

I know it's not.

I want to throw up the white flag of surrender right here, to taste more of that kiss he barely gave me.

And some part of it must show on my face, because he draws back and laughs. "Willpower, Vi."

It's a smoky sound that curls inside me, as though he's somehow infected me.

"I'm trying to remember why this is a bad idea."

"Oh, it's not. It's a very, very good idea," he croons. "But we're supposed to arrive in Stormhaven within the hour, and an hour's not long enough to do any of what I have planned."

I close my eyes. Images dance there, of the pair of us tangled together on heated sheets. "That isn't helping."

Thiago chuckles under his breath. "It wasn't supposed to. Come. Kyrian will be waiting for us."

I can't help watching him as he strides toward the center of the Hallow. Thiago wears power like a mantle, but there's a hint of old wounds showing beneath his careful words.

I wondered why he surrounded himself with the misfits and outcasts like Eris and Baylor. In my mother's court, they would have been shunned and despised, regardless of their powers.

Now I know.

Because he's an outcast himself. Even here, in the city he rules, they know him as the enemy.

THIAGO ACTIVATES THE HALLOW.

It's unusual to have one here, inside a building. They're usually found in mossy forests or atop old barrows. The stones that guard them like silent sentinels are still here, though the columns line the circular room.

"Ready?" Thiago asks, reaching out to take my hand.

For the Prince of Tides? Never. But I nod anyway.

Thiago gave me two weeks to help find this *leanabh an dàn*. I'm not going to let one of my mother's worst enemies bar me from helping.

Thirteen Hallows were created to lock the Old Ones away, but once their other use as portals was discovered, more were created. Not merely prisons, but means of transport between kingdoms.

This is not an origin Hallow.

It's clear this was built after the wars.

The world flashes past in a shimmer of green as the glyphs light up, and then my stomach starts to turn.

There's an odd hum within the portal. "Is that supposed to be doing that?"

Thiago frowns.

Power washes over us. Not so much like a soothing tide, as usual, but a raging sea. It sends me spinning, tumbling through a vortex of magic unlike anything I've ever known.

Waves of pure magic crash over me, drenching me in its warm liquid gush.

We're thrown forward, tossed about like jetsam caught in the barrel roll of a wave. I lose Thiago's hand, tumbling endlessly, endlessly—

This isn't normal.

It's never felt like this before.

A hand plucks at my hair, and then a woman appears before me, crafted almost singularly of seafoam. Green seaweed forms her hair, and her brows are dark and frowning over fierce eyes. "You are not welcome here, *miatha lin*."

She bares sharp teeth at me, lunging toward my throat.

I scream as her teeth sink into my tender flesh and punch her directly in the side of the face. It's enough to tear her loose long enough to break free. And then I'm spinning again, churned about like clothes in a copper wash pot. Salt water washes up my nose and down my throat, until it's all I can taste.

The portal spits me out on a rocky shore, coughing and gagging on seawater.

I'm still fighting, trying to wrestle my way free, only to discover the firm hands locked on my shoulders belong to Thiago.

"Vi!"

I spit out a mouthful of salt, only to find his fingers have captured my chin and he's tilting my face to the side. I slap it away, but he holds up bloodied fingers.

"What happened?" he demands.

The prince, as usual, looks like he just sauntered out of a bedroom. No sign of wet clothes, only slightly tousled hair. I'm sure I look like a drowned sailor.

"Did you see her?" I gasp, scraping bedraggled hair out of my face.

He offers me a hand. "See who? And what happened to you? Why are you wet?"

I tell him about the woman who tried to drown me, but his eyebrows merely draw together in a frown. "That's impossible."

"What's impossible?"

He glances at the jagged stones that stand on the rocky beach like solitary sentinels. "She sounds like one of the saltkissed, but they were banished along with the Father of Storms."

The saltkissed.

"But they're trapped." I look around. "Here. They were trapped here."

I know enough of my history to know where each of the Old Ones was trapped. The Father of Storms made his final stand on this beach before being lured between the standing stones.

Thiago presses his hand against the nearest stone. The tattoos on his throat writhe, so I know he's using his power, but nothing else manifests.

He shakes his head and lowers his hand. "I can't sense anything, but this is troubling. The portals take us into the World Between Worlds for the brief moments it takes for us to travel. If one of the saltkissed managed to manifest there, it might mean the prison walls are weakening."

"Do you think this has anything to do with Angharad?"

"I don't know."

We stare at each other.

There are a few too many troubling details coming to light of late. It can't be coincidence.

First, Angharad starts toying with Mistmere. Then we

hear whispers that a child born of the Old Ones might be walking the world. And now, the Hallow on Stormhaven Isle is reacting weirdly.

I reach out to touch one of the stones and hear the hiss of the saltkissed woman in my ears.

Yanking my hand back, I swallow hard.

"What did you feel?" Thiago's at my side in an instant, his callused hands capturing mine.

"I heard her again. It's as though... the Veil between both worlds is thin here. And she's waiting on the other side for me."

"Why you?" He searches my face.

"She called me *miatha lin.*"

Instantly, he frowns. "It's the language they spoke on this world before we arrived. The language of the Old Ones. 'Promise of one,' I think. I haven't spoken it in several hundred years. Perhaps Kyrian will have a better grasp than I do. He loves to lock himself away up there with his library and his brandies."

I stare at the stony cliffs that shear into the blue skies. Fierce, winged drakon soar through the skies and hover at cave mouths in the cliffs above us. They distract me for a second, but I'm not here for the fauna.

"What if there's something wrong with the Hallows?"

It's a question neither of us have dared broach.

Thiago's eyes darken. "Then we pray and hope that Maia hears us."

STORMHAVEN RESTS on a rocky crag overlooking the Innesmuch Sea.

The lord of the Kingdom of Stormlight has never been on good terms with my mother. Though really, who is?

And while Queen Adaia and Thiago might be bitter enemies, the enmity between her and Prince Kyrian is the stuff of legends. It's said that he loved a maid of the sea once, only to lose her when the oceans called her home. My mother had her minstrel compose a song about it to mock him, and Lord Kyrian sent her the minstrel's tongue and fingers in a box.

"Are you sure I should be here?" I'm not looking forward to it.

"Don't worry," Thiago drawls. "He doesn't bite."

I stare at the long, stone staircase that wends its way up the cliff face. "Do we have to...?"

"Yes." Thiago flashes me a smile. "Consider it your exercise for the day."

"You seem remarkably cheerful." I look at those stairs again. I can already feel my thighs groaning. Curse it.

"Here," he says, setting foot upon them. "I'll even go first, so you can stare at my ass the whole way."

"How very thoughtful of you."

I set myself to the climb. As suspected, it's brutal and merciless and I hate the prince more and more with each step. "This isn't helping your cause," I mutter as we near the top. Or at least, I hope it's the top. Every corner we turn, my hopes fade when I see another rise. "Why couldn't Kyrian have installed lifting platforms? I've seen them at Greycliffes. They're marvelous devices."

"Because," calls a voice rich with melody, "it amuses me to see my visitors huffing and puffing up my stairs. Especially if they're enemies. It takes a bit of the fight out of them."

I follow Thiago around the next curve of the cliff, and

the stairs finally flatten out into an expansive balcony overlooking the seas. Stone sea serpents wend their way along
the edge, forming a natural rail. I swear their polished brass
eyes watch me as I pass between them.

"Thiago." There's a tall, lean fae male waiting there, clad
in leather from top to toe and wearing a pirate's swagger. He
flashes a dangerous smile as he clasps Thiago's hand and
claps him on the back. "It's been a long time, my old friend."

"Not long enough, you bastard. I remember now why I
don't visit more often."

Seeing the two of them standing together is either a
woman's best fantasy, or a gift from Maia.

Kyrian's dark eyes flicker to me, his smile thinning a
little. "Princess Iskvien, you're as beautiful as the stars say
you are."

"Are you on speaking terms with them?"

"Every night," he purrs. "Haven't you heard me whisper
in your dreams?"

"One can hardly compete with the stars," I mutter. He's
not what I expected, at all. Nor is he the man haunting my
dreams.

"Don't make me throw you off this cliff," Thiago says.
"Vi's not the only one who had to climb those fucking
stairs."

"If the rumors are true, you wouldn't have had to."

"What rumors?" I ask.

Thiago's brows darken. "Ignore him. He's been sniffing
the sea breeze for too long. Empties his head."

Kyrian throws back his head and laughs.

There's a certain sense of earthy rawness to the sound, as
if the sea has given him a raspy undertone. Though his face
is formed of near perfection—those lips a little too full, and
his lashes a little too long—there's also something feral

about it. Not for him a court full of polished courtiers and bowing sycophants, I suspect. No, he looks like he'd be just as comfortable on the swaying deck of a ship as sitting on a throne. Comfortable anywhere he stood, even if it was a prison cell.

I wish I felt the same sense of confidence.

"Come this way," Kyrian calls, turning and striding toward the stone arches that seem to lead directly into a castle hewn into the rock. "I've had my servants send for refreshments. You seem as though you need them."

KYRIAN SINKS onto the enormous carved stone throne in the middle of his audience hall, kicking his legs over one arm and snapping his fingers for wine. "So tell me, to what do I owe the pleasure?"

"You'd know that if you bothered to show up for the alliance meeting." There's nothing to say Thiago is angry except for the cool, supercilious arch to his brow.

"I had better things to do rather than waste my time watching three petty bitches try to put me in my supposed place."

Servants spring forward, a pair of women wearing gowns of berry red that drape at the throat, leaving their backs and spines bare. Though they offer us refreshments, there's a fierceness in their eyes that leaves me in no doubt that they're not merely servants, and I'm fairly certain the golden ornaments in their hair have sharp ends.

"As much as they irritate me too, we need them," Thiago replies, accepting a glass.

"It's debatable." Kyrian's eyes flash fire and he glances at me.

"She knows."

There's a faint softening of the Prince of Tides' shoulders. He rubs his finger around the rim of his wineglass. "Year by year, it all plays out the same way. You must be weary of the game by now, old friend."

"Would you be weary? If that was Meriana?"

Kyrian's finger stills on the glass.

"No. I would not be weary. I would spend a thousand summers hunting the seas so I could cut that bitch's heart from her chest while she watched."

Meriana.

That was the name of the woman he'd once loved.

But it's clear that whatever emotions he felt toward her have long since faded.

"And I would spend a thousand winters waiting for my wife to recognize me, if that was what it took," Thiago replies in a deadly soft voice. "But she's right here, so perhaps you can stop talking over her head as if she's not."

Kyrian shoots me a disdainful smile. "I used to think love was a gift, but it's not. It's a poison, slowly ingested over years, and it's ultimately fatal. Remember that, Your Highness, when you must return home to your mother again. Because you're leading him to a slow, steady death as surely as the sun will set in the west, and I don't think the bastard has the strength to avoid his fate now."

The words stun me.

I think I understand Eris's anger toward me—she cares for her prince. But Kyrian's anger feels more intimate, as though he's seeing another face painted over mine and his words are intended for her.

That doesn't make them feel any less personal.

Or true.

I don't know what I feel toward Thiago—the entire revelation was such an upheaval I'm still finding my feet—but I know when he looks at me, he sees his entire world. It makes me feel safe and overwhelmed and nervous.

Nobody has ever loved me.

It's all I ever longed for when I was a little girl, and it feels as though that dream has been delivered on a gold platter, but I somehow missed the steps leading up to it.

I wanted someone who would never turn away from me. I wanted strong arms I could curl up in when night fell and I was alone with all those little thoughts that eat at me sometimes. I wanted someone to protect me, someone who would fight for me, someone who would always be there for me.

But what if I get him killed?

What if all I do is take and take and take, until there's nothing left?

Those dreams were a child's dreams, but I'm a woman now, and I know sometimes the world can be cruel.

"If you felt any sense of love for him, you would set him free," Kyrian continues. "Or you may as well put a blade in his heart right now and end it mercifully."

Those words hammer at me.

Because they echo my own thoughts.

And the only way to quell them is to lash out. "I can't remember what happened to this Meriana, or why you feel such vitriol toward her, but perhaps what you felt for her wasn't love, if you think of it as poison. And if anyone did the deed, then you did it to yourself."

His eyes drop to half-mast, heat flaring in their amber depths. "You dare?"

I sip my wine. Perhaps I can thank my mother for granting me the grace to face such malice with no reaction. "I thought we were exchanging insults? Did you want me to sit here in silence and shed a tear at your words? Perhaps I should simper a little?"

"You know, I never did see a resemblance to your mother until this moment, but you've well proven your—"

"That's enough," Thiago says in his midnight voice, the one that expects to be obeyed. "The both of you." He turns to Kyrian. "We came here as guests. As friends. And this is how you greet us?"

Kyrian's fingers twitch. "My apologies, Princess. I did not mean to offend you."

It's a lie, and we both know it.

But I'm genuinely sorry for my part in it. There's a deep reservoir of anger within me, a hot coal slowly gathering heat. But he's not the target. And I shouldn't take my anger out on him. I need to save it for my mother. "I'm sorry if my words caused you pain."

Kyrian waves the apology away. "Well, let's hear it. You didn't come all this way just to offend me."

Thiago wastes no time. "Angharad's been seen in Mistmere, trying to resurrect the Hallow."

"Why?"

"We don't know," Thiago replies. "Hence, why we're here."

Kyrian stares into his wine a little moodily. "Surely that bitch has better things to do than dabble with the Mother of Night."

"She's also looking for something she calls *leanabh an dàn*."

"Child of destiny," Kyrian says.

Thiago tells him the theory about a child belonging to the Old Ones, and how he thinks Angharad wants to use it to access some of the Old Ones powers.

"This is... troubling. I'll see what my sources have to say,"

Kyrian murmurs, pushing to his feet. "In the meantime, why don't you both enjoy the pleasures of Stormhaven? I'll have rooms prepared. Or is it just one room?"

There's no malice in his eyes, but the words are a challenge.

"Two," I say, just as Thiago says, "One."

We both look at each other.

"Two," I repeat in a softer voice, because I don't know that I have the willpower to deny him if we're forced to share a room.

And a bed.

26

The city that surrounds the base of the keep is carved from stone and weathered by eons of storms. But there's a sense of revelry in the back alleys, and paper lanterns are strung across narrow streets, giving it a sense of cheer. The city attracts those who find a living on the seas, though it's rarely a legitimate trade. Too many cutlasses strapped at everyone's hips, and gold winking in a fae smile.

Thiago leads me to a restaurant overlooking the Hallow, where there's a stone balcony that gives us both a semblance of privacy and a view. Vines snake across the strand of lanterns, and vibrant pink flowers dangle from their tips. Tiny little demi-fey the likes I've never seen before flit from flower to flower, sipping on the sweet nectar.

Kyrian promised he'd have more information on what Angharad is planning by morning, which leaves us with a night to explore the city.

And perhaps, to simply enjoy each other's company.

"A man of many talents," I mutter. "He can insult me in one breath and then promise us answers in the next."

Thiago's eyes narrow, and his fingers tap, just once, against the table. "Don't forget, you belong to me, Princess."

I lean forward, nursing the wine. It's made me feel bold. "I belong to myself, Your Highness. And you'd do well to remember it."

He captures my hand, toying with my fingers. "You've always been your own woman. It's what attracted me in the first place. But don't play games. Not with other men. Not now. Don't make me kill my friend."

My breath catches.

Is he jealous?

"I'm not playing games and I have no interest in your friend Kyrian," I tell him. "Nor do I have any interest in anyone else. One husband is enough, thank you."

"That's the first time you've called me that."

All this time he's been charming and seductive, but I've never gotten a glimpse of the real man. I didn't realize how much it bothers him that I'm holding him at arm's bay.

I've seen the armor.

I've seen every wink and smile he can offer.

But I've rarely seen a hint of vulnerability.

I fold a piece of thin, flat bread and sprinkle a handful of chopped tomatoes and soft cheese into it. "I'm trying."

"I know," he murmurs.

"You seem out of sorts."

"I'm usually in your bed by now." Thiago looks away, out across the star-strewn skies. "And that's not a complaint. I understand your request for two rooms. My insistence was purely for security reasons, though at least they're beside each other. But every year it takes a little longer for you to trust me. Every year, I count the days until you look at me with any sort of fondness. And every year, that day ticks closer to the time I must return you. How many years will it take, I wonder, before my wife no longer looks at me with love in her eyes?"

Silence falls between us.

"My mother does her job well. She fills my ears with poison and puts a knife in my hand and whispers of the threat you pose." Not to me. Never to me. "She paints pictures of war and how I could save my people from such harsh reality."

Because she knows I will always take the threat to my people harder than any harm against myself.

"I come to you thinking you're a monster." Only to find the man himself, with his seductive smiles and his curious charm. It makes me wonder: Have I even seen the real man yet? Or is he still stifling his true nature, trying to woo me, as it were. Trying to be soft and gentle and not to frighten me. "I need to know you," I whisper. "In all your facets. The good. The bad. The frightening. I know you can be kind, but that's not all of you. The other kingdoms wouldn't fear you so badly, if that was all of you."

His eyes dance back to mine. "I am not kind. I am a prince, and I must make hard decisions. But I will never hurt *you*, Vi. The other kingdoms fear what they don't understand, and I will always be an abomination in their eyes."

What does that mean?

"Why?" I demand. "Because my mother calls you Unseelie? Because of your Darkness. Your tattoos?"

If there is anything to fear of him, it is that.

"What are they?" I remember the snarling whisper of their voices. Five distinct voices, if I recall correctly.

Thiago's face shuts down. "They are the cost I paid to find myself in the position I now hold. And that is all, Vi. I don't want to talk about it."

"I won't tell my mother."

"I know." He forces a smile. "But tonight is for us. I want to enjoy it. Not speak of monstrous things and a bloody past. Please."

It's a small step.

This time he asks for me to set it aside.

"One day," I warn.

"One day I will tell you everything." Thiago reaches across to stroke my hand. "I promise."

There's no point arguing. It makes me insatiably curious, but then, I have my own secrets. I raise my glass to him and now. "Tonight is for us."

The server brings out steaming dish after steaming dish.

There are sweet loaves baked in some sort of leaf, and a spicy rice dish that complements the fish perfectly. Rich goat's cheese, thin wafers, and all manner of fruits spread across a platter that barely fits on the table. And finally, little cakes drizzled in honey, which I'm forced to lick from my fingers.

"Maia's breath, that was so good," I moan, once I'm finished and can no longer fit anything else inside me. "You may have to carry me to the castle."

"I was about to suggest the same."

I eye those broad shoulders. "I may need three mules and a wagon to do that."

His smile softens, though there's an odd sense of satisfaction to it rather than amusement.

"What?" I ask.

"Nothing."

My eyes narrow. "That wasn't nothing. You have that smile you sometimes wear, as if I've done something amusing."

"You seemed quiet today," Thiago replies. "It's nice to see

the familiar spark in your eyes. That's all. I wasn't sure how long it would take for you to accept this."

"How long does it usually take?"

"That depends. Usually, the spell unwinds the longer you're with me, and some memories start leeching in."

"I don't quite know what to make of all this," I admit. "I've spent weeks avoiding you, because I could sense something was wrong. You don't know what that feels like, to be aware of secrets whispered every time your back is turned."

It's almost a relief to know what they were all keeping from me.

"And... I don't know you." It's a soft, strained confession. "Oh, perhaps I've started to know you as a man, but not as my husband. And it feels like.... It feels...."

I don't want to put it into words that might hurt him.

Thiago captures my hand, his thumb rasping over the fleshy pad at the base of mine. "Truth," he says. "Always truth between us. Don't ever be afraid to say what you think to me. It might not be what I want to hear, but I'd much prefer that, rather than wondering if you're too afraid to speak plainly." He leans forward. "I know this has all been a shock. I know it's all new. I *know* you, Vi. And while I might wish I was in your bed, I'm content to wait until you're ready. You don't owe me anything you don't want to give tonight, Vi."

It releases some of the tension in my shoulders.

"It feels confusing." I squeeze his hand back. "I think I was almost more at ease with you when I didn't know the truth."

Because back then, there'd been no pressure.

No expectations.

What if I cannot love him?

I try to curl my fingers into a ball, but he won't let me.

"Give me time, Vi. That's all I ask."

Yes, but how much time do we have? I'm aware of the slow, stealthy march of days and nights, sweeping me toward an inevitable clash with my mother.

Those gentle fingers stroke their way across my palm. It sends shivers through me. "Perhaps I can set your mind at ease. Ask me anything, and I'll do my best to answer."

"Anything?"

"Anything," he repeats.

I consider my options. Not the Darkness. Not his bloodied past. *Us.* "I know you saw me in a vision, but I don't know.... Why me?"

Why had he fallen in love with me?

"I know you don't remember any of our courtship. I know you wonder how we could have fallen in love so swiftly. Three days is not an eternity, and yet we bound ourselves to each other forever. But all my life I have been called "other" and "abomination" and "impure." To be granted a vision of my one true love by Maia was a gift that made me feel as though I belonged, for Maia turns her face from those who darken the earth beneath their feet. She shuns the Unseelie, and if she'd gifted me, then I felt she must have found me worthy. That vision was all I had on nights where the blackness ate at my heart. It kept me going with the promise that one day I would find you. One day I would know love."

The words fill some gaping wound deep within me.

Because he's not the only one who felt as if he didn't belong, and yet I never had a vision. All I had was hope and the desperate longing to earn my mother's respect, if not her affection.

"And then I finally met you. You were the first woman who ever looked at me as if she saw past the whispers," he admits. "You didn't look at the tattoos. You didn't look at me with fear. You tipped your chin up and told me 'An Asturian *never* cowers before her enemy, so if you think your big, bad reputation scares me, then pray, think again.' I knew in that moment that you were mine, no matter what I had to do to have you."

"It sounds a little too perfect to be true."

Thiago smiles, his voice growing rough. "You did threaten to throw a bottle of wine at my head. It shattered a few of my illusions. In my vision, you were beautiful and kind and you smiled at me. And then when we met, you told me that if I even thought about putting my filthy Evernight hands on you again, you'd break my fingers, one by one."

Not even a hint of recognition fills me, but now I'm fairly certain he's telling me the truth.

"And now you're smiling," he whispers, brushing a strand of hair from my cheek. "I love seeing that smile. It's your secret smile, as if you don't want to be amused but you can't help yourself. It's *my* smile, the one you only give to me. The first time I won it from you, you looked like you wanted to murder me, even as you simply couldn't stop yourself from laughing."

"You don't strike me as that charming," I point out, trying to regain some equilibrium.

Thiago reaches forward to pour me more wine, his eyes shining with glee. "Ah, but you've been fighting me at every step, Princess. And I know all your weaknesses by now."

"Let me guess." I grasp the wine and lean closer. "My weakness is you?"

He doesn't look away as he snaps his fingers. "I'd like to say yes, but the truth is.... Sometimes you can resist me. I don't know how. It honestly baffles me. I thought I was irresistible. No. Your weakness is...."

The server clears her throat beside me, breaking our eye contact.

She holds a small plate on her tray. A decadent, steaming banana pudding sits in the center of the plate, oozing with a rich rum sauce that melts into the cream. The mere smell of it makes me salivate.

"Oh, no," I groan. "I couldn't eat another thing."

"Would you care to make a wager on that?" Thiago lifts a suggestive brow.

~

HE WINS.

I ate the pudding and scraped every hint of sauce from the plate. I probably would have licked it clean if we weren't in public.

And perhaps I have to admit he was right: he is charming me. Inch by reluctant inch, one smile at a time.

I thought myself immune to charm, but this is different. The males in my mother's court hounded Andraste and me the second we came of age. There were gifts and smiles and elegant platitudes. Poetry and dancing and smirking invitations to take a walk through the gardens. It was all so... premeditated.

I was always aware of the crown on my head and my mother watching from the distance. This lord would be good to "cultivate," she would suggest, as if the loss of my virginity was a bargaining chip used to win good fortune.

Years of facing such a pursuit turned me cold on the entire ordeal. I grew used to practiced flirtation and managed to guard myself with scathing retorts that held the worst of the offenders at bay.

It wasn't until Etan of the Goldenhills walked into my

life that I came close to understanding the difference between being hunted and being wooed. Unfortunately, it was too late for me to realize I was no less his quarry than I was to any of the others. He was merely better at hiding it.

This feels different.

Thiago doesn't care whether I'm a princess or not. Indeed, my relationship to my mother proves a hindrance more than a prize.

Which means... he wants me for *me*.

The tension's been brewing all night. Little touches as we walk the streets. Hot looks thrown across a crowded room.

And the way his fingers felt around my thigh as he leaned forward and threatened to kill his friend if he glanced my way....

It's not the sort of behavior I'd ever encourage, and yet I cannot deny a thrill lit through me. The prince is a dangerous opponent, and he's made it clear he intends to have me. No matter how long it takes.

And there's a part of me that wants to take that risk.

I'm not toying with a noble of my mother's court, who watches more for my mother's approval than for mine.

Nor am I dealing with a smirking royal from another court who sees me as his path to power.

No. When Thiago looks at me, the world drops away until all that's left is the promise in his eyes. One that speaks of pleasure and dominance and scalding kisses that would leave no doubt in either of our minds as to who's in control. *Forever, Vi*, he tells me.

I've never been pursued like this in my life.

"This way," he says, tugging me down an alley.

"Where are we going?"

"Nowhere," he whispers, twirling me until my back's against the nearest house.

His hand splays over the wall beside my head as he leans closer. Every hard inch of his body shields me from the wind, but he doesn't press closer. Doesn't move an inch, as if to prove there's no danger here.

Which is ridiculous, because he's the most dangerous male I've ever met.

"What are you doing?" I whisper.

Hot, smoldering eyes lock on me. "You owe me two kisses, if I'm correct, Princess."

"Two?"

"One a day, wasn't it? And we missed the other day." His other hand brushes against my mouth, and he smiles sinfully. "But don't blame me. I didn't make the rules."

I bite his fingers sharply, warning him this *princess* has teeth. "One kiss. If you miss your chance, then you lose it, Your Highness. Since I'm making the rules."

"An Asturian princess reneging on her own bargain? Consider me shocked." His finger trails down my lip, and then his hand curls around my throat, thumb stroking the smooth column of my neck.

I don't know why, but it's like he's lit my veins on fire. I want those hands to keep going.

"It's not reneging if you didn't bother to read the fine print."

He leans closer, his breath whispering over my lips, and sweet Maia, but every inch of me tingles in anticipation. "There was fine print, was there?"

"Section 2.1," I reply swiftly. "Any unclaimed kisses expire."

"Then I guess I'll have to make this one worth it."

His mouth fuses to mine.

All this time, he's let me take the lead, let me make the rules, let me keep our kisses fairly chaste. But this time, there's no denying he's through with playing nicely.

Every inch of him presses me against the wall, and he claims me with hot, hungry kisses. His tongue slicks against mine, teeth nipping, biting, hands pinning my wrists to the wall.

I can't catch my breath, but it seems I don't want to. A groan echoes in my throat. Sweet Maia, he's ruining me. I should push him away. Protest. But those hips grinding against mine remind me its been a long time since I've gotten naked with a man, and my libido's happily cheering him on. It wants me to grab a fistful of his hair and drag him back toward our rooms.

Just one more second.

One more minute.

And then one kiss segues into another.

"You're cheating," I protest, coming up for air.

"I always cheat." He breathes the words against my lips, hips grinding against me. "But technically—" He nips at my lip. "—we never broke contact."

Those firm lips nuzzle across my jaw, and somehow, some stranger has hold of my body. I arch my neck, moaning as his teeth graze the smooth column of my throat. Common sense is losing the battle against desire.

His hands slide down my arms, rough thumbs gliding over the sheer fabric covering my breasts.

No. No, this is bad.

I jerk against him, breaking the contact.

Thiago laughs softly. "There's no one here to watch if you give in to desire, Princess."

Only myself.

I rest my forehead against his chest, breathing hard. "I

think you just tricked me out of paying off any debt I owe. Actually, I think I'm ahead now."

"Oh no," he purrs. "One kiss a day. Any extras don't count toward your future debt. Section 2.3 of that fine print you mentioned."

"Fairly certain I never wrote that into the contract."

"Maybe you should read it again." There's laughter in his eyes, and whatever frustration urged him to push against a wall and plunder my mouth, it's clearly been sated.

Thiago takes my fingers, pressing featherlight kisses to the tips of them, watching me all the while.

Oh, he's dangerous.

Maybe it was a mistake to ask for two rooms. Perhaps it's time I face what lies between us, and not run from it.

A cold prickling sensation slithers down my spine just as I reach for him. It's like a dash of cold water to the face.

"Wait," I whisper.

He pays my warning no mind, his fingers capturing my chin. "You're not going to cry shy now, are you?"

I can't help feeling as though something's horribly wrong. Little goose pimples erupt along my arms, my stomach twisting as if I just ate something foul.

"No, wait. Something's wrong."

The prince is immediately all action, one hand sliding to his sword as he backs away. He turns in a circle, scanning the area, and I feel a moment of stupidity when there's nothing there. Nothing but the sound of people laughing several streets over.

"I know I... felt it."

"I believe you," he says. "Have you got a weapon?"

"Only my knife."

He nods. "Let's head back toward—"

There's something moving in the shadows of the alleyway. The prince stills like a predator catching the scent of prey.

The gorge rises in my throat as if I drank pure cod liver oil, and every inch of me feels dirty. I can't draw my knife quick enough.

"What *is* that?"

It looks like the ripple aftermath of a stone thrown into water, as if the air itself is suddenly fluid. There's something moving there.

Thiago drives forward, thrusting his sword into the ripple. Half his sword vanishes, as if it's plunged through time and space itself. I've never seen anything like it. It reminds me of a portal, though they're only to be found in the middle of a Hallow.

Harsh, raspy laughter shivers down my spine.

From behind me.

There's a blur of movement at my back as I spin, a creature leaping out of nowhere toward me. I lash out with the knife, but the blow glances off its arm. I can barely make sense of what I'm seeing as I try to dodge the swipe of its claws.

It's several feet taller than I am, and shockingly thin. A gaunt face flashes in front of me, large hollow sockets hiding the dark gleam of eyes. Some sort of black leather armor covers its body.

"Vi!" Thiago yells.

"Busy!" I block its next grab, snatching at its wrist to try and throw it past me. My fingers burn as if I've touched pure ice.

I flinch and the creature backhands me across the face.

It's like being hit by a runaway carriage. I stagger backward, my face hot and bruised and the world spinning around me.

"Get down!" the prince yells.

Call it instinct, but I hit the ground just as a wave of pure darkness washes over the top of me. The creature is thrown back into the wall, screaming a high-pitched scream as Thiago's Darkness shreds it.

Then it vanishes.

Thiago crouches at my side, hauling me to my feet. Shadows writhe around him like wings. "Let's move."

"What was that thing?"

"*Things.* There were two of them. And nothing good." He shoves me ahead of him, and we sprint down the alleyway.

The second we're in the main street I feel safer, but I can't help sensing that itch on the back of my neck that tells me we're being watched. A couple of fae fill the square, and there's no sign of our attackers, but I don't want to take any chances.

"Where to?" I ask, bending over and panting. My body's beginning to tremble with the aftermath of the fight, and the left side of my face is hot and swollen.

"Back to the palace."

"Are you sure?" It hasn't escaped my notice that the only one who knew where we were going is Kyrian. "You don't think it's suspicious that we're attacked in his city?"

"It wasn't Kyrian."

"Why? Because the pair of you are such good friends?"

"Because whatever they were, those things are Unseelie. And Kyrian despises the dark fae. He won't be in bed with them."

My brow says it all. "Isn't Stormhaven warded nine ways to the Underworld? How did they get in if the wards are activated?"

Thiago slows, raking a hand over his mouth. "They couldn't. Unless the wards were down."

"Who's in charge of the wards?"

He doesn't answer.

The wards that protect the city will be activated by someone high within the Prince of Tides' council.

"It's not Kyrian," he repeats firmly.

"As you wish." I'm not going to argue. Not with someone who's set their mind in stone.

He turns, and I catch a glimpse of blood welling on his sleeve.

"You're hurt." I grab his arm, turning it this way and that before he captures my hand.

"I'm fine, Vi. It's just a scratch."

"This is what you get for trying to lure me into dark alleys."

He peers around the wall, scanning the street before turning back to me with a tired smile. "Well, if I thought you wouldn't simply slam the door in my face when we returned, I'd have waited until we reached the palace."

I ignore that.

"What in the Horned One's name were they?"

The prince sheathes his knife, his face hard and his brow furrowed. I can tell what his answer will be before he even says it.

"I don't know."

27

Kyrian drew Thiago aside the second we returned, and the pair of them are holed up in Kyrian's study. The Prince of Tides was furious to discover the defenses of his city had been breached, but apparently, my insight isn't needed.

Rather than spend hours cursing him in my room, I head for Stormhaven's infamous library.

If the men are going to whisper secrets together, then I'm going to see if Kyrian's telling the truth.

Slipping through the double doors that leads to the library, I'm so focused on the mission that, when I finally light the lantern I brought, the library nearly stuns me.

It's a circular room, and books line the shelves. We're on the second floor, and as I head to the rail and glance over it, I realize there's another circular row of shelves below me, and looking up through the hollow tower, more above me.

"Erlking's cock," I breathe.

Say what I like about Kyrian, but his library's almost gorgeous enough to make a girl want to snuggle up to him.

There have to be more books here than in every other
library I've ever seen combined.

It's going to take me half a century to find the books I
want, unless he's got them catalogued in a predictable
manner.

I brush my fingertips over the leather spines of the
books, making my way along the shelves and searching for
books that might contain any mythology on the Old Ones.

The mark of the creature's fingers still itches on my arm,
the burn white against my skin. It was like nothing I've ever
seen before, and the handprint still tingles as if I've been
marked somehow.

I need to know what it was.

And I need to know more about this *leanabh an dàn*, if
I'm to save him or her.

Kyrian's library is ridiculously extensive for a piratical
lout. There's a number of bestiaries, historical manuals, and
explorer's journals on the second level, but nothing quite
details what I'm looking for. Down or up?

It's dark on the lower level, with locked glass cases
displaying rare—and probably dangerous—books. If I were
a betting woman, I'd say that's where he keeps his most
important books.

Slipping down the stairs, I set the lantern on one of the
shelves and examine the books. Whatever that creature was
that attacked us, it's got to be Unseelie.

The problem is that the Unseelie kingdom is comprised
of everything the Seelie Alliance deems impure.

All the other races that were cast into the darkness were
gathered under the rule of Sorcha, the first Unseelie queen.
Hordes of creatures native to this world flocked to her
banners. Dozens of creatures unknown crawled out of the
northern forests for a chance to go to war against the Seelie,

and many others were spawned when the Horned One cracked open the earth and unleashed them from the Underworld.

It could be anything, and yet the thought of its frozen touch tickles against my memory, as if I heard something once and just need to see mention of it again to prompt my recall.

Hours later, when the candle flickers low, fat globules of wax weeping down its side, I finally find an answer to my riddle. There's a grimoire in a glass cabinet with a lock that's easy to pick open. The cover is a leather so soft I don't want to know what's it's made from, and the pages whisper when I slowly open it. Merely touching it makes me shiver, but that old, familiar feeling is back.

The answer is in here somewhere.

Each page details magic dark and powerful, and with every page I turn, my breath becomes a little shallower. This is black magic. Summoning spells for the Old Ones. Blood sacrifices. A means to speak to the creatures of the Underworld.

It's an abomination, and it should have been burned, not locked away in a library somewhere.

But there are creatures in here, some I've never even heard of. Creatures from the Underworld painted in grotesque detail with horns, and extra eyes, and leering tongues.

And as I turn the next page, I finally see it painted across the page.

Fetch.

The Heartless: Created by the Horned One himself, they were summoned from the bowels of the Underworld and are of neither plane, but somehow both. They can walk through shadows and are invulnerable to any mortal weapon, including star-forged steel. Their only weakness lies in direct sunlight and they can only be killed by the blood of the purest. The only other option is to find the hearts that were cut from their chest in order to bind them, and burn them. They were used as hunters by Sorcha, and once their prey is marked, they cannot lose their trail and will remain inexplicably linked until one or the other dies.

Another chill runs down my spine as I slowly close the grimoire and examine the mark that seems to be sinking even deeper into my skin.

The creatures that attacked us are fetches.

And I've been marked.

I STEAL the grimoire from Kyrian's library and slip back to my bedchamber. There's no sign of anyone in the hallways, not even servants, but I can't help feeling as though something's watching me, and after what I read, I'm practically running by the time I reach our wing.

The light beneath Thiago's door paints a bright line across the carpets, but my room is pitch-black. I slip inside and lock the door, resting my spine against it.

"Did you enjoy your little rendezvous?"

A little shriek escapes me as Thiago clicks his fingers and lights the candles by my bed. He's stretched out on the mattress, one hand cupping the back of his head, the muscles in his biceps flexing as he watches me.

Erlking's hairy b—

I clap a hand to my racing heart and hastily shove the pair of books and my lantern on the nearest table. "What in the Underworld are you doing in my room?"

On my bed....

"Waiting for you to return, of course." He rolls onto his

side, fingers idly stroking the bedspread as if he wishes it were me. I ignore the soft caress and the way my skin prickles in anticipation. His gaze drops to the books I tried to secrete on the table. "Stealing some of Kyrian's books, were we?"

"I prefer the term 'borrowing'."

"I thought I told you to stay in your room." The sound of his voice is still a purr, but now it has a bit of edge to it.

"And I thought you wanted my help working out what Angharad is doing, but I'm fairly certain the pair of you shut the door in my face earlier."

He sits up. "So you thought you'd ignore me. Was that supposed to be retaliation?"

"I'm not thirteen," I reply archly. "If you and Kyrian want to keep your secrets, that's fine."

"I'm not trying to keep secrets from you. I wanted to talk to Kyrian without the pair of you spitting insults at each other."

"And I'm not going to sit here in the dark, waiting for you to throw me a hint. How else am I going to learn anything?"

"You do remember that we were attacked several hours ago?"

I hold up my arm, revealing the white fingerprints. "Really? I had no idea."

He pushes to his feet, and while I was firmly aware he wasn't wearing a shirt, the aggression in his stance highlights every flawless inch of him. It's like the candlelight is doing its best to revere each muscle.

"If the city isn't safe, then the palace might not be either. We don't know what those creatures were, or what they want."

"It almost sounds as if you think I'm stupid." I cross to

the fireplace, warming my hands. "They stepped out of the shadows, Thiago. I doubt they're going to balk at these stone walls—" I rap my knuckles on the fireplace for emphasis. "—just because they belong to my bedchamber. I was just as safe in the library as I was here. Oh, and you might not know what they are, but I do. Thanks to my little expedition."

He pauses.

"They're fetches."

"I know."

It stops me in my tracks. "You didn't think to tell me?"

"I've never seen them before," he snarls. "It wasn't until I was speaking with Kyrian that I realized Angharad's set her pack of hunters on your trail."

"My trail?"

A hint of strain shows around his mouth. "You didn't notice how they went straight for you?"

I'd been too busy fending them off. I'd assumed—

"Why me?"

"I don't know."

"You don't know? Or you don't intend to tell me? Since you're the Prince of Secrets...."

He whirls on me. "I don't *know*. The only leash they wear is Angharad's, which means she wants to get her hands on you for some reason."

Between my mother and the Unseelie Queen, I'm not certain which option is worse. "Do you think Angharad knows I was there? At Mistmere?"

"If she knows you were there, then she knows I was there. And yet it practically shoved me aside to get to you."

It makes no sense.

I have little enough magic. I'm not my mother's heir, nor am I likely to be named as such. I've never even come face-to-face with Angharad, other than that glimpse of her at the Queensmoot. The idea she even knows who I am is ridiculous.

Out of the two of us, I'd have thought her to be more interested in the prince. He's powerful, dangerous, and was one of the dominating factors in the Seelie winning the last war and driving the Unseelie Queens back.

He picks up a golden cuff from the bed. "I want you to wear this. It will help cloak your whereabouts and protect you. You might wear the fetch's mark, but this will muffle your precise location. It's why I went to see Kyrian. Though I meant for it to protect you from... another."

My mother.

I let him close the cuff around my wrist. The filigreed gold is finely woven in the shape of birds and feels warm against my skin, soothing the seeping chill from the finger-marks. "Thank you."

"You're welcome." With a sigh, he hauls a chair in front of the door and sinks into it.

"What are you doing?"

"Someone has to keep watch, Vi. They can walk through stone walls." He turns his face to stare through the arches that lead to the balcony, moonlight cutting across those sharp features. "And I refuse to lose you."

THIS TIME, the dream steals me away to a ruined castle.

Thirteen eyeless sorcerers kneel around a Hallow, chanting, and there's a black skull with horns in the middle of the circle. I step through the shadows and find myself watching them emotionlessly.

Skirts rustle like dry leaves, and then Angharad appears

from the nearest arch, a crow resting on her shoulder. "Well?" she demands.

The fetch bows before the queen. "I have found your sacrifice, my queen. She is marked."

It makes my heart flutter in my chest, as if some part of me is aware of the danger. I don't know why the fetch is in my dreams, but it feels like I'm staring out through its eyes.

It feels like this is not a dream at all.

"Fetch her for me," Angharad says. "The Hallow is nearly resurrected. I'll offer her heart to the Mother, and then She and I will make a deal."

I whimper.

There's no escape. All I can do is watch as the chanting begins to rise in tone.

"*Vi*," someone whispers, and I turn into a warm embrace. "*You're safe. You'll always be safe in my arms.*"

"Please." I'm tugging at something. Fighting my sheets. My flailing arms.

"*Vi, wake up.*"

There is no escape. I feel my body turn, stalking through the ring of sorcerers.

"*Wake up,*" says a whisper in my ear. Then there's a soft curse. "*Dream of me, Vi. Not them.*"

A gentle mouth brushes against mine.

The sensation tears me in two. One moment, I'm ducking down a long corridor, and the next my eyelashes are stirring, a large, muscular form kneeling over me. I can taste his breath on my lips and feel the stroke of his tongue.

My fingers clutch at his shoulders as I wake with a jerk.

"*Thiago.*"

He wraps me in his arms, drawing me against his chest. "Shh, Vi. Shh. You're safe."

"I was inside the fetch," I gasp. "And Angharad was speaking to me—to it, rather."

He runs a smooth hand down my spine. "They can't hurt you, Vi."

"Yes, they can," I snap. "They were speaking of using me as a sacrifice to resurrect the Mother of Night." My heart still pounds. "D-do you think it was real? Do you think I was somehow seeing through its eyes?"

"It's possible. Fetches create a bond with their mark. It's how they track them. Perhaps it uses that bond to see where you are and what you're doing. Perhaps you managed to follow the trail back to the hunter?" Every inch of Thiago goes still, as he strokes my back. "I won't let them hurt you, Vi. I won't let them have you."

"How are you going to stop them? They can walk through *shadows*." I push to my feet, wrapping my arms around myself. "Sunlight is their only weakness, or the blood of the purest, whatever that means."

Why me?

Why are they searching for me?

Thiago's face turns hard and cold, and the tattoos that crawl up his throat writhe. "There are ways to counter a creature of the shadows. Trust me, Vi. It will not have you. No matter what I must do."

28

K yrian waits in his inner tower, staring through the windows at the sea. There's a golden compass in his hands, and its needle points due west, though he swiftly snaps it shut when we enter.

"Well?" Thiago asks.

The Prince of Tides turns to face us, his windswept brown hair tied at his nape and his shirt open to mid-breast. "I've found her. Angharad has her pet sorcerers working on the Spell of Unmaking. You were right. She's up to something. They're looking for a sacrifice to break open the Hallow at Mistmere."

It's exactly what I saw last night in my dreams.

Thiago exchanges a glance with me, but he doesn't say anything. "A sacrifice? Why the Mother? If they thought they could break open a Hallow, I thought she'd go straight for the Horned One."

"Who knows?" Kyrian replies. "The Horned One was a special case. Bran the Mighty linked the pair of them, then drove the Sword of Unmaking straight through his own heart. It was enough to trap the Horned One in a deathlike trance before they closed the prison. Perhaps Angharad needs some way to bring him back from the edge before she releases him?"

"And the Mother has the power," Thiago says, cursing under his breath as he paces. "She has the skills. She created spell craft, so if there's anyone who knows how to break that link, it's her."

"Angharad seemed to think there was a specific sacrifice required," Kyrian says. "Do we have any idea who it is?"

Another little chill runs up my spine.

Thiago insisted I wear long sleeves, and I'm grateful for it now, as the blue silk covers the fetch's mark.

"No," Thiago lies, looking his friend in the eye. "No doubt a queen. Or a prince. Or someone of equal power. The Hallows required a powerful sacrifice to create the link to the prisons. No doubt they require one that's just as powerful to break them open. Either that, or one of the great relics like the Sword of Mourning. But most of them are lost."

I don't understand. I don't have the power required. My magic dwells beneath the surface, caged by the wards Thiago laid over me the night I nearly burned the bed. But it's no greater than that of any pure born fae. I know, because my mother had both Andraste and me tested when we were twelve.

And as far as I can tell, my memory loss begins and ends on the day I first met Thiago, so that previous memory must be real.

"Watch your back then, my friend," Kyrian says, slapping a hand on Thiago's shoulder.

"You too. And start preparing for war. I'll send my armies west, to Mistmere. We need to stop her before she can get the Hallow working."

"My ships are at your disposal," Kyrian replies. "And my men. Send word the second you're ready to attack." He turns to me. "In light of certain revelations, you may consider my grimoire a gift. I think you may need it, Your Highness, though next time... ask."

IT's a quiet trip back to Ceres.

Though the thought of travelling through the Hallow and meeting that saltkissed bitch haunts me, the trip is uneventful. The gold cuff on my arm goes ice-cold, but there's no frightening whirl of seawater, no screaming saltkissed hissing in my face.

I'm almost disappointed.

29

One day later we have word from the other kingdoms.

The queens have discussed our tale of Mistmere, and have decided to send their own emissaries. We're to meet them near Mistmere where we'll continue on foot. Each queen has sent ten retainers. No more. No less.

Even a single extra guard might be considered a threat against the other retinues, or a plot to exploit the situation.

"Maia help us if Angharad intends to invade and has an army awaiting us," Baylor says, pacing the shadowy forest outside the tents we've set up.

"At least it shall be a glorious death," Finn points out.

"Or a swift one," Eris mutters.

The edge of the swamp that runs into Mistmere lake is the best place to meet, as the brackish waters will hide our scent, and it's unlikely banes will be patrolling here. A castle turret sticks out of the water ahead of us, moss lining its crenellations. It looks like the swamp has swallowed a castle whole, and only the tip emerges.

Maybe it will swallow us whole too.

That's a cheery thought.

A light flickers in the top window, highlighting a pale face, and then it vanishes.

"They're here," I murmur, blowing warmth into my cupped hands. I forgot how cold it was this far north.

"It's about time." Eris wades into the shallows, pushing the boat out a little further. "It's not as though the fate of the seelie alliance rests upon the other kingdoms actually getting off their asses, for a change."

"Ah, Eris, my love," Finn says quietly, "You expect everything to be straightforward. It's your uncouth unseelie nature showing. This is Seelie. If we don't stab each other in the back, slit someone's throat while they sleep, toy with our allies' emotions, or promise everything and nothing in the one breath, then can we even call ourselves fae? The only good news is that at least we look good while we do it."

"Never trust a beautiful face," Eris murmurs, as if she learned the saying by rote as a child.

"And never trust a seelie smile," Finn adds.

"You smile all the time," I whisper.

"Precisely." The grin on his face doesn't shift. "Don't ever believe a word I say, my sweet princess. I'm a born liar."

"I suppose you *did* tell me how handsome and brave and amazing you were, when we first met."

Finn claps his hands over his heart, and staggers back as if mortally wounded.

Baylor merely sighs and rubs a hand over his eyes. "Here lie the hopes of Evernight. We're doomed."

A drift of shadow moves toward us in the night. Thiago dissolves out of nothing, looking as if he was born for nighttime.

"Is anyone here aware how far voices carry in the mist?"

he whisper-breathes, as the guards following him melt into stillness.

Instantly, the four of us stiffen.

"Get in the fucking boat." He includes me in his fierce look, though he does offer me an arm.

I can't help feeling a nervous flutter in my veins as we seat ourselves.

My mother will have sent her most loyal and her best. Andraste's standing in that turret. I know it with every fiber of my being, but the question is: Who else is with her?

One of her generals?

No, Mother won't want the confrontation with Eris or Baylor. Never reveal your cards, she always tells me. And she won't want any of her generals wondering about the unseelie we're facing. Her generals are firmly under her spell, but they're also responsible for the safety of Asturia. Any hint of a threat and all five of them would start asking questions Mother won't want to answer.

I can't help thinking of the conversation we had through the flames. I told her about Angharad and Mistmere, and yet she arrived at the alliance meeting acting as though the truth is something to smother, not face.

It doesn't make sense.

Why would she not want the rest of the alliance to know about Angharad? Every day my eyes open to a new truth, including the one that's been dwelling on my mind most.

My mother is acting as though she's working *with* the enemy.

But that's impossible.

She wouldn't. She hates the unseelie and sees them as beneath her. All my life she's warned against their lying, deceitful ways, and their filthy courts.

But what if she hates the prince more than she hates them?

What if she thinks she can use them to ruin him, and then sweep them aside afterwards?

Someone taught her to curse-twist the fae into banes.

And someone cursed me with the dark magic the unseelie possess.

It's a troubling knot and one I'll need time to unpick.

Fog sits like a blanket on the lake as we make our way across.

Baylor rows, the heavy flex of his shoulders rippling beneath the stark black leathers he wears. A leather thong ties half his hair back from his face, but there's no hiding the harsh slant of those cheekbones, or the glitter of his eyes as he watches me. I jerk my gaze away, but it's too late.

He knows I'm hiding something.

Then we're arriving at the small island that houses the turret. Thiago helps me ashore, and I realize I'm right. We're not standing on a stony beach, but the remnants of a castle wall. Moss and lichen coat the stones, and I can see the gleaming amber eyes of demi-fey watching us from nooks and crannies. Some of them flutter in the air with translucent wings that hum on the verge of hearing. Others hiss at us from between reeds. One gnaws on a freshly caught fish.

"Are you sure you're ready for this?" Thiago murmurs, squeezing my fingers.

Maybe he can sense my nerves, which means I'm not hiding them as well as I should be. "I'm ready."

This meeting is important. If we don't convince the other courts of the threat then we'll be standing alone against a possible unseelie invasion.

But when I climb the slick stairs, my sister is standing in the middle of the remains of the tower door, looking every inch a warrior princess.

My sister, who has lied to me every bit as much as my mother has.

And suddenly, I don't want peace.

I want war.

I'm TREMBLING BADLY as I sweep past Andraste into the tower.

It's all I can do not to look at her, not to vent the rage that bubbles beneath the surface.

In a way, her betrayal is the sharpest blow. I've always known my mother never cared for me. It didn't mean I didn't try to seek her approval, but when I constantly failed there was a small part of me that merely saw it as inevitable.

But Andraste....

She was the only one who had my back.

I loved her.

A part of me still does.

And as they say, the sharpest sting of betrayal is the fact it only ever comes from those you trust.

She reaches for my arm. "Vi—"

"Don't." I jerk away from her with a snarl. There are a thousand words I want to say to her, but none of them spring to the tip of my tongue. I'm so angry. I can't put them all together.

"Ah," says a mocking voice as my stepbrother, Edain, saunters down the tower stairs in all his finery. "The princess awakes." He spares an insolent smile for Thiago. "Does she love you, yet? Or is she still holding you at arm's length? *Tick tock*, Your Highness. You're running out of time."

It's too much.

I don't even know I'm moving until I drive a fist right into his stomach. Edain goes to one knee with a sharp exhale of breath, his red velvet tunic rumpling and his dark hair tumbling into his eyes. Then his sound of shock turns into a laugh and he slowly pushes to his feet. "I see you've lost none of your edge, dear sister. Nice blow."

"I *missed*."

"You've got your mother's touch for going right for a man's balls." The smile on his face seems wrong, somehow. Edain never looks bothered by anything—harsh words slough off him like rain off a roof. But there's an edge there I never saw before. "I wonder…. Do you have her gift for toying with a man's emotions?" He looks right past me, the words aimed at Thiago.

It stalls my answer in my throat.

Stops my fist in mid-air.

I know what my mother uses him for. They call him her pet at court and whisper about how he'll do anything to keep his position.

But I never realized it bothers him.

I used to look up to my sister, and wished my mother turned to me as often as she turned to Edain, but those were the wishes of a girl who'd long been neglected. I didn't see the poison she drowned them with. I didn't see the gilded cages they're trapped inside. Or the puppet strings woven around them.

Perhaps none of us shall escape Mother's twisted, tangled web without scars.

But I'm the only one who may actually escape her court.

And Edain knows it.

There's no escape for him. There's no mysterious prince

claiming to be his husband. No gorgeous palace awaiting, filled with the warmth of allies and friends. And Eris, who is neither, if one is to be honest.

Edain will continue to be Mother's whore, her pet, her lickspittle. And Andraste, who stands in the position I once dreamed of, shall forever bear the brunt of Mother's nasty little games.

I'm free.

It's a heady realization.

For all that Mother's taken from me, she can never truly steal the one thing I didn't realize I have: A chance.

My fist lowers. "You're right. The princess is awake now. And she's starting to see things clearly." I glance toward Thiago, and it feels as though the veils have been lifted from my eyes. "I pity you, Edain. All you have is this. You'll never escape the wounds she deals, if you continue to seek her favor. I'm well clear of such poison."

Edain looks at me sharply, and it's clear my words have done more than my fist ever could have. "You little fool." He shakes his head. "You actually think you're free of it."

"I think my mother had best watch her back. It doesn't matter how many times she steals my memories, I'll always come back to this moment. I will always hate her, and.... I will always see the prince for who he truly is."

Edain laughs, the sound so rich and mocking it jars down my spine. "She doesn't know, does she?"

"That's enough," Thiago says, moving toward my step-brother with menace dripping from him.

"Know what?"

Both men pause, gazes locked, as though they're mentally crossing sabers.

But it's Edain who turns to me with a sneer. "Save your

pity for yourself, Iskvien. Because while you might think you've found your chance for forever, your time is running out. If you think the queen has finished with you, then you're very much mistaken. She's just waiting for the game to roll to its final, inexorable conclusion."

"That's enough." Andraste's voice rings through the hollow core of the tower. "We have guests."

Ever the dutiful sister.

But I bite my tongue as I catch a glimpse of another boat skulking out of the mist. Muraid of Aska, judging by the stern slope of her shoulders, and those mismatched eyes. Queen Maren takes her to bed, it's whispered, though Muraid is her fiercest general.

Behind her, is a tall man wearing Queen Lucidia's emblem on his breast.

Time to focus on Mistmere.

Though I won't forget any of what happened here.

"WHAT DID EDAIN MEAN?" I grind out through gritted teeth, as the boat rows us toward Mistmere.

Other boats follow ours, though they're warded so well I can't see or hear them.

It's a good thing our boat is warded too, because there are words I need to say, and this may be the last moment of privacy we get.

Or as private as we can be, with Eris leaning in the prow watching the waters ahead as if she's waiting for an imminent attack. Finn clears his throat, setting his back into the oars, and Baylor has a sudden fascination with the moon.

Thiago tugs his leather gloves into place, his face impassive. "That is between your stepbrother and myself."

There hadn't been a chance to insist upon answers earlier, for the representatives for the other kingdoms had arrived, and if there's one thing you don't do, it's show Muraid of Aska your throat. I'd swallowed my frustration and greeted her with a smile, but I knew Thiago could sense the brewing storm within me.

"It seemed as though Edain was trying to suggest I *was* involved. I'd like to know what he meant by '*time is running out.*'"

"Later," he promises, leaning toward me. "We need to focus on—"

"No. Not later. Now."

Sometimes I forget how much bigger he is, but I'm not backing down. Not this time.

The prince stills, his eyes hooding. "Thirteen years," he says softly. "I bartered for thirteen years with you. It was all your mother would agree to. There are no more chances for you to remember me. This time when I return you, if you don't remember me then I forfeit my lands... and my life."

The world drops away.

"What do you mean, if I don't remember you?"

"The rules are clear. I must return you to your mother. Three days later the entire alliance meets at the Queensmoot, where you must make your choice." Thiago captures my gaze. "Your mother, or myself. You leave with one of us."

"You *agreed* to this bargain?"

It's a terrible bargain.

"I didn't know what she intended to do to you at the time. I couldn't fathom a world in which you would walk away from me."

I sink onto the bench seat of the boat, my knees trembling. "But if I don't remember you, then I'll never...." *I'll never choose you.*

"You *will* remember."

I wish I had his certainty.

"Why did you not tell me?"

"Because I wanted to enjoy my time with you," he snaps. "I wanted to spend these days in your arms, not worrying about the future."

"We could have been working toward a solution!"

"We've tried. Do you think I haven't done everything in my power to break the spell over the years?" A bitter smile touches his mouth. "It's not true love's kiss, let me assure you."

"What if there isn't a means to break it?" My chest feels tight. I cannot have his death on my conscience. "What if she...."

I can't say it.

Thiago kneels in front of me and takes my hands. "I have faith, Vi. You never want to see me hurt, no matter how much you think me the enemy. Even if you don't recognize me, I think some part of you will always know me. Maybe this is what the spell needs to break? Maybe if my life is at risk, then the curse will shatter?"

"*Maybe*?" Does he not see how wrong that sounds? To pin all our hopes on maybe? "What if I don't feel a thing? What if it's too late?"

"I have faith," he repeats.

"Well, I don't!"

"For once, the princess and I are in agreement," Eris mutters.

I'd forgotten about them, forgotten about them all. This is why she hates me. This is why she can't even look at me.

She knows I'm the millstone around the prince's neck, threatening to drag him to his death.

Thiago leans closer to me. "Later," he repeats, in a deathly quiet voice.

Behind him, I can just make out the foreshore of Mistmere. He's right. This isn't the time, or the place.

"Later."

The words are a promise made.

He tilts his head to me, one adversary to another. "There's the woman I married. There's my queen. Don't lose sight of her, Vi. Because I need her at my side. As much as your mother's curse must be dealt with, this takes priority. I won't allow another war." The boat glides to a smooth halt, and he leaps down into the shallows with barely a splash. "Now, come."

Darkness blurs his features as I accept his hand. I can sense the magic shivering beneath his skin like a quiet storm.

The others dismount, and we wade ashore toward the Hallow. Edain and Andraste are already there, waiting for us.

"Is this some sort of joke?" Edain demands loudly.

The words cut through the night like a whip crack.

Thiago was shielding us, but there's no aural shield surrounding Edain.

"Mother of Night," Eris curses, drawing her sword. "Are you *trying* to get us killed?"

Instantly, the guards surrounding my sister set hands to weapons. Andraste quells them with a single sharp flick of her hand. "Killed by what?"

It's only then that I notice the silence.

A frog croaks somewhere in the distance.

Wind whispers across the lake.

And as it blows, the mist stirs.

It doesn't disguise a damned thing.

Because there's nothing *to* disguise.

The Hallow is naught but ruins, covered in a thin layer of snow. Everything—the tents, the crane, the work teams—are gone.

Or, if one is kind, it looks as though they never existed.

30

Edain's sword clears his scabbard. "Is this supposed to be a trick? What mockery is this? There's nothing here. Nothing but broken stones and rubble."

I step forward. "It's no trick." Or at least, not from us. "There were teams of enslaved goblins here, and a troll...." I can see it all as clearly as day. The enormous crane the troll pushed.... It should have been right there.

But there's nothing but wind whispering through the long-abandoned streets. Nothing but an ancient tattered curtain flapping in a distant window.

Thiago kneels, brushing aside the fine layer of snow. His fingers pause as they find one of the ancient runes, the bronze pitted and scarred. "I'm not the only one with a gift for illusion."

"Enough." Edain laughs under his breath. "It's cold enough to freeze my fucking balls off, and you dragged us here for this mockery. I'm done. Andraste?"

Andraste's hand comes to rest upon her sword, but she's watching me. Not him.

"My queen will hear of this," Muraid sneers. She spits on the ground, then turns and stalks away, leading her contingent of fae warriors.

It's all falling apart.

My gaze meets Thiago's, as he slowly stands.

"How?" I whisper.

Angharad can't have just made an entire Hallow disappear. That would require magic beyond any that even the queens have.

"During the wars," Thiago murmurs, still glancing around, "an entire company of seelie warriors entered the ruins of Morghulis to make camp. It was long abandoned, or so they thought. Only one came out. He spoke of an empty ruin suddenly vanishing around him, as though someone swept the curtain aside to reveal an entire castle teeming with unseelie. They were there all along, he said. And we thought him mad."

Edain kicks at one of the sentinel stones that leers to the right like a drunken reveler. Snow shivers off the top of it. "Aye, Valarien of the Greenmantle." His lip curls. "I remember that story too. And it was just a story. No one has the power to make half a city vanish. There's nothing here. Nothing but trickery." He points his sword directly at Thiago. "Or is it treachery? I cannot help but notice you've gathered the powerful fae of each kingdom here, where they can be destroyed in one fell swoop. Guards!"

The Asturian guards snap to attention, their swords out and pointed toward us.

But I swear I heard something to the right....

A little metallic click, as though steel scraped on stone.

"What is it?" Thiago whispers hoarsely.

I hold up a hand, my head cocked to listen.

Silence. Nothing but silence.

Behind me, the others continue to argue.

"We're leaving," Andraste announces, and the tone of her voice is wary.

"I wouldn't lie to you," I tell her. "I saw it. There were banes everywhere. Tents. The Hallow was nearly complete."

Andraste looks at me, and I see the answer in her eyes. She thinks my mother's telling the truth. She thinks Thiago used his powers of illusion to fool me. "I'm sure you saw what you claim. But there's nothing here. How do you explain that? Think, Vi. Think with your head, and not your heart. He's lying to you. He always has. He has you so wrapped up in knots, you can't even see the truth anymore."

I grab her arm. "Maybe I should ask you about lies? Because in this entire situation, the only one who's told me the cursed truth has been him."

"If Angharad did resurrect the Hallow, then where is it?" Edain demands, the insolence sloughing off him and revealing those cunning eyes. I sometimes forget he's not the courtly sycophant he pretends to be.

"I don't know." I swallow hard, as I look around. I'm losing them. I know I am. "But it's been five days since the alliance held their meeting. Angharad has spies everywhere. She may have been given warning...."

And that's when my stomach drops right to my boots.

One queen has revealed access to dark magics she shouldn't know.

One queen stood in that meeting and sneered at the truth, even though I'd already warned her.

One queen wants to destroy the Prince of Evernight at all costs.

What if my mother told Angharad what we had seen? What if Angharad dismantled the Hallow with magic?

What if they *are* working together?

"We're done here," Andraste says softly, and she looks sincere. "I'm sorry, Vi. But this is our kingdom at stake. I have to report what I've seen. Edain, ready the boats."

She tugs her arm free from my grasp, and turns away from me.

I take a step after her, before halting.

There's no reaching her. No point even trying.

And I still haven't forgiven her.

Once upon a time I would have stormed after her, but I'm tired of reaching out, only to have doors slammed in my face.

Thiago pauses at my side, his solid presence warming me.

"She doesn't believe me."

"She doesn't want to believe you," he replies. "If she does, then she must face your mother, and your sister doesn't have the courage to do that. She's too busy playing the dutiful daughter."

"I don't understand," I tell him, looking around at the ruins. "I saw what I saw."

"So, did I," he replies grimly. "Come. These are dangerous territories. We need to return to camp, before we're caught out in the open."

"Wait." Valarien of the Greenmantle. It's not just a story. It's a warning wrapped in a nursery rhyme in my court.

NEVER RIDE NORTH, little fae, little fae;
  For the wolves are a-calling, said they, said they.
  Though you don't see them, or smell them, they're there;
  With slavering teeth and brindled back hair.

.   .   .

I TURN, staring through unblinking eyes.

THICK IS the spell that wraps round the keep;
   The visible silenced, until they must reap.
   Blood binds the spell, but it's blood that shall break it;
   From the old to the new, paint the marks that were writ.

I DRAW MY KNIFE, crossing to the center of the Hallow. "Blood. Blood breaks the spell. They'd need a queen's blood to activate a glamour of this size, and the Hallow.... The Hallow would power it."

"Vi." One word holds a wealth of meaning. Thiago's hand drops to the hilt of his sword.

"Trust me," I tell him, setting the tip of the knife to the fleshy pad of my finger.

Maia's blood flows through my veins. There's power there, even if I can barely channel it. *Old to the new....* It has to be. I slash my finger, hissing at the sting, then squeeze several drops of blood to the surface.

Blood drops into the snow, splashing hotly against the first glyph.

BOOM.

I feel a distant vibration, as though something shifts deep within the earth. Snow shivers off rooves and everyone staggers to find their footing.

"What was that?" Eris demands, looking as though a fetch walked over her grave.

"I don't know," Finn whispers, "and I do not *want* to know."

Thiago's head swivels, his hawkish gaze sweeping the ruins. "More," he says.

I squeeze another droplet of blood to the surface, and it splashes wetly against the glyph.

The very earth vibrates beneath our feet as though the Hallow is slowly waking. Shaking off the remnants of centuries of sleep with a groan, it shivers to life.

Light shimmers across the entire ruins.

It feels as though the clouds suddenly part, or perhaps shadows are merely being swept from my eyes. Inch by inch, the Hallow is revealed anew, and I gasp as the illusion breaks.

We're standing in the middle of thirteen fully erect sentinel stones. Canvas tents flap nearby, and the black banner of Angharad snaps in the wind.

Banes prowl the ruins on leashes, and goblins strain to hold them back as they watch us with hungry eyes and slavering jowls.

And there, with a shock of white hair and black robes stands Isem, Angharad's pet sorcerer.

"Erlking's cock," Finn breathes. "Where the fuck were they hiding?"

"To me," Thiago barks, the steel of his sword ringing as it clears his sheathe.

I stagger back against him, my dagger clenched in nerveless fingers. There are dozens of banes. And at least fifty swarthy goblins clad in leather and steel and feathers. No matter which way I turn, the Hallow is surrounded and there's no escape.

"Blow your fucking horn," Baylor snaps at Finn. "The others can't have gone far."

Finn lifts his golden horn to his lips, it's clear notes ringing through the sky.

I can't help thinking of Edain's sneer. Of Andraste's stony features.

Will they even help?

One last drop of blood hits the snow, and the Hallow comes alive beneath my feet.

Isem snaps his fingers, his eerie colorless gaze locking upon me. Upon that drop of blood. "Bring me the princess. Alive, preferably."

"And the others?" growls a goblin, with a black tattoo obliterating the right side of its face.

Isem smiles. "You did say we were running short of meat for the banes."

31

The snap of chains landing on the ground is terrifying, as the goblins release the banes. The slavering beasts launch toward us, and I can't draw my star-forged sword quick enough. My mind is calculating odds, even as I fall into a defensive stance.

We're overwhelmed by numbers and trapped within the Hallow.

There's no way we can survive.

"Blow the horn again!" Thiago yells.

Finn does, but my heart is racing.

They didn't come.

My sister would have heard that horn from miles away.

Eris draws the two swords strapped to her back, her dark braids swinging. "Stay behind me."

Gladly.

I'm good with a sword, but I can feel my hands trembling with excitement and nerves. Master Hammond prepared me for every possible foe, but it's one thing to face a challenge in a training ring, and quite another to be staring into the maw of bloody ruin.

Steel rings and Eris throws herself forward, both swords flashing. A bane's head hits the ground, blood gushing from its decapitated body, but she's rolling under it, steel lashing out to hamstring two others.

I gape at her prowess for half a second to and then I'm facing my own threat.

Two goblins fan out, swinging the chains they used to bind the banes. They tower over me. They even make Thiago seem short, which means they must be nearly seven feet tall, and their arms and shoulders bulge with thick muscle. A motley assortment of leather adorns them, though the one on the right has a chest-piece made of bones laid over the top. Neither of them bears tattoos on their cheeks, which mean they're of the Clanless, the outcasts that were exiled from the mountain halls.

It also means they obey no rules or laws of their people.

Golden, cat-slit eyes lock on me and one grins, revealing teeth he's sharpened into points. "Alive," he yells to the other, and I realize they're not planning to kill me.

They're planning to deliver me to Isem in chains, which is an entirely worse fate.

When the sun sinks into the final darkness....

One chain lashes toward me, and I use the sword to deflect it. A blur comes at my head from the other direction, the second goblin using the first to distract me. Ducking beneath its chain, I feel cold iron brush against my cheek with a stinging kiss, and then I throw myself into a roll across the slate of the Hallow's floor.

A swordsman who sits still is a dead swordsman, Master Hammond's words ring in my ears.

It's like my body has a will of its own. I scramble to my feet, leaping over the top of the whiplash of the first chain. Another dive and roll, and then I'm right within the goblin's reach, driving the sword straight up beneath its sternum.

Its breath hisses from it in shock, but it manages to bring its bony forehead down into mine with a crunch.

Mother of Night.

The shock of it flings me off my feet, my ears ringing. Pain floods through me, and when I blink, I'm flat on my back, struggling to breathe. Another blur comes at me, and I roll in terror, but it's merely a head tumbling past me.

"Get up." Eris is there, hauling me to my feet, her eyes locked on the fight.

Disorientation makes me stagger. Both goblins are down. One with my sword through its chest, and the other in a crumpled heap. Or... two crumpled heaps.

One significantly shorter than the other.

"Move," Eris says, as another chain swings toward us.

I duck below it, grabbing the hilt of my sword and wrenching it from the goblin's chest.

Eris snatches the end of the chain and hauls her opponent toward her. The bastard staggers forward, where she smashes the hilt of her sword into his filed teeth. Blood sprays and he screams, and then she's driving her boot up into his face.

The goblin hits the ground, and Eris barely glances at him as she stabs him through the throat, then wraps the chain around her fist and punches a bane in the face with it.

"Are you laughing?" I gasp, as I scramble to keep up with her.

Blood flecks her face and her eyes are wild and triumphant. "That prick shit his pants when he saw me. You should have seen his face, before I removed his head. Here." She pushes me into Thiago's arms. "Look after your wife while I clean up this mess."

And then she's gone, howling with glee as she wades back into battle.

I was wrong. Eris does know how to smile, and it's the most terrifying thing I've ever seen.

"Are you all right?" Each breath I take ravages my lungs, but he's covered in blood.

Thiago grins. "Not mine. Here. Watch my back."

He sets his back to mine and we face the oncoming onslaught of more banes.

There's nothing but the fight ringing in my ears, as blood splashes across the floor of the Hallow. I feel Thiago's back against mine, and it gives me a confidence I've never known. I'm not a princess, protected by her guards. I am Death, and every blow I strike, every spray of arterial blood that drenches my tunic, only makes the blood in my veins pump harder. There's something exhilarating about this dance of steel. It's so very simple. You move and you live. You stop and you die. You focus only on the next move, the next foe.

I've never felt so alive.

Back to back we fight, with Baylor covering the left and Finn to our right. Eris is out there somewhere, a one-woman killing spree with a maniacal laugh. For a moment, I think we're going to survive.

And then Finn staggers, going to one knee as an arrow protrudes from his thigh. It's a critical breach in our defenses.

"Get up!" Thiago snaps.

Finn pushes to his feet and snaps the arrow in half with a wince, but it's clear he can't balance.

"Eris!" Thiago bellows.

"Coming!"

I'm crushed between fur and flesh, the stink of a bane's raw breath hissing in my face as it slams me back into Thiago. It's all I can do to drive my knee up into vulnerable flesh to gain some space. My sword is trapped between us and the second it winces, I slash back the other way, right across its abdomen. My sword is so heavy my arm aches, and the blow is sloppy.

As it falls away, it grabs my wrist.

Kicking it in the face, I try to hang on, but the fight is taking its toll. I can't feel my fingers.

"Vi!" Thiago yells, and I turn just in time to see a fist driving toward my face.

It's like being hit by a runaway horse. My sword is gone, my ears ringing, and then I'm bundled into someone's arms.

"Got her!" grunts the goblin that hit me.

He slings me over his shoulder, and the world jolts around me.

"Vi!" Thiago yells, and then he's leaping over a pair of fallen banes, his cloak seeming to grow larger, to spread into amorphous wings.

A dozen goblins intercept him as though they were waiting for this moment. I catch a single glimpse of his eyes as our gazes meet, and then he's buried beneath monstrous flesh.

Hitting and kicking, I try to free myself, but the goblin is immovable.

I bite its throat, and it tastes utterly fucking wretched, but all that earns me is a slap across my ears.

"Be still, little fae. Or I'll break your fingers."

"Thiago!" I scream.

Shadows writhe and the goblins that tackled Thiago start thrashing on the floor. Something flings them through the air—a punch of raw power, perhaps—and then the prince is climbing to his feet, his eyes gleaming pure black and merciless.

But it's too late.

Goblins close ranks around us, and as the one carrying me dumps me onto my feet, another grabs my wrist to slap chains on me.

It's too much.

I turn into a spitting, hissing ball of rage and manage to tear free for three precious seconds.

"Catch her!"

I duck beneath a meaty arm, and jump backwards as a dagger swipes through the air, narrowly avoiding my abdomen. Someone grabs at my hand and I wrench it free, yelping as my hand rips through a metal gauntlet.

Then I'm back through the stones, clutching my bleeding hand to my chest.

A pulse whispers through my veins. The Hallow is alive, its power stroking against my senses. *Use me,* it seems to suggest.

Travelling via a Hallow is dangerous at the best of times. But this one.... Is it even working? Angharad may have resurrected the sentinel stones, but the very alignment of them must be perfect, their angle connecting to the sentinel stones of other Hallows, for it to have any chance at working.

Finn goes down beneath a ferocious wolf-like creature with teeth as long as my fingers. Eris appears, covering Baylor as they keep a pair of goblins off Thiago's back. All four of them are within the Hallow's circumference. Good enough for me.

Torn apart by the Hallow's portal, or torn apart by banes. Which one offers the best chance of survival?

I thrust my bloodied hand against the rune that refers to the Isle of Sorrow.

And then the world implodes in upon us, and Mistmere vanishes.

I SLAM BACK into being on a bed of moss that cushions my fall.

Every inch of me feels like it was taken apart and put back together again by amateurs. *Mother of Night.* I hurt from the tip of my toes to the roots of my hair.

But we're not the only ones the Hallow transported.

Crawling to my hands and knees, I watch as Baylor smoothly decapitates a pair of goblins. Part of a bane twitches at my feet. It was only halfway inside the Hallow's stones when I activated it.

My sword is gone, but there's no need for it.

Thiago clambers to his feet from beneath a pile of slaughtered goblins, and Finn is kneeling by Eris's side, wincing as he claps a hand to the arrowhead in his thigh. The rest of our enemies are dead—without reinforcements, Thiago and Baylor swiftly took care of them.

Thiago strides toward me, his face hard. He snatches at my bloodied palm. "You're not hurt?"

"Nothing but scratches." I wince, rubbing my tongue over tender teeth. "And a few bruises."

"Here." He cups my face in his palms, heat spreading through me.

I want to curl into it, especially when the pain evaporates, but I can't quite look at his face.

All I can remember is what it looked like during that fight. Those black eyes. Those swirling tattoos. In that moment, I saw him as our enemies did.

He's not seelie.

I've never been so sure of that in my life, though what he *is* remains uncertain. There were definitely wings.

"You didn't unleash your Darkness."

Thiago hesitates. "I can't always control it."

And in such close quarters, there was no telling whether it would fell friend or foe.

"What happened? I was just about to throw my fucking dagger at Isem's throat when the world disappeared." Eris pushes to her feet, dripping gore, her eyes wild as she looks around. "Where are we?"

"The Isle of Sorrows," I croak. "It was the only rune I could reach."

Thiago slides a sidelong look toward me. "You activated the Hallow?"

"It was the only thing I could think of."

His thumb strokes across the bloodied cuts on my fingers. "You took a risk."

"A calculated risk. Would you prefer to be in the belly of a bane?"

"If Angharad hadn't consecrated the ground again, and tied the power of the leyline to the stones, then we would have been pulverized into a thousand particles when the Hallow imploded. I've seen it happen before."

"The Hallow was awake."

His thumb pauses. "How did you know that?"

The same way I knew the Hallow at Stormhaven wasn't right.

It never occurred to me that others might not be able to feel the Hallow's vibrations.

"I just... did."

Everyone's watching me.

"Well, I, for one, am cursed glad you did," Finn says, slinging an arm around Eris's shoulders. "Eris, my love, can you help me to that log? I need to sit down before I fall down."

"Since when did I become your crutch?"

"Since you're far prettier than Baylor," Finn replies promptly.

"That's debatable," she replies.

"Yes, but he has curves in all the wrong places."

"You touch my curves and I'll break your fingers."

"But I do my best work with my fingers," Finn protests.

Baylor helps him sit down. "Do you never shut up?"

"Only when I've got my mouth full." Sweat beads on his temples, but Finn's still smiling, and he's speaking faster than usual. I know bravado when I see it.

And so do the others.

"Here." Eris whips one of the leather armguards from her wrist and shoves it between his teeth. "Bite down on this."

"Is it going to hurk?" he manages to grind out around it.

"Oh, it won't hurt me at all," she replies with a grin. "I just want you to stop talking."

The tension dissolves as Eris squats in front of Finn, slicing the gaping hole in his trousers wider, so she can examine the arrowhead embedded in his thigh.

But I know the prince is still watching me, a faint frown embedded between his brows.

This line of questioning isn't over.

And I don't know that I have the answers he clearly wants.

Somehow, I can feel the Hallows when no one else can.

Just like the Old Ones can.

32

"It's later."

The words are soft with danger. But it's the kind of danger that comes wrapped around a warrior male with a promise in his eyes. Thiago rests his shoulder against the doorjamb to my bedchamber in Ceres, his eyes sleepy and insolent, but I know he's not here to discuss the Hallow, or Angharad.

One day he gave me. One day to rest and recover.

One day to hide in my rooms as I tried to process everything that had happened at Mistmere.

But he's never been one to hide from me. Not for long.

"It is." I close the book I'm reading with a snap. "One day closer to the moment my mother takes your head. Perhaps she'll parade it on a pike. Or hang it above her throne."

His eyes narrow as if to say, *oh-so-that's-the-way-it's-going-to-be*.

"One day closer to the day you choose me."

"Is your sense of confidence usually so inflated? Or are you just so insufferably smug you can't see the risk?" My voice roughens. Curse it. I've been dwelling on this all day, and I wanted to sound logical and calm. "You made a deal that will cost you your life, and I will be the catalyst of your death! And you didn't think to tell me?"

I want to fling the book at him.

Thiago slides onto the bed, taking the book from me as if he can read my mind. "You don't love me. Not yet. I wanted to give you the chance to fall for me, without you feeling that you must."

"I don't...." I don't know what to feel. Confused, mostly. I grind the palms of my hands against my eyes. "I trust you." It's a whisper. "And you're charming and dangerous and... you're like some sort of storm that's swept into my life and blown me so far off course, I cannot see the shore anymore. Everything has changed. Everything feels like some sort of horribly wonderful dream I've found myself trapped in." I draw my knees up to my chest, resting my chin on the top of them. "And then there's you. Both the catalyst for this upheaval, and my one safe haven in the storm. And I honestly don't know what I feel."

"You can't keep your eyes off me. That's a start."

I lower my palms. He's smiling.

"You're the one that keeps parading in front of me in various forms of skin-tight leather," I accuse. "Was I not meant to look?"

"Oh, no," he purrs. "You were definitely meant to notice."

Leaning forward, he brushes his lips against my cheek. He's so close, I could turn and press my mouth to his, and turn this into something else.

I want to.

But there are still words to be said.

"Curse you," I whisper, turning my face just so, my lips brushing against his. "I'm trying to be angry with you."

"You owe me nothing, Vi. Not your feelings, not yourself, not if you don't want me." His lashes flutter against my skin. "I love you. I will always love you. But this kind of love does not demand anything from you, this kind of love is not a cage. If you cannot bring yourself to give your heart to me again, then know this: You hold no blame for any of this. I loved you. And *I* made a dangerous, foolish bargain with your mother, because I was so certain of our destiny, I could not see the trap around me. Your heart is a gift but if you cannot give it to me, it will never change how I feel about you. You bear no responsibility for any of this."

And then he captures my face and deepens the kiss.

It's so familiar. So intoxicating. I want to drown myself in him, and ignore all the doubts that plague me.

I want to pull him down onto the bed and take whatever chances we have.

But I *can't* forget.

I shove him away angrily. "That pretty little speech sounds as though you want me to remember your words when all is said and done. And clearly, I loved you enough to defy my mother. So, yes, I feel some guilt. I need to fix this. Or I'll never forgive myself."

Nobody has ever risked their own life for mine.

"Trust in fate, Vi. Maia didn't grant me a vision of you only to punish us. We were written in the stars."

"I'm going to hit you with this book," I tell him, reaching for it. "Destiny is not an answer to this problem. You make your own destiny. It's the one time I agree with my mother."

"Any solution we seek is twice as likely to get us killed," he growls. "We've tried everything on this side of Seelie. The only possible means to break the curse are either dark magic, or bargains with eldritch beings, and you know what that means."

Unseelie.

"So you haven't tried *everything*."

"It's not safe to venture into Unseelie."

My mind starts racing. Normally, I'd agree with him, but this is his potential *execution* we're speaking about, and I don't share his hopes in my memory. "We could take precautions. Or Eris. She seems to enjoy murdering unseelie creatures."

"It's not safe *for me* to enter Unseelie."

My breath comes slowly. He's alluded to his past, though he swore he wouldn't tell me the truth until the curse is broken.

"In what way?" I ask carefully. "Vengeful creatures who've sworn to have your head? Or the... Darkness?"

"Both."

"How dangerous?"

"I couldn't help you. Vi. Not even to save your life. I wouldn't be able to use my powers there, for fear they'd overwhelm me. Or for fear my enemies would feel it and come for me. I would be virtually defenseless." His face shuts down. "And there's no point discussing this, for we're not going to find any answers there."

Reaching out, he yanks the book out of my grasp.

"*The Age of Myth and Magic*." He turns the book over. "If you wanted to know what it was like before the great wars, you could have asked."

That's not why I chose the book. "Excellent diversion."

"I thought so too." He finds the page I was reading and opens it, his eyebrows almost hitting his hairline. "I stand corrected. You're not reading about the wars." He turns the book this way and that, as I try to snatch it from his grasp. "I would say 'By the Erlking's hairy balls', but I see they're quite well trimmed. And.... Intimidatingly enormous."

I finally get one hand on the book, but he fends me off with ridiculous ease.

"Give it back!"

"Another bookmarked page," he teases, rifling the pages. "The Grimm. Not quite as well-endowed as the Erlking, though one can hardly tell with that scythe he's wielding. Are you sure this is suitable bedtime reading, Vi? If you wanted to scratch a certain itch, you should have called."

"If I wanted to scratch an itch, I'd scratch it."

His eyes heat.

And I grab the book with both hands.

"Don't let me stop you." He tackles me to the bed.

We roll, a motley assortment of limbs and hard flesh. I lose the book, but it no longer matters. Thiago pins me to the bed, wrists held on either side, and I can't help surrendering.

We're both breathing hard.

"Is this a better distraction?" he whispers, letting me go.

"Maybe." I reach up and grab a fistful of hair, dragging his mouth toward mine for a lazy kiss.

Tension quivers through him. His tongue is firm and demanding, and I moan a little as his weight presses me into the mattress.

Breaking the kiss, he rests his forehead against my shoulder. "You ruin me, Vi. I should go. Before I break my word."

He rolls toward the edge of the bed.

"Thiago...." I catch at his fingers.

Sitting on the edge of the bed, he glances over his shoulder at me. "Yes?"

Somehow, I find the courage to put my wishes into words. I would rather face a dozen howling goblins, than admit to my feelings, but.... "You should stay."

He glances down at our linked fingers. "In what capacity?"

"Guard my dreams," I whisper, though it's more than that.

I want to fall asleep in his arms, feeling his breath stir against my neck and his heartbeat kick against my back. I want what I've only experienced in those soft moments between sleep and waking—a single stolen moment of surrender, before the dream vanishes, leaving only the ghostly sensation of his touch in my bed.

Thiago turns, sliding back beneath the sheets and opening his arms to me. "As you wish."

And I don't think about it.

I just curl into those strong arms and try to imagine a future where I could spend every night like this. No longer alone. No longer guarded. Safe. And loved.

Three weeks remain. And now I have incentive to break this fucking curse, no matter what I must do.

Tick tock.

MORNING DAWNS, bringing with it a soft golden light that paints ripples across Thiago's chest. Waking in his arms might be my new favorite thing, though I'll never admit it. Lifting my head slightly, I examine his restful face, those eyelashes dark against his olive skin. My fingers stir, tempted to brush against his chiseled lips.

They're so perfect, though perhaps my judgement has something to do with his kisses.

If I didn't know better, I'd almost think I was besotted.

"You snore when you're exhausted," he says suddenly,

and I jerk my fingers back with a squeak, as those lashes flutter open. "I'd almost forgotten."

"I do *not*."

"Like a troll."

Stabbing him in the ribs with a finger, I scowl at his sexy smile. Every inch of him is sleepy and rumpled. I like him best like this, I think.

He captures my fingers and bites them lightly, his gaze falling to my throat.

"Nope, nope, nope!" I push at him as he leans closer with a heated look in his eyes. "Don't you dare. I haven't brushed my teeth yet. And it's morning."

I throw the blankets off, but he throws them back over me and pins them there.

"So it is."

"Morning," I rasp. "Which means one less day to break this curse."

Thiago stills, the muscle in his biceps flexing as he hovers over me. "I thought we'd discussed this."

"The discussion wasn't finished. You told me there's nothing in Seelie that can break the curse. That leaves the north." I push myself upright. "Tell me everything we've tried in the past."

And so he does.

Sorcerers. Magi. Witches. None of them can break the curse. None of them even know what the spell is, or who cast it. Baylor thought it was Unseelie work, which definitely means dark magic.

"So, there's no hope then." It's starting to hit me. I'm going to lose him. I'm going to lose myself.

Thiago takes so long to reply that I almost suspect he's not going to.

"There's someone we can ask."

"Why does it sound like you'd rather gouge your eyes out with a spoon?"

He grimaces, his biceps flexing as he rolls his head toward me. "Because it involves going deep into Unseelie territory and seeking out one of its most dangerous members. There's a reason I've not taken this path in the past. And I can't help you. I can't protect you."

Deep into the heart of Unseelie. He's not the only one who hesitates. The Unseelie kingdoms are filled with creatures that would eat you alive. And that's probably one of the more merciful deaths.

"Who?"

"The Morai."

It's not a name I know.

"They're three ancient Unseelie," he tells me, "who can grant you answers to any three questions you ask. You just have to be careful you're asking the right questions."

I draw my knees to my chest, my hair tumbling over my shoulders.

Unseelie. The answer lies there. It has to.

I glance at him. "You don't need to protect me. You've spent thirteen years trying to be my shield. Maybe it's time I became yours."

His face darkens, but I press my finger to his lips to stall him.

"Let me be your queen. Let me do this."

Thiago bites my finger. "You know not what you're facing."

"It can't be worse than my mother." I toss the blankets aside, slipping from the bed. "And we have no time to lose. Get out of bed. Let's rouse the others. We have a trip to plan."

33

"Does anyone else not see the problem with this?" Eris demands, as we gather at the Hallow in Valerian.

Cold wind bites through my cloak. Whatever magic wards the city doesn't quite cover the Hallow. Snow dusts its marble floors, covering the ancient bronze symbols that help channel its power. The Valerian Hallow lies directly along the ley line that runs to the Unseelie Hallow we want to arrive at.

"Come," Finn declares, "it will be a glorious death. They'll sing of us in the ballads as the Unseelie drink their wine from our skulls."

"See," she points out. "Even he agrees with me."

Thiago remains quiet by my side.

He's been quiet ever since he announced our plans to venture into the Unseelie territories. Eris, Finn, and Thalia have filled the void with their incessant chatter, but beneath their brightness I can hear the faintest undercurrent of nerves.

I can't forget he left Baylor behind "just in case."

If we all fall, then someone needs to hold the Kingdom of Evernight together. Someone needs to hold my mother at bay and speak for the Alliance. Whilst Baylor's Unseelie born, he's the only one my mother might fear enough to restrain her worst impulses.

"This is madness," Eris says.

"What would you suggest?" Thiago demands. "The Morai are the only step we haven't explored in the past."

As much as Eris rubs me the wrong way, I don't doubt her loyalty to Thiago. Her lips firm. "There's a reason for that."

"What reason?" I ask.

They all look at me.

The danger of journeying into Unseelie doesn't need to be explained, but until this moment, the Morai were the target, not the danger.

"The Morai were here when the Old Ones first walked the realms," Eris admits grudgingly. "They can't access the power of the ley lines, but even the Old Ones stepped cautiously around them. Each visitor is granted one visit—and only one—to access their visions, in exchange for a gift of blood."

To offer a creature your blood, hair, or nails is tantamount to offering them a means to control you, if they're strong enough.

"They need the blood for the visions," Thiago says, correctly interpreting my expression.

"I don't find that remotely creepy," I mutter, especially considering I'm the one who's been chosen to visit the Morai.

Thiago's used his opportunity already and said he can't go near them. Apparently, he didn't like what he saw, and neither did they. If they catch even a single hint he's in the area, there may be a confrontation.

"Is she joking?" Eris asks. "She had best be joking. They make the hair on the back of my neck rise, and I'm not afraid of anything."

"She's joking," Thalia says, fist clenching and unclenching around the staff she wields.

"You'll be safe," Thiago assures me as we take our places within the Hallow. "The Morai have their own rules. They cannot harm a traveler who comes seeking answers—"

"Not until they've given those answers," Eris mutters. "Getting in isn't the problem. Getting out is."

"Which is why I brought you," he says.

Eris glances at the sky, as if she's praying directly to Maia. "I don't know what I did to deserve this, but I promise I won't do it again."

"It's because you're so powerful and dangerous," Finn tells her. "Even the Morai quiver when they hear Eris of Silvernaught is in their woods."

Eris cuts him a look that clearly says, *Die.*

Finn winks at her. "I'll hold your hand if you get scared of the dark."

Which is the other glorious piece of this puzzle. Apparently, the Morai live in an underground cavern system.

I swallow as Thiago powers the glyphs that activate the Hallow.

I can do this. After everything he's done for me, the least I can do is try.

"There are bats," Eris mutters. "I hate bats."

I clench my eyes shut. She *had* to mention it.

"You'll be fine," Thalia assures me, squeezing my hand quickly. "Thiago isn't about to lose you to the Morai. They'll have the answers you need to break the curse. I *know* it.

Think of how delighted your mother will be when you defeat her."

Bats. I give her a look.

"Trust me," Thiago says, and then heat and power shoot through the bronze glyphs, straight into the sky, and the world vanishes in a whip crack of sensation.

WE ARRIVE at the Hallow at Scarshaven, deep in Unseelie territory. The abrupt shift from endless evening skies to late afternoon is jarring, and the hiss as everyone simultaneously draws their sword sounds ridiculously loud in the air.

The Hallow stands in the middle of a swamp, and mist clings to the air.

Everything is a rich, verdant green, and the irritating *crick-crick* of an insect chirrups through the mist. Enormous trees jut out of the water, moss clinging to their branches. The island we're standing on features three stone bridges leading to either land or other islands. There's no way to tell which is which, though one of the bridges has long since crumbled into fragments.

Something moves in the water.

Bubbles slowly wend their way toward the island we're standing on.

Finn frowns. "Is that—"

"Move," Thiago says, shoving me in the back.

According to Kyrian's sources, Scarshaven is almost abandoned and our best bet to arrive deep in the heart of Unseelie without being noticed. No member of the Seelie courts has been this way in centuries, however, so we have to hope Kyrian's intelligence is correct.

It's also directly in the territory of Blaedwyn, one of the fiercest Unseelie queens.

They say her heart turned to stone the moment she used the Sword of Mourning to drive the Erlking into the Underworld, and it's been that way ever since. Though she was once Seelie, she was driven from the south and cast out of the alliance. She's no friend of ours.

"Which way?" I whisper.

Thiago strides across the bridge to my left, the one that leads directly into the mist. Shadows beckon there, so of course this is the path we must take.

The journey out of the swamp takes over an hour, and silence masks our footsteps. Anything could be hiding in the mist, and our chances of succeeding rely purely upon stealth. An army couldn't take this place, but perhaps a small party of five can slip through it unnoticed.

The black ash trees give way to birches and maples, and the ground soon becomes drier.

It's... beautiful in a wild, feral kind of way.

Waterfalls drip from far distant cliffs, and thickets of thorns climb their way around stone ruins. There are low-lying walls running through the underbrush, as though the forest slowly reclaimed an ancient town that once lay here. Demi-fey skitter through the thickets, hissing at us and whispering to each other as they watch.

If this is Unseelie, then I'm beginning to wonder if the stories were all lies.

They say when the Old Ones walked the land, they brought darkness into the hearts of the fae they met. They cast curses to twist fae into creatures that became ugly and evil, creatures that would do their bidding. They lay with them and from these creatures sprang the Unseelie.

The very nature of the beasts changed the lands, as the

fae are all connected to the earth, and the queens' magic most of all.

Magic blackened the skies, the forests became hungry, and the earth violent.

But this is... not what I expected.

"It's so beautiful here. I thought we'd be walking into a barren, scorched land full of monsters."

"When you want to start a war," Thiago says softly, at my side, "then you need to unite your people behind a cause. And what is a more powerful tool than fear? Fear of the other. Fear of the unknown. You call them monsters and creatures and Unseelie, and your people will flock to your banners. You show them the bloody carcasses they leave behind, and your people will raise their weapons and vow to eradicate them. You change all the stories until the only ones that are spoken speak of the monstrousness of the enemy."

He helps me over a rotting log. "But there were other stories, once. The Unseelie were bound to the land more than we ever were. They worshipped nature and they grew to worship the Old Ones, as their parents did. Their powers were fiercer and more elemental. They turn away none, no matter how ugly or curse-twisted or violent. They worshipped strength. They were the howl in the night, and the chill on the back of your neck, but they were also the shadows dancing around a bonfire, and the ones who picked up those babies left in the forest to die so they could nurse them as their own."

I glance at him sharply. "They raise those children?"

There's always a mother who fears the prophecy spoken over their child at birth. Or misshapen, ugly curse-twisted creatures born to a fae woman. Changelings, they call them, left in their cribs by the Unseelie, but I sometimes wonder if they're the price of our magic.

It's always bothered me to hear of those babies left in the forest for nature to grant them justice.

"They raise them all," he says. "Perhaps not as you or I would raise them, but they take each and every one. Old Mother Hibbert prowls the night, listening for the cries of abandoned babies, and she sends her sprites to spirit them away."

Old Mother Hibbert is one of the creatures we fear. I grew up listening wide-eyed to stories of how she'd steal me away if I wasn't tucked in my bed come sundown.

I never knew she took the children we cast aside.

It's troubling. Because my mother lets her minstrels sing songs of Old Mother Hibbert—and others—in her court, and I've seen the horror and fear in my people's eyes when they listen.

"We must guard our hearts against the treachery of the Unseelie," she always says. *"They're monsters, Iskvien, and they must be subdued before they come to take what is ours."*

Does she truly believe her words, or was she merely warping the truth to keep my eyes firmly shuttered?

It makes me wonder about the great wars.

They came to enslave us.

They came to take what was ours.

They served the Horned One, who'd grown in stature among his people and commanded two of the queens.

They wanted to destroy us all.

Is any of it true?

"You fought for the Seelie Alliance during the wars, but you don't consider the Unseelie to be monsters. I don't understand."

"Of course, they're monsters," he replies, with a bitter

twist to his smile. "But are they the monsters we consider them to be? What *are* monsters, Vi?"

I don't have an answer to that.

"What drove them south?" he continues.

"The Horned One," I mutter, though now I'm not sure.

"Aye. He conquered most of the north and turned his gaze south. Do you know what he called us? The bright and shining ones who sought to steal the Unseelie's lands and magic. And maybe he was right. The Seelie had begun to eye the rich, fertile lands across the mountains. They wanted to conquer the 'northern filth'. Long before my time, there were clashes. The northern half of Mistmere and Evernight were once Unseelie. Valerian was one of their major cities. When the Horned One turned his hordes south, they came to reclaim what had been stolen from them."

"You sound as though you almost feel sorry for them."

Thiago slips through the forest on a wraith's feet, barely even disturbing the leaves. "I don't know what to think, Vi. There were atrocities committed on both sides. And which side is right? Which side is wrong? It depends what you believe. It depends what you're heard and seen with your own eyes. As I said, stories change, depending on the one speaking them. Wars are woven with lies. They're fought with weapons and swords, but they're started with words. I know what words can do to a person, or even a people. Now imagine what it can do to history."

I think of everything my mother has said of the Prince of Evernight.

Monster. Bastard. Usurper.

Unseelie.

And before I was given to him, I called him those names too. I feared and hated him, and I had no reason to do so, beyond that which I was taught from the cradle.

"My mother said you overthrew your queen and then killed her sons. She said you came from nowhere to serve your queen as her warlord and then you betrayed her. You were one of Araya's... favorites."

Lovers, is the word my mother used.

Thiago's shoulders stiffen. "Is that a question?"

"Yes."

This wicked prince can be both cruel and kind. And I married him. I loved him. I don't know what I feel right now, but there's hints of those feelings still left inside me. If I'm to make sense of everything I feel, then I need to know the truth.

"I was Araya's warlord," he replies, eyes focusing on the forest as if he can't look at me right now. "I was never her lover, no matter what the stories say."

"She granted you favors beyond those she gifted others."

His lips twist bitterly. "Yes. But I think I'll keep the reason why to myself, if you don't mind."

"And if I do?"

"Then I'll tell you. One day. The day you cast your mother's lies aside and choose me in the gathering."

"I'll hold you to that bargain," I warn.

"And I'll pay the price freely."

If I cast off the curse and remember him.

"Tell me of Araya's sons then," I continue. "They say you overthrew them in single combat."

"You're full of questions today."

"You're the one who speaks of wars and lies. All I know are lies. Perhaps I want to know the truth. Your truth."

"Araya had two trueborn sons, Emyr and Arawn. Emyr was cruel, but he was generally expected to be named his mother's heir. He was big, and strong, and virile. He spent hours practicing his sword work and rode at my side, countermanding every order I made. He thought himself a warrior, but he wanted to be a conqueror. I hated him with every ounce of my being. Arawn was his opposite. Smart, agile, a lean whip of a man who spent most of his time on politics or in books.

"A month before she was murdered, Araya called her sons together and announced that Arawn would be her heir instead. I was there. As her warlord, I needed to know who to back. And I think she wanted me to be the shield between Emyr and Arawn, for any fight between them would end with Arawn's death. He was never a fighter."

"So Emyr killed her."

"No." The words are soft. Full of malice. "Emyr was never smart enough to plot her murder. The queen was no fool. If Emyr had done it, he would have driven a sword straight through her chest, taken the crown from her head, and then sat upon her throne, bloody sword and all."

"Arawn, then?"

"I was the one who found her, slain on her throne room floor. Someone had cut her throat from behind. And Araya was the most dangerous woman I've ever met." He falls silent for a moment, as if he's picturing it again. "To get near her, her killer had to be someone she knew. Someone she would never suspect nor defend herself against. Someone smart, who could lay the blame at another's feet. Someone who had something to gain." Thiago glances toward me. "I can never prove it, but Arawn was the next one through the throne room doors with an entire complement of guards. They found me there, kneeling by her side with her blood wetting my fingers. Emyr came through the other door, just as the guards fanned out." His lips quirk. "I don't know who was more surprised. Emyr challenged me. Of course, he challenged me. All those years we'd sparred together, and he still couldn't see his death looming. I cut him down within minutes and fought my way free of the castle.

"It was almost perfectly plotted. Cast me as her murderer, and use me to kill his brother. Arawn named me traitor and set about hunting me down, but he forgot one crucial fact... I was Araya's warlord. Most of the army belonged to me, and I had Eris and Baylor by my side. The other two warbands split and sided with Arawn. It meant we had to fight our own, but I was younger then. Furious and lost in grief. I knew he'd done it. The smarmy little prick always did like to prove how clever he was. But I didn't want to ride against our friends and allies. When we arranged ourselves on the field, I offered a chance of single combat so no blood would be spilled. Arawn refused to meet me on the battlefield himself, but he sent his finest warrior, and I cut them down."

His voice softens. "If there's one thing an army respects, it's sacrifice. I had wagered everything I had on that duel. I could have ridden through those that stood against me—I had the numbers—but I chose to spare them instead. And when Gawad fell, by the terms of the duel, I was a free man. But Arawn ordered his generals to take my head. It was the second mistake he made. Trial by combat is unassailable. And he'd gone back on his word. So they brought me his head, instead."

And he became the usurper. The bastard. The murderer.

His armies worshipped him, and those in his court counted him as both prince and friend, but the people in Ceres.... I couldn't forget the pain in his voice when he spoke of their disdain for him.

And for what? A lie. A petty, scheming prince's aborted attempt to take a throne.

Thiago's never overthrown that mantle. He probably never will.

It's true.

Words have a power even a blade can't match.

Finn slips through the forest, appearing out of nowhere. "We're nearly there."

"Nothing ahead?" Thiago asks.

Finn shakes his head. "Nothing but bones littering the forest floors and hanging in warning from the trees. Even the squirrels avoid this area, and judging from the spiderwebs, they have good cause."

Spiderwebs. I give Thiago a long, hard look, which he ignores. There was no mention of spiderwebs.

"And Blaedwyn?" he asks.

"I can see her castle through the trees, but there's no sign of her guards." Finn scrubs at his mouth. "Her banner is hanging from the tallest tower."

Which means she's home.

Another complication.

Thiago turns to me. "Are you ready?"

The sooner I get in, get the answers I need, and get out, the sooner we can slip unnoticed from these cursed lands.

"Let's get this done," I tell him.

We move out, and Finn leads us directly to a chasm in the side of the mountain ahead. He's right. Bones hang from charms in the trees, swinging in the wind. Someone's drilled hollows in them, so as the wind catches them, they give an eerie whistle.

But it's the spiderwebs that cling to every rock and tree that cause me the main concern.

"What size does a spider have to be to create a web like

that?" I hiss as Finn slices through one that bars the way ahead.

"I really, really don't want to know," Thalia mutters.

"You're not the one who's going to have to find out," says Eris, looking as grim as I've ever seen her.

I eye the sheen of sweat on her forehead. Is Eris—the almighty Destroyer—actually nervous?

"Here we are," Thiago says as Finn hacks through the last of the webs.

A cave appears. Moss hangs over the opening, and spider silk glistens in the late afternoon sunlight. It's dark and gaping, like the hollow mouth further north that allegedly leads directly into the Underworld.

"Look at me." Thiago's hands cup my chin, and he turns my face to his. "I can't go in there with you, Vi. Not even to save your life. I've already been once, and the Morai vowed a second visit would be my undoing. They cannot lie. What they see is bound to come true." He hesitates. "You don't have to do this."

If this is the only way to gain answers, then yes, I do.

This curse isn't merely a wedge between us, it's an obliteration of who I am. I want those memories back. I want to be able to look my mother in the eye and ask her why. And I want my magic.

Swallowing hard, I lock down every little scrap of fear that shivers through me and rest my hand on the hilt of my sword. "Spiders? Ha. You know what spiders are afraid of?"

His brows draw together.

"Fire," I tell him, clicking my fingers and sending a spark into the air. "If I'm not back before nightfall, then give my mother my regards."

34

The cavern's enormous, and silvery threads decorate every surface. Torchlight reflects back off droplets of mist that cling to each strand, and as I look up, I see the gossamer threads go all the way to the roof of the enormous cavern above me.

Webs.

The entire cave system is covered in spiderwebs.

On a scale of one to burn-it-fucking-alive, my feelings about spiders are firmly on the flammable end of the scale.

"It could be hundreds of tiny little spiders," I tell myself as I creep along the passage. Sticky strands burn away before my torch, but I can feel some of them clinging to my hair. "Maybe even a thousand of them."

It's not.

I know it's not, but the art is in tricking your mind into believing it.

The caves lead deep underground, and I follow the main cavern all the way down, ignoring the smaller caves that branch off. Spiderwebs cover their gaping mouths, and I pass numerous dried husks encased in fine silver thread.

Some of them still move.

If I pay the price, then I'll be safe, Thiago said, and the flask of warm blood—mine—is strapped to my hip.

Down and down we go, until the air is still and cold. The only light is the torch I carry, and I swear I can hear things scuttling in my wake.

But I am not going to think about that right now.

Finally, I reach an enormous cavern that gapes into infinity. In the distance, I can make out a dais where three shadows move against the canvas of an enormous loom coated with spider silk.

He'd warned me about what I'd find, but even so, the reality is grotesque.

The Morai are part spider, part... something else. Their bloated bodies scuttle about on long, spindly legs, though their torsos and faces appear humanoid. The upper arms glisten with spider silk, and their eyes are bound with simple linen. Rumor has it they gouged them out many moons ago, after they glimpsed a future they were never meant to see.

The three of them freeze, bodies slowly undulating before the enormous loom. Their heads turn toward me as one, and the first one sniffs the air, letting out a hiss of delight.

"Sisters three, what have we here?" it asks.

"Smells like... dinner." One of them scuttles toward me, its reddened lips wet with saliva, and I wave the torch at it threateningly. Fire's the only thing that can keep them at bay.

The Dreamweaver forges fate in her grasping hands. The web she sees can only be woven by the Threadcutter, and the Shadowbinder is the one who manipulates the fabric of the future.

"I come seeking answers, O Great Ones," I call, because a little flattery never hurts anyone.

"Answers, sisters," whispers the first one. "It wants answers. To what questions, one must ask?"

"A thorny curse," chortles another.

"A deranged queen."

"A heart left shattered."

They fall silent, quivering with anticipation as they watch me. Well, now. That was creepy.

"Ah, it is surprised," one whispers. "Did it not know we see all? We see the past."

"We see the future."

"And we see the now." The last sister inches toward me, pincers abstractedly weaving what looks to be a net.

I wave the torch again. "Stay back."

"Did you bring the price of a reading?" asks one.

"Hot and warm, I can smell it," whispers another.

"The blood, the blood, so sweet and wet." The last sister traces her clawed chelicerae over her lips as if she can already taste it, and if that wasn't enough to make my gorge rise, then nothing else will do it.

"I brought your blood price," I call, holding up the leather flask and praying my nerve lasts. "But in return, I want answers three."

Thiago told me what to ask for.

And whatever you do, don't run, he'd added.

"Answers three."

"It's a bold, greedy little thing."

"It dares much."

They creep closer, lips drawing back from sharp teeth.

"*It* has sharp iron," I call back boldly, "and fire."

"Fire dies."

"Iron rusts."

"And bodies bleed."

"All true." I swallow hard, lifting my hand. Magic, don't fail me now. "But this fire can't be quenched."

A snap of my fingers and the spark inside me ignites. Flame whirls into life, chasing the crisp nothingness of broken webs and dreams.

The Morai draw back with a collective hiss, their shadows painted large upon the walls. Sweat drips down my forehead as I step forward, the flames dancing in circles around my feet. They like weak prey and easy meat, but they're cowards at heart, Thiago told me, and will retreat if I'm bold.

"Give it," one hisses, retreating halfway up the wall.

"And we'll grant thee answers three."

"But mind you ask carefully."

I hurl the flask, and they fight over it, splashing my blood across their faces and lips, greedily sucking it from their pincers.

"There is a curse upon me," I tell them very carefully, "that steals my memories every time I return to my mother. I need to know if it can be broken."

The Shadowbinder plucks at the threads on her web, halfheartedly spinning something into life. "All curses can be broken."

"All contracts can be voided," says the Threadcutter.

"All magic can be undone."

I'd thought so. There's always a loophole, and yet it's a relief to hear it spoken. "How do I break the curse?"

"End yourself and you end the curse."

"Kill the one who cast it."

"Seek one who is more powerful to break it."

Two of those options are worth exploring. "Who cast the curse?"

Silence.

One of them smiles. "The Queen of Thorns."

It's a breathless feeling to hear it spoken aloud. "My mother doesn't work blood magic. It's Unseelie magic. It's forbidden."

It's old, powerful magic that blackens your soul. Every working you perform slowly corrupts you, until *you're* the monster in the forest or the witch who needs to be burned.

"Do you call us liars?" one of the Morai hisses.

Whatever you do, do not insult them, Thiago had warned.

"Of course not." I bow my head, but my mind is reeling. "I spoke from surprise. I would never.... I can't believe she...."

I've known the truth for days, though accepting it is another matter. I know her heart. I know her soul. Betrayed by her daughter? With her enemy gaining the upper hand upon her? Of course, she'd do it.

She wouldn't even flinch.

"How did my mother learn this sort of curse magic?"

They quiver and sway.

"You asked for answers three, and we have given them," one of the Morai says slyly.

"I believe I asked two questions," I say carefully. "The first was a statement of fact. Not a question. I said, 'I need to know if it can be broken.' You volunteered the answers."

There's a collective hiss.

"It's a tricksy little beast," says the Shadowbinder. "It had best mind its tongue, that we don't find it delicious to eat."

"How did my mother learn this sort of curse magic?" I repeat.

"She was taught by a master."

"She was taught by a monster."

"She was taught by a sorcerer who is owned by the Horned One."

Isem. Angharad's pet sorcerer.

Of all the truths I've learned today, this one is the most shocking. My breath catches. My mother's working directly with the Unseelie. While I might imagine her casting the curse, this.... This is beyond betrayal. If anyone were to discover proof of her actions, she'd be overthrown. Not even her alliances with the Queen of Aska and the Queen of Ravenal would protect her. Even they would not tolerate this.

I must have driven her mad.

"It has the truth now, sisters," the Threadweaver whispers, turning her blindfolded eyes upon me. "Now what will it do with it?"

Kill my mother, and I'll have an end to this wretched curse.

Or find someone more powerful than she to overturn it.

But who has that sort of power?

I'm not lying when I say my mother is one of the most powerful fae in the Seelie Alliance. Queens are tied to the land and wield its power. We'd never get close enough to kill her. And to break her spell work....

Thiago might be strong enough, but he's not a spell worker. Nor are any of the other queens. Armed with both the land's power and Isem's sorcery and cursework, my mother would be well-nigh invincible.

The Shadowbinder touches one last droplet of blood to her lips, and then gasps.

"What's wrong, sister?" The Dreamweaver demands. "What has it done?"

"It is not what it has done, but what it will do," she hisses.

I stare between them. "What will I do?"

The Shadowbinder inches closer, her stark face hungry. "You will break the world, *leanabh an dàn*."

Leanabh an dàn.

My heart freefalls into my feet. There'd been a suspicion, earned the day we drove Angharad back at Mistmere, but I'd never yet let myself entertain the possibility. I couldn't.

And I don't have the time to contemplate it now.

My hand goes to my sword. As far as prophecies go, it's a wretched one.

"You will unleash chaos and ruin upon your people."

"You will bring about the end of Unseelie."

"What shall we do, sisters three?" whispers the Dreamweaver.

The Threadbinder edges closer to me. "Kill it and save the world."

"Eat it all up and forestall ruin," says the Shadowbinder.

"Bury its bones," the Dreamweaver whispers, "and never let them see the light of day."

I wave the torch, backing toward the caves. "Stay where you are. I paid the price."

"But you never bargained for safe passage out of here," says the Dreamweaver with a leer as she lunges toward me.

I whip my flames into a protective circle with my magic, sweat dripping down my face. The Morai shriek and scuttle backwards, but I don't have the strength—or the skill, to fan my flames.

Instantly, their faces turn, all three of them focusing on something behind me.

A torch bobs in the darkness as if someone is running toward us.

Something's wrong. *The only reason Thiago would have sent someone to fetch me is if we're under attack.*

The three Morai sniff the air.

"Ah," says the Shadowspinner, grinning through her bloodred lips. "The Bastard. We warned him what would happen if he ever returned."

"We'd suck the meat from his bones and drink his marrow," another hisses.

"And unleash the burden he bears."

They scurry toward the torchbearer.

"Thiago!" I yell, trying to smother my flame circle.

It wanes, but doesn't smolder. Curse it. I leap over the flames and bolt after the Morai, drawing my sword as I run.

The Morai clamber the walls of the tunnel, one of them scuttling along the roof.

I shout a warning, but there's no way I'll be able to reach him in time.

Then I realize the newcomer's too short to be my husband.

Eris sprints toward me, her eyes black in the darkness of the tunnel. She spots the first Morai and launches herself at the wall. Springing off it with one boot, she slashes her sword through the carapace of the one on the roof.

Cold, black ichor splashes across the walls and my face, and then the Morai screams and falls to the floor.

"Go! I'll cover you!" Eris lunges forward with her blade, and for a second her shadow on the wall looms large, monstrous teeth gaping.

The Shadowspinner recoils, clutching at one of her sisters. "It's her!" she screams. "The Devourer!"

"Sullied One," another hisses, and then they're all drawing back, crouching low as if to try and avoid her attention.

Sullied One? I shoot her a glance and see a flicker of hurt in her eyes, then Eris realizes I'm watching and her expression smoothes.

"You can stay and be spider bait if you like," she snaps, "but we've got a hunting party on our trail."

"A hunting party?"

"Thiago thinks it belongs to Blaedwyn. We need to get out of here."

I eye the hissing Morai. "Gladly."

35

The woods are still and quiet when we finally escape.

I don't dare put my sword away, jumping at every chime of the wind through those hollow bones as we make our way back to where we left the others. I can still hear the furious shriek of the Morai in my ears as Eris poured a trail of brandy across the entirety of the tunnel and I set fire to it.

All those dried husks and spiderwebs caught fire, and the stink of burning hair and clothes still clings to me.

Eris leads, slipping through the woods with a focus I've never seen on her before. Crouching before a thicket of thorns, she gestures for me to join her.

Below lies the clearing where Thiago said he'd wait.

It's empty.

"Where are they?" I breathe.

Eris points to a tree, and I catch sight of an arrow embedded in the trunk. The second I see it, my eyes start to make sense of what I'm seeing. Hoofmarks churn the dark loam, and there's a wink of silver across the clearing, as if someone lost an epaulet.

My heart drops. "What happened?"

Eris slips through the treeline, and I follow as she skirts the clearing and finds a trail stomping through the underbrush.

She slowly straightens, looking furious.

"Blaedwyn happened. She's taken them. Nobody else could have countered Thiago and survived. And with that fucking sword at her side, she's invincible."

And he can't use his power.

"What now?"

Eris turns on me, and for a moment, I swear she's going to use her sword on me. "Now we discover just how far you'll go to prove yourself worthy. Thiago instructed me to see you back through the Hallow if things went wrong. I swore an oath to do so, on my obedience to the crown, but technically, as his wife, you *are* the crown."

My eyes narrow. "What are you trying to say?"

"Do I obey my orders and whisk you back to safety while your husband loses his head?" she asks coolly. "Or does *the crown* have other orders?"

"You seem awfully interested in his survival."

"Thiago gave me a home when others would have burned me at the stake," she snaps. "I would die for him. The question is: Would you?"

I eye the trail leading toward Malagath, the ancient seat of Blaedwyn the Merciless. A sigh escapes me. "How angry do you think he's going to be?"

Her shoulders ease as she realizes what I intend. "With me? Furious. With you?" Her eyes light up. "Beyond."

"Think positively," I chide as I start along the trail. "We might all die and never have to look him in the eye again."

ERIS and I track the hunting party back to Malagath.

The castle ruins perch on the edge of a cliff like a vulture, hump-necked and crumbling. Vines snake their way toward the keep, forming a dangerous labyrinth. The only safe way in is the main road, which snakes up the hillside, but anyone coming would be seen for miles. Sunset is starting to bleed across the skies, but the fae can see in the dark, and the Unseelie consider themselves at home there.

I eye the labyrinth.

There's got to be a thousand wrong turns in there and numerous dangerous beasties, but what are our options?

Eris paces, wearing her frustration like a shroud that darkens her face. Of all the people to be stuck with on a rescue mission....

"I don't suppose you can fly?" I ask.

"I don't suppose you can fight?"

My fingers curl into my palms. I'm better with a bow than a sword, but I can hold my own. Any daughter of Adaia must be able to, though Andraste could beat me nine times out of ten. "I'm competent. We need to get closer."

The pair of us slip back into the forest, creeping toward the road.

A slow, steady ringing of bells has been echoing for minutes now, and I don't know what it means, but hopefully it will mask any sounds we make.

It might also mask any sounds someone following us might make.

The thought makes me nervous, but then, I do have someone at my side that the Morai were afraid of.

"What do you think is happening?" Lights beckon

through the trees as we parallel the road, staying a safe distance away from it.

Eris crouches and watches. The lights bob and flicker. Torches. I think they're torches. And someone is singing, though the song has a ribald flavor that reminds me of a tavern.

"Unbelievable," Eris breathes. "It's Raven's Flight."

Raven's Flight is the night the Unseelie celebrate the Raven King. There are masks and bonfires and feasts. Dancing and fucking and ribaldry.

We edge closer.

Our luck couldn't have been better.

Yes, there's hundreds of Unseelie flocking to the castle to celebrate, but on the other hand, there's hundreds of Unseelie flocking to the castle to celebrate. Two more travelers might be overlooked.

The trickle of travelers stretches along the road, where they laugh and cavort and threaten each other in loud, leering voices.

Most of them are masked already, and I realize I'm staring at a basilisk. To see its face is to know death, so they cover them at all times, only revealing them when they intend to kill. Behind it, a trio of fae wearing large black cloaks and polished silver masks keep a respectful distance.

"I have an idea."

Eris follows my gaze. "This is a *bad* idea."

"We need a way in, don't we? I don't think relying on your charm and grace is going to cut it."

She snorts. "If we get caught, I can't protect you."

"Who said I need protection?"

"Does a goblin like gold?"

One of these days.... "If you have a better idea, *the crown* will happily hear it."

Eris and I stare each other down. She finally looks away, the muscle in her jaw flexing. "Fine. Those three." She points to the masked fae trailing behind the basilisk. "You distract them. I'll kill them."

THE PLOY WORKS WELL. Too well.

We're inside the castle, and the guards barely glanced at us in our borrowed finery. Something's going to go wrong. This is too easy.

Blaedwyn's the least dangerous of the Unseelie queens, though one should never underestimate her.

She's over five hundred years old, and there are tales of her heroics—the ones that cost her soul. Fair Blaedwyn, the Seelie princess who buried the Sword of the Mourning in the Erlking's chest, vanquishing him into an Otherworld prison. The princess who sacrificed herself in order to ply the ancient relic of power and trap an Old One.

Wielding the relics comes with a cost.

The sword warped her and turned her into this... creature.

Now she's cruel and vicious and far more powerful than she ever was. The sword still hangs at her hip, and even from here, I can sense its malevolence vibrating through the air. It binds her to Mrog the Warmonger, who is said to bring turbulence and hatred wherever he rides.

She's never been defeated whilst she has that sword in her hand.

The Unseelie of her court howl and rampage through the ballroom in celebration, flinging horns of mead everywhere.

Blaedwyn herself sits on her throne, one leg crossed

over the other as she watches her court revel. Her raven hair is braided in myriad little plaits that are all bound together, and raven feathers hang from the end of each plait. Kohl darkens her eyes, making her look like some sort of bird of prey.

Hanging above her in a gilded cage is Thalia, though there's no sign of Finn or Thiago. Every now and then, one of their Unseelie captors stabs a spear through the bottom of the cage, cackling as Thalia's forced to dance to avoid being skewered from below. Though it's unkind to leave her there, at least she's alive.

"Where is he?" I whisper, trying to blend into the vines that snake their way up the walls. I'd know if he was dead, wouldn't I?

If we were written in the stars as he claims we were, then I would feel something so monumental as his death. Surely.

A troll stomps past, casting us a leering smile, and both Eris and I freeze. The club it wields is bound with heavy iron spikes, and its rank scent is strong enough to almost knock me over.

"I can't see him." Eris lifts her head and sniffs the air. "Though I can smell him."

"Through that?" I nearly gag. "How can you smell anything after that great hairy unwashed armpit just strolled by?"

"With great difficulty. He was here, and there was blood, but not enough of it to mean his throat was cut." Eris hesitates, her gaze sliding toward Blaedwyn. "If she knows she's captured the Prince of Evernight, then I doubt she'll kill him. He's too useful."

"The Alliance would never trade them power or lands in exchange for him."

"No. But...." There's something she's not telling me. "If

they can turn him, then it's possible he might... become their vassal. And Unseelie's biggest weapon."

"Thiago?" My voice rises a little in disbelief. "Working for the Unseelie queens?"

He'd never cast aside his kingdom, his people.

He'd never cast *me* aside, which is what he'd effectively be doing.

"The Darkness inside him is not from the light courts," she whispers, and this time I see the desperation in her eyes. "He holds it at bay with great difficulty, but every day is a battle. If he were overwhelmed, then it's possible it wouldn't be Thiago left standing, but the creatures inside him. And they would very much like to destroy every last fae that lives in the south."

I know virtually nothing about the things he calls the Darkness, but I can remember the snarl of their voices and their grasping hands. I can remember every single word they whispered in my ear.

"They're powerful, Princess, and whilst they're trapped inside him, the world is safe. But make no mistake. If even a single one of them gains control of his body, we may as well kiss our lives goodbye. He could walk through the gap in the mountains, walk right into Seelie, and destroy anything they sent his way."

A shiver runs through me. "So she won't kill him, she'll seek to use him. Can he control his daemons? Or can she break him?"

Eris looks unhappy. "Both. Neither. I don't know. I don't want to find out."

I stare around the gathering.

Perhaps Blaedwyn doesn't yet know who she holds in her castle, but I'd much prefer she didn't find out.

"We need to move. And fast." I glance toward poor

Thalia, still swinging in her cage. "If I create a distraction, can you track Thiago down and free him?"

A hand locks on my arm as I take a step toward the dais. "What do you intend to do?"

My gaze falls upon Blaedwyn's sword where it's propped against her throne. "I'm going to steal that bitch's sword."

36

The best laid plans are the simplest.

I slip through the crowd, gaining a layout of the throne room. There are at least three exits, and the one I don't want to take leads directly into the labyrinth.

Eris's argument lingers in my ears. The Sword of Mourning is no simple sword. Its power is immense and tied directly to the Hallows and the ley lines. It alone is the key to opening the Erlking's prison world, and only a creature with the power to control it can set hand to its hilt.

The cost of failure is phenomenal.

Wielding it once cost Blaedwyn her light-blessed soul.

And as far as Eris knows, I don't have anywhere near the power to even touch it.

As far as *I* know, I don't have the power to touch it.

But I guess there's only one way to discover if I truly am this *leanabh an dàn*.

Slipping through the crowd, I dance and sway, staggering a little for good effect. The revelers are starting to succumb to the wagonloads of mead. The floors are slippery, and I'm nearly crushed by the crowd as I finally make my way to the side of the dais.

Draining the goblet I stole, I haul my arm back and hurl it at Thalia's cage. "Dance, you wretched Seelie bitch!"

The goblet hits the bars with a clang, and a half dozen Unseelie burst into laughter at Thalia's furious look. She cuts me an icy sneer, and I slip my mask from my face just long enough to wink at her.

Thalia freezes.

Then I slip back into the shadows until I can be certain no one is watching me too closely.

A troll found my act amusing and repeats it, with mead spraying across the crowd. A pair of hobgoblins take offense to being drenched, and suddenly a fight breaks out, knives flashing and the troll's club rising in the air.

Blaedwyn laughs as half the dancers are swept aside in a sudden melee.

I dart forward, capturing Thalia's attention.

"*Sing*," I mouth.

Thalia grabs at the bars of her cage, staring at me desperately. From the draw of her brows, she has no idea what I want her to do.

I point to the sword, then to Blaedwyn, then to her. And then I pretend to sing.

A hobgoblin slams into me, spinning me out of the way. "Clear the path," it snarls.

By the time I look back, Thalia is nodding.

The troll ends the fight with a sweep of its mighty club. Three of the Unseelie fall, and this time they don't get up.

"Fight me," it roars, huffing and snarling with rage, but the crowd is eyeing those broken bodies, and almost as one, the argument dies before its begun.

"Take it outside, Brutu," Blaedwyn calls. "Before you break any more of my tables."

Trolls have little intelligence, and this one is worked into a rage. But it takes one look at her, with her glittering, merciless eyes, and then it stomps away through the crowd.

"Queen Blaedwyn," Thalia suddenly calls, rattling on her cage bars. "I warn you to let me go, or else see your court suffer."

All eyes turn toward her.

Blaedwyn leans forward on her throne, her elbows resting on her knees. I need her to move away from the throne, but she merely smiles. "Why, the little bird has finally found its voice again. Pray tell, little bird, what shall you do if I deny you?"

Thalia visibly swallows. "I shall sing death down upon your people, and drive them mad."

The entire crowd roars with laughter.

Blaedwyn pushes to her feet, sauntering toward the middle of the dais. "The only ones who can sing death are bound to the sea or locked away with the Father of Storms. The saltkissed cannot walk the earth, little bird."

"But I am not wholly saltkissed," Thalia says in a firm voice.

And then she starts to sing.

The first few notes are pure bliss. Her voice. Sweet Maia, her voice. But then the octave shifts, and suddenly every pane of glass left in the windows high above us shatter.

Unseelie scream and bellow, fleeing for the doors and finding themselves trapped. Glass shards rain down upon the crowd, and finally, Thalia stops, her song cutting off with a sharp note.

"Do you want to hear me go higher?" she suggests.

Blaedwyn alone stands unstunned. Her eyes narrow, as I

slip behind the dais.

"It's a lovely performance," Blaedwyn calls, snapping her fingers for one of her servants as though she has no worries in the world. "Though I think I shall call your bluff. For that is what it is, is it not? If you could sing death, little bird, then you would have struck my riders down in the forest where you were captured. No saltkissed allows herself to be taken alive. No. I think you're lying."

She takes a goblet of mead from the server's platter.

I slip from the shadows and crouch behind the throne, my back set to the bleached wood. Every inch of me is tense, waiting for the merest hint of an outcry, but none comes.

"Indeed," the queen mocks, "I think I'm starting to remember a little rumor I once heard on the wind. Prince Thiago of Evernight has a cousin who was born a bastard of the sea, does he not? The girl could sing, or so it was said, until she made a pact with a mad witch who stole the power in her voice. And she never goes anywhere without her cousin. Grimsby, tell me.... Those two warriors you threw in the dungeon. Is one of them covered in tattoos?"

"I-I couldn't say, my queen," calls a lord to the right.

"Then find out." Blaedwyn snarls.

A brief glimpse shows the sword, resting against the arm of the throne. Sweat drips down my spine. It's now or never. I can't afford for her to discover who her prisoners are.

I gather my muscles, prepared to grab for it, when a sudden cry goes through the room.

"My queen," yells a loud voice. "I have found an intruder!"

Blaedwyn lowers the goblet from her lips. All across the room, heads turn, and the crowd parts.

My outstretched hand freezes.

Eris is forced forward, her hands clasped behind her

head and her eyes glittering with rage. A fae male wearing the same black robe and silver mask she disguised herself with, prods her forward with a sword to her spine. One of his irises is black, and the other a pearlescent silver that makes me queasy.

"This woman wears the bloodstained rags of my brethren," the fae declares, his mismatched eyes locking on Blaedwyn. "Though she's not of my clan."

"Bloodstained rags," Blaedwyn muses. "An intruder, by the look of it. A thief. Or is she here to rescue her prince?"

The crowd gasps.

It's not the distraction I was hoping for—curse Eris—but the Unseelie queen has her back to me, and her sword is but an inch away from me.

Time to set the plan in motion.

"But who would rescue Thiago?" Blaedwyn mocks. "Oh, look at those black, soulless eyes. *Yes.* I've heard of you too, Devourer. I've long itched to match my sword against your own. They say you cannot be beaten by battle, yet here you stand, bested by the lowest of my guard."

Eris stands still, her eyes locked on the queen, and I know she's deliberately ignoring what I'm doing. "Do you consider me bested?" she asks, cocking her head. "What if this was the plan, in order to get close to you?"

I've almost missed hearing the disdain in that voice.

"Then you're a fool," Blaedwyn tells her.

She's only three feet in front of me.

"I think that sword's warped your brain," Eris says. She slowly lowers her hands. "I wonder, can you be beaten in battle without it?"

"You'll never find out," the queen promises.

"Won't I?" There's a sense of satisfaction in Eris's voice as I make my move.

Lunging forward, I grab Blaedwyn and yank her back against me, holding a knife to her throat. "Don't move."

A collective gasp rolls around the room.

Blaedwyn freezes.

"I'm not having a good month," I whisper in her ear. "I suggest you answer my questions. Or I'll cut your throat with star-forged steel. Where are you keeping the prince and his man?"

"Oh my," she whispers back. "Another little mouse, rustling in the shadows. What a treacherous plot I've discovered."

"The prince," I growl, letting her feel the sharp edge of the knife.

"The dungeons," Blaedwyn replies. "Where else would I keep the Royal Prick?"

"Send someone to fetch them. If they don't return unharmed, then I'll do unto you what is done to them."

"So bold," she taunts. "I wonder..., could it be the prince's wife? They say he'll eat a thousand souls before he lets her go, but will she return the favor? Will she risk her own life for his when she can barely remember him?"

"I don't know." My grip in her hair tightens. "But I'm fairly certain I'll risk yours. Send someone to fetch him."

The bitch smiles and pushes into the blade. Blood weeps down her throat as my knife digs into her skin. "Do you know the problem with your little declaration?"

"What?"

"I've already walked in the shadows of the Gray. You can't kill me," she snarls, then drives her elbow back toward my face.

I turn at the last second and take the blow on my cheek instead of my nose. Pain ricochets through my face, but it's not the blinding pain it could have been.

The floor rises up to meet me, and the breath slams from my lungs as I slide across the polished stone of the dais.

Blaedwyn stalks toward me, the hem of her cloak rasping along the floor. She reaches for the sword in her sheath, and then pauses as her hand finds nothing.

"Missing something?" I demand, crawling inelegantly to my feet. Casting my cloak out of the way, I reveal the sword strapped to my hip.

Pure, utter coldness turns her eyes dark. "You little fool. Go ahead. Draw it against me. No hand can touch it but mine, though I'll enjoy watching your suffering."

There is no going back. Only forward. I have no other chance than this.

Grabbing hold of the hilt, I draw the Sword of Mourning with a steely rasp. The second the last inch of iron clears the sheathe, the rasp turns into a high-pitched squeal and the weight of the sword drives the tip of it toward the cold slate floors.

The sound of that ringing is like a knife straight to the brain. All around me, the rest of Blaedwyn's court stagger to their knees, their hands clapped over their ears, but I don't dare take my hands off it.

I can't anyway.

Pain roars through me, cleaving straight through my soul. I see armies rise and fall. I see throats cut and bodies dancing in the breeze as they jerk in the gibbet. I see Unseelie capering, their bodies fucking and grinding, and through it all, right back through a thousand flashing images of death, I see the shock of betrayal on a man's snarling face as my hand drives the sword through his chest, and I sob out a whispered, "*I'm sorry.*"

It's not me.

Nor do I recognize the stranger who falls, his enormous body slamming back onto the tiles of the Hallow, his blood spraying the stones.

The room explodes around me as power surges through me. I can hear the grumble of the ley line far, far beneath me.

Someone is screaming.

I think, perhaps, it might be me.

But images are flashing past my eyes. I see the creature fall a thousand times, his eyes wounded and surprisingly fae, as the woman whispers again and again, "*I'm sorry.*"

"*I'm sorry.*"

"*I'm sorry.*"

We weep a thousand tears, and I fear I'll never escape the weight of the sword.

Then darkness encroaches.

A woman walks out of the darkness, garbed in an endless black cloak. She shifts the cowl back from her face, her midnight-dark eyes warming as she beholds me.

"*Ah,*" she whispers as she closes my fingers around the Sword of Mourning, "*There you are.*"

The pain vanishes.

The knife is yanked from my brain.

I find myself standing on the dais, slowly lifting the tip of the sword as the weight of it lightens.

Blaedwyn gapes up at me from where she's lying flat on her back at my feet. The entire crowd is down, and the walls crumble from the shock of detonation.

Then Eris is there, shoving Thalia ahead of her.

"Move!" she yells, shoving me toward the arch behind the throne.

Through the castle wall and into the labyrinth.

37

"We're lost," I say, hacking at a thorny tangle of vines with my old sword. It shears away from the wall of the labyrinth, but other vines hiss at me and take its place, knotting the wall into an even tighter array of greenery.

Behind us, the howls of rampaging Unseelie echo through the labyrinth. Blaedwyn unleashed her host upon us, and I can hear them growing ever closer. There's no way we can survive an entire war host, though with the walls of the maze so close, they can only come at us two abreast.

And while I have the Sword of Mourning sheathed at my hip, I don't dare use it.

"Eris." Thalia turns to her with a pleading look in her eyes.

"No."

The word is hard, final.

"What other options do we have?" Thalia snaps. "If the Unseelie face you in your other form, they'll scatter like scavengers."

"It's not the Unseelie who have to worry," Eris bites out.

"What are you both talking about?"

Eris looks at me coldly. "I have something inside me, something that can terrorize the entire Unseelie host and send them fleeing. But it comes at a cost. The last time I let myself channel my *other* half, I slaughtered an entire battlefield."

I don't see the problem with that. "A few hundred less Unseelie in the world isn't going to be a major problem."

"An *entire* battlefield," she repeats. "Enemy and ally alike. Friend and foe." For a moment, horror darkens her eyes, as if she's seeing it all over again. "I destroyed everyone who followed me onto that battlefield and when I walked out, I was the only thing living. I barely manage to cage it after all the glut of blood. I don't know if I can come back to myself again. It's been centuries, but every day it pushes at the cage, I can feel it growing hungrier. There's no point asking me to unleash my dark side, because if I do, then I'm going to be the only thing left alive in this entire kingdom. And even then, *I* might not be me."

"They called her the Eater of Souls," Thalia whispers.

The Devourer.

My mind suddenly trips over a long-forgotten memory. One of our tutors was obsessed with history, and I vaguely recall hearing of a battlefield where only one survivor walked away. Nevernight, they call it now, and even the ground lies fallow, as if the glut of blood drowned every blade of grass that stood there.

Thalia hesitates. "Thiago—"

"Is at half strength," Eris replies calmly, "and we both know it. He's no match for me, not right now. He's also still trapped in the dungeon."

"And I'm useless," Thalia says bitterly, "after that bitch stole my voice."

I make a small circular gesture in the air. "Let's pretend you haven't told me all of these stories before. Blaedwyn said a witch stole your voice. What does that mean?"

"It's a long story," Thalia replies, "and there's not enough time to tell it. If we get out of this, you and I shall raid Thiago's wine cellars and dwell on the bad old times."

"Use the sword," Eris says. "They won't hunt us if you stand against them with that"—she nods uneasily toward my hip—"in your hand."

I can't explain the shiver of fear I felt when that mysterious woman put the sword in my hand in that vision. "It drove Blaedwyn mad. I think it best if I *don't* touch it."

A troll suddenly bellows behind us, and then it's lumbering around the corner of the maze. It lifts its head and howls, as if to alert the host.

"Erlking's hairy balls."

Eris shoves me behind her and then leaps forward, her sword flashing in the dim light. I grab the hilt of my own sword, but a hand grabs my wrist.

"No!" Thalia says. "She can handle it. We'll just get in her way."

It's a struggle to stay out of the fight, but it soon becomes clear she's right. Eris isn't just fighting the troll, she's destroying him. She moves like a flash of lightning, ducking and weaving the massive swings of its ironbound club before sliding to her knees beneath a dangerous swing and slashing her blade through the tendon behind its ankle.

The troll bellows in pain and smashes into the thorny wall of the labyrinth, crushing it. An opening suddenly appears, just as its friends come around the corner.

"This way!" I yell, hauling Thalia through the opening.

A pair of startled hobgoblins glance our way, but I sweep

their axes aside. The clang of steel echoes behind me, and I know Eris is covering our backs.

A horn suddenly cuts through the air, and everything goes quiet. One second the maze is full of snarls and angry voices, and the next you could hear a mouse creeping.

"Did anyone else just feel a shiver run down their spine?" I mutter.

The labyrinth quivers, leaves rustling and thorny vines lashing angrily as they subside. Ravens take flight, cawing wildly. Even the wind seems to conspire against us, hissing through the leaves as if it's suddenly part of the hunt.

We all stare in the direction of the horn, and I can hear my heartbeat racing in my ears.

"What do you think that means?" Thalia asks.

"Death to all who enter here?" It's a guess, but I could be wrong.

"It's Blaedwyn's horn," Eris said, then curses under her breath. She glances about wildly, but there's seemingly no escape. "If she's entered the maze, then we're done for. Unless you use the sword."

"How many times must I say no?"

We scramble through the lashing maze, thorny whips scourging the skin from my arms and face. Around the next corner, we find ourselves in a dead end and slide to a halt.

Behind us, the horn rings again, and this time a cheer goes up.

"So, Eris has the power to destroy all our enemies, but can't let herself do that," I gasp, "and you could sing them into submission if you still had your powers. But you don't."

And I'm about as useful as a snowball in the wake of a volcano.

Thiago and Finn are locked up.

A raging queen is on our trail, along with a pack of

bloodthirsty Unseelie, and we have no way of fending her off—

A horrible thought occurs to me.

We have no means to defeat Blaedwyn.

"I have an idea." The words just blurt out of me. "It's a horrible idea, and I need the two of you to convince me not to do it."

"What?" Thalia asks.

"If I tell you, then you have to talk me out of it," I yell as we skid into a thorny corner of the maze.

"You weren't locked in a cage!" Thalia yells. "I'll let you do anything."

I tell them.

Thalia's eyes nearly pop out of her head. "You think *he's* a solution?"

"You said anything," I point out.

"Thiago will kill you. Blaedwyn will kill you. It's a terrible idea!" Thalia says.

It's Eris who surprises me though. A horrible, horrible smile crosses her mouth. "And it just might work."

Sprinting through the maze, I lead the chase while Thalia and Eris slip away to safety. I'm the one Blaedwyn wants, after all. If she gets her hands on me, she has both the Queen of Thorns and the Prince of Evernight by the throat.

I reach out with my senses, trying to grasp that elusive whisper of power I've been able to feel ever since we arrived. The Hallow pulses somewhere ahead of me.

Power calls to me.

It quivers deep beneath the earth, the ley line lying dormant like some enormous torrent of magic that wants to be used. I can sense where it pushes toward the surface, the power of the ley line channeled through the Hallow.

That's where I need to go.

The only thing stopping me is the maze.

I turn a corner, intent upon the Hallow, and realize the hair on the back of my spine has risen. Wrong way. I know it as instinctively as I can sense the air on my skin.

Bolting back the other way, I feel the pull of the Hallow. It wants me to find it. It wants me to give myself over to the rush of power. Racing through dozens of narrowing passages, I finally leap through a hole in the hedge and find myself in a grassy field.

Skidding down the slope, I bolt between a pair of the enormous lintel stones just as lightning lashes the horizon.

This is the worst idea I've ever had, but if it works…. It might be the only way to escape Blaedwyn and her Unseelie host.

I'm alone as I wait in the Hallow for my pursuers. Thiago will kill me if he realizes I suggested using me as bait, but if one is being positive, at least he'll be alive and free to kill me.

The ground quivers, and Blaedwyn's horn screams through the air.

The Unseelie burst from the maze, howling and gibbering as they spot me.

Blaedwyn stalks up the hill toward the Hallow where she defeated the Erlking, the thorny vines rustling in her wake as if they're alive and aware. You can almost hear them whispering.

"Princess," she says smoothly, holding a strung bow in her right hand.

"Your Highness." I'm not above common courtesy.

"It's over," she says, with a smile that bares her teeth, as she draws an arrow from her quiver. "Angharad will be thrilled to see what I've managed to get my hands on. The Prince of Evernight and his little wife, all in one."

"You have to capture me first."

Her eyes narrow. "Put the sword on the ground, and you won't be hurt."

I grip the Sword of Mourning's hilt in one hand and hold the sheath with the other. "As I recall, it knocked you on your ass last time. Think it can do so again?"

Blaedwyn smoothly sets the arrow to her bow and nocks it. "Think you can draw it before I put an arrow through your throat?"

"I set one trap for you," I reply. "Do you think I've had time to set another? Do you think it will snap closed before you can let fly?"

I tweak the power beneath me, and the Hallow vibrates.

She glances toward the stones. "Didn't you realize you need to power the Hallow first?"

To use the portals, the correct runes need to be activated in order to channel power and open the pathway to the Hallow you intend to arrive at. I shrug. I can feel the power of the Hallow alive and awake beneath my feet, waiting for me to call it to life.

And while I intend to open a portal, this one isn't to another Hallow.

I draw the sword. This time there's no detonation. This time there's no visions. Blaedwyn's answering smile is chilling, as if she didn't think I could be this stupid.

"You can't defeat me," she points out. "I wielded that sword long before you were a speck on the edge of consciousness."

The Sword of Mourning rings as if it cuts through the air itself, a high-pitched whine almost on the edge of hearing. It's vibrating in my hands, forcing me to grit my teeth.

Blaedwyn holds up a hand, and the sword's tip jerks toward her.

It's all I can do to hang onto it.

"You're invincible with that sword," I cry. "I know. No mortal being could stand against you and hope to survive." I suddenly smile, swiping my palm down the sharp edge of the blade. "But look where I'm standing. I think I know someone who can defeat you. And someone who might be very, very interested in seeing you again."

I slam my bloody palm against the nearest ward stone. It's the one with the symbol for *Uraz* on it. If you squint, the rune *almost* looks like something with horns.

My blood ignites the Hallow, but this time it's not opening a portal to another Hallow. The ley line beneath us trembles as if it senses a new pattern in the runes. I've never felt so closely linked to it, and for a moment, it almost seems as though I can *touch* that power.

I don't, because I'm not an idiot and would prefer not to be incinerated.

The Hallow starts shaking.

Dust and chips of stone shiver off the ward stones. The ground trembles, forcing me to soften my knees to maintain my stance.

Blaedwyn looks down sharply, then her gaze jerks to mine and her face goes white. "What are you *doing*?"

Lines of light sear through the snow on the ground, the heat melting it in an instant. The marble floor of the Hallow is suddenly visible, and every bronze glyph carved into the marble glows.

"Don't!" Blaedwyn screams, as she nearly goes to her knees.

I drive the Sword of Mourning right into the middle glyph.

It's the key, after all.

Only a kingly sacrifice has the power to break the prison open—or one of the great relics.

"Surprise, bitch." I grab onto one of the ward stones for balance as power suddenly erupts through the Hallow, and a blinding line of light forms right in the middle.

And then the Erlking steps through from his prison in the Underworld, sucking all of the oxygen from the air.

THE ERLKING IS ENORMOUS.

Violent, gleeful eyes lock on me with an intensity that almost makes me step back. That look says *run, mortal.* It speaks to every ounce of my being that's ever frozen when you hear something moving out there in the woods. It lifts all the hairs down my spine, and my lungs seize as he steps through the rift in the world.

Because while it says run, that look also says I just might want to be captured.

Every inch of him is built to conquer, to take, to hunt. The feral slash of his cheekbones and the cruel curve of his mouth speak of a primitive kind of carnality that make me want to swallow.

And his eyes are the eyes I saw in that vision.

I was in Blaedwyn's head when she betrayed him.

"Freedom," he whispers, holding his hand out as if he hasn't felt air on his skin in centuries. Dressed in strict black hunting leathers, he wears a cape of raven feathers. A crown made of golden antlers settles on his brow, and his long, tangled hair has golden beads woven through it.

Of all the Old Ones, he's both the most dangerous and the most mercurial, but also one of the only ones we might survive. He was Master of the Wild Hunt, and though his prey never escaped him, he was also known to be benevolent toward those with pure intentions.

"You freed me," he says, turning his focus back upon me. "And so I owe you a boon." Cruelty tilts that mouth in a wicked curve. "But speak wisely, little one, for I shall warn you only once—my gifts hold a sting."

"A mighty favor, Great One." I bow my head. "And one which I shall hold in stead, for I want for nothing in this moment."

"If you want for nothing, then why did you free me?"

"I brought you a gift," I say, pointing toward Blaedwyn.

She's scrambling down the slope, fleeing as if the Wild Hunt is already on her heels. I can't say I blame her. The wind is already whistling, as though a ghostly horde follows him. She's the sole reason he spent centuries locked away in the Underworld.

The Erlking stills, his falcon-dark eyes locking upon her.

His answering smile terrifies me. "And now I owe you two boons, child." He snaps his fingers and a pair of golden antlers sear themselves into the back of my hand like a tattoo. "All you need do is call for me, and I shall appear."

And then the wind whips around him and he vanishes in a swirl of ravens.

38

The castle is a hive of mayhem when I return, slashing my way through the brambles like some prince come to rescue his princess. I left the Sword of Mourning buried to the hilt in the middle of the Hallow. Let he who draws it know its misfortune.

I don't want it.

Unseelie flee in all directions, and the wind whistles through the half-broken spires as if some otherworldly being is attacking the castle with the elements.

Stones fall as an arch crumbles, crushing a pair of hobgoblins beneath it. The thorns in the maze creep away from the castle's flanks as if to distance themselves, and fire flares in the top tower of the keep.

Hopefully, Eris and Thalia managed to break the others out of their rotting cells before the Erlking arrived.

I sprint through the bailey, cutting down a pair of hissing Sorrows that try to flank me. "Eris?" There's no answer. Only the wind, cutting now, like a knife. "Thiago?"

Thiago strides out of the tower, shadows rippling around him like a cloak—or a pair of wings. In that instant I see him as the Unseelie do; a fierce warlord who looks unstoppable. There's nothing Seelie in his expression, and his eyes are completely black with the Darkness within him.

"What in Maia's name did you do?" he yells, the fierce wind whipping his torn shirt behind him like a banner.

I can't help myself.

I rush forward and throw myself into his arms. He practically lifts me off my feet, his arms closing around me like a trap. Despite his anger, I can feel the tension in him ease the second he holds me.

"What would I not do?" I whisper, and then capture his face in my hands before claiming a swift, furious kiss. "You promised you'd come for me. I could do no less."

"Vi," he says, eyes darting around. "What—"

"It's a long story," I yell, tugging him toward the gates. "And now is definitely not the time to discuss it. Hurry. Before he brings the rest of the castle down."

"Did it work?" Eris yells, staggering out of some doorway. She has her shoulder under Finn's arm, and his face is pale, blood matting his hair.

Thalia guards their backs, wielding two razor-sharp daggers with enough dexterity to convince me she knows how to use them.

"It worked!" I point to the stones that crumble around us. "I think Blaedwyn's locked herself away in the tower. I also think we're now the least of her concerns. But it might be wise to get as far away from here as we can."

⁓

THE HALLOW SPITS us out in Valerian.

The entire city is blanketed in snow and darkness. A deathly quiet fills the air, a vast difference from the shrieking beasts that lumbered through the swamp toward the Hallow at Scarshaven.

Thiago wastes no time. "What did you do?"

This is where the payment comes due. I glance toward the others, and when Eris winces, I know I'm in trouble. "You see.... The first plan failed. I stole the Sword of Mourning from Blaedwyn, but then she set her entire court to hunting us. And I didn't dare use the sword. So I... made a contingency plan."

Thiago grabs my wrist, flipping it to reveal the pair of golden antlers marked on my skin. His nostrils flare, and then his gaze captures mine, burning with intensity. "What. Did. You. Do?"

"I had no choice!" I snap, tearing my wrist from his touch. "We couldn't escape, and Eris didn't dare release herself. I could barely hold the fucking sword, let alone wield it. The only thing I could think of was to unleash *him*."

He turns on Eris, hot fury smoldering within him. Just one push, and I think he's going to erupt. "I gave you sanctuary. I put my life on the line to save yours, and *this* is how you repay me?"

She flinches.

I grab his forearm. "It's not her fault. If you want to blame someone, then blame me. It was my idea. I was the one who released him. I was the one who made the bargain with him."

Every inch of him quivers with suppressed rage as he turns his head toward me. Despite myself, I swallow. I've never seen this side of him. He's always been so careful to play at the charming suitor, the wicked prince. I've heard all the stories, all the rumors, but I've never seen the darkness that lurks inside him.

Not until now.

Slowly, I let his wrist go and tip my chin up to stare him in the eye. His are completely black, but I've seen the Darkness within him and I know he'd risk his own life to save me from it.

I'm not afraid of you.

An Asturian princess does not yield.

"Blame me," I tell him softly. "Or perhaps you should be thanking me, considering I daresay Blaedwyn would be mounting your head on her castle wall if we hadn't rescued you. Your *Highness*."

For a moment, I think I've pushed him too far.

Then he turns and stalks away, his illusions slipping just enough to give me a glimpse of his wings.

They're pure black, made of soft black feathers that gleam beneath the moonlight. One blink, and then they're gone again, as if he realized he'd lost control.

"Get your asses to the castle," he snaps. "We need to clean up and gather in the war room so I can fix this fucking mess."

I can't help myself. "You're welcome!"

39

I t's a cold trip back to the castle, where the group disperses to lick their individual wounds.

I watch Eris march away, her shoulders stiff, and I'm tempted to go after her, but there's someone else I need to deal with first.

Of course, tracking down my elusive husband is easier said than done.

He's not in his chambers, the library, the tower, or even the ruins of the ballroom. Indeed, he's in none of his usual haunts.

I turn to leave the ballroom, and there's Baylor, watching me from the top of the stairs.

I clap a hand to my chest. "You startled me."

His mouth firms. "I'm sorry. I... Have I done something to offend you?"

"What? No." I look past him, but there's no escape.

"You flee every time I enter the room," he says. "You refuse to meet my gaze. I don't know why." His expression grows pained. "I thought us friends, but you haven't been the same this time."

Friends.

Sweet Maia.

I close my eyes. I owe him this. I owe him the truth.

The words blurt out of me. "He's dead."

"Who?" His brows draw together in a frown.

"Your brother. Lysander." The truth has been haunting me for weeks. I can't stop the words. They spill from my lips, as Baylor's eyebrows lift higher at each twist of my tale. "My sister killed him. I didn't know who he was, only that he somehow knew me. I'm so sorry. So, so sorry. I shouldn't have kept the truth from you."

Stunned silence greets me.

Then Baylor releases a sigh. "Dead." He gives a rough laugh. "He's not dead, Your Highness."

It's not the answer I expected.

"He is," I whisper. "I kept his amulet. It's in my jewelry box in Ceres."

"What did you do with the body?"

I blink. "I think my sister buried him in the forest." It's exactly what Andraste *would* do.

Baylor steps forward. "I forget how much you don't know." He captures my hand, and rests it against his chest. "Neither Lysander nor I can truly die, Vi. Feel my heart."

His chest is hollow. Empty.

Nothing beats there.

I tug my hand back in shock.

"We were never fae," he admits roughly. "I was born into a different body than this one. I was born with the howl in my veins and the scream of rage in my soul. I was once one of the hounds who rode with the Grimm, when he stalked this world. Over time we learned to shift skins, to better hunt our prey. The fae. But when the Grimm was trapped in his Hallow, we were set free. The Seelie Alliance wanted to destroy us, but Thiago bartered for our lives. We serve him now and forever, but as long as the Grimm still exists, then we cannot truly die. My brother would have risen from his grave with the moon. He's still out there. Somewhere. Thank you for telling me."

My shoulders slump. "I should have told you sooner."

I can't believe the guilt and grief I felt has no true purpose. He's alive. Lysander is alive.

Baylor's smile is a brief flash in the night. "Now you have no reason to hide from me."

"I wasn't—" I pause. I was.

I grace him with a hesitant smile.

"Go," he tells me gruffly. "Find your prince. If I know him, he's licking his wounds in the baths. He loves you, Vi. Don't be too hard on him. He's just worried. And thank you. Now I know where to look."

ONE OF THE demi-fey peers out from behind the tangle of thorns in what's left of the observatory and I gesture it closer with my fingers.

"Do you know where the baths are? I'm looking for the prince."

It blinks at me, cocking its head.

"The prince?" I mimic a big, scowling menace, and flap my arms.

Ah. Its eyes widen, and then it scampers along the hallway, leading me lower into the castle, where the heated baths lie. Crouching outside the door to the steam room, it wends its way through my legs like a cat.

An expectant cat.

"I don't have any milk or honey right now," I tell it. "But I'll set some in a saucer at the foot of my bed later."

It gives me a look that can best be described as *you'd better*, and then it flounces away.

Inside the bath chamber the air is sticky and hot. Steam drifts from the enormous pools I haven't had a chance to use yet, providing an excellent curtain for Thiago's activities.

He turns at the sound of my footsteps, green eyes flashing.

I can just make out a hint of wet flesh and the dark shadow of wings. Despite myself, I'm curious to see more of them. He's always shrouded in that cursed cloak or his illusions.

"We need to talk," I tell him.

He's been avoiding me ever since he yelled at me.

Thiago stands up, water dripping from his elbows as he wipes it from his face. I rest my hands on my hips, staring him in the eyes with a resolve that's starting to weaken. *Do not look down. Do not. Do not. Do not....*

Curse it.

My cheeks heat and I force myself to focus on his eyes. They're very pretty eyes, but they're no match for the rest of him. All that sleek muscle and smooth skin just begging to be touched or licked.... There's no softness about him. He was built to be a predator, built to prowl, to overwhelm. Every inch of him is hard and carved of sleek edges.

And as he wades toward me, water caressing those slick muscles, I realize that he's been kind and charming and polite with me so far. The patient suitor. But right now, with the Darkness blackening his eyes, he's clearly cast aside such aspirations.

Right now, I'm dealing with the Prince of Evernight.

One who looks at me as if he's thinking of punishing me

for my ruse with the Erlking. Only…. I think I'd quite enjoy what he has planned.

"Then talk," he tells me.

I clear my throat, trying to gather my scattered thoughts. "Can you get dressed?"

"What's wrong?"

You're naked. And I'm trying really hard to focus.

"It's difficult to have this conversation when you're naked."

"You mean, you want to yell at me and yet, you can't keep your eyes off me."

Something like that.

"No," he says, enunciating the word. "I'm having a bath. You can either join me and scrub my back, or you can wait for me upstairs at my leisure."

At my leisure…. I scowl. "I know we're married, but do you think I'm going to sit upstairs in your chambers like a good little girl and wait for you to tell me how wrong I was?" I lean forward. "Because if so, I think you must have hit your head in that castle. Or is it the fact *I* rescued *you* the one you're having trouble dealing with?"

Thiago rubs at his jaw, fingers scraping over the dark stubble as he growls, "I swear to Maia, you were sent to punish me."

It's a little bit disheartening to be considered punishment.

I know we've been dancing around each other for weeks, even months, but… there's a little piece of me that started to believe his declarations. It's a heady feeling to know someone loves you enough to sacrifice everything. I'd even started to believe that maybe there was a piece of myself worth loving.

Or maybe I'm just a fool who wants to believe.

"I never asked for this," I say hotly. "I never wanted to be a pawn between you and my mother. And you're right. Maybe I should leave this argument where it lies and go upstairs, but if you think I'm going to be waiting for you to finish it, then pray, think again."

I turn toward the door, boots hammering as fast as my heart.

"Vi!"

The door slams in my face with a gush of wind.

I yank at the handle, but there's no shifting it. And I don't have enough magic to break his hold on it. Burning it to cinders is not a good idea. Certainly not one a mature princess can afford to entertain, no matter how tempting it is. Hammering a fist against it, I pause once, palm pressed to the wood, before turning back around.

"Open the door."

The words almost sound calm.

"No."

Oh, he's going to regret this. "That was the only time I'll ask. Next time, I'll get a fucking axe."

Thiago wades closer to the edge of the pool. "Aren't you tired of running?"

It's not the first time he's accused me of that.

I plant my feet. "Fine. I'm not running this time. Let's talk. Let's punish each other."

"Vi." He curls his fingers into a fist, his jaw locking tight as he clamps down on whatever he intended to say. Finally, he opens his fist. "I didn't mean to say it like that. You're more than that to me. You're more than a pawn. More than punishment. And you know you are. I would walk away from this war with your mother in a heartbeat if I thought she'd leave us in peace. But I can't keep fighting a war on two fronts. I can't keep fighting you as well as your mother.

We have just over three weeks before time runs out, and this time, it's forever.

"You made a reckless decision today, and I don't know how to even explain how dangerous it was. And here you are with those two marks upon your hand, and all I can see are the consequences. All I can see is myself losing you."

"We had no other choice—"

"There are always other choices. Do you have any idea what you've done?"

"No, I don't!" I shoot back. "All you've done is yell at me. I know the Old Ones were locked away, but the Erlking is the Master of the Wild Hunt. He's dangerous, but he's not—"

"You were not born into a world where the Old Ones walk the nights. You've never had to bar your windows or blow out all the candles in your home because the Wild Hunt is howling through the trees and it's hungry. You think he's benevolent? He takes what he wants, Vi, and you're cursed lucky he didn't decide he wanted you. Yet."

I rub at the marks on my hand. "He owes *me* two boons."

"Does that make you feel safer?" Thiago sinks into the water with malevolent grace. "If you use those marks, you risk capturing his attention. I'm sure he was distracted by the sight of Blaedwyn, but you're beautiful, powerful, and stubborn. All things that rouse his predatory instincts. I can only pray he'll be distracted long enough to forget you."

It makes me swallow.

I know what the stories say about the Erlking.

He lives in his own realm—side by side with the mortal realm—and he sends forth his hunt every full moon. Nothing is safe. Sometimes you're prey, designed for his bow and his sword. Or sometimes, if you're lucky, you're a distraction. Offer him mead, offer him a dance, or offer him your virtue. It's all the same to him. A night of bedsport and laughter, and you might wake and consider yourself lucky. Male, female, it doesn't matter. He left behind a trail of broken hearts and no doubt dozens of bastard offspring.

It was only the very rare few that he stole.

And they were never seen again.

Some say time moves differently in his realm, and so mere hours have passed in relation to dozens of years here. Some say, if you drank his mead or his wine, you were bound to stay in his world forever. Or some simply say he never let them go.

Nobody really knows the answer to that.

Thiago continues, "The Old Ones were locked away for good reason, Vi. You've never looked across a battlefield and seen your own people taken to be slaves to the Horned One. Or worse, food. You've never kissed the floor at the Mother of Night's feet and hoped she couldn't sense your dissent. You've never risked the seas, wondering if the Father of Storms and his saltkissed will drag your ship under.

"They were creatures who tapped into the raw, elemental power of the ley lines. With all that power, they were well-nigh invincible. They were cruel, and rapacious, and inhuman. They don't think like we do. They have no empathy, no ability to see us as anything beyond livestock. They played with us like pawns, and when the Horned One sent the Unseelie south to conquer our peoples, the only option we had was war. Why do you think we locked them away? The entire Seelie Alliance rode as one, and we couldn't kill even *one* of them. The only option we had was to trick them into the circles and lock them away. It took years of planning to simultaneously lure them into that trap, and you just blithely released the Erlking!"

"Would you have rather died?" I snap. "Because that was our only other option."

"*Yes!*"

The word echoes around the chamber, ricocheting like a slap to the face. My mouth drops open.

"What?"

He tips his chin up proudly. "You weren't there, Iskvien. You don't know what it was like."

Not Princess. Not Vi. But my full name.

It's the first time I think he's ever called me that, and though I would have preferred it several months ago, now it feel like a rejection.

"I risked everything I had to trap them all those years ago. So the cost of my life would have been a small blessing to keep them contained."

"But.... It's only one of them," I whisper, rubbing at the marks. "We can trap him again. Or—"

"Kill him? Blaedwyn drove the Sword of Mourning—a weapon forged with all the power of the Alliance—directly into his chest, and it merely stunned him." Thiago forges through the water. "I'm the most dangerous male in the south, and I don't think I can stop him, Vi. If he comes for you, then I will do what I can. But our best hope is distraction. I don't want to lose you."

And he's afraid he might.

It finally sinks in.

All I've ever heard are stories. He's right. I don't know what it was like. They're merely legends to me. But if Thiago —with all his power, all his might—doubts he can keep me safe, then perhaps he's right.

Perhaps they are best left alone.

"I'm sorry," I whisper, sinking to my knees by the side of the pool. "I didn't mean to cause so much damage. It was just—Blaedwyn was hunting us through the maze, and I knew we couldn't escape her. It seemed our only option at the time."

His voice roughens as he pauses by the edge of the pool. "You always were reckless. You'd never have married me if you weren't."

"Do you regret it?"

The words blurt from my mouth, all my lingering doubts swarming me in an instant.

He looks up sharply. "Marrying you?"

I can't help speaking what's been on mind ever since I discovered the truth. "All I've ever brought you is pain." The words feel thick in my throat. "All I've ever done is hurt you."

He speaks of punishment, and he's right.

"*Never.*"

I reach for his hand, and he captures my fingers, giving them a light squeeze.

"You are my light, Vi. You're my breath, the beating of my heart, the smile on my lips." He brings my hand to his mouth and presses a hot, open-mouthed kiss to the palm. "You're the beacon I use to find my way back to land when the Darkness threatens to drag me under. You keep me whole. You make me laugh. You remind me of what I am and what I want to be."

I don't quite understand what he's talking about, but the words soften that lump in my throat so I can finally swallow.

"I love you, Vi. You are my everything, and despite the pain, despite the rage, there's not a day that has passed since our marriage that I haven't considered myself blessed by the gods for being given to you."

The brush of his mouth stirs things low in my body, but his words are an arrow straight through the heart.

They dissolve the doubt that festers there like poison.

I wish I could tell you I love you, but I'm so afraid I'll lose it.

I release a slow, shuddering breath. It's more than I can handle right now. "You're not just saying that to get me in the water with you?"

He knows me well enough to understand I'm overwhelmed. Backing off, he gives me a sinful smile. "Caught," he says softly.

And we're both hiding behind masks in that moment.

"I'm sorry," I whisper.

"So am I."

Silence ticks away the seconds.

Hot steam envelops us, but all I can see is him. Those green eyes are dangerous, tempting me to throw caution to the wind and join him.

"Come in, fair maid." He flicks water at me.

I rest my chin on my knees. Entering that water is akin to giving in, and we both know it. There's no coming back from this moment, no more second-guessing myself. "Why would I? I'm enjoying the view."

"It's better in here."

Oh, I'll bet it is.

As if to tease me further, he fans his arms back and forth, splashing ripples of water against his chest. Every inch of him is perfection, and I want to touch him so badly I ache.

"You're a dangerous man," I tell him through narrow eyes.

Thiago smiles. "You have no idea, Princess."

"I'm starting to." I slip my boot off and dip my toe in the steaming waters. Sweet Maia. My eyes almost roll backwards in my head. It's deliciously hot and tempting. Thiago's not the only one wearing almost a week's worth of grime.

"Good?" he asks.

"Terribly good."

Too late, I realize he's been circling closer. One hand locks around my calf, and he gives me a wicked grin as he hauls me into the water, clothes and all. I go under with a splash, heat enveloping me and my arms flailing.

The second I come up, I'm in his arms, and there's no escaping.

"What are you doing?" I gasp.

"You looked dirty." He brushes his thumb against my nose and looks at it, as if he can see dirt. "I thought I might be able to help you get all clean."

I splash him in the face.

There's an instant where he looks startled, and then a wave of water is coming in my direction.

It turns into all-out war.

I don't know what's taken over me, but I can't help laughing as I splash him. Water flies back at me, almost blinding in its intensity. I smash plumes of it directly in his face, and somehow win the first round.

Or maybe that was only a ruse to lure me closer, for suddenly I'm the one being drowned.

"Stop!" I yell, but there's no surcease.

Leaping upon him, I try and shove his head under the water, but he's so impossibly strong. So big. Too late, I realize exactly how badly I've erred.

Thiago captures both my hands. I lock my legs around his waist, determined to escape, but there's no shifting him.

My back hits the edge of the pool, and its only then, when he pins my wrists there, that I realize how trapped I am.

And how naked he is.

Suddenly, I can feel him, pressed hot and hard between my legs. The thin leather leggings are no barrier. Nor is my wet shirt. My nipples press against his chest, and we both still, caught in the sudden realization we were doomed the second he hauled me into the water.

This is the moment.

My smile dies, laughter forgotten in the wake of the sudden flare of desire I feel. I can see it in his eyes too, dangerously green beneath those thick, wet lashes.

"Vi," he whispers, his gaze dropping to my mouth.

My heart rabbits in my chest. Every inch of me hovers in indecision. This is no mere kiss he's asking for. Everything changes from this point on.

I know I have his heart. I know I've had it from the moment he first saw me, but I've never dared give him mine. Not this time. And I want him. I want him so desperately that I ache.

"You owe me a kiss," he teases.

"I owe you two. I'm fairly certain its past midnight."

His smile melts me. "Well, I wasn't counting, but I won't say no."

"Liar," I breathe. "You've got a tally nailed to your bedroom wall."

His fingers curl through mine, no longer pinning me, but relentless all the same. And I can feel the hard edge of his wedding band. The one he wears for me. The one he's worn from the moment we married.

I could tell myself a thousand times this is dangerous, that we were never meant to be. I could use our kingdoms as an excuse, use my mother, my curse, all of it, to deny what I feel. But it's a lie, and if there's one thing I've always striven to do, it's to tell the truth.

I can't help myself.

I kiss him.

Pushing against his hold, pushing hungrily into his

mouth, it's like I set something loose inside him, for he responds in kind. His hands slide down my ribs, tangling in wet fabric. There's too many layers between us, and a thwarted moan escapes me. I want those hands on my skin. No, I need them. I want his mouth, his touch, the bite of his teeth—

Thiago laughs, and I realize I'm biting his lower lip, as if to convey exactly what I need.

"Anyone would think you were the one who's spent all these years wanting what he can't have," he whispers, the stubble on his cheek scraping my jaw as he nips at my chin.

"Who said you can't have it?"

His eyes darken. "I guess that decision is yours. It's always yours."

And then he bites my chin, his lips grazing my throat as he works his way down.

I arch my head back, moaning a little. "You're making it very difficult to make a clear-headed judgement here."

Those lips pause. "Better?"

"Don't stop." I grab a fistful of his hair and kiss his mouth. "Don't you dare stop."

I can feel his smile against my mouth but there's no time to think of anything more, for his tongue lashes against mine, and his hands finally find the hem of my shirt and tug it free of my leggings.

Then all I can feel are the roughened calluses on his hands as they glide up my stomach, higher—

His thumb finds the bindings that cover my breasts, and I almost let forth a snarl of thwarted rage.

"Are you sure, Vi?" he whispers in my ear. "Because if we go any further, then I'm not going to let you go. I'm not going to let you out of my bed. You will be *mine*."

The possessiveness of that statement makes my heart

skip a beat. He's so steadfast and sure, so certain of *us*. I wish I had an ounce of his certainty, and none of the doubts that whisper poison in my mind. When I'm in his arms, I can't hear those doubts. Maybe he's right. Maybe I should stay there, in his embrace. In his bed. In his… heart.

Am I sure?

Yes. A thousand times *yes*.

As if in answer, I grab the hem of my shirt and haul it over my head. It lands somewhere behind me on the tiles with a wet slap. Then my hands are back on his skin, gliding over the sleek wet muscles of his shoulders. He's enormous. The bulk of his trapezius muscles alone would take me all week to lick.

I'm game to try to conquer the task though.

"I'm sure. Do you think I'd release the Erlking for any old prince?"

His eyes darken, and maybe it's too soon for that jest.

Indeed, as he captures my mouth, my suspicions are confirmed. His kiss is almost bruising, one hand locking on my jaw as if to pin me there. Every hard inch of him presses me into the wall, and then his teeth graze down my throat and a gasp escapes me as he shoves the binder down and captures my nipple in his mouth. It's too much and not enough, and damn the Underworld, but I want more. I want everything. I want him like I've never wanted in my life.

"Please." I'm undulating against him, grinding shame-lessly against the hard thrust of his erection.

Thiago laughs softly. "You never were patient."

Patient? I grab a fistful of his hair.

"I want you. Now."

If there's an easy way to get wet leather leggings off, then I'm sure the Old Ones are laughing at me right now. Thiago has to take over, grabbing me by the hips and sitting me on the edge of the pool as he tears them down my legs. Thumbs dig into my thighs as he parts them and steps between them. The tiles are cold on my ass, but he doesn't give me a chance to overthink it.

Instead, his mouth is on mine again. Rough palms skate up the sides of my waist as he deftly removes my undergarments. He shreds the silk between my thighs with a hiss, his eyes dark with pure desire.

"Fuck, I've missed this." Hands curling under my ass, he hauls me closer.

I have precisely two seconds to realize what his intentions are, and then the roughness of his stubble marks my inner thighs.

Blessed Mother of Night.

Thiago's hot mouth moves over my core, and his tongue is just as good as he proclaimed it. All I can see is his dark head moving between my thighs, and then a flash of heat spears through me. The hot, slick glide of his tongue flickers against my clit, but it's the way he suckles and eats at me that drives me wild. I can barely breathe as his fingers slide inside me, stroking and teasing.

It feels like pure, utter tenderness.

It feels like worship.

He makes me beg for mercy, fingers curling in his hair. I arch my spine and slam my head on the tiles, and still he doesn't relent. Every inch of me strains for release, but he knows it. He keeps me on the edge, his tongue tracing small, teasing circles, and his green eyes watching me with such wicked intent I know he's enjoying every moment of this.

"Please! Mother of Mercy, please!" I writhe on the tiles, desperate and aching.

"As you wish, my love."

His hot breath whispers over me, and then his tongue is exactly where I want it.

I plunge over the edge of that cliff, crying out as lightning strikes through me. There's no relief from his mouth. He licks and suckles, shoving me recklessly into ecstasy. It's too much. Not enough. And Thiago drives aftershock after aftershock through me, until I'm a sobbing mess shattered by pleasure.

It's only afterwards, when I come to with my head resting against his chest, warm and relaxed in his arms, that I realize he's dragged me back into the water.

Soft kisses brush against my temples. "Can you remember your name yet?" he teases.

I lift my head off his chest, drowning in those smug green eyes. "I know you probably don't want to hear this, but there's a little piece of me that considers myself lucky to learn how good your tongue is for the first time, again and again and again."

His mouth should be immortalized.

"Oh, we're not done yet, Princess."

He captures my lips in another slow, drugging kiss, but I've got other ideas.

"My turn," I whisper, shoving him back against the wall.

He allows me to pin him there. "Do your worst."

Water skates down his body, caressing each muscle. I lick my way down his throat, and Thiago makes a rough sound that ignites me. It's like he's helpless beneath my touch. This vicious, dark prince who could destroy the world if he desired it melts in my hands.

My hand glides down his abdomen, and then it's curling around his cock.

Thiago hisses as I flex my grip, twisting and working him

with a tight fist. A bead of cum dwells on the tip of him, and I glide my thumb over it, smearing it across him.

"I've waited months for this," he breathes, staring into my eyes. Grabbing my wrists, he lifts me back against the wall of the pool. "*Months.* I need to be inside you."

It's not a question.

And if it was, I answered that long ago.

"You're mine. Say it."

I shake my head, but then he's biting my throat, rocking against me. The slick threat of his erection grinds against my clitoris, both a taunt and a demand.

"*Say it,*" he breathes.

I bite my lip, desperate to chase that elusive pleasure he's offering. I can't help myself. My mind holds no memories of him, but my body is a slick instrument he plays with familiarity. It knows him. It wants him. Bowing my head, I rest my forehead against his. "I'm yours."

Then he surges forward, the tip of him breaching me.

And all I know is pleasure.

40

We lie in bed, Thiago's fingers stroking down my spine. I've never felt safer than this moment in his arms. But there's a lingering question that casts doubt over me like a cloud.

"You're Unseelie," I whisper, into the night.

I've wondered about it a million times, but he's too perfectly formed. It's only when his wings appear and his eyes darken that his Unseelie aspects rise to the surface, and I've never heard of anyone being able to do that before.

Those fingers still, and then resume their gentle caress. "Where did you hear a lie like that?"

He didn't deny it.

I roll over in his arms. "Is it a lie?"

Shadows darken his face, and he glances down at my lips.

"If you can't trust me with the truth, then what sort of marriage do we have?"

"It's not you I can't trust."

Or not the me that exists in this moment.

Thiago sits up in bed, shadows caressing the ripple of his abdomen. Reluctance bleeds through his pores.

"You've never asked me that before," he says.

"Maybe I never dared. I could see it in your face when we were fleeing Blaedwyn's castle. And most Seelie don't have wings, but some do." I brush my hands against the sleek smooth skin of his back, where his wings should be. "Your eyes go dark when these appear."

He shudders, as if the sensation of my hands is too much. With a shiver that contorts his face, the wings appear. And the tattoos on his chest darken.

My breath catches as I behold them.

Those feathers are sleek and glossy, and spun from pure midnight. I always thought—or was told—that the Unseelie are ugly, beastly creatures, but he's not. He's beautiful in a way that makes my heart race.

"May I touch them?"

He nods.

And then my hands brush against them. "Do you fly?"

"I can." His voice roughens. "Sometimes I need to escape the city and I head north, to the mountains where the goblin clans reside. There's nothing more freeing than hurtling yourself through those icy peaks, risking death on the wind."

"But you don't dare cross into Unseelie."

"No. I don't."

He vanishes his wings. It almost seems as though some of his vitality and power disappear. He's utter perfection in any form, but I love the wildness of his other side, the feral carnality of it.

"Your shadows. Your Darkness. It's your Unseelie side fighting to break free, isn't it?" It's the reason I've never seen those sorts of tattoos before. They're not from the Seelie courts.

Thiago laces his fingers through mine. "I'll tell you the truth one day, I promise. If you stand before your mother's court and choose me, then I will tell you the truth."

But not before.

I tug my fingers from his. It's clear he doesn't think we'll be able to break the curse. "Believe in us. Believe in *me*!"

Thiago draws back, his mouth set in a thin line. "I've spent every day of the last thirteen years believing in you. That doesn't negate the truth—everything we've tried has failed."

"The Morai said—"

"The Morai speak in riddles," he snarls. "Their words cannot always be trusted."

It makes me wonder what they promised him when he sought them out. There's a reason they warned him never to return. I cross my arms over my chest, determined not to take offense. "They can't lie."

I'd told him everything as we lay in each other's arms. But I hadn't realized he didn't feel the same surge of hope I felt.

"It doesn't mean they speak the truth," he warns. "There are a thousand ways to word something, to make a fool believe."

"Are you calling me a fool?"

Thiago freezes, as if he realizes he's gone too far. "I think you want to believe them," he replies carefully.

If I don't believe them, then we have no hope.

And hope is the only thing I can live for.

But it's suddenly clear that whatever hope he held is gone, dying away like a guttering candle. I can't entirely blame him. How many times have I promised my love? How many times have I forgotten it? The years have clearly taken their toll.

"Perhaps I was the fool," he says, "who wanted to believe." He turns away from me, the muscles in his broad back quivering with anger as grabs the poker by the fireplace and stabs at the fire. "They promised me the love of my life, though they never promised her heart in return. They said I could have a piece of her, but only a piece. I never understood what that meant until you forgot me the first time."

Crossing the carpets, I wrap my arms around him. His wings are gone, the darkness inside him vanishing. There's only the prince, with his wicked eyes and his guarded heart.

"I'm sorry."

I hate the way my mother stole him from me.

And a little lick of fear curls inside me at the thought she might do it again.

How do I fight a curse when I have barely any control of my magic?

How can I promise my heart when she might take it from me?

End your life.

End hers.

Or find something with the power to undo the curse.

"If I could lock you away," he whispers, thumb stroking my hand, "then I would. I would defy your mother, defy the entire alliance if it meant forever in your arms."

Though I yearn to linger in his embrace, I shake my head. The other courts are too powerful, and he gave his word. "If you defy the treaty and keep me, then you play directly into my mother's hands. If you kill her, then Asturia will march. And I won't be the reason our peoples go to war." I lick dry lips. "We could find someone who could break the spell—"

"And what would they expect in return? No." His hands tighten over mine. "We could flee."

Flee? I draw back sharply as he turns to face me. "Where?"

The answer's in his eyes. North. We could go north. Cast aside all allegiances and run into the Unseelie lands. We'd be on our own, constantly hunted by both of our kinds, but we might find freedom for a while. A chance to be together.

"No." I curl my fingers around his hand. "You're not the only thing my mother stole from me."

And I want it all.

My power. My magic. It feels like she's stolen an entire lifetime from me, and I want the truth.

"We face her. Together," I whisper.

Thiago brushes his thumb against my lips. This time, he doesn't bother to shield me from the bleakness that crosses his expression. "Forever, Vi. You will always be mine."

How long does forever last?

I don't want to answer that.

I lean closer, capturing his mouth, my tongue dancing with his. All hot and sleek. The caress deepens until he's inside me again.

Forever will last as long as we're in each other's arms. And maybe I don't remember him, but as I gasp for breath, shattered by pleasure, I can't help stroking my hands up his back, feeling the thick muscle where his wings should meet his shoulders.

This prince is mine, and I will curse the entire world to keep him.

No matter what I must do.

HOURS LATER, my fingers trace the tattoos that drift across Thiago's chest. Tension lingers in him at the touch, though he allows it, and his tattoos have started shifting in response, as if they enjoy being stroked.

I can never forget their voices. The hunger in them, the viciousness. There's no light in this Darkness of his, and yet some part of it yearns to be touched by light. Accepting him means accepting them.

"Does it bother you?" he asks.

To be married to an Unseelie prince masquerading as Seelie? It might have bothered me a few weeks ago, before I knew him for who he was. Before I faced the Morai and my own truths.

"For thirteen years, you've been patient enough to wait for me," I tell him. "You believed in me, even when I knew you not. You believed in *us*. I can do nothing else but return that trust."

Pleasure softens my fierce prince's face. He captures my mouth with a swift kiss. "I forget what it's like to be with you. You give me hope."

I can feel the heated press of his desire against me. "That's not all I give you. Clearly. I won't be able to walk tomorrow."

Thiago rolls over me, sinking between my thighs and resting his elbows beside my shoulders. "Were you planning on going somewhere? I was intending not to leave this bed for at least five days."

"Then I definitely won't be able to walk."

He kisses the side of my jaw, his stubble prickling me. "I'll carry you."

A laugh escapes me, and I cup his jaw. This is what

happiness is. The laughter eases as I stare into his eyes and realize the days are running out. That infernal clock in my head is ticking ever closer to the Samhain rites, when I'll have to face my mother again.

I don't want to let this moment go.

I want to bathe in it until the shadows of the future can't touch me. I want to drink it in and use it as my shield against the coming confrontation.

I want a moment to remember, a moment that will brand itself on my skin until nothing can make me forget it.

"Kiss me," I demand.

"As you wish," he breathes, leaning in for a long, heated kiss.

And for the next few hours he makes me forget it all.

The curse. The approaching deadline. My mother's wrath.

Only this exists.

Only us.

Only this promise of darkness.

41

D ays pass. Then a week.

We spend the nights buried in each other's arms, trying to ignore the tick of the clock. The days are given to courtly business. Angharad may have been driven back at Mistmere, but she's out there somewhere, and Thiago is determined to find her. He sent an entire warband to clear the ruins and they returned yesterday, smiling with victory.

So far, there's been no word of the Erlking, though the full moon has not yet come again, and, judging from how quiet Blaedwyn seems to be, I suspect he's busy.

We argue about how to trap him again, and whether the Alliance should be alerted. But the Alliance seems to be shattered, my mother's connection to Angharad making us wary. And the other queens may use the information to strike a cruel blow, rather than as the warning it should be.

With Thiago's mind busy, I give myself over to the idea of breaking the curse. I know Thiago's last hope lies in his faith that this time will be different, but I can't accept that.

My mother's stolen him from me *twelve* times.

I don't want to make it thirteen.

Seven days until the rites, and I can feel the panic in my touch when I haul him into bed at night. At six days, I bury my nails in his back and make such marks they're still there the next day. At five days, I tear the library apart, looking for answers. I still have Kyrian's grimoire, but I've been through it a thousand times, and there's nothing but lore about the Old Ones and black magic.

And then the morning of the third day dawns, and the moment I wake, I know this *has* to be the day I find an answer.

Or else, all is lost.

Thiago is arguing with Baylor in the stables as I hurry along the bridge that leads to the library. Most of the words are muted, but I can hear enough to know they're arguing about Mistmere and the forthcoming rites.

I don't want to speak of them anymore.

I am done with dwelling on my mother and her curse. I need a solution.

It's in the library that the truth first starts to stare me in the eye.

Killing my mother isn't an option. She's too powerful, and even if I could bring myself to take that step, I know she'll have a contingency in place. She'll never let us have a moment of peace, even from beyond the grave.

But the Morai gave me another means to break the curse. *Seek one who is more powerful....* Thiago doesn't want to take that option. He fears the consequences, but what am I supposed to do?

Kill myself?

Watch him die?

Murder my mother?

As far as I can see, finding someone who can break the spell is our only possible solution, but who? My mother's a direct descendant of Maia, power bred through her line through the ages. The Queen of Nightmares is her equal, but no friend of mine. The Unseelie queens are clearly working with my mother, and Isem, the only sorcerer with the skill to curse-twist, has no reason to help us.

Besides, Angharad and Isem want to cut my heart out of my chest to summon the Mother of Night.

That leaves me with Prince Kyrian and Thiago, and if either of them was strong enough to break the curse, they would have done it.

The golden antlers on my hand wink in the candlelight as I turn the pages of the grimoire one last time. I'm owed two favors by the Erlking, but he's no sorcerer. Powerful enough, yes. Could he break the curse? Possibly. Would he destroy my mind in the process? Also, possible.

I turn the page, and there it is.

The answer I've been looking for.

The paper's so old, it almost crumbles beneath my touch. Gilt lines the edges, and the image in the center is etched in black and silver ink. A serene face stares out from beneath a cowl, those black eyes locking on me as if the figure can see directly through the pages of the book. A triple moon is painted over her shoulder; a crescent, a full moon, and a waning one.

Maiden. Mother. Crone.

The Mother of Night.

And as I turn the page, I swear she's the woman I saw in my vision the night I drew the Sword of Mourning.

The second I blink the resemblance is gone. But a shiver of excitement lights through me.

Years and years ago, when she walked the realms, she was worshipped as a goddess that granted her powers to those who pledged their allegiance. She was the one who forged spell craft and taught it to the fae. The first sorcerer. The first curse worker.

Granted, such powers were not given freely.

No, they came at a cost.

But if I don't take a risk right now, then at the end of the week, I'm going to watch my mother execute my husband, and I'm not even going to know who he is.

I slam the book shut, nervousness rising in my chest.

If I turn down this path, then there's no escaping the consequences.

I'll have enough power to defeat my mother, but I'll be bound to pay the price the Mother insists upon. Magic is never free.

And yet, I might be able to save my husband's life.

Thiago's spent so many years sacrificing everything, just for me. He fought for us when I didn't. Or couldn't.

If you go down this path, then you'll lose him.

He was furious that I released the Erlking. *Never again, Iskvien. The Old Ones were locked away for a reason....*

I set the book down with a heavy thud. "I'm going to lose him either way," I whisper to myself.

At least he'll be alive.

And I don't have to release her. Just... entice her with a little bargain.

With that thought, my resolve firms.

Angharad wanted to use the power of the Mother of Night to break the Horned One free of his prison. The Hallow in Mistmere is resurrected, which means Angharad will be able to forge a link to the Mother if she returns.

All I need is the Hallow, some blood, and a little luck.

But there's no way Thiago will allow me to make this sacrifice.

So maybe I'll need a few other items as well, including a surly, vicious warrior who doesn't seem to like me very much.

42

"This is a terrible idea," Eris mutters as she holds my horse's bridle.

I swing down from the saddle, looking around. There's no sign of any Unseelie. The war party Thiago sent this way has done its job well and cleared the ruins. Mistmere lies abandoned, silent as a grave beneath the full moon.

"Agreed," I snap, "but if you've got a better plan, then I'll be quite happy to assist you."

She shuts her mouth and looks away, her jaw trembling. I don't know why I didn't see it before, but she's not the emotionless rock she pretends to be.

Thiago gave me a home when others would have burned me at the stake.

It meant more to her than I'll ever know. She pledged her life to him, and now she's watching helplessly as he hurtles toward almost certain doom.

I rest a hand on her arm. "I promise I'll do everything in my power to save him."

"I wouldn't be here if I didn't think you would." Visibly

gathering herself, she ties my horse next to hers. "Let's do this, bitchspawn. Save the sniveling for later."

Right. I almost forgot myself there.

Hauling my pack, with all its supplies, over my shoulders, I head for the Hallow.

Eris stalks ahead of me, her eyes roving the darkness, searching for any threat. Her shadow stretches ahead of her, growing longer and longer, and I swear it's starting to look a little inhuman. The hint of wings flare, as if whatever she hides within her is stretching.

"You're not going turn into the Devourer on me, are you?"

Eris realizes what I'm looking at, and all of a sudden, her shadow shrinks to its normal size and shape. She gives me a look that might have shriveled my insides a couple of months ago, before I realized she uses those icy glares to keep others away. "Just play your part. I'll play mine."

We reach the Hallow, and the enormity of what I'm about to do starts to set in.

This is the moment.

If I go through with this, then there's no turning back.

All the stones stand in place, ropes and pulleys holding them upright. Moonlight glints on their runes as I circle them, looking down at the piece of paper I tore from that book.

There's the crescent moon on one column; the circle and arrow on another, that represents the full moon. I just need to find the waning moon, the crone....

And there it is, three columns over.

"Found them?" Eris asks, as she sets out the candles and lights them.

"Found them." I can't help feeling the portent in those words.

I set the piece of paper aside, mentally preparing myself. And then I take a deep breath and enter the circle.

The ley line quivers.

Somewhere, deep beneath the earth, I can feel power whispering to me. It's almost as if some enormous force has turned its head toward me, waiting with bated breath for me to make the next move. I don't want to think about what that force might be.

I slice the dagger across my finger, and blood wells. "If this doesn't work, then ride back to Valerian and tell Thiago I loved him enough to try."

"Along with the fact that I rode with you and let you get yourself killed? Thanks," Eris snorts.

I shoot her a smile. In another lifetime we might almost have been friends. "If I die, then I bequeath the Erlking's oath to you. Along with my collection of lurid romantic tales."

Eris rolls her eyes. "Just do it, will you?"

I lean down, examining the stone at my feet. Thirteen grooves are cut into the tiles, and as I squeeze my hand over the center well, I feel the air around me suddenly stir. The Hallow needed a kingly sacrifice to trap an Old One, but if I'm right, then I won't need to kill anyone. It worked at the Erlking's Hallow.

Blood calls to blood.

Like to like.

Leanabh an dàn. I think I finally know what that means.

Blood drips from my clenched fist into the small well, and as if by magic, it shoots along all thirteen grooves toward the standing stones. The ground is shaking, little shards of stone shuddering across the tiles. A hollow boom echoes through the earth, as if entire continental plates shift beneath us.

"Vi," Eris says nervously, one hand settling on her sword.

"It's working," I whisper, painting blood across all three runes I've identified.

I don't get a chance to even smile.

Light blazes from every glyph carved into the stones. The ley line suddenly ignites, raw power shooting toward the stars. Wind rushes past me, my hair whipping around my face.

But it's the sensation of something reaching for me and grabbing my mind, my magic, that makes me flinch.

"Princess!" Eris screams, but it sounds so far away.

Finally, something whispers in my ear.

Something dark and dangerous, with a laugh like dry leaves rustling against each other. I have a moment of sheer terror, a moment where I realize I may have made a crucial mistake in thinking this being can be bargained with.

And then the Hallow implodes, taking me with it.

I FALL.

It lasts both seconds and eons, until I'm barely aware of the world flashing past me. Little claws pick at my mind, unravelling pieces of me, as if a dozen hungry creatures are eating those memories and finding sustenance.

I see my sister and me running through a meadow as girls. Laughing, carefree, and happy. My mother watches the pair of us like a hawk from the edges of the meadow.

Then the memories twist, and I'm screaming at my mother, "Give her back! Give her back!"

Another flicker. "You little slut," my mother hisses, lifting her hand to lash me with her claws. But it's Andraste who captures her wrist and forces her back.

"Think about it," my sister yells, standing toe-to-toe with the queen. "You can use this. You can trick the prince into a trap of your own choosing."

And though it terrifies me at the time, I know I've been granted clemency.

Again and again, I hurtle through memories I've never seen before. My sister. My mother. My stepbrother. Thiago. Thalia. Eris. Even Finn and Baylor. The Mother examines them all until my head feels like it's going to explode.

Splashing into ice-cold water slams me back into my body.

It covers my face and I thrash, every primal instinct demanding I fight my way to the surface. It tastes like burned magic and feels as thick in my lungs as liquid mercury. I'm drowning in it, coughing and choking on the tendrils that steal their way past my lips.

Something hauls me up. I break the surface with a gasp, and the thick liquid sluices down my face as I cough and splutter, taking in the world around me.

A soaring, cavernous roof arches into darkness above me, and the waters seemed to stretch forever. Or no, not water. I can feel it enveloping me like a gelatinous coating of slime. The taste of it lingers on my tongue, and everywhere it touches feels alive, so alive.

Pure power.

An icy, underground lake of magic that glows a faint silvery blue in patches. In the distance, a dark, shadowy island lurks in the water, but there's no sign of anyone else. No sign of the Mother.

Blessed Maia, where am I?

The water—for want of a better word—warms around me, growing brighter as if all the light within it floods toward me. My fingertips tingle, nipples furling into tight buds as my body begins to absorb the power. It leaves me breathless, exhilaration firing along my nerves. Suddenly, I'm floating in one of those silvery blue patches.

But with the light comes darkness.

Shadows ripple far below me like leviathan sensing prey, and something brushes against my foot. I jerk it toward me, heart suddenly thundering.

I'm not alone.

I just don't know what else is with me.

"Eris?" A brief glance around shows I'm on my own.

Well, you are in another world.

All that power flooding through me feels invigorating. I reach for it, and it blooms within me like a flower, long denied sunlight and water. A soft cry of wonder escapes me. *This* is what it feels like to have magic?

For the first time in my life, I feel as though I could conquer the world. All those years of trying—and failing—to wield my power, and here it is, mine for the taking.

I'm so wrapped up in the sensation that I don't realize the danger.

The shadows swarm like a pool of ferocious fish, as if suddenly realizing what I am. I scream as they drive toward me, casting the magic wide—

A single thought and the world blurs, stretching me out thin and then slamming me back into my physical body.

I fall to my hands and knees in the shallows, a good forty feet from where I'd been. A glance back reveals that glowing patch of light, the light winking out as though dozens of fireflies were snuffed out by the second. A swarm of shadows thrash and churn the water, drinking down the light until it finally vanishes.

I don't want to be here when they realize where I've gone.

Sloshing out of the lake, I collapse on the shore and pant. For the love of Light, that had been close. And the magic—I lift shaking hands, surprised to see tiny flecks of light swimming through my veins, visible even through my skin.

It's the first time I've felt that kind of power. I want more.

"Well, well, well." A laugh echoes hollowly behind me. "Look what fell into my pool. A little fish, drowning in the deeps."

Scrambling to my feet, I reach for my knife as I spin around.

There's nothing there.

Neither the knife, nor the owner of the voice.

Only a rocky shore piled with broken limestone pillars that look like they've been snapped off halfway down. Hints of ancient glyphs beckon along the stone, the same ones that adorned the circle stones of Mistmere.

Yarbra. Accult. Sylas. And more, hidden beneath a coating of moss.

Power words meant to contain something within their circle.

"What's wrong, little dove?" mocks the voice. It comes from the top of the rise. "Can't you see me? But then, you're looking with the wrong eyes...."

"If there's one thing I hate, it's smug, creepy ownerless voices," I call.

Silence.

"Then come and find me."

I don't think I'm imagining the hint of a snarl.

"Who are you?" I demand, striding up the rocky slope.

"Has the mortal world forgotten me already?"

A figure materializes from the shadows that wreathe the throne that sits on the top of the hill.

I expected to confront a horror, but the creature that emerges from the cowl is the most beautiful being I've ever imagined. The Mother's skin gleams like moonlight on polished alabaster, and her eyes are as black and velvety as the night sky. Raven dark hair falls in a spill around her shoulders, though little horns peek through at her temples.

There's an ancient sense of knowing in those eyes, as if the Mother has seen stars rise and fall over the eons.

As if she can see right through me.

Every thought, every hidden desire, every envious little shred of my soul.

"Ah, Daughter of Darkness. How apt that you should be the one who found me."

Daughter of Darkness? "Why would you call me that?"

It's one thing to suspect there's the old blood in my veins, but....

"Do you not know who your father is?" the Mother whispers as she seats herself on the throne.

Every part of me stills. Only the quickening beat of my heart betrays me. "Connall of Saltmist."

A visiting noble from the Far Isles, one who was never seen again. Children are rare among the long-lived fae, but it only took one chance encounter for my mother to begin to bloom with me.

This time I'm not imagining the smirk in the Mother's voice. "Is that what she told you?"

I still.

It can't be a lie. My mother would not lie about that. She wouldn't.

But I can't help thinking of all the other lies, and her disappointment in me. "*You were born to power,*" the queen always whispered. "*You disappoint me, daughter. You can barely light a candle.*"

And I'd tried, curse her.

I'd tried so hard.

"Can you not sense it?" the Mother of Night whispers seductively. "The power of the ley lines, the earth beneath your feet. The power that made this world. You can sense it on the breeze, luring you toward your destiny. No mere fae gave you that gift. No puling lordling spilled life into your mother's womb. You were born with the moon in your eyes and the breath of the gods firing through your veins. You were born to rule the stars and consume the world. You're so close to quickening that even the earth can feel it. Have you not felt it calling to you? Have you not felt it trembling beneath your boots?"

As if her words stir the power, I feel it pulling at me as though my boots are magnets. It's a horrifying, breathless moment, and I refuse it. I *refuse* it.

"*No.*"

"*Yes.* I've spent years whispering in the shadows and bending the Unseelie queens to my will. All to bring you here to me in this moment." The Mother leans forward on her throne. "You are the key to my redemption. You were born to set us free."

"No." I back away.

"You cannot escape your destiny."

Watch me.

"You're lying." I hear Thiago's words all over again: *We need to find this child of the Old Ones. And we need to end it.* "I barely have *any* magic. My father was Connall of Saltmist."

"Connall of Saltmist never existed," she says with a sneer. "Your sire was one of ours, freed from his prison for one night only. You know the rules: Never lie with a man on the night the Hallows open. Never walk in the dark on Samhain. Never leave a light burning in the windows. Your mother spat in the face of tradition and thought to host a masked ball on Samhain. She practically sent us an invitation. And one of us took it, to plant a babe in her belly."

She settles on her throne with a satisfied smile. "And now here you are, kneeling before me as supplicant."

Never. "I came to offer you a bargain. Nothing more."

"You came to set us free. Nothing less."

This was a mistake.

Thiago warned me: Never bargain with the Old Ones. Never trust them. Never court their attention.

And I was so foolish. I saw this as the answer to all my fears.

The Mother of Night can set us free, but what will she demand as repayment?

And how do I escape, now I'm here?

"Ah," she says. "You finally see the truth. You cannot escape me. Not without giving me what I want. Deny me and you will stay here with me. Forever."

They're trapped here.

Their powers are bound.

She can't force me to free them; all she can do is try and coerce me.

"If I can't escape, then here I stay," I tell her. Perhaps it's for the best, anyway? I can't make a choice, if I'm not there to make it. My mother can't steal my memories again. And Thiago....

Thiago lives.

Her eyes narrow. "I can make you regret that decision."

My nails curl into my fingers. *Breathe. Just breathe.* "I'm sure you can. But I came to offer you a bargain. Aren't you interested in playing?"

That's how it always begins with the Old Ones. And now I

know what she wants. Freedom. Well, she's not getting it. Thiago taught me the truth of that. But if she thinks I was born to deliver her back into the world, then that's a starting point.

"A bargain." The faintest of smiles crosses her face. "Go on, *leanabh an dàn.*"

"You first."

"Very well." She taps her fingers on her throne with a smile like a purring cat. "Perhaps I can tell you the truth of your begetting?" A faint pause. "But no, that's not what you want. Not yet, anyway.

"Or perhaps I can offer you power. You crave it," she whispers. "Magic. You yearn for magic. I can give you your magic...." I gasp as it floods through me, burning like a supernova. The Mother clicks her fingers, and the sensation vanishes, leaving me empty and void. "Or I can take it away."

I'm hollow and empty and on my knees.

But for one precious second, I was more. I was *everything* I've ever wanted to be.

"Power," she whispers. "Enough power to face your mother on your own terms. Enough power to take what is rightfully yours. You could claim her throne. You could rule your kingdom. You could rule the entire Alliance with what I could give you."

I think of Thiago, who sacrificed everything, year after year, just for me.

With the power the Mother gives me, I wouldn't have to beg her to break the curse. I could shatter it myself and ruin my mother. We could rule both Asturia and Evernight together.

The other kingdoms would not allow that, some part of me whispers.

There would still be war, only we would be fighting it on at least three fronts.

And what would Thiago say in the face of such power?

He'd demand to know where it came from.

"Does he have to know?" the Mother whispers, as if she can read my every thought. "The curse steals your memories of him. Why not twist it? Why not take a single memory from him? He never has to know you were not born with this power."

I could have it all.

Magic. A throne. Thiago.

I came here, knowing I would lose him, but with this offer, I wouldn't have to.

It's so incredibly tempting.

The Old Ones like to whisper empty promises. Beware their gifts, for they all have a sting.

"No." Slowly, I push to my feet. "All I want is for you to undo the curse. The rest I can manage on my own."

Large, unblinking eyes lock upon me. "He will never forgive you for this."

I know.

But I could never let him love me knowing I had stolen a piece of him, the same way my mother had stolen from me.

"If I steal his memories, then I am no better than my mother. That isn't love. It's fear. And I won't live its lie. I just want the curse broken."

She tilts her head as if examining me anew. And then she smiles.

"So, we are agreed," she says, "upon the gift. Now, we must come to terms with the price."

I swallow hard. "Name it."

There is little I can offer—that I will offer. Nothing that hurts my people, or the people of Evernight. The price must only affect me. I'm even willing to grant her my soul upon my death, if need be, but she surprises me.

"I want your firstborn child."

I see a glimpse of a child's face, her eyes dark and blinking. I've never dared put the idea into words, but there's a little piece of me that yearns to hold that baby in my arms. "*No.*" It's a mother's instinct—even if I'm not yet one—that burns through me, fierce and protective. "That is not an option. I will not give you my future child."

"Come now," she says. "If such a child does not yet exist, how does the loss affect you?"

"Find. Another. Option."

"My freedom," she whispers, leaning forward in a predatory manner.

"*No.*"

The Mother smiles. "So, you come here, into my realm, with nothing to offer me. You will not grant me my freedom, and you will not gift me the fate of your firstborn. What do you have to offer?"

It's here. I tremble. "My soul upon my death."

At least I won't die immediately.

The Mother stills as if incredibly tempted, but then she shakes her head. "A powerful gift, but no, I think not."

What?

I gape at her. The gift of a soul will grant her immeasurable power, especially if my father was an Old One. Why would she not want it?

Because I won't give her the freedom she craves? Or because she seeks to push my back against the wall?

"Then name a price I'll be willing to pay," I tell her.

The Mother falls still. "The Crown of Shadows."

I vaguely recall Thiago saying something about several relics that were conduits for the Old Ones' powers. One was the Sword of Mourning that Blaedwyn wielded against the Erlking; another was the Crown of Shadows, missing all these years.... I swear there was some other mention of it, perhaps in Kyrian's grimoire, but I cannot bring it to mind.

"It's lost to the world."

"No," she says. "Only lost to mortal memory. It still exists. I can feel it pulsing with power, calling to me. Bring me the Crown of Shadows within the year, and I shall be satisfied. If you do not, then I shall take your firstborn as payment. And do not deny me again. I am done bargaining with you."

It's not a good bargain.

The crown could be anywhere, and if it's lost to mortal memory, then how in Maia's name am I going to find it? Unless.... She specifically said 'mortal memory', but there are those in the world who are immortal. The Morai, for one, though I've used my chance with them.

And there's time to find it, whereas time is running out for Thiago and me.

Three days, and I must return to my mother. Three days and she will finally have the excuse she needs to destroy my husband.

Versus one year to free myself of this meddlesome bargain.

And if I don't find the crown, well, I started bleeding last night. There is no child for her to take. And maybe there never will be, if Thiago cannot forgive me for this.

"Agreed," I whisper.

43

I don't want to go back to my mother, but I have no choice.

If I stay in Ceres, then I condemn my people and the people of Evernight to war. Thousands will die, and it's likely the other three kingdoms will be drawn into the battle too.

There are those among my mother's court who crave her power and position, but I've never seen it as anything other than a burden. To rule is to serve your kingdom. And while the crown may pass to Andraste, its burdens haven't escaped me.

Adaia might relish a war—perhaps that's the excuse she's wanted all along—but I will not give her reason to start it.

We pause at the Hallow as Thiago prepares to say his goodbyes. I'm still bleeding, but our last encounter remains printed on my skin, and even if my mother steals my memories, I'm sure I'll still feel his touch. Perhaps I'll look at those bruises and wonder who loved me hard enough to leave such marks on my skin.

"This is it," I whisper, not wanting to let his hands go.

My mother's riders wait for me outside the Hallow, grim-faced and tense. I count heads and realize with a sinking heart that neither my mother nor my sister is among them.

They sent the fucking guards.

They couldn't even be bothered to escort me in person.

"I believe in you, Vi," he whispers, brushing his fingers against my cheek. "Maia gave me the promise of you. I have to have faith in that. I have to have faith in us."

Squeezing Thiago's fingers, I give him the only gift I can. "I love you. I always will. And no matter how many times she steals my memories, she cannot take that away from us. I'll always come back to you. I'll always fall for you. 'Til the stars burn into nothingness and the sun no longer rises, you are mine, and I am yours. Remember that: I would do anything for you."

Even make this terrible bargain.

I only hope he can forgive me one day.

"Forever, Vi," he promises, capturing my face between his hands and bequeathing me one last blistering kiss. "I'll be waiting for you."

Waiting for me to return to the Queensmoot in three more days and finally make my choice.

I just hope this succeeds.

It's like seeing everything through new eyes.

Mother's gleaming, watchful eyes as she resides on her throne like a bloated spider watching us approach. My step-brother, Edain, reclining at her feet with a look of boredom on his face, despite his hot, hungry eyes that take in everything. Andraste, stoic and emotionless at the foot of the dais, her hand on the hilt of her sword and a golden circlet on her brow, as if she's already been proclaimed princess-heir. Why did I never notice any of it? The rot in Hawthorne Castle stretches deep.

"Daughter."

How dare she call me that?

Rage burns, like a heated coal deep inside me. It's banked now, by necessity, not choice, but I know it will flare to life if given the slightest chance.

"Mother."

She looks me up and down, taking in the glittering black gown I wear. "I have had a bath prepared. You look like you've rolled in filth."

"I enjoyed every moment of it, Mother."

Her eyes glitter. It's hate I see there. For a second I waver, the little girl in my heart still wishing for impossible things.

But then I shake my head.

I am not unloved.

I have friends in the Evernight court. I have Thiago, and he loves me enough to fill the empty hole my mother has left. I will beat her, and I will take the happiness that is owed to me, no matter what I must do.

"Leave my sight," she hisses. "You disgust me."

"Not yet. Aren't you going to welcome me home, Mother?" Mounting the dais, I take her hands in mine and lean closer, seemingly to brush a kiss to her cheek. "I will never forgive you," I whisper in her ear.

"Forgive *me*?" She goes to jerk her hands away, but I have hold of them, my nails biting into her palms.

"Yes." I draw back, just enough to meet her eyes. "I promise you this, and I swear it thrice. I will be the end of you and your reign. I will not rest until you have nothing but ashes in your life. I will take back everything you stole from me, and I will repay the debt threefold."

I let her go, a smile pasted on my face as I step back. "Let's end this mockery. I think I will take that bath, after all."

Fury mottles her skin, but she's never one to show it. I see the nobles in her court leaning forward hungrily, as if to catch a hint of what we whisper, but I'm already walking away.

"Let us celebrate the safe return of my daughter," my mother calls behind me, clapping for musicians.

The court becomes a sweeping whirl of light and laughter that sounds like nails on slate to me.

All I have is hope that I haven't merely bargained with a devil for no reason.

This time, the curse must break.

I won't accept any other outcome.

I HATE my mother's balls. I loathe them with a passion. It's one thing to be on display like a prized pet, quite another to walk alone through a room full of people who watch and whisper every time you turn around.

But appearances must be kept.

Andraste finds me amidst the revelry I'm trying to ignore.

"Drink," she insists, pushing the goblet of wine into my hand.

It's instantly suspect.

"Thank you." I take the goblet but don't so much as sniff it. "I've missed the taste of betrayal."

Andraste looks away. "Not here."

"If not here, then where?" I ask coolly. "Or will I even get the chance? How does she do it, I wonder. I've been here twelve times. I know what she does. I must have been on the alert each and every time, yet she still slips beneath my guard. I keep wondering how that happens."

"Curse you, Vi." There's a pleasant smile on her face as she surveys the ballroom. "There are too many eyes watching us."

"Tell me one thing," I say, not taking my eyes off our mother. "What was the cost of the coronet on your brow? Was it my happiness? My memories? My husband?" I can't help hesitating. "Us?"

"It's not like that," she insists.

"No?" The rage stretches its wings inside me. "Do you remember when we were little girls and you would creep into my bed because you were terrified the boggart was going to whisk you away in the night?"

Our old tutor had used such a creature to terrorize us into obeying him, and Andraste had slept in my bed for months before mother found out.

"Do you remember the times I would slip you bread and water when Mother had you locked away in the oubliette?"

She looks away from me. "Yes."

"And when we planned an elaborate escape for the demi-fey that mother's cousin, Matisse, kept locked in a cage?" I could list a thousand such incidents when we were children. "When did we lose that?"

I know the answer now, of course.

I lost her the night I met him.

I lost her the minute I gave my heart to the enemy.

But she's the one who turned her back on me.

Andraste turns on me with a hiss. "You *betrayed* her, Vi.

How do you think you kept your head over such a move? You want to know the truth? The curse was *my* idea. She was going to give you to the goblins as their pet, and I talked her into this. Yes, you lost your memories. Yes, you lost him. But you were still alive. You still had a chance."

It stuns me. "I lost everything."

"Not everything," she returns, her eyes glittering furiously. "Do you think I gained anything when Mother gifted me with her favor? You had his love. I was there the night they made the pact. He would have torn the world apart for you, and I? I lost my sister. I lost my heart." Her voice softens. "My soul. Do you know what she's had me do over the course of the years? The blood these hands have worn? I let her turn me into what I am so you could keep your head on your shoulders. I did it for you. No crown is a gift to its wearer, and hers shall be even heavier than most."

"I hope it weighs you down."

"Drink," she tells me again, her eyes glittering fiercely. "It won't hurt for much longer. All you have to do is forget."

It's my sister who brings me such sweet poison.

I refuse to let the tears in my eyes fall. "She's going to kill him if I cannot remember him."

"He made his choice."

"And so did you. Remember that. For I will never forgive you. Perhaps I'll forget this moment, but I know you never will. Remember it forever. That's my curse upon you. We will never be sisters again."

Andraste looks as if I struck her, and I wonder how many times I've said those words. "So be it. Hate me if you must, but at least you'll be alive to do so. Now, drink."

I have little choice. If I don't drink, then I daresay I will be held down, and the potion poured down my throat. I have to trust in my bargain. I have to trust in the Mother's power.

So I lift the cup to my lips and swallow my obliteration.

44

My eyes blink open.

Sunlight pours through my bedroom window in Hawthorne Castle. My head aches like I drank far too much elderberry wine, and while I have barely any recollection of the night before, I do recall one thing.

Andraste giving me a glass of wine.

Strange. She must have put aside her enmity of me for one precious night. I know we've been at odds of late, though perhaps we can make amends. It feels like a peace offering, and a part of me longs for it. I'm tired of fighting with her. I'm tired of feeling like an axe hovers over my head.

Servants flutter through the doors, looking hesitantly in my direction.

"The queen insists you dress, Your Highness," one of them says. "Today is a day for... celebration."

"Judging by the ache in my temples, I think I celebrated too hard last night," I drawl, flinging aside the covers and slipping from my bed.

They exchange looks.

"It's... been three days," one whispers. "Since the ball."

Three days? Good grief. I must have been ill.

"Did she say what we're celebrating?"

Instantly, the nearest maid goes pale. "N-no, Your Highness."

No doubt she's terrified of my mother.

Aren't we all?

As a child, my nurses tried to scare me with tales of the boggart who would steal me away at night, but those stories never frightened me. Why would they, when I'd faced Adaia's wrath time and time again?

I feared the darkness of the oubliette, with only the company of its bats to keep me sane.

I feared to love a single servant, for fear she'd send them away or remove their heads.

I feared her wrath when I failed, time and time again, to make use of my recalcitrant magic.

But myths and books were my companions. I loved to read of the Old Ones, despite the warnings against them. I loved to dream of the dangerous Unseelie courts, filled with riotous hobgoblins and Sorrows. I even wished—just once —that Old Mother Hibbert would steal me away and place a changeling in my bed.

Alas, there's no escape from my mother.

"What should I wear?"

Both servants nearly fall over themselves trying to dress me.

The queen insists I dress in red and gold, which are Asturian colors, but my fingers linger on a gown of midnight silk instead. Someone's shoved it in the very back of the wardrobe, and the glitter of tiny chips of diamonds woven in the skirts catch my eye.

"This one," I say.

"But the queen—"

"This one." I pull it out of the wardrobe, feeling the furious urge to wear it. "I'll tell my mother I spilled wine on the red."

Both servants bow, looking stricken, but I'll wear the blame.

Andraste paces the hallway outside my room, one hand clasped negligently on the hilt of her sword. The second I open the door, she stiffens.

"Wearing a rut in the hallway?" I muse. "Someone had a bad night."

Judging by the shadows beneath her eyes, she fell afoul of the same batch of wine I did.

"How do you feel?" she asks warily.

"Terrible. Is there something I should be aware of? The servants looked like they wanted to leap from my bedroom window when I dressed myself, and now you're hovering in the hallway. Is Mother in one of her moods?"

"No," she says shortly. "She's... quite satisfied."

"Heads must be about to roll," I say, rolling my eyes, and perhaps it's my imagination, but my sister looks ill. "What? Are they?"

"Yes," she says curtly.

"Who?"

"You'll find out at the Queensmoot. Come on. The carriage is waiting."

The Queensmoot?

But it's not an equinox. That's the only time the Alliance comes together, unless....

Major political decisions are afoot.

I catch her wrist as she turns to leave. "What's going on?"

"You'll find out."

"Andi, please." I hate the way my voice softens. Of all the things my mother has named my weaknesses, this one is the worst. It's been so long since we've even spoken like this, and there's a piece of me that's desperate to use this chance to fix what cannot be fixed. "I miss you. I miss my sister. I miss these moments."

Andraste tears her hand loose. "That wasn't what you were saying the other night."

"I don't know what I was saying at the ball." My temples ache again. "Too much wine, I think."

"You were the one who reminded me we can never be sisters again."

"I was drunk," I insist.

For one long hesitant moment, she looks like she wants to throw her arms around me.

"I don't know why we've been at such odds," I press. "I don't want the crown. I never have. If you were to wear it, I would never stand in your way. I would support you, no matter what decisions you made. We could be sisters again—"

"*Don't.*" She pushes past me, then pauses, clearly fighting her emotions. "Maybe you don't remember what caused our fight, but I do. And I will never forget it."

"Andi—"

"No," she says fiercely, her eyes shining with unshed tears. "I won't hear it. You're wanted at the Queensmoot."

I can't help trying one more time. "I'm sorry. For whatever I've done that caused such grief."

"So am I," she breathes before practically fleeing from me.

～

THE RULERS of the Seelie Alliance are all gathered at the Queensmoot, including Kyrian, the Prince of Tides. The last I'd heard, he'd sworn to have my mother's head if he ever saw her again, yet here he sits, stony-faced and demanding, his eyes locked firmly upon me as if nothing else exists.

The moment throws me.

He stares at me for a long moment, raising a brow.

I return the sentiment, determined not to yield. He's no friend of my mother's, and his attention can only be a bad thing.

Prince Kyrian seems disappointed with my defiance and gives me a mocking smile. "As inconstant as your mother."

What a strange thing to say.

The Queen of Aska strokes the hawk resting on her leather glove, her eyes half-closed but watchful. Amusement rests on her pursed lips, though I'd hate to be the cause of it. Queen Maren makes my mother seem sane, and most of the fae call her the Queen of Nightmares when they're certain she can't hear them.

At her side is Lucidia, the Queen of Ravenal. She stares ahead of her through blind eyes the color of an alpine lake, and I've never seen one of the fae with such withered white hair or parched dry skin. She wears age like a mantle, and I can't help wondering how many summers she's seen. The fae don't usually age. Instead, when they reach their end, they wither quickly and fade, like a bloom plucked from the vine.

It doesn't make her any less dangerous.

There's only one face missing, though I've never seen him in person. All I've heard are rumors.

The Prince of Evernight is my mother's dearest enemy and would never lose the chance to taunt her face-to-face.

Whispers suddenly cease, and the chorus of a dozen fae

suddenly sucking in a sharp breath sounds as loud as a shout. Fae peer over each other's shoulders as movement swims through the courtiers directly opposite us.

"What's going on?" I whisper.

Andraste ignores me, staring stonily ahead.

"At last," my mother murmurs, and triumph lights her eyes.

The crowd opposite us parts, and the Evernight delegation finally arrives.

I understand the urge to take a sharp breath. There's a fae male in the lead wearing black enameled armor, embellished with glittering chips of obsidian. He towers over the warriors at his side, and I swear, as his cloak swirls around his calves, for a moment it looks like a pair of wings.

He's staring directly at me, as though no one else exists.

"*Vi,*" he mouths.

The crowd vanishes, and for one precious shining moment I feel the hand of fate grasp the back of my neck. A shiver runs down my spine. There's something about his face that makes my heart skip a beat. I have this horrible, breathless sensation inside me, as if fate took a direct side-step into my path and there's no avoiding it.

And then a stab of pain through my temples nearly brings me to my knees.

I blink, and stagger sideways.

Andraste's hand locks around my wrist, forcing me to straighten. "Stand," she hisses.

And then the pain is gone, and so too is the sensation I felt.

Some of my mother's courtiers hiss at the prince. Others smile malignantly. He ignores them, wading through the crowd as though they're but flotsam and jetsam that seek to hinder the inexorable surge of the tide.

I can't take my eyes off him.

"Vi," he says, again, stopping but five feet in front of me.

My mother's herald raises his staff and drives it into the stone at his feet. Once. Twice. Thrice. A hollow boom echoes through the stone beneath us, and then silence falls.

"Just breathe and this will be all done in a moment," Andraste murmurs. "I know you don't understand, but it will be done soon. It will all be done."

As I turn toward her in confusion, the crowd draws back. Andraste withdraws with them, her face expressionless.

Suddenly, I'm alone in the center of the Hallow with the Prince of Evernight on one side of me and my mother on the other.

He steps forward, reaching for me. "Do you—"

"Enough," snaps my mother. "We are bound to silence. Any attempt to sway proceedings will end in a forfeit." Her smile twists. "Though I would welcome such an attempt."

My head swivels between them.

I feel like the bone caught between a pair of fighting dogs, though I've no idea how I became the prize.

"Let the test begin," says the Queen of Aska.

"Let the test begin," says the Queen of Ravenal.

"Let the test begin," says the Prince of Tides, though he, at least, looks sad.

"I know you don't understand what's going on, Princess, but this is a challenge between the Prince of Evernight and your mother," the herald assures me with a faint, placating smile. "Please answer our questions truthfully, and this will all be done in a few minutes."

"Very well," I say, drawing my spine as straight as I can manage as I return the prince's stare with one of my own. I know my mother well enough to know this is not merely a test between her and the prince, but one meant for me as well.

"Do you know the prince?" my mother taunts.

I look at his face again, an uneasy sensation crawling down my spine. The "no" is on my lips, but there's some part of me that hesitates. Perhaps there's a look about his eyes—a desperate sort of pleading.

The prince takes a step toward me. "Vi—"

"Speak again at your own peril," my mother snaps.

"If you can speak, then so may I," he returns.

"Agreed," says the Prince of Tides, earning a scornful look from my mother.

"Agreed," repeats the Queen of Ravenal.

The tension that fills the Hallow feels like nails down my spine.

"Curse you," he whispers. "Look at me, Vi. Look at me."

I can't look away. My fingernails drive into my palms, and there's a horrible sensation inside me, as if something's threatening to tear its way free. Perhaps a scream, for it certainly feels that way.

He stares at me with pure belief burning in those green depths, as if he's trying to tell me something.

"I-I don't know," I whisper.

"Could you love him?"

It seems a trick question—which is precisely what my mother is most fond of.

"Though I find it doubtful," I reply carefully, "I cannot say it would be impossible. I have never known love, but who is to say where it shall strike?"

Our eyes meet.

And I can't help feeling as though I've failed in some way.

"*Do* you love him now?" my mother insists, resting both

hands on the edge of her throne and leaning forward
intently.

It seems as though the entire court holds its breath.
Hungry eyes watch me with anticipation. The only one who
seems in any way empathetic is Kyrian, the Prince of Tides.
He sees the answer in my face, and his gaze flickers down,
hidden by his lashes.

"I don't understand...." The Prince of Evernight's a
stranger. The enemy. What does she want from me? "I
barely know him."

"Answer the question," she thunders. "Yes or no,
Iskvien?"

"*No.*"

My answer echoes through the sudden silence like a
door slamming.

"Vi." The prince makes a move toward me, anguish
written all over his face. "You know me. You do. You love me.
She's stolen your mem—"

"Gag him," my mother commands.

The Queen of Aska snaps her fingers, and a golden band
of magic snaps across the prince's mouth. Glowing mana-
cles form around his wrists, jerking his arms behind his
back, and something forces him to his knees.

"The Alliance must be satisfied," Adaia purrs, leaning
back in her throne. "The Prince of Evernight has gambled
with his kingdom and lost. His life is forfeit."

Emptiness spirals through me. This is wrong, somehow.

I know him as my enemy, but to see him on his knees
like this, fighting against those magical bonds, awakens
something inside me that I don't understand.

My temples ache.

I drive my palms against the hollow sockets surrounding

my eyes in an attempt to alleviate the pain, but it only makes it worse.

What is wrong with me?

What is going on?

"His life is forfeit," the Queen of Aska says with a malicious smile.

"His life is forfeit," the Queen of Ravenal agrees.

Everyone turns to the Prince of Tides, who curls his lip in a sneer. "I disagree. The rules were broken. Many times. If the Queen of Asturia cannot win without cheating, then I call it a loss."

"It doesn't matter, little princeling," my mother sneers. "Two of the ruling alliance have voted. Yours doesn't count." She turns to the Prince of Evernight. "Kill him. Then bring me his head. I want to mount it above my throne."

Mother's retainers start howling and laughing.

I am going to be the cause of this stranger's death, and still he looks at me as if I'm the center of his world.

"*I forgive you.*"

It's the faintest trace of sad words whispered on the breeze, though I know they somehow came from him.

The hobgoblins that serve my mother scamper around the enemy, darting in with leers to stick him with small knives.

Someone hauls on the chain around his throat. The prince flinches away from a knife, blood welling on his cheek, but his desperate eyes still search for me. Condemning me with a glance.

"Stop." It's a bare whisper. I can't stand to watch this, knowing I'm to blame. "This doesn't have to end this way."

"His kingdom and his life," my mother calls. "Those were his terms. Be silent, daughter. You've done enough."

She snaps her fingers and her executioner steps forward, snapping the leather sheath from his axe.

Hobgoblins haul him forward until his chest and face slam into the stone of the Hallow's floors, his cheek grinding into the runes carved there.

The Prince of Tides looks at me. "Long live true love," he sneers before turning and walking away.

My arms start itching. I dig my fingernails into my palms, trying not to draw mother's attention. Curse it. How can I stop this?

I grab Andraste by the wrist. "Do something. Stop this!"

"I can't," she replies sharply.

"She'll listen to you! You have magic. You have her ear. This is… this is wrong. It feels wrong." I'm nearly shredding my arms with my fingernails. "*Please.* Please! If there's any part of you that ever loved me, please stop this."

Andraste swallows. "You set this into motion, Vi. You're the only one who can stop it."

"I set it…?" I shake my head. "Why are you doing this to me? She'll listen to you. You're the one she adores. You're her favorite."

Andraste hesitates.

"I will never forgive you for this." The pain is drilling, drilling, deep into my soul. I can barely see her face. "I cannot have his death on my conscience. I cannot."

She captures my hand, tugging it from my eye. "What's wrong?"

"It hurts." I curl in half, crippled by the pain. A scream lies trapped in my throat.

"Curse you," Andraste mutters. She turns. "Mother."

The hobgoblins fall silent, the lack of noise leaving my ears ringing.

The executioner pauses, his axe gleaming razor sharp.

"I ask... for mercy," Andraste pleads, going to her knees and bowing. "Let him be exiled into the north, where he belongs."

There's a stillness on my mother's face that warns me even before she speaks. "You disappoint me, daughter. You share your sister's weaknesses."

"An Asturian before all else," Andraste says. "My loyalty lies with you, but it also lies with her. You speak of weaknesses, but I call it strength to speak for my own." Slowly, she looks up. "You have won. Many times over. Ask for exile."

"When a thief steals from our court, we do not grant mercy," the queen hisses. "When he kidnaps one of our own, we do not think of exile—"

"Is it theft or kidnapping if what he stole left willingly?" Andraste dares to ask. "And I ask for mercy, not for his sake, but for hers."

The other queens exchange slow glances that speak a thousand words.

But my ears are ringing with the sound of Andraste's voice.

Is it theft or kidnapping if what he stole left willingly?

One by one, glyphs light up against my skin. The itch worsens. They feel like they're burning, right through to the bone. I try to stifle a scream. There's one between my eyes, branded on my skull.

My head, my head....

I'm slowly being unraveled, thread by thread, until there shall be nothing remaining.

"What's happening to her?" someone whispers.

Light shines from the glyphs. And then there's a rumbling from beneath the ground, as if something ancient stirs.

"No mercy," my mother intones, pushing to her feet. Her eyes blaze with fury. "No weakness. Executioner! Kill him!"

"*The bargain is made,*" echoes a hollow voice in my ears. "*The bargain is met. Strike the veils from thine eyes. Remember,* leanabh an dàn. *Remember it all.*"

Hammer strikes of memory slam through me, one after the other. The prince rolling toward me on a bed of heather, desire darkening his eyes as he claims my mouth for a kiss. A stolen kiss behind the stones of the Hallow. Swords clashing as we duel. Arguing in a ballroom I don't recognize.

"Thiago," I whisper.

It's all coming back to me.

One by one, until I can barely see, let alone think. But through it all, I see the axe rise over the executioner's head.

"Wait!"

It's too late. The axe begins to fall.

Desperation strikes me. Energy rumbles through the ground beneath my feet—an ancient ley line thrumming with quiet power—and I open myself up to it.

And through it, I hear the Mother of Night laugh.

I remember it all.

The last three months. My desperate search for an answer. The bargain.

And more....

Leanabh an dàn, she called me.

All along, I've been terrified they'll discover what I am.

But maybe I'm not the one who should fear.

Because the Old Ones could access the power of the ley lines, and I have their blood in my veins.

Magic bursts from me in a gush, white light obliterating the Queensmoot and throwing everyone backward. It brings me nearly to my knees. The power is like a broken dam, gushing through me as if it's been waiting eons to be released. Torrents and torrents, burning so brightly I can't believe it doesn't incinerate me.

"*Vengeance, dark and bloody.... It's finally mine to take.*" The Mother of Night whispers in my mind. "*Crush their bones. Destroy these filthy ingrates that sought to trap me. Me. I will have them on their knees....*"

"No!" I scream.

She's in my head, messing with my thoughts, my power. She finds the burning ember of rage I feel toward my mother, and glee lights through her as she fans the flames.

I see my mother, hands flared out as she tries to shield herself and her retainers from the flood of raw power. Our eyes meet, and for a single second I see fear reflected there.

"*Yes,*" hisses the Mother of Night. "*Kill her for what she's taken from me. From us.*"

All these years my mother's lied to me, mocked me, made me feel as worthless as a worm, when she was the one who wasn't worthy of *me*. She took everything from me. My husband. My mind. My magic.

And now I'm going to take it all back.

"Vi!" Thiago screams.

I blink and see him crawling toward me through the gush of light and energy pouring through the Hallow. His cloak looks raw and tattered, as if the magic is tearing at him. The magic chains binding and gagging him are gone.

"Vi, stop! You're going to tear the Hallow apart, and everyone here, with it."

What is stronger? My love for Thiago, or my fury at my mother?

Anger is a flame that burns everything. You may destroy your enemy with it, my nurse's voice murmurs in my head, *but you'll also destroy yourself.*

I clench my fists, reining in the fury and choking the

Mother of Night down. We may be directly linked now, but I'm still the one in control. And until I pay my tithe, I can't allow her to gain one foothold in this world.

Or within me.

The power flickers and then dies in a sudden quenching of light, leaving me wrung dry and shaking.

My eyes are night-blind, but I can hear shocked gasps and startled cries.

Fear. I can practically taste it.

When my vision returns, it's not Thiago or my mother I see first, but Andraste, staring at me in horror.

"What are you?" she whispers.

She who knows me the best.

The axe is gone. Solid iron melted into slag by my magic. The enormous troll who wielded it has vanished. All that remains is blood sprayed against the stone steps that ring the Queensmoot. Shadows scorch the earth where some of the lesser fae once stood. Only those with enough power to shield survive, slowly lowering their arms in shock and horror.

Thiago lifts his head.

"What... did you do?" he rasps, eyeing the glyphs burned into my skin.

"What was necessary." I capture his face in my hands and press a desperate kiss to his lips. "I love you." Our mouths meet again, mashing against each other in our urgency. "I remember you!" It's almost a sob. "I remember you."

"Vi, get out of here."

I turn, trying to see what's caught his attention.

"Abomination," my mother spits, forcing herself to stand. Her crown of thorns quivers with her anger, but for once, I feel almost as tall as she is.

"You should know, Mother. You were the one who begat me."

"I should have drowned you at birth when you came out *wrong*." She rises to her full height, and thorns spring from the ground, curling around the hem of her charred skirts. "Herald. Blow your horn."

The herald lifts his horn and a long, sweet note cuts through the air.

The entire crowd stands with bated breath.

"Adaia," the Queen of Aska warns.

My mother's smile chills my blood as a chorus of answering howls echoes around the Hallow's standing stones. Banes. Dozens of them, by the sound of it. Shadows stream across the bracken-covered hills that surround us. Enormous, writhing beasts conjured from all manner of monstrosities.

"You dare bring those creatures here?" says the Queen of Ravenal.

The Queensmoot is sacrosanct, its laws written in stone thousands of years ago. To break its laws means risking everything, for the Alliance will not stand against it.

But if there's no one left to speak of war and broken laws, then who will question her?

I should have known.

My mother doesn't *lose*. No matter what she must do.

"Vi," Thiago says, pushing me behind him and drawing his sword. "Are you armed?"

Only with the knife she gave me to kill him. Instinct must have made me bring it. "Not really."

And then chaos descends as banes tear through the outer flanks of hobgoblins and courtiers.

45

"Stay behind me!" Thiago yells, settling into a defensive stance.

The first few moments are mayhem.

Fae scream and scramble for cover, trampling each other in their wake. Hobgoblins go down, ripped to shreds by beasts that were curse-twisted for war.

The Queen of Aska turns furious eyes upon my mother and starts to conjure a cloud of darkness between her hands.

"Walk away," my mother tells her coldly. "You and your court are free to leave."

Queen Maren considers it. The darkness between her hands dissipates. "We will talk once this is done."

A wise decision on my mother's behalf, for Maren did not earn her title lightly.

Lucidia is not so lucky. Turning toward the approaching pack, she doesn't see the bane that stalks her from behind.

"Look out!" I cry, but as she turns, its teeth sink into her throat and she goes down with a startled cry, buried in more snapping banes.

"We need to retreat." Thiago shoves me back through the stones.

Retreat isn't in either of our natures, but a swift glance proves him right. The Queensmoot is—or *was*—a place for peace.

To bear steel on this hallowed turf is against all the rules.

To draw blood is cause enough for execution.

Each queen or prince is only entitled to twenty-five courtiers, guards, or retainers. And right now, they're all being overrun. Nobody was prepared for this. The break in tradition is catastrophic.

I knew my mother had ambitions, but to watch them play out like this.... She knew. She planned for this. She always intended to strike at the Alliance and place herself firmly on a throne that rules the entire south.

If she'd succeeded, then Thiago, Kyrian, and Lucidia would all be dead.

I nod as Thiago starts to cut a path back to his people. Retreat is the only option.

"Vi!" Thalia yells from the melee ahead.

"There they are!" I tell him, pointing toward her pale face.

The only problem is, between us lurks an entire pack of banes, tearing into a gaggle of Lucidia's courtiers.

"Can you summon your magic again?" Thiago demands, catching sight of a bane lunging toward us. Timing it perfectly, he steps to the side just as he brings the sword down. Steel slices through matted fur, and the bane's headless corpse crumples to the ground.

"No."

I'm too far from the Hallow that channels the ley line's power.

And I don't know if I dare open that link again. Judging from the tremble in my arms and legs, I'm facing the backlash of handling so much raw magic, and I can *feel* the Mother of Night there, just waiting to close her trap.

Finn appears out of nowhere, mounted on a dappled gray stallion. "Here," he yells, tossing me one of his swords.

I turn to wade into the battle, but a hand reaches down and grabs me by the back of my dress, hauling me up.

With a squeal, I land in Finn's lap.

"Get her out of here," Thiago yells.

"Don't you dare!" I elbow Finn in the side. "Thiago!"

He's turning to face a pair of banes with his hands held low at his sides. What in Maia's name did he do with his sword? He's virtually defenseless.

"Thiago!"

He doesn't turn. Doesn't look at me. Merely walks forward.

"While I'd usually enjoy having a beautiful woman in my arms," Finn mutters, "I think I'd prefer it if she wasn't trying to emasculate me."

"If you try and haul me out of here," I snarl, "then an elbow will be the least of your troubles. Ride after him."

"Princess, as much as I'd like to oblige," Finn says, grabbing the reins and wheeling the gray around, "he's not the one in any danger."

Wisps of fog stir around Thiago's hem. The shadows at his feet stretch and grow. Every step he takes, he seems an inch taller. The cloak starts to twitch, and then enormous glossy black wings unfurl.

My breath catches in my throat.

I am an army, he said once.

And I remember those snapping, snarling voices that fill

his shadows. I remember the way his eyes turned pure black and dark runes sprang up all over his skin.

"Ride," I tell Finn. "I'll cover your back."

Slinging one leg over the pommel, I haul a handful of my skirts up so I can grip the saddle.

I glance back only once, as the stallion launches forward, smashing a pair of dueling fae nobles out of the way. Thiago vanishes within a cloud of darkness that leaps hungrily forward, consuming everything in his path.

He may be Unseelie.

He may be a monster.

But he's my monster.

I kick one of Mother's guards in the face, and he flips backward in a stir of red and gold. Asturian colors, though I've turned my back on them forever.

It hurts, just a little, though I'm sure the black and silver of the Evernight court will suit me better.

Then we're free of the melee and streaking through the bracken.

Howls echo behind us. Then pained yelps and the sound of a bane's high-pitched scream.

This time, I don't dare look back.

THE COST of channeling the Mother of Night's power is heavy.

I can barely see by the time Thiago returns to Valerian, carrying me through the portal in his arms. He'd found us by the Hallow, and I vaguely recall fainting forward into his arms.

"Why Valerian?" I whisper.

He hesitates as he sets me down. "Because I don't know

if I can entirely trust everyone in Ceres. And it's the first place your mother will attack."

I shudder, staggering sideways.

"You broke the curse," he says, his eyes locking on me intently. "But you didn't remember me until it was too late."

I look away. Now comes the time of reckoning.

"End yourself," he whispers. "Kill the queen. Or find something with more power to break the spell. I should have paid closer attention to you in those last few days. What did you do? *Why?*"

"I made a pact with the Mother of Night. She would give me the power to break the curse—"

"And in return?" he demands harshly.

"In return, I have a year to find the Crown of Shadows and present it to her. Or...." I can't say it.

"Or?"

"Or I must bequeath her our firstborn child."

For a second, he looks as though I've punched him in the face. Fury lights his eyes. "You *what*?"

"I had no choice." The very thought makes me feel ill. Could I have made a better bargain? I've tossed and turned over the thought every night since I made it, but the truth is, I would cut off my own arm before I ever gave a child to the Mother of Night. I will find the Crown of Shadows.

Making this deal was the only way I could buy myself some time.

"I offered my soul, but she wouldn't take it."

"Curse you, Vi! Why?"

"Because I couldn't bear to watch you die, and I was afraid your faith in me was misplaced. I needed an answer. I needed a guarantee. And I didn't set her free. I wouldn't promise her that," I tell him. "We have a year. And as long as

I don't fall with child in the meantime, then we're safe. She cannot take what does not exist."

"The Mother of Night wouldn't make a bargain unless she thought she had something to gain from it," he snarls. "If she made a deal that involves a child of ours, then she considers it to be more than a possibility. You could be with child now."

"I'm not," I assure him. "I'm not a fool. I would never have accepted if there was any doubt."

He rakes his hands through his hair. "You don't understand. What were you thinking?" he yells. "Or *were* you thinking?"

Days of worrying about how I'm going to save him, and this is his response? I tip my chin up in anger. "I was thinking that my mother was going to execute you right in front of me and I wouldn't have even shed a cursed tear until it was too late."

"You would have remembered—"

"I'm glad one of us is certain of that," I shoot, "because I wasn't. And even if I did, I didn't have the power to challenge my mother."

"All you had to do was free me—"

"And start a war?" I point out, though the irony of my mother's betrayal does occur to me. "Because I'm fairly certain if I'd remembered you, we would have had to fight our way out of there. Or *you* would have had to fight our way out of there, and I didn't even know what condition you'd be in. What if you were beaten? Unconscious? Your magic chained? What then? I am tired of hiding behind you. I am tired of not being able to face her. My mother doesn't *lose*, Thiago. She will fight until the last breath leaves her body. And she would have rather seen me dead than happy in your arms. I had to make her fear me. I had to have the power to confront her, and I didn't have any other options to get it from."

"She's the Mother of All Darkness, curse you!"

"Really? I had absolutely no idea."

"The more you channel her power, the greater the hold she'll have on you," he warns.

It didn't occur to me that he'd think the power I was channeling at the Hallow would be hers. As much as I want to tell him the truth, he was the one who considers it mercy to kill the *leanabh an dàn*.

The truth dies on my lips.

I just need a little time. I just need to convince him I'll never do it. I'll never set them free. The Erlking is enough. I understand the damage they can cause. I'll tell him. One day.

"I won't use her power again. I promise."

I knew what the price would be if I traveled this path, but what was the alternative? Watch him die? Wake up, many years from now, sobbing in my bed when I finally remember?

No. *No.* Every lesson my mother has ever given me taught me to fight, and to fight dirty. Time was always our enemy, and now I've bought us another year of it.

"We have a year," I repeat. "And my mother lost. You have the disputed territories and—"

"I don't give a fuck about the land." He scrapes at his face, fury still harsh across his expression. I can tell he wants to punch a wall or something, but he doesn't like behaving like a savage.

The thought makes me blink.

I don't know how I know that, but I do.

And just like that, the fire in his eyes banks. "We need to plan. We'll call in my people. Prepare to fortify ourselves against Adaia's armies."

Relief floods through me. *We.* He said *we.* "You don't want to dissolve the marriage?"

"*Dissolve* it?"

"Since it appears you are married to a monster." They're lighthearted words, but even I hear the depth of emotion underscoring them.

Two steps and he's right in front of me, though I don't know if his hands quiver with the desire to put them on me or to push me away. "You're not a monster."

Aren't I?

"Forever, Vi." His voice roughens. "That was the promise I made. No matter what the cost is. No matter what I must do to keep you. You belong to me, and I to you, until the moon falls from the sky and the tides no longer churn. Forever."

I remember those words, spoken the night we bound our hands together and married. The memories are still incomplete, broken fragments that slip through at the oddest moment, but some seem seared into my mind.

Until now, I've been channeling the exhilaration of the meeting, fueled by fear and rage and exhilaration. But with those words, I want to throw myself into his arms and cry.

I don't cry. I hate crying.

But for some reason, my eyes grow hot.

And then he's cursing under his breath and snatching me into his arms.

"This is where you belong, Vi." A kiss to my temples. He squeezes me so tightly I could swear he'll never let me go. "I know this is still new to you, but I waited centuries for you. I'm not about to turn away from you just because you bound yourself to the Mother of Night. You used her to break the curse and gain power. I can continue to be furious about that, or... we use it to protect you. Besides"—he lifts my chin and brushes my lip with his thumb—"you still owe me a kiss. Three, if I'm counting correctly."

"You're going to hold me to that?"

"Always."

I capture his face in both hands and claim his mouth with a desperation born of fear. He's not going to turn away from me. One kiss. Two. I paint them all over his mouth.

"I promise I will never hurt you," I whisper. "I'll never make a pact with the Old Ones again. We'll find the Crown of Shadows and give it to that bitch, and then forget all about her."

His eyes are stormy seas as he holds my face between his hands. "It's not that easy, Vi. No one has seen the Crown of Shadows since the wars."

"We've faced impossible odds before."

"And if we do find it, then giving it to the Mother is dangerous," he says. "As far as I know, it was used only as a conduit for a fae to access the Old One's powers, but if she wants it, then she thinks she can use it for more. I'll stake my entire kingdom on it."

"No more gambling with kingdoms, please. Or your life."

The faintest of smiles touches his mouth. "No more making deals with Old Ones."

"Done. Done. Done. I promise thrice."

"Then done," he whispers, resting his forehead against mine. "Done. Done. I promise thrice."

Finn clears his throat behind us. "As lovely as it is to see the pair of you back where you both belong, we may have to start moving. The Hallow's not safe. It could spit anyone into our midst right now."

Thiago's face goes hard. "You're right. Let's go home." He takes my hand and starts leading me toward the ruined castle in Valerian.

"And then?" Finn asks.

"Prepare for war. Adaia made her move. Now it's time to make ours."

Dear Reader,

Thank you so much for reading! Iskvien and Thiago's story continues in **CROWN OF DARKNESS** in 2020.

True love will face the ultimate challenge when a dark goddess rises, secrets threaten to tear them apart, and a queen will stop at nothing to gain revenge.

I hope we meet again between the pages of another book!

Cheers,
Bec McMaster

P.S While waiting for CROWN OF DARKNESS, why not read one of Bec McMaster's other fantasy-fueled romances, HEART OF FIRE?

An exiled *dreki* prince meets his match in a farmer's daughter with the gift of magic, but danger threatens when a dragon-hunter arrives on Iceland's shores.

Expect pulse-pounding action and adventure in HEART OF FIRE, the thrilling first novel in a fast-paced fantasy romance series.

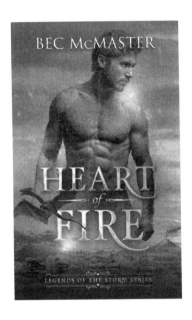

READ NOW

ALSO BY BEC MCMASTER

DARK COURT RISING

Promise of Darkness

Crown of Darkness (coming 2020)

Curse of Darkness (coming)

LEGENDS OF THE STORM SERIES

Heart Of Fire

Storm of Desire

Clash of Storms

Storm of Fury (coming 2020)

COURT OF DREAMS SAGA

Thief of Dreams

Thief of Shadows (coming)

Thief of Souls (coming)

LONDON STEAMPUNK SERIES

Kiss Of Steel

Heart Of Iron

My Lady Quicksilver

Forged By Desire

Of Silk And Steam

Novellas in same series:

Tarnished Knight

The Clockwork Menace

ABOUT THE AUTHOR

BEC MCMASTER is a writer, a dreamer, and a travel addict. If she's not sitting in front of the computer, she's probably plotting her next overseas trip, and hopes to see the whole world, whether it's by paper, plane, or imagination.

Bec grew up on a steady diet of '80s fantasy movies like *Ladyhawke*, *Labyrinth*, and *The Princess Bride*, and loves creating epic, fantasy-fueled romances where even the darkest hero can find love. She lives in Australia with her very own hero, and her daughter.

Read more at www.becmcmaster.com

Printed in Great Britain
by Amazon